PRISONER OF LOVE

He did not release the coiled rope. "Can I trust you to *keep* your word, Miss Dale?"

Devina gave a short, bitter laugh. "You'll soon find out, won't you?"

A chill moved down Devina's spine as the helplessness of her situation registered fully in her mind. Her captor's reaction was to pull her closer against him, and Devina was again reminded of the power in the arms that had so easily subdued her.

Devina summoned the last residue of strength within her. She would not let this land intimidate her. As for this man, whoever he was, he was no match for her, as he would soon see....

Other *Leisure* and *Love Spell* books by
Elaine Barbieri:
CAPTIVE ECSTASY
DANCE OF THE FLAME
DANGEROUS VIRTUES SERIES:
HONESTY
PURITY
CHASTITY

ELAINE BARBIERI

TARNISHED·ANGEL

LOVE SPELL BOOKS   NEW YORK CITY

To my father, Andrew Favati, who was everything a father should be and who taught me that love is in giving, love is in laughing, and love is in understanding.
I miss you, Pop.

LOVE SPELL®

February 1998

Published by

Dorchester Publishing Co., Inc.
276 Fifth Avenue
New York, NY 10001

ISBN 0-505-52250-0

The name "Love Spell" and its logo are trademarks of Dorchester Publishing Co., Inc.

Printed in the United States of America.

CHAPTER 1

DRIVEN BY SHEER desperation, Devina thrust her perfectly coiffed head out the window of the rapidly moving stagecoach and took a deep, full breath. Seconds later she pulled her head back inside, coughing and sputtering, her eyes and throat filled with residue from the perpetual cloud of red dust that rose from the dry Arizona road. She struggled to regain her breath, fanning the air wildly with a delicate hand, blinking almost comically as tears streamed from her smarting eyes, streaking the fine layer of grit covering her face and hair. Breathing normally at last, she groaned and wrinkled her aristocratic nose, creating an expressively pained grimace, her patience having expired in the wake of this last imposition on her limited forbearance. Her gaze focused pointedly on the sleeping passenger slumped beside her. Oh, damn! Was there no escaping his ghastly stench?

She had been only too conscious of the choking dust that had enveloped the stage since the beginning of its journey on the rough sunswept road that morning. Was she not covered with at least an inch of the distasteful sandy substance? Even as she poked her head out the window, she had realized she would only be exchanging one intolerable situation for another; but fool that she was, she had momentarily convinced herself anything was preferable to the foul odor emanating from the derelict cowboy beside her.

Devina gave the sleeping man another quick look out the corner of her eye. He swayed in complete relaxation as the

1

coach's great wheels rolled from one jarring rut to another. Unkempt, unshaven, his hard thigh pressing annoyingly against hers, he was either totally oblivious or totally uncaring of the hardship that his odoriferous presence caused his fellow passengers.

Another frustrated groan escaped Devina's lips. Surely a man could not reek so strongly from just consuming alcohol. Judging from the smell of him, the unconscious degenerate must have bathed in it! It was no wonder he had been sleeping so soundly. She was surprised that she and the other two unfortunate passengers had not been anesthetized merely from breathing the fumes!

Devina shot a glance toward the silent couple seated across from her. Just past middle age, quiet and unassuming, they appeared to be weathering the ordeal far better than she. Incredible as it seemed in view of her own nausea, they appeared almost immune to the offensive odor permeating the coach!

Devina returned a narrowed gaze to the mainspring of her discomfort and surveyed the man disapprovingly. Faded clothing marked with the stain and grime of the trail, worn boots, a broad-brimmed hat pulled down over his forehead, shielding his heavily bearded face from view . . . Her seatmate was obviously thoroughly disreputable—a wastrel, a drunken saddle tramp. As if that was not enough, the obnoxious individual was beginning to add to her discomfort by sprawling over the entire seat, pushing her farther and farther toward the corner with each rut they struck.

A sudden bump in the road threw the unknown cowboy even more offensively close. Crushed against the wall of the coach, Devina gave a sharp gasp, but the angry comment that jumped to her lips was stunned into silence by a fleeting glimpse of the man's startlingly keen dark eyes as they flicked open to glance into hers. Lurching back with the next bump in the road, the drunken cowboy ended their intimacy without apology.

Oh, that was the final straw! Furious, cutting words rose to Devina's lips, only to be stopped as the man gave a low snort and lapsed back into his drunken stupor, sliding onto the skirt of her stylish green traveling ensemble as he did so!

Frustration sent hot color surging to Devina's cheeks. She had taken enough! The damned inebriate would take no further advantage of her! Grasping her skirt in both hands, she gave a hard pull. It refused to budge, and her flush darkened. Shooting a look of mute appeal toward the couple across from her, she felt her last shred of control slip away. Asleep! They were asleep!

Her color high, her eyes blazing, Devina gritted her teeth with determination. She took a deep breath and gave the reeking cowboy a powerful shove, then pulled on the portion of skirt on which he was sitting.

She was free! Sweet triumph surged through her veins—until the intoxicated man grumbled and then slumped toward her, squeezing her firmly into the corner of the seat once again. His eyelids fluttered briefly, and his dark eyes appeared to focus on a point outside the window before dropping closed.

Devina was incensed! Damn him! He was all but crushing her!

Her great silver-blue eyes narrowed into menacing slits as she turned toward her sleeping nemesis. A low, unladylike growl escaped her lips. Too infuriated to show caution, she drew back a delicate, tightly clenched fist and punched her unconscious adversary's shoulder with all her might.

No response!

Perspiration was beginning to dot Devina's forehead and upper lip. Her smart green chapeau, adorned with two white doves on the wing, sat crazily askew. The springy silver-blond curls she had arranged so carefully now adhered wetly to her temples. A heated fury was assuming control of her senses.

This man, this damned odoriferous beast, had turned the cramped coach into a torture chamber! He had nauseated her with his stench, crushed her unmercifully with his hard-muscled body, and was now pushing her out the door!

In a voice that bore not the slightest resemblance to her normal cultured tone, Devina issued a concise, cracking command: *"Move!"*

Pushing at the heavy arm pinning her against the wall, she continued with growing intensity, "I paid for this seat, damn it! You're sitting in *it* and on *me!* Get over on your own side!"

She stared heatedly at the cowboy's partially hidden face. A flash of pure gratification suffused her as he turned his back in obedient silence and faced the opposite window.

Devina was elated! She had her own portion of the seat to herself at last! Triumphantly adjusting her hat and attempting to ignore the rank odor of stale whiskey that still pervaded the coach, she took a deep, satisfied breath.

She was staring at the curve of the cowboy's back when she began to feel the first glimmer of disquiet. Although the drunken cowboy still lay in his own corner, she sensed an almost imperceptible tensing of his limbs. The broad shoulders, which had been slumped forward to afford more comfort on the hard seat, were gradually straightening. His bearded chin no longer rested on his chest, but had been elevated just enough to allow him an unrestricted view of the passing countryside. She could not see the man's face, but she was convinced his eyes were no longer closed, that he was staring alertly, expectantly out the window.

An inexplicable awareness sharpened Devina's senses, and apprehension overwhelmed her. With a startling flash of clarity she was certain her whiskey-soaked seatmate was alert and completely sober!

Devina shot a quick glance toward the elderly couple seated across from her. They were still sleeping. She glanced back to the man beside her. He stiffened, as if something or someone in the landscape had caught his attention. Devina's heart began racing. Unexpectedly, in a single fluid movement the cowboy straightened up and swung around to face her fully for the first time. Dark, alert eyes held her mesmerized in the split second it took him to reach down into his boot and withdraw a gun!

A shaft of sunlight glinted menacingly on the barrel pointed in her direction. Devina gasped. He had fooled them all completely! He wasn't a senseless drunk!

In a rapid movement, the cowboy's arm snaked out to encircle Devina's waist. Pulling her roughly onto his lap, he held her breathless, her back pinned against the wall of his chest. He pressed the hard muzzle of his gun into her ribs.

"Don't move! Do exactly as I say or you won't live to get that breath of fresh air you've been looking for. My gun doesn't have any conscience where women are concerned, and neither do I."

Not waiting for a response, he pulled her even tighter against him. Simultaneously, he raised his gun and fired two shots through the roof of the coach, then shouted a brief, harsh command to the driver to bring the vehicle to a halt. He darted a quick, silencing glance toward the elderly couple who had been startled awake to face his drawn gun.

The stage began braking, and the cowboy jammed his gun back into Devina's side. His eyes on the roof of the coach, the gunman shouted into the sudden unnatural silence as the stage shuddered to a halt: "All right, you two on top, throw your guns on the ground. Don't try anything or this fine lady sitting here on my lap will breathe her last breath."

A b⁻ief silence was followed by the low rumble of voices. A few more seconds passed before the glint of sunlight on steel flashing past the window revealed the driver and guard had complied with the gunman's orders. The arm around Devina's waist tightened.

The gun pressed more sharply into her side as her captor addressed the men on top once more: "Well, I guess the lady is going to have to persuade you fellows to throw down *all* your guns." His tone increasing in menace, he growled in a voice meant for her alone, "It's up to you."

A deep rage tempered Devina's fear. Not only had this odious person made a complete fool of her with his drunken cowboy act, he was now about to make her a party to his crime by forcing her to speak in his behalf!

The gun barrel was cutting painfully into her side, and Devina fought to suppress her quaking. The swine . . . She had not a doubt in the world this beast would shoot her if she did not comply with his instructions. Men of his type had no conscience. She would have to swallow her pride, she decided, so as to live long enough to see him pay for this crime and for his treatment of her.

The hammer on the gun at her side clicked warningly. The gunman's voice was heavy with menace. "Well?"

Hating herself for submitting to the gunman's threats, Devina raised her voice in a surprisingly steady shout: "You men on top, throw down all your weapons. He has a gun at my side, and he means what he says!"

There was a short pause. Then a grudging acknowledgment sounded from atop and a rifle fell past the window, followed by a handgun.

Apparently satisfied, the gunman spoke again. "That's better. Now, get down carefully and stand with your hands up. You're being watched, so don't think you can get away with anything."

As if awaiting his signal, three masked men rode out from behind cover a short distance from the road. Their guns were drawn, and one of the outlaws was leading a riderless horse. Waiting until the men on top had reached the ground and were being covered by his accomplices' guns, Devina's captor looked to the terrified couple across from them. His voice softened when he addressed them, even as he secured Devina more cruelly against him.

"I want you both to step down and go stand beside the driver and guard. You don't have to worry. Nothing will happen to you if you do as you're told."

Devina's eyes followed the older couple as they moved to her captor's orders. She realized her captor's attention was now focused on her.

His voice grated low and threateningly into her ear. "And now there's only you and me left in here."

Sliding her off his lap, the gunman turned her to face him. Startled at the strength of the features barely discernible beneath his heavy beard, Devina felt the full impact of his steady dark-eyed gaze. She swallowed tightly.

"What's the matter?" the gunman asked. "Nothing to say? You were a lot braver when you thought I was a helpless drunk. You didn't mind letting me know how offensive you found me then, did you?"

His taunt ignited a spark inside Devina that forced all caution from her mind. She reacted with cutting anger. "I was disgusted with you when I thought you to be a slovenly drunk. Now that I know what you truly are, I find you even more repulsive."

The gunman's harsh features tightened, and Devina fought to control her quaking. She raised her chin in stubborn defiance. She would not allow this criminal to force her to cower.

The gunman's response was a short, sinister statement. "Repulsive, perhaps, but in control . . . of you."

The gunman turned abruptly and stepped down from the coach. Jamming his gun into his belt, he turned back and reached inside the coach to swing Devina roughly to the ground beside him. His grip on her arm held her at his side.

The masked robbers had already begun moving silently about their tasks, one man gathering up the discarded guns, another scaling the coach to throw the strongbox to the ground while the third stood guard. A quick shot into the box splintered the lock. All eyes moved intently to the strongbox when the lid was raised. Out of the corner of her eye, Devina saw the stagecoach guard make a quick move toward the nearest masked man.

"No, you don't, John Henry!"

His arm snaking out even as he spoke, Devina's captor pulled her up tight against him. Pressing his gun to her ribs, he held her securely against his lean, hard length as he continued menacingly, "Don't try anything foolish. You wouldn't want to put this lady in danger, would you?"

Humiliation at her role of helpless hostage added a new sharpness to her tongue as Devina snapped, "How very *brave* you are. Do all you *brave* western gunmen hide behind women's skirts?" Fuming when he did not respond, Devina continued acidly, "You needn't answer. It's obvious you're quite at home conducting yourself in this manner."

The gunman purred into Devina's ear, "That's right, ma'am. I'm just as comfortable behind a woman's skirts as I am under them."

A flush rose to Devina's cheeks, and she snapped her lips tightly closed. The gunman's short, whispered response made two things abundantly clear, despite the strain of the moment. The first was that she could not afford to trade insults with her captor. The second was that her earlier observation had indeed been correct: Her captor did not reek of alcohol because he had consumed it. The breath that washed her cheek was clean and sweet. He had obviously doused himself in whiskey. His slovenly attire and grooming, as well as his feigned drunkenness, were part of his strategy to keep everyone off guard until the coach arrived at the place where his henchmen awaited him. He had taken over the coach without a single shot being fired. Oh, this fellow was smart, all right . . .

Devina had no further time for conjecture as the masked men loaded the last of the sacks from the strongbox onto their saddles and turned toward her captor.

"We're ready to go."

Dragging her with him, Devina's captor strode toward his horse.

A new fear gripped Devina and her heart began a wildly erratic beat. She struggled furiously as he pulled her along. "Wha . . . what do you think you're doing? Let me go!"

Releasing her as he reached his horse, he gave her a contemptuous glance. "Don't flatter yourself. You've served your purpose. I have no intention of taking you with me. You wouldn't be worth the trouble. Get over there with the others, and make it fast!"

An uncontrollable flush reflected Devina's humiliation as she turned to face the other passengers. Walking on trembling legs with as much dignity as she could muster, she did not turn around even at the sound of the thieves' rapid departure.

Abruptly, Devina realized she was shuddering. Grudgingly,

she accepted the support of the short, burly guard as the driver attended to the elderly couple.

"Are you all right, ma'am?"

"Other than having been manhandled by a repulsive, foul-smelling thief who threatened my life, I suppose I'm all right."

His heavily jowled face reddening, the guard bobbed his head apologetically. "I'm sorry, ma'am. I wasn't expectin' anyone to be hidin' in the coach. There was nothin' I could do."

But Devina would not suffer the guard's excuses or his concern. She was extremely shaken, for all her pretended calm. That vile beast had taunted her as he held her life in his hands and then had dismissed her with contempt.

The sudden memory of dark, intense eyes returned to mock her. Her color high, Devina shook off the guard's supporting hand. Turning, she addressed the driver. "I can see no reason for us to stand here on this dusty road in the blazing sun." Turning with a quick glance toward the elderly couple who had weathered the whole ordeal admirably, she raised her chin with determination. "I should think these two people would agree that we've wasted enough time here as it is and that it's time to go on."

Ignoring the driver's startled expression as well as the persistent weakness in her knees, Devina turned and walked back to the stage.

Seated inside minutes later, Devina turned to stare blindly out the window. She could still feel the pressure of the arm that had held her prisoner. The bruises, where the strong fingers had bitten into her arm as her captor held her to his side, throbbed painfully. She closed her eyes, and her heart skipped a beat as she recalled the sensation of the hard muzzle of the gun against her ribs. She had never been so frightened . . .

A vision of the hard black eyes arose in her mind, threatening, mocking her. Devina opened her eyes. Realizing she was shaking, she felt rage suffuse her anew. A low, common thief terrorizing her, telling her that she was not worth his trouble . . . If it was the last thing she ever did, she would make the beast eat his words. She would make him pay . . .

Succumbing to the nagging force inside him, Ross Morrison reined his mount to a sudden halt on a rise of land a short distance away. He turned his horse around, his mind unconsciously registering the sound of continuing hoofbeats behind him as his companions made good their escape.

His expression intent, he cantered to the edge of the rise, his eyes falling on the tableau in the distance: a stagecoach motionless on the winding, dusty road, the horses standing restlessly in their traces, small figures engaged in conversation a few feet away.

Fuming with an inner heat, Ross settled his gaze on the slender figure he sought. Pulling her shoulders erect, the woman shrugged off the support of the guard with apparent disdain. His keen eyes caught the slight elevation of her chin as she spoke. Her air of unquestioning command came cleanly across the distance between them. In the space of a second, she turned and walked back toward the stage, her head erect, her proud, narrow shoulders purposefully squared.

The heat inside him intensified, and Ross made an effort to control his disturbing reaction to the woman he watched so intently. It angered him that the spoiled little witch had been right in her assumption: For the space of a few short minutes, as he had held her tight against him, had breathed in her fragrance, he *had* actually entertained the thought of taking her with him! The realization left him strangely shaken.

Ross had never been a ladies' man. His encounters with women had been infrequent and casual. Three years in Yuma Prison had sharpened his need for the touch of womanly flesh, but he had satisfied himself with the more than willing whores in the towns he had visited since his release. One woman was as good as another in that respect. He had learned long ago that women were not to be depended upon—his own mother had been the best teacher of that basic truth.

Still intent on the woman walking purposefully toward the stage, Ross gritted his teeth against the strangely conflicting emotions that assailed him. His contempt for women of her type was deeply ingrained—wealthy, pampered eastern-bred women who could endure the rigors of the western frontier beside their men for only as long as their creature comforts were not impaired. His own mother had been cast from that same mold, and he did not even remember her face.

Ross's frown tightened. What was it about this particular woman that made him unwilling to ride off and leave her behind? Certainly it wasn't her appearance. She was a beautiful

woman, if you cared for her type, but picture-book beauty—
silver-blond hair, small, fine features, and blue eyes, no matter
how direct and expressive—had never appealed to him. He
preferred earthy beauties, women with vibrant coloring. What's
more, he liked tall women, and that haughty witch was too petite
for his taste. But persistent memory forced him to admit there
had been nothing angular about the body he had held so tightly
against him. He could still feel the warmth of those lush curves
cushioning the tension in his muscular frame. He felt a spontaneous tightening in his groin as his mind teased him with the
thought of how it would feel to bury himself deep within that
softness.

The snort that escaped Ross's lips was one of self-contempt.
So, he was not above experiencing sexual desire, despite his
aversion to the type of woman she personified. From the first,
she had openly declared her distaste for the mode of travel she
had been "forced" to take to Tombstone after coming to the end
of the rail lines. Already seated on the stage, pretending a
drunken sleep, he had overheard her well-voiced complaints
about the breakdown of the larger coach on which she had
traveled the first day of her journey. She had insistently protested
the use of the "outdated" smaller vehicle and the "primitive"
comforts it would afford. Those same protests had allowed the
older couple to board ahead of her and take the seat across from
him, leaving her the seat at his side.

She had proved herself worthy of his first negative reaction to
her during the time they had traveled together. Granted, he had
gone to great lengths to disguise himself. Sporting long hair and
a full beard, his old clothes liberally doused with red-eye, he had
smelled almost as bad as he looked. He had also been unrecognizable;
he wanted his release from prison, after serving only three years
of his sentence, to remain a secret at present.

Through half-closed eyes he had watched the petite witch's
reaction as she stepped up daintily into the coach. He had felt a
perverse amusement as she realized she would have to sit at his
side. Perfectly groomed and elegantly attired in a traveling outfit
that had doubtless cost the equivalent of three months' salary for
the average miner, she had taken a short sniff and grimaced
almost comically before sitting down and allowing him the wid-
est possible berth.

But if he had chosen to make her even more uncomfortable for the duration of their aborted journey, she had succeeded in inflaming his fury with her silent assumption of superiority. He had read that same attitude in the eyes of mining company executives from New York and San Francisco when they arrived in Tombstone in their sleekly tailored gabardine suits a few years before, their pockets bulging with out-of-town wealth. With their smooth talk, they had succeeded in methodically buying up the properties of independent investors. Even the discoverers of the Tombstone lode—the Schieffelin brothers and their friend and developer, Dick Gird—had sold out to those big-time operators.

A familiar bitterness tightened Ross's dark expression. Was it any wonder that his father had not stood a chance? A victim of smooth talk and empty promises, he had signed away his claim, only to realize when it was too late that the complicated legal document had not included a promise of future income from the proceeds of the mine. In the end, all he had had to show for his strike was a small cash settlement and visions of a future that would never materialize.

The demise of a dream had broken his father's heart. Ross's own attempt to obtain justice from Till-Dale Enterprises had resulted in his being unjustly accused of having caused an accident at the mine that had taken six lives. Perjuring witnesses, falsified papers, and a high-priced lawyer with a contempt for justice had put him in Yuma for five years. Brad Morrison had not lived to see him weather the first.

Ross's dark eyes followed the woman's slender figure as she mounted the steps of the stage and sat imperiously inside. Her face was in the shadow, but a flash of silver-blond hair at the window tightened the knots in Ross's stomach. Unbidden, memory returned the sensation of that fine, light-colored silk brushing his cheek, returned the sweet scent that had teased his nostrils as he held her intimately close. He remembered the feel of her round buttocks against his thighs as she had sat on his lap. He remembered his arm had spanned the minute dimensions of her waist with room to spare, and he recalled only too vividly the tantalizing warmth of her breasts brushing the tense muscles of his forearm with each rapid, anxious breath she took.

Ross swallowed hard and shook off his wandering thoughts. He did not know the arrogant young woman's name, but she was one of a breed he thoroughly despised. He could afford to waste no more time thinking about her. He had taken another step against Till-Dale Enterprises today. The payroll for the mines Harvey Dale had swindled away from his father and other honest prospectors in the area was presently being carried away by his men as their horses galloped toward the mountain.

The sound of hoofbeats behind him turned Ross's attention to the approaching horseman. Waiting only until the rider had drawn up alongside him, he snapped, "What are you doing back here, Jake? I told you to go on with the boys and take the money to the hideout."

Jake Walsh's youthful face reflected his incredulity. "What am *I* doin' here? What in hell are *you* doin'? You're watchin' that stage like a hungry vulture, like you got all the time in the world. You just stole the payroll, dammit! You're supposed to be ridin' in the opposite direction!" Pausing a moment, Jake continued in a lower voice, "If you're so interested in that blonde, you should've brought her along. Hell, that would be better than hangin' back here, waitin' to get caught like a damn . . ."

Jake's voice dwindled as a warning flashed in Ross's eyes. He assessed the hardening of his friend's jaw and the telltale muscle ticking in his cheek.

Ross wheeled his horse around. He caught Jake's eye, holding it for long silent seconds before mumbling, "Hell, you never could take orders. You'll never change."

Releasing a tense breath as Ross spurred his horse in the direction of the Dragoon Mountains, Jake shook his head. Within seconds he was following behind him.

CHAPTER II

DEVINA STOOD BESIDE the stagecoach on which she had just arrived in Tombstone. A hot late-afternoon sun beat down on her shoulders, increasing her discomfort, and she raised a weary hand to her brow. The still air reverberated with the raucous honky-tonk music and shrill laughter spilling from the numerous saloons lining the street behind her. The unrelenting pounding of carpenters' hammers echoed mercilessly inside her head, and she squinted against the noisy rumble of the heavily laden ore wagons that moved past to settle yet another layer of fine red dust on her stiff shoulders. The rhythmic racket of the stamping mills in the distance added to a pervading din that brought a new level of pain to Devina's aching head.

A crowd of curious townspeople had responded to the stage's thunderous arrival. Ignoring the narrowing circle of onlookers, Devina watched her father's expression as he approached. She had never seen him so furious.

Meticulously dressed in a sleekly tailored suit, his gleaming silver hair covered by a fashionable bowler hat, Harvey Dale was in a silent rage. His handsome mature face still as stone except for the small tic in his smooth-shaven cheek, he spoke in a tightly controlled voice. "You're certain you're all right, Devina?"

"Yes, Father, I'm fine."

Taking her arm, Harvey Dale turned his full fury on the tensely waiting guard. "All right, John Henry, I want a full explanation, now! How did you manage to lose my payroll?"

13

"I didn't have no chance, Mr. Dale. I wasn't expectin'—"

"You were armed, weren't you?" The sarcasm in Dale's voice bringing a bright flush to the burly guard's face, Harvey Dale continued with growing heat, "It was my understanding that 'you are one of the best riflemen around. Or was that all just a lot of talk to make me feel safe in entrusting my payroll to Wells Fargo?"

"Yes, sir, I was armed." A responsive anger sparked John Henry's small eyes as he pulled his broad frame up to its full height. "And, yes, sir, I do lay claim to bein' one of the best rifle shots in these parts. But I didn't have no chance to—"

"What do you mean you didn't have a chance? It was your job to defend that stage and that money with your life! And you tell me you didn't even get off a shot! What in hell is wrong with you? You were hired to—"

"Father, the man had no choice." Devina could no longer witness her father's attack on the undeserving guard without protest. Expressionless, she met the full heat of her father's anger as he turned again in her direction.

"Stay out of this, Devina. This man acted in wanton disregard for his responsibility. He—"

"No, Father, you're wrong. The thief held a gun to my side and—"

"A gun to your side!" The unnatural flush suddenly draining from his face, Harvey Dale threw a quick glance in John Henry's direction.

"That's right, Mr. Dale. One of the robbers—I think he was the leader—made out to be a passenger. I didn't see or hear nothin' until he fired two shots through the roof of the coach and said he'd shoot Miss Dale if Buck didn't rein up. To my mind, we didn't have no choice. That fella had a tight hold on your daughter, and his gun was against her ribs. He wasn't about to let her go. It seemed to me he was the type of fella who wouldn't hesitate to shoot her if I made a move."

"Is this true, Devina?" Dale demanded, his expression registering the full impact of the guard's words. "The leader held you captive? Threatened your life?"

"Yes, it's true."

His hand tightening spasmodically on her arm, Harvey Dale assessed his daughter's face more closely, noting for the first time her unnatural pallor and the pained narrowing of her expressive eyes. Making an obvious attempt to control his rage, he said, "We'll discuss this later, John Henry." Then he urged Devina onto the board sidewalk. Supporting her with his arm, he guided her around the crowd of onlookers and matched his stride to hers while still managing to propel her insistently forward.

"Father, where are we going? It's been a long, exhausting trip. If you don't mind, I'd like to—"

"Devina Elizabeth Dale"—the use of her full name warned her that her father was still angry—"I am not the fool you think me to be." Ignoring her spontaneous protest, Harvey Dale continued tightly, "I am well aware that you had no desire to join me here in Tombstone, that you would have preferred to remain in New York where you could enjoy the social scene to which you have become accustomed."

"Father, I—"

"Kindly, do not interrupt me, Devina. You are a beautiful young woman. You are wealthy and well educated. You will marry well. Your presence here in Tombstone will not affect that certainty. I intend to see to that. It is also my intention to see that nothing interferes with the brilliant future guaranteed to you as my daughter." Harvey sent her a meaningful glance before continuing. "When I say 'nothing,' Devina, I include in that category your own irresponsibility!"

"Father—"

"You have disobeyed me from the first, Devina! Mrs. Watson was a responsible woman. I searched long and hard, studied countless letters of application, recommendations, references, before deciding to hire her to accompany you to Tombstone. Yet you defied propriety and me by dismissing her and making the journey alone!"

"Mrs. Watson became ill."

"How convenient for you!"

"Oh, Father, she was an obnoxious woman, always giving me orders! She attached herself to me like second skin, refused to allow me out of her sight! She was driving me mad with, 'Your father instructed me to do this, your father instructed me to do that!' "

"And of course that was too much for you to bear."

"Yes, Father, it was. In any case, Mrs. Watson did become ill."

"And when you saw your opportunity, you took it and started off without her."

"Yes."

"And in the process nearly paid with your life!"

Stunned, Devina shook her head. A shadow of a smile cracked her stiff expression. "Surely, you don't think Mrs. Watson could have helped me during the holdup, Father? The man took everyone by surprise. What could Mrs. Watson have done? Oh, I suppose she could have rolled over and crushed the thief with her enormous bulk, but I doubt she would have had the presence of mind to—"

"Do not be sarcastic, Devina!"

"Father, you never met her. If you had, you would have congratulated me for my ingenuity in escaping her!"

"I sincerely doubt that." Slowing as they came to the corner of Fourth and Allen, Harvey Dale lowered his gaze to again meet hers. A startling vulnerability flicked across his face as he said, "I . . . I would like to say something that I should have made clear from the outset, Devina, when you objected to joining me here in this 'frontier wilderness.' You are my only child, and I love you deeply. I have no wish to spend my life separated from you, no matter how difficult you can be at times. It is expedient for me to remain in Tombstone to affect the greatest return on my investment here, but I have missed you sorely and I want you with me. The realization that you have been made to suffer because of my demand that you join me is the source of considerable pain to me; but I give you my word, you will not suffer again as you did today. I also promise you will enjoy your stay in Tombstone, even if I must change Tombstone to your liking in order for you to do so."

A warm heat gathered beneath Devina's eyelids, and she swallowed hard against it. She was almost grateful to the hard-eyed thief for having been successful, if temporarily, in tempering the war of wills that had raged between her father and her for the past few years. Despite her brave front, she was extremely shaken and haunted by the memory of the gun pressed against her ribs, the deep, sinister voice in her ear. The image of those dark eyes, which had dismissed her so contemptuously, lingered strangely in her mind. A sense of outrage swelled anew inside her, prompting her soft response. "Father, there is something you could do that would make Tombstone much more to my liking."

Committed to his words, Harvey Dale nodded his assent.

"I want to see that criminal, the leader of the men who robbed the stage, behind bars. I want to prove to him that . . ." Emotion unexpectedly filled her throat, and Devina was unable to go on.

Visibly affected by his daughter's agitation, Harvey Dale slid a protective arm around her waist. His voice was low, intense. "You have my word, Devina. That criminal will pay, and pay dearly, for his ill treatment of you."

Embarrassed by her unexpected lapse, Devina was unable to respond as her father continued softly.

"But now there's something you can do for me, Devina. I'd like you to accompany me to Dr. Carter's office. It is just a few doors down the street. It will relieve my mind immeasurably."

"Oh, Father . . ."

"You are extremely pale, Devina. I fear that you are more shaken than you will admit."

"I'll be fine after I get a little rest, Father."

"Dr. Carter's office is only a few doors away."

The concern in his gaze more than she could dismiss, Devina gave a small shrug. "All right, Father. If it will make you feel better."

Relief twitched lightly at Harvey Dale's thin lips as he escorted her down the street. His sharp knock on the door was met by a muffled response.

"Come in."

Her vision temporarily limited as she stepped from the bright sunlight into the dark interior of the office, Devina glanced at the broad-shouldered shirtsleeved figure crouched over a cabinet filled with medicine bottles. She was suddenly as impatient with her father's concern as she was with the man who kept them waiting while he finished scribbling in a small notebook. This was a waste of time. She was perfectly well. All she needed was a brief rest and she would be as good as new.

Harvey Dale began speaking as the man straightened and turned in their direction. "Charles, I would like you to meet my daughter, Devina. She has had a trying experience on her journey to Tombstone, and I'd like you to . . ."

The tall man turned fully toward them and Harvey Dale's words faded from Devina's hearing. A low gasp escaped her throat. The man's eyes were black, and startlingly familiar. He advanced toward her, and Devina's hand went to her throat, shock driving the breath from her lungs. His dark eyes locked onto her frozen gaze, Devina fought to catch her breath.

It was he, the gunman, the man on the stage.

But the broad hands that reached out to grasp her firmly were gentle for all their strength. The low voice, so startlingly familiar, was coolly professional, reassuring. He ushered her to a chair and held a vial under her nose. Her head snapped up when she inhaled its pungent scent.

The dark eyes again met hers. Large and distinctly slanted above bold cheekbones, they were still heart-stoppingly similar to the eyes that haunted her memory. But kindness and concern were reflected in these eyes, in direct contrast to the cold contempt in the gaze that hovered in the back of her mind.

"How are you feeling, Miss Dale? Has your head cleared?"

Nodding, still unable to speak, Devina assessed the man crouching beside her as he pressed his fingers against her wrist. She was barely aware of her father's low tone as he spoke quickly, efficiently summarizing the events that had led up to their visit. Her gaze remained frozen on the doctor's face as her vision slowly adjusted to the light.

A flash of embarrassment accompanied realization of her error as Devina studied the young doctor's face more calmly. How could have she have been so mistaken?

Granted, this man was of the same height and build as the stage robber, but his dark hair was cut fashionably short and gleamed with cleanliness, even in the limited light of the room. He was clean-shaven, allowing an unrestricted view of strong features in a sharply planed face that was compelling rather than handsome. She raised her eyes again to his. Oh, yes, the similarity was there in those dark, expressive eyes, but all threat was gone when the warmth of this man's smile creased their corners, lighting their dark depths.

Shaking off her lingering distress at the eerily familiar tone of the doctor's voice, Devina was suddenly chagrined. For all her brave display, she had allowed fear to control her, to make her see demons where there were none. Determined not to reveal her foolish mistake, Devina turned toward her father, only to be startled at his pallor as he stood hesitantly at her side.

"Father, are you all right?"

Her simple question sent a flush of color to Harvey Dale's stiff face as he directed his response to the young doctor at her side.

"My daughter asks if I'm well, Charles, when indeed it is she who almost fainted a few moments ago. So I pose the same question to you. She is extremely shaken, as you can well see. I worry for the state of her nerves. Perhaps a tonic to relax her . . ."

After regarding Devina intently for long silent minutes, Charles Carter said, "Harvey, you needn't be too anxious about your daughter's temporary upset. Miss Dale appears to be a strong and healthy young woman. As you can see, her color has already returned, and her concern for you indicates that she is once again thinking quite clearly. I suggest you take her home and allow her to rest. I'll give her a powder to use should she be unable to sleep. If she feels it necessary, I can stop by to visit her tomorrow. I think we will be able to get a truer picture of her problem then, if indeed there is one."

"You are certain that she is all right?"

"Your daughter has undergone a frightening experience, Harvey, but I doubt she'll suffer any lasting effects from it. The best treatment for her right now is rest. I suggest that you have your carriage drawn up in front of my office to save Miss Dale any unnecessary steps. Then a light supper and some sleep. She'll need no further treatment."

Harvey Dale excused himself and walked quickly out the door. Still silent, Devina returned her gaze to Charles Carter as he pulled a chair to her side, sat down, and smiled into her eyes.

"I'm very pleased to meet you, Miss Dale."

An uncharacteristic flush coloring her face, Devina gave a small laugh. She had not expected the smooth charm this frontier doctor exhibited. "I must admit I feel very much at a disadvantage, Dr. Carter. I am not accustomed to fainting at the sight of a strange man."

"This business on the stage, would you care to tell me more about it?"

"Truly, I would rather not." Agitation stirring anew at the simple mention of the incident, Devina shook her head. "I was personally threatened, held captive with a gun at my ribs. I'm afraid I was more upset by the incident than I realized."

A strange flicker in the young doctor's dark eyes caused Devina a moment's concern before he replied quietly, "Somehow I have the feeling the full impact of the incident didn't hit you until you walked into this room. I hope I haven't been responsible for upsetting you in any way."

Startled at the doctor's perceptiveness, Devina shook her head. "Of course not. You've been very kind."

The rattle of a carriage could be heard outside the door, and Charles Carter turned in its direction. A small frown creased his face as Harvey Dale's voice accompanied the sound of footsteps outside the door. "It seems your father has not hesitated in his return, Miss Dale." Unexpectedly placing his hand on hers, Charles Carter offered her a small smile. "I would very much like to call you Devina, if that meets with your approval."

The sudden warmth in the young doctor's regard returned a sense of normalcy to the situation, and Devina smiled. "Of course, if I may call you Charles."

Rising as her father entered the office, Devina was about to speak when an excited cowboy burst into the room.

"Doc, there's been a shootin' at the Orient. You'd better come quick."

Devina felt her smile drain from her lips, and her heartbeat grew ragged. At the cowboy's words, all the cordiality had vanished from Charles Carter's eyes, and she found herself looking into the cold onyx gaze of the gunman once more. But Charles allowed her little time to indulge her fantasy as he grabbed his bag and nodded a brief farewell. Within minutes he was moving through the doorway.

Her heart was still beating raggedly when Devina lifted her eyes to her father's. Turning, she walked toward the doorway on legs that still quaked beneath her.

Furious with her own strange debility, Devina seethed in silence. She would conquer this fixation, would forget those cold, dark eyes that had burned into her soul. Willing the strength back into her weak knees, she stepped out onto the sidewalk and hurried toward the waiting carriage. She would not allow fear to become her master.

CHAPTER III

SHOCK HOLDING HIM motionless for long moments, Ross Morrison slowly raised his head. Incredulous, he focused his gaze on Jake Walsh's sober face as he stood in the doorway of the cabin. When a second sense had made him send Jake into Tombstone for information immediately after the robbery, he had not expected Jake to come racing back at daybreak to tell him . . .

"Devina Dale, Harvey Dale's daughter? You're telling me I had her in my hands and I let her go?"

"Hell, I was just as surprised as you when I heard she was the woman on the stage! Nobody knew she was comin' in yesterday. From what I understand, not even Harvey Dale knew."

His gaze following Jake's progress into the room, Ross shook his head. Agitation quickened his breath, and he rose to his feet.

"I had her in my hands and I let her go. Hell, I had it all right here in my hands. I should have known, should have realized . . ."

"Realized what? None of us knew Harvey Dale's daughter was comin' out west to live with her father."

"I knew from the moment I saw her . . . There was something about her, the way she carried herself, the way she spoke. That damned attitude of superiority, as if she was two steps up from the rest of the world."

The memory of Harvey Dale's face returned to Ross's mind, and he felt a flush of pure hatred suffuse him. He continued in a low voice, uncertain and uncaring if Jake was still listening.

21

"Dale has that way of looking at a man with contempt, as if a man's a fool to think he stands a chance against him and his money. He looked at my father that way on that last day in court when he walked off free and clear with my father's claim. And he looked at me that way the day I was convicted and sentenced to prison on the evidence he'd paid for. The hardest part of it all was knowing he was right. Pa and I never stood a chance against him."

Familiar with Ross's hatred for Harvey Dale, Jake did not like the direction Ross's mind was taking. Anxious to stem his friend's rising frustration, Jake interrupted Ross's low monologue. "Yeah, I know about all that, Ross, but I didn't come back with the news just to stir you up. Dale was real busy in Tombstone after he took his daughter home. He's madder than a hornet and he's hatchin' up somethin'. I figured you ought to know so you could be on the lookout." Jake paused with a brief shrug. "When you come right down to it, what good would it have done if you had known who the Dale woman was from the start?"

Ross's eyes took on a sudden menace. He gave a low, mirthless laugh. "What good? I would've listened to you, old friend, and brought her with me."

"You know I didn't mean what I said, Ross." Jake shook his head in denial. "You know damned well you were right when you said that woman wouldn't be worth the trouble."

"That was before I knew who she was."

"She still wouldn't be worth the trouble. What would you gain? Hell, Dale's mad enough that we're hittin' him in the pocketbook. We don't need him puttin' any more pressure on the sheriff. He's only got one daughter."

"And my father only had one life."

"Ross, the girl's innocent. She didn't have anythin' to do with what her father did to your pa or to you."

Ross's response was a low growl. "That girl hasn't had an innocent day in her life." Unwilling to discuss the matter further, Ross turned and walked to the door, where he paused in contemplative silence.

Jake snapped his mouth shut tight. His light brows furrowed into a frown. Two and a half years as Ross's cellmate in Yuma Prison had taught him that it was useless to argue with him when he was in one of his dark moods. Silence now and a quiet, persuasive argument later would be far more effective.

But that realization afforded Jake little peace of mind. He had sensed that somehow, this robbery had been different. Ross had been too tense after this one. In the three months since they had been released from prison they had managed to relieve Till-Dale of six payrolls. Each time, Ross had been jubilant, knowing he was another step closer to causing a financial crisis at Till-Dale. Not so with this last robbery.

His disquiet growing, Jake watched as Ross turned from the door and began restlessly pacing the small cabin. Jake's frown deepened. He hadn't liked Ross's reaction to Devina Dale. He liked it even less now that they had found out who she was. That girl would be trouble for Ross, and Ross needed no more trouble, especially from a Dale. He had suffered enough.

Fragmented memories flashed across Jake's mind. Isolation, dark cells, hunger, and hard, grueling, unrelieved labor. Ross had suffered it all right along with him, and Ross had saved his life several times during those days in prison when he had been too weak to defend himself.

Jake swallowed tightly. Beads of perspiration induced by harsh memories covered his forehead, and he brushed them away with his arm. He'd give his life for Ross Morrison, and he'd be damned if he'd let Ross go off half cocked and end up in prison again. He'd talk to Ross later, when he was in a mood to listen.

His restless prowling suddenly coming to a halt, Ross walked purposefully to the doorway.

"Where are you going, Ross?"

Turning around abruptly, Ross glared darkly in his friend's direction. Hesitating before he responded, he reached into the bucket by the door and withdrew a bar of soap and a razor.

"If it's any of your damned business, I'm going to cool myself off." Reaching up, he tugged at his ragged black beard. "And I'm going to get rid of this thing. It's too damned hot. I've had enough of it. Besides, it's too easy to recognize, now that the passengers in the coach had a close look at me."

"But you know what's going to happen if you shave. You're going to . . ."

A small smile curved Ross's lips. "I know exactly what I'm doing, Jake."

Turning abruptly, Ross strode from the cabin. Walking past Mack and Harry as they tended to their horses, he gave them a brief nod, unaware that Jake's concerned gaze still followed him.

• • •

Crystal beads of water reflected a rainbow's hue on Ross's strong, naked length as he walked calmly from the pool a short time later. Flexing the muscles of his powerful chest and shoulders, he ran a callused palm over his smoothly shaven cheek. Damn, that felt good! The long hair and beard had been uncomfortable.

Ross gave a short laugh. Mack and Henry said he was obsessed with being clean. They said he had chosen this dilapidated prospector's cabin as a hideout simply because there was a shallow natural pool nearby. They had been partly right. Memories of three years in Yuma returned—working long hours in the hot sun, wearing the same clothes for endless days, subsisting on food that was little more than edible, sometimes not even that, enduring conditions that were fit for neither man nor beast. He had earned the luxury of a daily bath. And he had learned a hard lesson: He had learned to survive.

He had also learned that he would never again be in a position where another man would have complete control over his life. His respect for the law was gone. The law was nothing more than a tool the rich used to protect their wealth. A poor man had only his mind and his strength of will to protect him, and Ross had determined in those three lost years that his will would never again be subject to others.

He had come out of prison a different man, a stronger man, harder. And he had come out determined to bring Harvey Dale to his knees.

So, the woman he had held hostage so briefly was Devina Dale. Devina. Of course. A common name like Mary or Sally would not do for the daughter of Harvey Dale. Jake had said that Harvey Dale was enraged when his daughter arrived in town thoroughly shaken by the holdup. Strange, he thought. Miss Devina Dale had not appeared all that shaken to him. She had refused to submit to his threat, retained her arrogance to the last. He remembered with particular vividness her erect, proud posture when he released her to join the other passengers. And he remembered only too vividly the struggle that had raged within him as he had fought the desire to ride up behind her, sweep her onto his horse, and carry her away.

He had told her she was not worth the trouble. Those words rang hollow in the back of his mind. He should have trusted his instincts, as blind as they had been. He had sensed then that she would be worth whatever trouble she gave him.

The sun was warm against his flesh and he closed his eyes and rubbed his face dry. His black eyes slanted upward above bold cheekbones framed by dark arched brows. Clean-shaven, his features were strong, compelling, his jaw hard and determined.

Ross began dressing. He had put his time in the pool to good use. He had emerged refreshed, clean-shaven, and with a plan. Devina Dale was the key to that plan.

A familiar spark ignited inside Ross at the thought of Devina Dale. It grew to a warm heat with the memory of her sweet scent, the womanly softness that had filled his arms. He remembered the haughty spirit in those great blue eyes as they flashed heatedly into his. He would enjoy taming her almost as much as he would enjoy making Harvey Dale suffer as he and his father had suffered.

Fully dressed, Ross walked rapidly back toward the cabin. Avid anticipation curved his lips into a smile.

Devina slowly descended the carpeted staircase. She gazed at the elaborate stained-glass panel above the front door, temporarily mesmerized by its exquisite beauty. Countless pieces of delicate colored glass, cut and arranged to form the pattern of the dawn of a new day. The muted hues at the base, blended with unmistakable artistry, gradually stirred to life, growing into a heated blaze of color with a subtlety of technique that was unique, breathtaking! The work of a master.

A brilliant morning sun shone through the panes, enhancing the dazzling composition before her, and Devina paused a little longer to indulge herself in the glorious wash of color that bathed the foyer. With a last lingering glance she continued down the staircase. If she were to be truly honest, she would have to admit that the artistic stained-glass window was just one of the many surprises that had awaited her when she entered her father's residence in Tombstone.

A few steps more brought her onto a lush Brussels carpet, and her mind unconsciously registered the depth of the pile, the beauty of the pattern. She raised her eyes to the crystal chandelier, trailed her glance down the walls, which were covered with rich silk. The mahogany furniture was elegant enough to grace the far more grandiose Dale mansion in New York, and an exquisite Ming vase stood on a small table in the corner.

This unexpected elegance, so casually displayed, appeared to mark the entire house. Devina's bedroom was unusually large and boasted an enormous canopy bed, an elaborately carved fireplace, and massive mahogany furniture. The yellow silk coverlet, bed curtains, and window draperies told her the room had been decorated with her taste in mind. The thoughtfulness touched her deeply. She was surprised her father had remembered that yellow was her favorite color.

As she approached the sunlit morning room at the far end of the hallway, she realized this house probably would afford her many more surprises.

She had not expected this touch of civilization when she received her father's command to join him in Tombstone . . . and a command it had been. Resentment, deep and profound, had been her response. During all those years in exclusive boarding schools, Devina had borne the loneliness and had dug deep inside herself for the strength to use it to her own advantage. And finally she had overcome it, become strong, self-reliant, determined not to be dependent on her father's love . . . or, indeed, on anyone's love. Love was a trap. It had been a trap for her beautiful, long-suffering mother, who had lived for Harvey Dale, enduring his neglect, his countless affairs without a word of recrimination.

No, she could never see herself in Mama's place, as much as she had loved Mama for her gentleness, her understanding, and even her self-sacrifice. With all the wisdom she had earned from her broken twelve-year-old heart, she had determined, when her mother died, that she would not try to fill her shoes, not for her father or any man. Only those like Harvey Dale survived—the strong, the ruthless, those who used love. She, too, was determined to survive.

So she had embraced the life her father had forced upon her, turned her eyes toward education, the arts. Possessing no talent herself, she had become deeply appreciative of the talent of others, without ever becoming subservient to that appreciation. A few months before, at eighteen, she had graduated from school and been firmly ensconced in the home of an extremely indulgent Aunt Emily. She had been cognizant of her many assets, the fact that she was an acknowledged beauty, wealthy, sought after by countless extremely eligible bachelors—and several not so eligible but very interesting rakes. She had been a woman at last, ready to enter society and take full advantage of the options open to her.

Then had come Father's command to join him on the uncivilized southwestern frontier. She had been outraged! Tombstone! Even if the primitive mining town had not had a horrendous reputation, its name alone would have conjured up ghastly visions of a life she had no intention of enduring. Had she spent all those years in learning to appreciate the beautiful things in life only to be buried in a territory inhabited by savages and barbarians, a place that possessed not an iota of the elegance and appreciation of beauty to which she was so firmly devoted?

Outrage soared anew inside Devina. Her father's surprising statement of the day before had touched a spot deep inside her that had been an aching void for too long. He had said he loved her deeply. But the truth was that she was aware of his limited capacity to love. She had no doubt he had sincerely loved Mama, too . . . in his fashion.

Devina slowed her step, once more allowing her eyes to travel over the sunlit hallway and the unexpected touches of elegance. The wild, uncivilized Tombstone, a town lawless enough to have incurred the concern of President Arthur himself, was certainly not evident here.

Abruptly, as if to negate her most recent thought, Devina was revisited by the vision of cold, dark eyes, penetrating, ruthless eyes that had successfully invaded her dreams all night long. A chill passed down her spine as memory returned with heart-stopping clarity the sound of a deep voice filled with threat: *Repulsive, but in control . . . of you . . .*

She remembered the sensation of a hard chest against her back, his sinewy thighs supporting hers. She remembered the bite of the gun barrel against her ribs. She remembered . . .

More shaken by the memory than she cared to admit, Devina was reaching out a trembling hand to steady herself when sudden realization assaulted her: She was shuddering! A flush of true fury coming to her aid, Devina curled her shaking fingers into a tight fist and dropped her hand to her side. Taking a deep, determined breath, she straightened her back and resolutely raised her chin. What had come over her? Would she allow a common criminal—an ignorant, uneducated derelict—to intimidate her? For all her brave talk when she had faced him squarely, she was now reacting like a spineless faint-hearted ninny!

Suddenly grateful that there were no witnesses to her shameful weakness, Devina paused a moment longer as her anger continued to build, filling her with strengthening resolution. Once more she was assailed by memory: *You wouldn't be worth the trouble* . . .

Why did those words continue to resound in her mind?

Shrugging off the disturbing question, Devina took another deep breath and sought to slow the rapid pounding of her heart. With a searing hatred of which she had not realized she was capable, she renewed her silent vow: She would see the cowardly bully who had manhandled and insulted her brought to justice, and she would smile as he was forced to retract every word he had uttered to her.

No longer shaking, Devina raised a steady hand to smooth the upward sweep of her hair. A stiff smile on her delicate lips, she stepped into the sunlit morning room.

The sound of a light step in the doorway raised Harvey Dale's well-groomed silver head as Devina stepped into the morning room. He assessed her exquisite countenance with true concern as he rose to his feet. Yes, she looked well and strong. Relief, love, and pride surged through him in a startlingly strong flood as he pulled himself up to his impressive height. His patrician features creased into the engaging smile that had turned the head of many a sensible matron.

Devina, his darling daughter . . . he had missed her so dreadfully. Indulging himself a few moments longer, Harvey allowed his gaze to touch Devina's perfect cameolike features. Those crystal-clear blue eyes, those delicate winged brows, the lush sweep of her dark lashes were all so like her mother's. Her cheekbones, sculptured so exquisitely, the fine lines of her profile, those finely drawn lips. Only her hair was different, a glowing halo of silver-blond, similar to the color his own had been. Had her hair been dark, Devina would have been the image of her mother, his own dear Regina.

Regina . . . queen. Yes, his beautiful wife had truly been a queen, and he had loved her dearly. He had not realized how very deep had been his love until he lost her. But he had long ago ceased berating himself for allowing his own self-indulgence to cause Regina to suffer during the many years of their marriage. He had come to terms with his regrets by finally reassuring himself that Regina had realized his character was flawed but had loved him anyway.

A flicker of anxiety moved across Harvey's mind. To his everlasting torment, he was fully aware that such was not the case with Devina. Devina had been twelve, intelligent and perceptive, when her mother had died. The many nights when he had not returned home to her mother's bed, and her mother's subsequent unhappiness, had not escaped her. Nor had they been forgiven. In a flush of childish rage and sorrow after her mother's death, Devina had screamed her fury at his faithlessness. Her knowledge and pain had caused a rift between them, which he had attempted to eliminate by overindulging her, but that particular solution had provided him nothing but grief. Finally realizing that he had lost control of the situation and that, indeed, the situation was worsening, he had listened to well-meant advice and sent Devina away to boarding school.

Admittedly, her absence had allowed him more time for business pursuits, and other more intimate pursuits as well. With the aid of time and distance, the animosity between Devina and himself had begun to fade, and he would have been able to convince himself all was once again well had he not sensed an unyielding, impenetrable reserve in her attitude toward him. He had finally come to the painful realization that the loving, trusting child that Devina once had been no longer existed. It was then that he had realized he would give up everything he had worked so hard to achieve just to see unqualified love for him shining in Devina's eyes.

As she had become stronger and more independent, her strength of will had grown as unyielding as her determination to defy his orders. But despite her opposition, Harvey Dale had remained adamant. He had not done well by Regina; he had resolved to do better by Devina.

He had followed through with his plans for Devina by assuming an inconsistently strict posture. Now, despite the mistakes and regrets of the past, Devina was back with him. She was intelligent, well educated, beautiful, and, he acknowledged regretfully, spoiled to a fault.

But he had meant what he said: He loved her deeply. He was aware that this depth of feeling was foreign to his nature, and he was at a loss to explain it. But whether it was simply because she was his daughter, of his own flesh, or because he saw himself so clearly reflected in her despite her lack of physical resemblance to him, he was uncertain. He only knew the pain of her rejection had been as soul-shaking as the joy she had given him, and it had never quite faded from his mind. Devina was the one person in the world he loved more than he loved himself. She was his beautiful child. Would she never again love him unreservedly in return?

Stepping forward as Devina reached the table, Harvey took her hand. Succumbing to impulse, he bent his head to receive her kiss. Devina's hesitation, however minuscule, triggered an uncontrollable sadness within him.

Stiff pride coming to his rescue, Harvey seated Devina politely and resumed his own seat. He picked up a small silver bell and shook it absentmindedly as he studied Devina's face more closely. At second glance, she did not look as well as he thought. Her color was a bit too bright, her smile strained. He did not bother to turn as he spoke to the uniformed servant who appeared at his side.

"Molly, Miss Devina is ready for breakfast."

"No, Molly, please don't bother. I'm not hungry this morning."

A flicker of annoyance nudged at Harvey. "Devina, you really should eat something. You've eaten very little since you arrived . . . understandable after the fright you suffered, but this morning . . ."

Devina's expression took on a familiar stiffness. "The 'fright' I suffered has nothing to do with my lack of appetite, Father. If I suffered any disability at all, it was due to the intense heat, the choking dust, and the unbearably long journey in that abominable coach. I very rarely have anything more than a cup of tea and perhaps a slice of toast for breakfast."

Harvey turned to the servant. "Bring tea and toast for Miss Devina, Molly . . . and orange marmalade." He held Devina's gaze with his own as he continued lightly, "Orange marmalade is one of Miss Devina's favorites."

Was he wrong, or did he see a momentary softening of Devina's expression? A moment later, certain he had been mistaken, Harvey decided to pursue a different tack.

"I regret that I'll have to leave you today, Devina. Unfortunately, this latest robbery has caused complications that I must handle personally."

"This *latest* robbery?"

'Cursing himself for his slip, Harvey shook his head. "It's nothing I care to discuss with you, Devina. I think it would be best if you concerned yourself with learning more about the social activities of Tombstone so you might settle yourself in more comfortably."

"Father, I disagree." The flicker of annoyance that had moved across his daughter's beautiful face turned into a full-fledged frown. "Since I was intimately involved in this robbery, I think it only sensible that I be informed of just exactly what has been going on here in Tombstone."

Harvey's expression tightened as well. "You were 'intimately involved' in that robbery only because of your defiance, Devina. Had you not changed the traveling arrangements I made, you would not have arrived on the coach that carried the payroll. And I tell you now that I shall not allow such a thing to happen again."

Suddenly realizing the situation was fast progressing into another open confrontation, Harvey gave a short laugh. "As for my telling you what has been going on, surely you're not ignorant of Tombstone's reputation, Devina. Your very explicit correspondence from New York has led me to understand the opposite. I believe your initial objection to joining me here was that you did not want to live 'under the lawless conditions that exist on the southwestern frontier.' "

Devina's frown deepened, and Harvey had a strong suspicion that he was not going to be able to avoid answering her question.

"Father, I cannot believe you sent me to school and educated me without expecting that I would emerge capable of thinking for myself. You know exactly what I mean, and I would appreciate a candid response from you in return. I should hate to have to get my information secondhand."

Harvey took a deep breath and stroked his slender silver mustache. He was not accustomed to being opposed at every word, but Devina was correct: She had a right to know.

"Well, the truth is, Devina, Till-Dale Enterprises appears to be under attack. Our payrolls have been stolen six times in the last three months."

"What makes you think it isn't just a coincidence? From what we've been led to believe back east, stagecoach robberies are a common occurrence in Tombstone."

"I thought the same thing at first, but while larger payrolls of other companies have gone unmolested, Till-Dale payrolls have not managed to get through.''

Devina paused, and Harvey watched as the myriad possibilities flashed across her expressive face. "Perhaps someone within your organization . . ."

"I doubt that."

"Can you think of anyone who might have a grudge against Till-Dale, Father? Someone who—''

Harvey's short laugh interrupted Devina's seriously voiced question. "Devina, if the truth be known and if I cared to enumerate, the list of those who consider themselves my enemy would be longer than my arm." Taking notice of his daughter's disapproving expression, he added in a more serious vein, "Certainly you realize I could not have achieved such prominence in the business world without leaving behind me any number of people who insist that part of my wealth belongs to them."

Devina appeared to consider his statement in silence. Then, as a sudden thought struck her, she shook her head. "I don't know why I didn't remember this before, Father. The thief, the man who held me hostage, he used the guard's name. I remember distinctly! He said, 'No, you don't, John Henry!' "

Harvey could not restrain his laughter. "Dear, I'm afraid there are very few people in this territory who don't know John Henry Thomas. In any case, dear, George and I will get to the bottom of things. We have overcome obstacles greater than this in the past." Pausing as Devina maintained her silence, Harvey waited until the unsmiling gray-haired maid had placed Devina's tea and toast on the table and turned her enormous bulk back to the kitchen before continuing.

"In the meantime, there are any number of things you might do to find entertainment in Tombstone, Devina. We have quite an active society here. The Terpsichorean Club for instance, or the Shakespeare Circle. We are quite a bit more cultured here in Tombstone than you have been led to understand. Believe it or not, dear, the New York production of Sardou's *Divorçons* is presently playing at Schieffelin Hall. Perhaps we will attend later in the week."

Devina made no comment. She picked at her toast and Harvey began to feel a surging frustration. He had forgotten how truly difficult his daughter could be.

Raising her eyes unexpectedly to his, Devina offered in a

surprisingly congenial voice, "Perhaps, but in truth, I would like to spend some time becoming accustomed to the town. I thought perhaps I would take a walk."

So relieved was Harvey at his daughter's apparent change of heart that it took a moment for him to react to her statement.

"No, I'm afraid that's out of the question right now, Devina."

"Out of the question?" Devina's expression lost all semblance of congeniality.

"I would prefer that you wait until I can hire a personal maid to act as your companion."

"Companion! Father, I'm not a child! I'm perfectly capable of walking—"

"I said it's out of the question, Devina." The unpredictable turns of their conversation were wearing on his limited patience, and Harvey straightened his shoulders in an unconsciously revealing gesture that caused his daughter's small nose to twitch with vexation. He paused and continued with an attempt at a smile. "Tombstone is, after all, different from any other town of your experience, dear, and you are quite beautiful. I would not want you wandering into any situations—"

"Father, I repeat, I am not a child!"

Realizing the last threads of his composure were slipping away, Harvey raised himself to his feet and said with great control, "You will not leave this house until I can provide you with a companion. I will take care of the matter on the way to the office this morning."

Making a last effort to part with his daughter on a more harmonious note, Harvey continued, "In the meantime, you might help me with a little matter. I've ordered any number of impressive pieces for this house, since I insist that my living conditions reflect a style consistent with my position here in Tombstone. But, in truth, I've had very little time to see that these pieces are well placed and to finish the refurbishing as I should like. I'd appreciate your expertise in rearranging things here, completing the decorating. It was my intention to have some sort of open house for my friends once this place was ready, but somehow, time has slipped away from me. Perhaps now that you're here, Devina, I might get my life into some semblance of order. I would sincerely appreciate your help, dear."

Releasing a silent, tense breath as Devina nodded, Harvey

stepped away from the table with a broadening smile. "You may tour the town tomorrow at the very latest, dear. You have my word on it. Until later . . ."

Taking his leave, Harvey walked rapidly toward the front door. He closed it behind him with a distinct sense of relief. How could he have forgotten? No one had ever challenged him like Devina, with her perceptiveness and her mercurial changes of mood. He had the feeling that whatever the future had to offer him now that she was back at his side, life would never be dull.

Listening as the door closed behind her father, Devina unconsciously straightened her shoulders. She dropped one hand to her lap, her manners faultless even as she stared unseeingly through the window into the yard beyond. Correct posture and proper table manners had been thoroughly ingrained in her at school: "Miss Dale, we do not slump at the table . . . Miss Dale, we raise our fork to our mouth. We do not lower our head to meet our food."

Devina dropped her eyes to the table. Her gaze fell on the small crystal container resting on the spotless white tablecloth. Orange marmalade. Orange marmalade and yellow drapes. Devina remembered her father's engaging smile. It had contained just the right mixture of sincerity and concern. Oh, yes, Father was a master at overcoming a woman's resistance. His technique was the result of long practice. His past gave ample proof of his ability.

Dismissing that thought as another surfaced within her mind, Devina again experienced a flare of annoyance. So she needed a companion when she walked the streets of Tombstone. Ridiculous!

Without warning, a dark, sinister gaze reappeared in Devina's mind's eye, startling her. But this time the penetrating eyes were mocking, and Devina felt a hot flush rise to her cheeks. Checking herself, she halted her rapid emotional response. No, she would not allow the mocking eyes or her own irritation at her father's autocratic attitude to force her into unwise behavior. She had learned the hard way that such a course of action was invariably to her own detriment. Father obviously had little respect for her intelligence and ingenuity, and those intrusive eyes—Devina took a deep breath—had no respect for her at all. She would prove them both wrong.

She would demonstrate her maturity by waiting a day, as her

father had requested, before beginning her tour of Tombstone. She would amuse herself by becoming accustomed to the household today. In truth, there were many things she needed to do. Father's request for aid in decorating the house, no matter its devious intent, had sparked her interest. She had always found the thought of spending Father's money intriguing. If he did not provide the "companion" by evening, she would go about town tomorrow on her own. She usually ended up doing as she pleased in any case.

Her decision made, Devina shrugged off the dark-eyed gaze that hovered at the back of her mind and picked up her knife. With a sober expression that reflected her resolve, she reached for the small crystal container and began spreading orange marmalade liberally on her toast.

Harvey Dale adjusted the high, stiff collar of his shirt. In a quick, efficient movement, he fingered his cravat, checking its folds, and adjusted the tilt of his stylish bowler. Such was his ritual each morning before stepping out onto the street, despite the time he usually spent before the mirror prior to leaving his room. After all, a man in his position—an equal partner in Till-Dale Enterprises, one of the largest mining companies in this portion of the country, a man who was socially prominent, who was the president of the prestigious Tombstone Club—could not afford to look less than his best. But, in truth, if he had been a common clerk or teller in a bank, he would still have maintained an impeccable personal appearance. Harvey was vain.

Having long before acknowledged that vice, Harvey had added it, without thought or distress, to the other numerous and acknowledged flaws in his character. Surely a man could not help but be vain when he knew he was handsome? He had been an appealing child, a good-looking adolescent, and he was well aware that he was a devastatingly handsome adult. His good looks had gotten him far, and he had played them for all their worth.

Harvey took great pride in the fact that his body was still firm, free of the fat and sagging muscle that usually accompanied middle age. He was also aware that his heavy silver mane and well-manicured mustache were just as attractive to the opposite sex as they had been in their original youthful color. He had at first observed with distaste the lines maturity had added to his faultless countenance, but later on had discovered that many women were attracted to mature men. With that realization, his already considerable ego had received another unneeded lift.

As for business, there was no doubt his appearance added to his credibility as one of the richest men in this part of the country. He looked the part, played the part, every inch the man he appeared to be. He was handsome, rich, well known in the financial community, where he was considered shrewd and almost invincible. He had long ago decided he would do anything he deemed necessary to maintain his position and expand his wealth, and he had followed that philosophy avidly all of his life.

Which brought him to his presently unsettling state of affairs. The fury he had suppressed in deference to his daughter's presence now surged to life, flooding his smooth-shaven cheeks with color. He had evaded Devina's questions about the latest robbery because he had not wished her to see how very frustrated he was by the apparent success of the vendetta being waged against him. Yes, he had enemies, but up until now they had been ineffective against him. The situation was beginning to change. Six payrolls had been stolen, and in the face of Till-Dale's current shortage of liquid assets, he was beginning to feel the pinch.

But Harvey's fury did not stem entirely from financial concerns. A new dimension had been added to his rage with the realization that a criminal—a common thief—had actually had the audacity to abuse his beautiful daughter, to threaten her life!

Harvey took a deep breath and made an effort to bring his emotions under control. It would do no good to allow anger to rule his thoughts. Instead, he would intensify his efforts to identify the men who waged a war against him. When that was accomplished, he would have them hunted down. He would see them imprisoned for the crimes they had committed against him, and for the unpardonable affront of touching Devina.

Harvey turned onto Third Street. The congenial manner he had exhibited at the breakfast table for Devina's benefit had been replaced by the stiff arrogance that had become his trademark, and he grimaced as the buildings at the intersection of Toughnut Street and Third came into view. He would take care of his business in this unpleasant section of town, and then he would meet with George Tillson, his partner and attorney. George was as close a friend as Harvey would allow. Together they had formed Till-Dale Enterprises and brought it to its present position, and together they would be victorious over the common thieves who threatened them.

But first things first.

Stepping up onto the board sidewalk, Harvey walked arrogantly into a small cheese and Chinese delicacies store. He glanced around impatiently, ignoring the various Oriental objects on display. He felt a personal flash of satisfaction as a silent clerk appeared, only to turn and melt immediately back through the doorway at the rear of the shop. Yes, that little Chinese lackey knew Harvey Dale would deal with no one but the person in charge, and that person was doubtless in the back, supervising the organized gambling in the rear room.

Harvey gave a low snort as his mind was touched by a reluctant admiration for China Mary's business establishment. It offered gambling—fan-tan, mostly, amply supervised by unofficial Chinese policemen—prostitution, opium dens, work contracts for the five hundred Orientals in Tombstone, and hop for the women of the red-light district, a traffic that had given this section of town its name: Hop Town. One person—China Mary—ran it all and supervised Tong affairs as well.

The curtain to the rear of the store stirred gently, then parted to allow a short, ample feminine figure to pass through. Clad in the rich silks and rare jewelry that were her trademark, China Mary approached with a silent, brisk step. Stopping just short of him, the lamp overhead clearly illuminating the liberal streaking of gray in her dark, tightly bound hair, China Mary smiled, her face creasing into myriad lines.

"Ah, Mr. Dale, what may I do for you today?"

Harvey's neglect of the amenities was a calculated insult as he spoke with barely concealed condescension. "My daughter has just arrived from the East. I need a servant for her, a woman who can be trusted. I need someone special, Mary, not the usual run of dirty laborers you provide for doing laundry and other menial chores. I need someone who will be able to function as a personal maid for her. My daughter is well educated and intelligent. She will not suffer a slow, ignorant, unclean person around her."

Harvey noted with silent satisfaction the narrowing of China Mary's small eyes. China Mary was respected in some parts of Tombstone. Some spoke of her generosity to those in need—

Americans as well as her own people—but to him, she was nothing more than a Chinese immigrant who had managed to raise herself a step above the muck in which the rest of her people were mired. But he knew Mary could be trusted to keep her word. It was her word, in fact, that had kept her bound to him in payment of a debt that surpassed financial considerations. He had made sure she would be a long time in repaying it.

Harvey's sharp eyes pinned her. "Do you know of someone who will be able to fill those qualifications?"

Hesitating only briefly, Mary nodded. "I know just the person you seek."

Satisfaction twitched at the corner of Harvey's mouth. "I'll need her at my house today."

"Yes, Mr. Dale. It will be done."

Harvey was beginning to feel better already. He perused China Mary's face with half-closed eyes, noting and enjoying the hint of subservience in her demeanor, which he knew she displayed for no one other than him. His power over this woman, whose command of the Oriental community was unchallenged, was a heady stimulant.

"Is there anything else I may do for you, Mr. Dale?"

Harvey paused, his eyes moving to the narrow staircase at the far end of the dimly lit store. The thought of the small room upstairs, where he had spent many sensual hours, unexpectedly set his heart racing. A telltale stirring in his loins caused him to reach into the pocket of his waistcoat and withdraw an elaborately filigreed watch. He flicked open the cover in an offhand manner that he hoped appeared casual. It would not do to betray his growing physical arousal. He did not wish to allow Mary that much power over him.

Realizing he had not even seen the Roman numerals on the expensive timepiece, Harvey nodded. "Yes, I think so. I seem to have an hour to spare this morning."

China Mary's face remained unchanged, her smile fixed, but Harvey was not fooled. Sensing her reaction to his words, he spoke slowly, drawing out the time so he might achieve full satisfaction from the woman's discomfort. "I think I should like to go upstairs."

China Mary was no longer smiling. "Perhaps a visit to the very comfortable dwelling next door. Mei Ling and Gin Lon would be honored by your presence."

"I have no use for professional prostitutes, most especially of your race. No, I choose to wander in a more chaste garden. I should like to bask in the beauty of a graceful lily."

"The one whom you seek is not available this day."

"Make her available."

"She has gone on a personal errand; I know not where."

"You know everything that goes on in Tombstone, Mary. Get her back here. Now."

Her eyes holding his in open challenge for the briefest second, Mary gave a short nod.

"That's better." Turning toward the narrow staircase that beckoned him, Harvey took only two steps, then turned to garner Mary's gaze once more. "I do not expect to be kept waiting for longer than five minutes, Mary. I need not remind you that you will do well not to disappoint me."

Waiting only a moment longer for her nod of acquiescence, Harvey was soon ascending the narrow staircase.

His face covered with a sheen of perspiration, Ross glanced up toward the unrelenting sun and muttered a curse under his breath. He adjusted his position as he lay on his stomach on the hard-packed ground, sending a quick glance around him to again curse the rolling landscape, which was entirely devoid of trees. Where was the breeze that could usually be counted upon to adequately cool a man before he expired from the heat? This morning, of all mornings, the air was perfectly still.

Ross trained his spyglass on the Dale house in the distance. Having arrived a short time before, he had tethered his horse on the far side of the hill, climbed to the top of the rise, found a position suitable for silent observation, and made himself as comfortable as possible. He had known he was in for a long siege, but he had not realized how very uncomfortable it would be.

Damn, he had not figured the haughty Miss Dale to be a recluse. He had expected that she would be moving about town by now. His annoyance flared, and Ross reminded himself that this was but the first day of a surveillance he expected would be of considerable duration. When Miss Dale's routine was established and he had decided which time of day she would be most vulnerable, he would take action.

Continuing his perusal of the impressive Dale residence, Ross gave a low snort. The biggest house in Tombstone, in the center of the elegant northeastern corner of town. Of course, Harvey Dale would be satisfied with nothing less. Dale had no compunction about spending other people's money.

A sign of movement at the rear door of the house interrupted Ross's thoughts. He adjusted his glass so he might more clearly see the figure that emerged. A low, spontaneous gasp escaped his lips as Devina Dale stepped out into the morning sunlight. The rapid escalation of his heartbeat revealing his affected state, Ross again adjusted his glass in an attempt to achieve sharper focus.

Firmly refusing to acknowledge his own intense reaction to Devina Dale, even at a distance, Ross watched as she walked slowly down the two steps into the yard. She was perusing the countryside. Her concentration on a point in his direction afforded him an unrestricted view of her face, and his heart leaped in his chest. The tilt of her chin was almost regal, and she wore her hair piled high atop her head. He had never seen hair quite that color before, a peculiar shade of pale blond that was almost silver. It glowed in the brilliant light, a soft, glimmering halo.

She was standing so still. Her smooth, perfect face was sober. She continued to look in his direction unseeingly, her mind obviously far from the hills into which she stared. What was she thinking?

Ross gave a short impatient snort. What in hell was the matter with him, anyway? The little tart was probably thinking of her home, wherever that was—New York, most likely. She was probably thinking how unfair it was that she had been forced to associate with the barely civilized residents of this small, uninteresting frontier town.

Yes, he had not forgotten the cutting words she'd used in her harangue of the guiltless stationmaster prior to boarding that smaller coach in Benson. The poor man's ears were probably still ringing.

Refusing to lower his glass while Devina Dale looked in his direction, Ross uttered a low, incredulous sound. How could a man as corrupt as Harvey Dale have produced a daughter who looked like an angel? And she did appear angelic, all right, especially in that soft blue dress, which even at a distance he could tell was the same shade as her brilliant eyes. Ross's lips tightened. What a waste—the face of an angel, the heart of a shrew. Well, a little patience and he'd have the opportunity to express his opinion of Devina Dale directly to her face . . .

A bustle of movement in the rear doorway of the house interrupted Ross's thoughts as a large woman appeared. Devina Dale turned toward her and shook her head. The woman went back inside the house.

His eye glued to his glass, Ross followed Devina's slender figure until it disappeared through the rear doorway. Unable to look away, he willed her to come out once more, but she did not. Ross waited a few minutes longer, then finally lowered his glass. Despite himself, he could not shake an inexplicable sense of loss.

Harvey paced the small, meticulously neat room with annoyed anticipation. He checked his watch with a frown, finally removing his fashionable bowler to toss it atop the circular table in the corner. He disliked waiting. Most especially, he disliked waiting under these circumstances.

Harvey flicked his glance around the room in careless appraisal. He had been in this room many times, yet he never failed to be amazed at the skill with which it was decorated, despite the foreign flavor of its composition. Silk wall hangings, lacquered furniture, the intimate attention to detail that was characteristic of the Oriental mind, whether in the workplace or in the creation of beauty. The room would have been considered lovely by one who enjoyed an exotic flavor. But he most definitely was not one of them. He silently admitted that the decor of the room reflected the personality of its inhabitant. The admission annoyed him almost as much as did his own presence in the room that morning. For the hundredth time he wondered what he was doing here.

His fine gray mustache twitched with irritation. He had had no intention of climbing the narrow staircase this morning. His thoughts had been elsewhere, firmly ensconced in other matters, but somehow . . .

Despite himself, Harvey walked the few steps to the delicately painted wardrobe in the corner. He pulled open the door, his eyes dropping to the fine Oriental silk garments inside. The pale shades were in sharp contrast to the brilliant colors worn by China Mary. They reflected a refinement of taste that was yet another cause of his fascination for . . .

The sound of a light step at the door alerted Harvey to a presence in the hallway the moment before the knob turned. Closing the wardrobe, he turned as the door opened slowly.

His breath catching in his throat, Harvey watched in silence as a tall, delicately boned young woman paused in the open doorway. The exquisite planes of her face remained momentarily still before moving into a smile. With a characteristic grace of movement, the woman completed her entrance and turned to close the door gently behind her. She took two short steps forward and bowed slightly before she spoke. The soft, musical tone of her voice heightened his desire as it touched his ears.

"I was informed that you requested my presence. I am most happy to see you again, Mr. Dale."

Momentarily unable to respond, Harvey indulged himself in the total visual assault that was this young woman. More delicate than a fine Oriental porcelain figurine, she never failed to fill him with a sense of awe. Hair the color and texture of black silk was carefully braided and twisted above her ears in an elaborate hairstyle that he would have viewed with disdain on any other woman. But the coiffure only added to the delight of Lily's beauty, calling attention to her smooth unlined skin, the fragile contours of her face. His gaze touched the fine straight brows, delicate slashes above mysterious eyes, which never failed to intrigue him. He let his eyes trace her fine features and the scrupulous line of her cheek before they moved at last to her thin, well-drawn crimson lips, lips he had tasted many times.

Oriental perfection was Lily, truly the exquisite flower for which she was named. It seemed inconceivable that this tall, slender beauty was daughter to China Mary.

Harvey made an effort to rein his growing passion. In his attempt to rationalize the irresistible allure Lily held for him, he had decided the fact that she was the coveted daughter of China Mary definitely played a part. Strangely, considering his natural abhorrence of all others of her race, he had desired Lily from the moment he first saw her. In his wildest dreams he had never contemplated taking a woman of an inferior people to his body, but Lily was different. There was nothing inferior about Lily . . . nothing but the color of her skin, and even that was beautiful. Smooth, even-toned, it was softer than any he had ever touched. He remembered how this incomparable flower had come into his hands.

China Mary had come to him for financial aid several years before, after having been turned down by every other source in town. He had sensed a silent strength in her, his shrewd business mind immediately judging her a good risk, but he had not stopped there. A second sense had caused him to look further into China Mary's background, and in a maneuver of incredible brilliance, he had managed to lay his hands on some papers that could send her back to her native land to suffer harsh punishment. He had obtained those papers and concealed them in a spot where they would be immediately brought to the attention of the authorities should anything unexpected happen to him. That action, as well as the money he had ultimately advanced her, had earned him China Mary's unqualified cooperation and unfailing compliance with any request he made of her.

He was still applauding the stroke of genius which had guaranteed him that when financial considerations had been repaid, she would still be bound to him.

China Mary's power within the Chinese community had grown. Her control of work contracts for her people, the fact that not a person of her race worked in town without her permission, gave her access to information that was unavailable to most people, and Harvey found occasion to use that fund of knowledge to his advantage. But he did not realize the full potential of his power over China Mary until he first saw Lily.

He still remembered China Mary's protests when he indicated his desire for her darling daughter. She went into a silent rage, and after several controlled clashes between them, he was certain she was planning to abandon all she had achieved rather than allow him access to her precious jewel. Then, on the night when he was all but sure Mary was planning to leave, Lily had come to his office without her mother's knowledge and offered herself to him. She had come to him because she was unwilling to allow her mother to sacrifice all she had achieved in this new land.

A chill passed down Harvey's erect spine at the memory of his discovery that Lily was a virgin. He experienced again in retrospect the same sense of exhilaration he had experienced that first night. Lily, an exquisite Asian flower, plucked from the garden of innocence by his own experienced hand.

His body responding predictably to his thoughts, Harvey quickly covered the distance between himself and the beauteous Oriental woman. He looked down into Lily's magnificent countenance, his eyes moving over her perfect smile. A sudden uncomfortable realization assailed him. He had indeed conquered this young woman, taken her innocence and bound her to him—but fate had played a ghastly trick on him. It was now Harvey himself who was truly subservient, a slave to the need she had fostered within him. Hard as he had tried to deny his hunger for her, he knew that only Lily's smooth, flawless, golden flesh could satisfy him. The mere thought of her was enough to whet an appetite that seemed to grow rather than diminish with time.

Perversely, he had begun to hold China Mary accountable for his unexpected addiction to her daughter. He was driven by a desire to punish someone for his dependence, and that someone was China Mary.

Unwilling to hold himself separate from Lily any longer, Harvey did not choose to respond to her greeting. Instead, he reached out and drew her silently into his arms. He held her close to him, aware of the rapid thudding of his heart against her breast, revealing more than any words he might speak. Yes, China Mary would suffer for this addiction, for he most surely could not blame this splendid young blossom who turned to him as if to the sun, yielding to his slightest whim, like a slender flower swaying in the breeze.

Unable to speak for the emotion that choked his throat, Harvey set Lily away from himself at last. His trembling hands moved to the closure of the modest silken garment she wore. He released the small silver buttons that secured the neckline of her robe, untied with clumsy hands the wide silk sash that bound her narrow waist. He pushed the garment from her shoulders, his breathing becoming more ragged as the shimmering fabric fell to the floor around her feet. He stripped away her undergarments with obvious impatience and stepped back in silence so he might observe her nakedness more clearly.

His eyes moved hotly over Lily's willowy body, taking in the gentle slope of her shoulders, her small round breasts. Graceful, slender, like a delicate reed . . .

Lily's musical voice brought his eyes to her face, then to her small mouth as she spoke.

"Do I please you, Mr. Dale?"

Realizing he had not yet spoken a word, and unwilling to allow this near-child to realize the full power she had over him, he nodded. Anger at his own debility forced a new harshness to his tone. "You know I like what I see, Lily."

"Yes, I know." Not bothering to conceal her satisfaction at his response, Lily raised her small hands to her hair. Her eyes moving to his mouth, she undid the plaits slowly, her pink tongue flicking out to wet her lips in a manner that increased his heartbeat to a thunder in his ears.

When the unbound silk of Lily's raven tresses spilled over her pale flesh, Harvey was near to gasping. As she raised her hands to him in silent invitation, he realized that she had again effortlessly reduced him to mindless desire.

"Do you want me, Mr. Dale?"

It was a game they had played many times before, but the thought touched Harvey that this time there was a subtle difference. Control had shifted. Control now lay in the delicate hands raised so innocently toward him. He could do no more than nod his response.

"Then you must take me, Mr. Dale. Come, I will help you."

The graceful hands moved to his chest. Her movements free of subservience even in the service they performed, Lily stripped away his coat. Her fingers moved to his cravat, his waistcoat, his shirt, and they were discarded. Lily's light touch moved to his trousers, releasing the closure. She knelt to strip his body free of the remainder of his clothes. Still on her knees, she straightened her slender back to enclose his tumescence between her palms. She kissed it lightly, her small mouth curving in a smile as his spontaneous gasp broke the silence of the room. It occurred to him that Lily was enjoying her power over him, but he was helpless against the realization.

Slowly, with great deliberation, Lily touched him again with her lips. Harvey murmured a short protest. No, he needed to control, not be controlled. Hating himself for his weakness, he submitted to her ministrations. Ecstasy rose, began to flower, filling his mind with fragmented pictures, colors . . . Lily . . . Lily . . . she was—

And then the ecstasy was withdrawn. Left teetering unsated at the apex of rapture, Harvey opened his heavy eyelids to see a subtle difference in Lily's demeanor as she rose to stand before him.

"Lily . . ." His voice a hoarse gasp, Harvey shook his head. "Lily, please—"

Her dark gaze holding his, Lily interrupted softly, " 'Please,' Mr. Dale?"

Hating himself, Harvey heard his voice rasp once more, "Please . . ."

"You must be more explicit, Mr. Dale."

Harvey shook his head. "You . . . you cannot go so far without . . . You must . . ."

"I do not understand."

Realizing he was shuddering, Harvey felt rage touch his helpless state. "You will not play this game!"

"I do not know what you mean, Mr. Dale."

Harvey shook his head, his breathing too irregular for him to continue.

Lily's hand moved to stroke him. Harvey stifled his vocal reaction, but Lily urged softly, "Speak, Mr. Dale."

Lily's hand was moving knowledgeably against him, and Harvey's eyes weakly closed. He heard a low, musical laugh and opened his eyes.

"Mr. Dale, I am waiting for you to tell me how I may please you."

Harvey's voice was grating, unfamiliar to his own ears. "Bring me ecstasy, Lily, and I will give it to you in return."

Lily's brief hesitation was a calculated, silent threat that did not escape him even in his agitated state. When she spoke again, her voice held a coy note, "Mr. Dale, is that all you wish to tell me?"

Harvey paused to catch his breath. "Lily . . . I can bear little more."

"Yes, Mr. Dale, I know."

She turned and moved quickly toward the broad bed in the corner of the room. She lay gracefully upon it and, turning, raised her arms to him in invitation. Her voice touched his ears in a softly sensual appeal.

"Come to me, Mr. Dale. Come, and I will give you what you seek, and more . . . so much more."

Within a moment Harvey was standing beside Lily's bed. He stared down at her naked, unblemished beauty and stifled a contemptuous laugh. But his contempt was self-directed. Oh, yes, he had taken Lily's innocence, and he had tutored her well in the ways of love . . . too well. In her subtle anger at being summoned with arrogance, she was demonstrating that he, who manipulated people to his own end, could be manipulated in return. The realization that his exquisite Lily did indeed possess such a startling measure of control over him was difficult to accept.

For a few brief moments longer, Harvey stood drinking in Lily's naked splendor. She raised a skilled hand to stroke the back of his thigh, the curve of his buttock. His anger melted and his desire grew. Even as he lowered his body over hers, he rationalized that the control she exercised was a loving, giving control. She practiced it on him alone, and as long as it did not grow too strong . . .

Harvey's body was melting into hers, and a thrill shot up his spine as Lily released a soft, ecstatic sigh. Oh, yes, he would allow her to enjoy her manipulation, for he enjoyed it as well.

Drawing back, he thrust deep within her, his elation rising at her breathless gasp. He thrust again and again. A voice in the back of his mind drummed with the familiar rhythm of his passion, *Enjoy . . . enjoy . . . enjoy . . .* Yes, he would enjoy his Oriental flower. He would savor the nectar of his magnificent blossom . . . and yes, he would, for a time, cast aside all thought of the pain its thorns could inflict.

In the hallway outside her daughter's bedroom door, China Mary's short, broad figure paused. She listened in silence to the sound of her daughter's cooing voice. She knew that tone well, and a bitter smile crossed her lips.

Lily, the daughter for whom she lived, had sacrificed her innocence. Then she had informed her mother that she had accepted her fate—but only temporarily, and not without malice.

China Mary knew the game her daughter was so artfully playing. Lily was committed to making Harvey Dale her slave. From the sounds presently emanating from within, she was certain Lily was making her anger felt at being summoned like the servant Harvey Dale wished to make of her.

China Mary paused in her thoughts. More sounds—this time Harvey Dale's voice, low in supplication. He was pleading! Lily had accomplished that which her mother had yet been unable to do. But the flush of triumph was brief, for the game was not yet over.

China Mary took a deep breath and turned away from the bedroom door. It would not do to torture herself. Better to turn her thoughts to other, more promising matters.

So, Harvey Dale needed a woman to serve as his daughter's

maid and companion. She knew of a woman who was suited to the position, but before she sent her to Harvey Dale, she would make very certain that the woman remembered where her first loyalties lay.

A hard smile flicked across Mary's lips. She descended the staircase before her, squeezing her bulk around its curves, and stepped down on the first floor once more. Raising her hand, she snapped her fingers. Her eyes glittered as a gray-bearded Oriental responded to her summons.

"Ming Keng, summon Lai Hua to me immediately."

With a short nod, Ming Keng turned. Within seconds the slight old man was moving down the street to her command. Following his progress with a keen eye until he disappeared from sight, China Mary took another deep, steadying breath. The small smile that finally curved her lips was inspired by neither joy nor amusement.

Yes, Harvey Dale, your arrogance and your contempt will be your undoing. You will see, Harvey Dale, you will see . . .

CHAPTER IV

JAKE WALSH SHIFTED on the hard ground but continued to watch the Dale residence, as Ross had done the day before. Unconsciously brushing an insect off his shirtsleeve, he grimaced at the unrelenting heat of morning and extended his arm to grasp the spyglass lying beside him. His grimace turned into a full-fledged frown. As he had countless times since he had arrived on the hillside outside Tombstone at dawn, he raised the glass to his eye and muttered a low curse under his breath.

Damn Ross and his schemes! He had taken over the job of watching the Dale household for a day at Ross's request, but he wasn't cut out to be a watchdog, or anything close to it. If Ross was so interested in Devina Dale's comings and goings, he would have to watch her himself after this.

Jake gave a low snort as his intense scrutiny revealed nothing more than a large woman emerging from the back door to dump rubbish into a bin in the yard.

Disgusted, Jake lowered the spyglass to the ground beside him. He took off his hat and ran his hand impatiently through his light, sun-streaked hair. His fair complexion felt flushed, and he wiped the perspiration from his brow with the back of his arm. He didn't like the way things were going. He didn't like it at all.

Damn, he had never seen Ross so intense, so completely wrapped up in his thoughts. He hadn't been the same since he'd found out the blonde on the coach was Devina Dale. Jake paused to amend that thought. No, Ross hadn't really been the same

49

since he met the Dale girl. He had been having trouble getting
her out of his mind even before he found out who she was, but
now that he knew . . . Jake shook his head.

He didn't like Ross's plans for the girl, either. They were too
risky. If things went as he planned, they'd have Dale just where
they wanted him, but there was no way they'd be able to keep
the girl from identifying them afterward. Hell, then they'd be on
the run and they'd—

But who was that? Reaching for the spyglass, Jake focused it
on the small figure approaching the Dale residence. He caught
his breath as the figure moved quickly around to the rear entrance of the house and paused at the door. Within a few
minutes, the large woman responded. After an exchange of
words, the woman pushed open the door to allow the smaller
woman entrance.

Jake paused for a long moment before again lowering his glass
to the ground. Continuing a squinting, unconscious surveillance
of the house, he shook his head in disbelief. If this meant what
he thought it meant . . .

Jake gave a short laugh, which brought a spark to the weary
blue of his eyes. Ross Morrison was one lucky bastard! Hell,
maybe this was a sign! Maybe Ross wasn't so crazy after all.
Maybe this whole thing would work out to their advantage, just
like Ross said.

His flash of optimism fading just as quickly as it had come,
Jake took a deep breath. The only thing he knew for sure was
that he was in this thing with Ross to the end.

Adjusting his position on the hard ground and cursing the heat
of the morning sun, Jake raised the glass and continued his
scrutiny of the Dale household.

Anyway, right now, it looked as if things were starting to go
Ross's way.

Bright morning sunlight shone through the windows of the
staid, dour room that served as her father's library as Devina, her
light eyes wide, turned away from the diminutive Oriental girl
and faced her father. Her attempt to control her astonishment
was decidedly inadequate.

"Father, you must be joking!"

Harvey Dale's brow knit into a frown. "Why would I be
joking? Lai Hua comes very highly recommended. She will

serve as your personal maid and also as your guide and companion until you become more accustomed to Tombstone. I am assured that her work will be more than satisfactory."

Darting a quick smile toward the petite girl who listened to their exchange in silence, Devina tried once more. "I don't doubt that Lai Hua will be adequate as a personal maid, but, Father, really, she's so tiny! Do you really expect that she's capable of providing protection against the lawless elements of Tombstone you seemed so determined to shield me from? Truly, should she and I walk together on the streets, I think it would be I, rather than she, who would need to do the protecting."

"Nonsense!"

"Father, take another look, please! I stand at least three inches taller than this woman, and top her weight by at least twenty pounds."

Harvey darted an annoyed glance toward the Oriental girl, who listened patiently as she was being discussed. In truth, he had been as startled as his daughter when Molly had ushered Lai Hua into the library a short time earlier, stating that she had identified herself as Miss Dale's new personal maid.

He had surveyed the young Oriental woman carefully. She was indeed small, under five feet, but for all her size, he had noted a keen intelligence in her expression. His subsequent interview had assured him that the girl was extremely well spoken, with only the slightest trace of the accent that made conversation with some of her race almost unintelligible. She was also surprisingly well educated and seemingly of a cheerful disposition that had not been discouraged by his darkest frowns.

Having satisfied himself that Lai Hua met those particular qualifications he had stipulated, he had stepped back and surveyed her physical appearance once more. Small, yes, but not as young as she appeared. A quiet maturity shone on her youthful face that doubtless far surpassed her age in years. He also sensed an instinctive loyalty, which he felt he could well manipulate to his advantage. The other qualification, which she filled admirably, was cleanliness. She had not about her the odor he had come to associate with the common laborer. Instead, she smelled rather pleasant, far better than Molly, who sometimes offended his sensitive nose severely. Yes, she smelled of some flower. Was it jasmine, or perhaps white lilacs?

A few more pointed questions determined that China Mary

had indeed chosen well. The girl knew Tombstone, was well aware of the boundaries set for the upper-class citizen. She would be an excellent guide and, he suspected, an amusing companion for Devina. Yes, China Mary had better instincts than he realized. This quiet, unobtrusive girl would doubtless function with greater efficiency on the job than the overbearing woman he himself had selected to chaperon Devina on her trip west.

Having finally decided that the girl would do, Harvey found himself annoyed to realize that Devina considered his efforts a joke. He responded sharply to his daughter's comment.

"Devina, I am well aware that Lai Hua is shorter and slighter than you are, but I did not hire her as your bodyguard! If that had been my intention, I could just as well have assigned Molly to accompany you around town."

Devina was becoming annoyed. "Well, what was your intention, Father? You were so concerned about my welfare yesterday that you refused to consent to my walking the streets alone."

"My intention was to see that you did not stray into areas of the town that are unsuitable for a young woman of your upbringing."

"Father . . ."

"Kindly do not use that tone on me, Devina. Tombstone is unlike any town to which you've been exposed in your sheltered life."

"Father, I have not been as sheltered as you seem to think."

"Indeed?"

The arching of her father's brow was more than she could endure, and Devina threw up her hands. Muttering low under her breath, she forced a smile. "All right, Father, anything you say. Lai Hua looks to be a very pleasant person, and I approve of your choice. Now, may we get on with breakfast?"

"Yes, let's get on with it." Nodding at his daughter's sudden acceptance of his judgment, Harvey dismissed Lai Hua with a careless wave of his hand.

A few minutes later, Harvey regretted his sharpness and attempted a smile. "In all honesty, Devina, I had hoped to introduce you to Tombstone myself this morning, but I made a late start yesterday and was able to accomplish very little, contrary to my intentions."

"A late start?"

His eyes suddenly intent upon his plate, Harvey nodded. "Yes, I . . . uh . . . I was deterred by important business, which occupied most of my morning. It left me little time, or energy for that matter."

Quick to pick up on his hesitation, Devina pressed with concern, "Little energy? Are you feeling unwell, Father?"

Devina frowned at the almost imperceptible twitch of her father's mustache as he devoted his attention even more intently to his breakfast.

"Yes, quite well. I think I just . . . uh . . . overdid a bit yesterday. In any event, I feel quite well today, and I expect to make considerable headway in discovering those guilty of this assault on Till-Dale Enterprises. Unfortunately, that leaves you to find your way around Tombstone alone this morning, but I would enjoy it very much if you would join me for lunch at the Can-Can Restaurant this afternoon."

"The Can-Can?"

"Yes, Lai Hua knows where it is. Shall we meet at noon?"

"Noon will be fine."

Obviously pleased with the improved tenor of their exchange, Harvey stood abruptly. "I suppose I shall have to be going if I'm to accomplish all I hope to today. I'll see you at twelve, Devina."

Emerging onto the street a few moments later, Harvey strode toward Allen Street.

Devina's pace was brisk as she walked along the busy Tombstone street. Her heels clicked against the boardwalk with each step, the hollow echo of the sound registering in the back of her mind as she smiled inwardly with satisfaction at the many interested glances she drew. But she was accustomed to admiring glances. She was well aware that she was a beautiful woman who excited comment wherever she went, and she had dressed with extreme care for this, her first outing in Tombstone.

Cocking her head in a fleeting moment of uncertainty, she was again struck with the nagging thought that perhaps the color of her dramatically stylish ensemble was a bit bold, but she had been unable to resist it when she had seen it displayed in the window of Madame Boneil's fashionable boutique. Pink had always been one of her favorite colors. It complemented her delicate coloring, the creamy tint of her flawless complexion, the glimmering silver-blond of her hair. If the pink in this particular outfit was a bit brighter than the shade she usually wore, if the black lace inserts in the shoulders and bodice of the close-fitting jacket were a little more revealing than she would have preferred, if the fringe on the draped skirt happened to wave a bit flirtatiously when she walked, it meant very little, since she liked the way she looked.

Perhaps a bit outrageously, she had also yielded to Madame Boneil's urging and bought a saucy chapeau that was little more than a twist of pink silk, black lace, and stiff ebony feathers, which she had frowningly commented to madame would be more comfortable on a raven's wing than on her head. But in the end she had been won over by the total effect of madame's creation, and had even added to it a pink parasol and matching gloves. Yes, she had wanted to announce to Tombstone and all the people in it that she had arrived, and if she was to judge by the reaction she was exciting on the street, she had more than accomplished her purpose.

Devina turned from her thoughts to contemplate the tiny Oriental woman walking silently beside her. Devina could not resist a smile. She was exceedingly grateful that she had taken the time to acquaint herself with the maid her father had so imperiously assigned to her that morning. Not having had previous experience with a person of Lai Hua's race, she had been fascinated. The girl was bright and informative, once her natural shyness had been overcome, and, in an inexplicable way, a bit mysterious. But Devina's natural curiosity about Tombstone had allowed her little time to dwell on Lai Hua, other than to acknowledge instinctively that she would be secure in following the girl's lead around the surprising frontier town.

Lai Hua and she had emerged from the house onto the street a short time before, and Devina had silently scrutinized the residential area in which her new home was situated. Pleasant and comparatively quiet, it was obviously the section where the wealthier residents chose to live. A quick glance had confirmed that the Dale home was the largest on the street.

Lai Hua's quick step had led them across Third Street and on to Fremont. She had begun to suspect that Lai Hua's direction had been influenced by strict admonitions from her father. She had carefully been led past Schieffelin Hall, and her earnest guide had echoed her father's comment that many New York productions appeared on its fine stage. Her tour had continued past the office of the Tombstone *Epitaph,* which Lai Hua had referred to as the best newspaper in town. In deference to Lai Hua's zeal for her task, Devina had stifled the comment that the publication appeared to be appropriately named in light of Tombstone's dubious reputation. They had then turned onto Fourth Street, passing the post office and the Can-Can Restaurant, where she was to meet her father at twelve. She was singularly unimpressed by the Can-Can's appearance and by the town as a whole until she reached the corner of Allen and Fourth, where the true circus began.

And a circus it was. The din and confusion Devina remembered from the day of her arrival had not abated. Indeed, if anything, it appeared to have intensified in the press of activities of a new business day. The main street was congested with a throng of ore wagons from the mines, which were only a stone's throw from the main street; freight wagons hauling all manner of merchandise to and from business establishments on the main thoroughfare; and family conveyances coming and going among the shops. As she stood in silent observation, the peal of a school bell in the distance signaled an unexpected surge of young students along the board sidewalk. Several large, excited dogs of dubious pedigree running and barking at their flying heels added considerably to the melee, and Devina was decidedly grateful when the last of the reckless youngsters passed.

Devina shifted her glance toward three businessmen conversing a short distance away. Spotlessly garbed, their stylish suits in stark contrast to the simpler garments worn by the other residents of the town, they paid little attention to two tattered, bewhiskered prospectors loudly arguing the merits of ore samples a few feet from them. Equally unaffected and totally uninterested in the rapid deterioration of the two men's discussion, three young matrons strolled past, involved in an exchange of their own. A brawny fellow with a blacksmith's apron covering his massive chest strode past, his ferocious glance unswerving as three painted ladies of questionable profession crossed the street behind him and walked in the opposite direction.

Strolling on in silence, Devina attempted to assess the occupations of those she passed. Surely the two sallow-complexioned fellows with brawny upper bodies and dirty fingernails were miners; the serious fellow with the leather apron was a cobbler; the swarthy man with the stained white coat and pants must be a cook; and the fellow in the long white apron who ran up behind the cook to tug at his arm was a waiter. Devina wrinkled her nose in distaste. Neither the waiter nor the cook appeared to be very clean. She hoped they were not typical of the help employed by the better restaurants in town.

Her gaze moved to a group of men who had just reined up on the street and were dismounting to tether their horses to a hitching post. She stiffened. They were unsavory characters—unshaven, unsmiling, with trail-stained clothes and guns slung low on their hips. The third man in the group—a tall, wiry fellow—paused and turned fully in her direction. Averting her gaze as his eyes swept her assessingly, Devina was startled to realize it was not the glance of this unknown man's small bloodshot eyes that caused a tremor to move down her spine; it was the memory his appearance evoked, the memory of those chilling dark eyes that still hovered in the back of her mind.

Beginning to believe she would never be free of the unpredictable assault of that remembered gaze, Devina turned to Lai Hua.

Sensitive to her mistress's rapid change of mood, Lai Hua inquired politely, "Does Miss Devina wish to go on?"

Raising her chin and forcing a smile, Devina nodded. "Yes, Miss Devina most certainly does."

Smiling in return, Lai Hua continued onward as Devina confirmed her earlier thoughts. Yes, Lai Hua would be pleasant to have around. And she was such a pretty little thing, with such an unusual type of beauty. Petite to the point of being almost doll-like, her face perpetuated that appearance with its tiny features and smooth, even-toned complexion. And her hair, carefully bound at the back of her neck, was so straight, so shiny, so dark, it was almost unreal.

Her attention diverted by an attractive store window display, Devina became engrossed in studying the various offerings as they continued down the street. Admittedly, Tombstone had far more to offer its residents than she had expected. She paused at a store whose sign read Heintzelman's Jewelry. Tombstone made an extremely good attempt to appear civilized. On this stretch of street alone she had passed what appeared to be two very well accoutered hotels, a livery, a butcher shop, a telegraph office, a furniture store, and a rather elegant clothier. She had not yet crossed the street, but she assumed she would find more of the same on the other side.

But Devina was very aware that there was more to civilization than a few well-decorated shop windows. Despite its grandiose reputation and the wealth that flowed through its dusty streets, Tombstone was surely nothing more than a backward mining town, definitely lacking in culture for all the touting of Schieffelin Hall's merits.

Devina discounted her father's concern for her safety. Some of the men who walked Tombstone's streets appeared to be of a rougher breed than she was accustomed to meeting in the East, but most of them seemed to be hardworking men, intent on their business and interested only in mixing with others of their sort. The greatest threat she had experienced since entering the town that morning had been the memory of haunting dark eyes, and that particular threat she was determined to eliminate.

Suddenly bored with the merchandise displayed before her, Devina turned to assess the establishments on the opposite side of the main thoroughfare. Not too much of interest . . .

Devina's scanning gaze stopped short on a small sign across the street. She took a short breath: Wells, Fargo and Company. Her father had said that John Henry Thomas was an employee of Wells Fargo. Annoyance touched her mind as Devina recalled the manner in which her father had laughingly dismissed her mention of the stagecoach guard the previous day. She knew her father considered her interest in finding the thieves and her desire to help nothing more than interference in his affairs. The thought rankled. If she had been a son instead of a daughter, he would not have dismissed her comments so offhandedly.

She had had time to think since that remark which had so amused her father. Yes, the man who had robbed the payroll had known John Henry Thomas. So it was not inconceivable that John Henry Thomas also knew the man, whether he realized it or not. She could not bring herself to believe that the stagecoach guard was actually involved in the robberies, but that did not mean she couldn't coax him into remembering something which might be of help. Perhaps if she spoke to him, attempted to jog his memory . . . In any case, it was worth a try.

Abruptly recalling Lai Hua's presence beside her, Devina turned toward her. "I have some business at the Wells Fargo office, Lai Hua. I'm going to—"

"No, no, Miss Devina. You cannot go to Wells Fargo."

Devina frowned. She disliked being told what she could or could not do, even if Lai Hua was obviously only following her father's orders. "You're mistaken, Lai Hua. I can and I will go to Wells Fargo. I have some business there."

Appearing flustered, Lai Hua shook her head. "No, Miss Devina. Mr. Dale will not like it. He say—"

"My father seems to think I'm totally incapable of taking care of myself, Lai Hua. I am not. I do not need him or you to think for me." Her anger softening at the confusion in Lai Hua's troubled face, Devina hesitated before continuing. "I don't want to make you uncomfortable, Lai Hua, but I intend to go across the street and talk to the manager of Wells Fargo about the robbery of the stage on which I arrived. It will do you no good to try to talk me out of it."

"Miss Devina, you do not understand—"

"I understand that I intend to cross the street, as I have just stated. You may accompany me if you wish, Lai Hua, or you may remain here."

Not allowing Lai Hua's obviously flustered state to affect her, Devina resolutely turned away and stepped down into the street. She fanned the choking dust from her nostrils, as yet another ore wagon rumbled by. She pressed her lips tightly shut, only to feel gritty particles grate between her teeth. Oh, this unpleasant town! How could one remain clean and comfortable in such a place?

Determined to take advantage of a short break in the heavy stream of traffic, Devina braved the still unsettled dust the moment the ore wagon had passed. The sound of small steps behind her registered in the back of her mind as she quickly made her way to the other side of the street.

Turning to shoot Lai Hua a small smile as she stepped up onto the board sidewalk, Devina dodged two husky men as they pushed their way out through the swinging doors of the Occidental Saloon and emerged onto the walk beside her. Her delicate nostrils quivered daintily as she brushed past them. The two cowboys smelled of horses, sweat, and liquor, and she grimaced

at the thoroughly repulsive combination of odors. Raising her
chin, she continued on down the walk, her gaze trained on the
small sign a few doors away.

Once more swinging doors pushed wide to her left, but this
time Devina was ready for the figure that emerged amid bawdy
comments from yet another saloon. Pausing to allow the man to
step out of her way, Devina was annoyed to see the fellow stand
arrogantly in her path. Raising a haughty gaze to his face,
Devina realized it was the same man who had reined up and
stared so assessingly at her earlier. She remembered that narrow,
unshaven face and those bloodshot eyes. She also remembered
the insolent manner in which his gaze had traveled over her
body, lingering far too long on the black lace inserts that covered
her breasts.

A warm heat touching her cheeks, Devina flashed the offensive cowboy a scathing glance. The insensitive fellow merely
laughed! Her color darkening, Devina straightened her narrow
shoulders to an almost military posture. "I beg your pardon.
Would you mind . . . ?"

The smirking cowboy's hands snaked out unexpectedly, closing on her shoulders as he pulled her toward him with a low,
insinuating murmur. "You don't have to beg me for nothin',
darlin', nothin' at all. Old Bart'll be happy to give you just about
anythin' you want, and maybe a little bit more than you expect,
too."

Startled as the cowboy attempted to pull her closer still,
Devina halted his encompassing embrace by jamming her palms
against his chest. Her voice was filled with loathing. "Let me
go, you, you filthy beast! Let me go!"

A spark of menace lit the small eyes so close to hers.

"Don't you go gettin' all high and mighty on me, girl. I'm
thinkin' you ain't the kind that comes cheap, but I can afford to
pay your price. My pockets are full right now, and I don't mind
payin' top dollar if the merchandise is worth it. Of course, I
might like to try a sample aforehand, so's I know what I'm
gettin'."

"A sample!"

A quick swipe of the cowboy's hand dispensed with Devina's
defensive posture, and within moments his sour breath was
against her cheek, his mouth seeking hers. Devina began strug-

gling wildly, only to find her struggles ineffective against the cowboy's superior strength. His sweaty unshaven face drew closer, his wet lips grazing her cheek. She was making a last frantic attempt to escape when a deep, familiar voice sounded sharply behind her.

"Bart, I think you've made a mistake here. You'd better stop now before you make an even bigger one."

The mouth so close to hers tightened into an angry line. The rheumy eyes narrowed into slits. "And I'm thinkin' what I do is none of your damned business, Doc."

Relief swept Devina's senses. Charles Carter! He would make this filthy cowboy release her! But Devina's jubilation was short-lived as the cowboy's grip shifted to encircle her waist and he hauled her to his side. Held roughly in the crook of his arm, Devina saw that the cowboy's other hand was hovering near the gun hanging low on his hip.

"I'm not armed, Bart, and I don't expect you'd want our little talk to come to that in any case." Her eyes darting to Charles Carter's face, Devina was incredulous to see the hint of a smile that flicked across his well-shaped lips as he continued, "Bart, that young woman you've got tucked under your arm isn't what you think she is. She's new in town. I'm sure she didn't realize a respectable lady doesn't walk on this side of the street."

"Respectable lady?" The cowboy slanted a short glance out of the corner of his eye toward Devina's flushed face. "Hell, there ain't no lady I ever seen that dresses like this here girl. And ain't no lady I know who looks at a man like she does, and wiggles her sweet little behind like this one."

Incensed at the cowboy's remarks, Devina lashed out at him furiously. "How would you know how a lady acts? You've probably never met a real lady in your life!"

"Devina, please . . ."

Snapping her furious gaze back to Charles Carter, Devina felt her anger flare anew at the amusement growing more apparent on his face with each passing moment. Her eyes narrowed into slits, and when she replied, her voice was little more than a growl. "I do not find this situation amusing, Charles."

Beginning to appear confused, the cowboy gradually relaxed his gun hand. He shook his head, still refusing to loosen his grip around Devina's waist. "You know this girl, Doc?"

"Yes, I know her, Bart. This young lady is Devina Dale, Harvey Dale's daughter."

Devina felt the shock of Charles's statement echo through the cowboy's wiry frame.

"Harvey Dale's daughter!" Releasing her with a suddenness that almost upset her balance, the cowboy stepped back. "Hell, I done some work for Mr. Dale a while back, and I don't want no trouble with him." His astonishment turning to anger, the cowboy turned an accusing gaze on Devina. "Seems to me a man like Harvey Dale would have more sense than to turn his daughter loose on the streets lookin' and actin' for all the world like one of Blond Marie's girls."

Her gaze snapping to Charles once more, Devina inquired with barely controlled anger, "Who is this Blond Marie?"

Extending his arm, Charles drew Devina to his side. His lips twitching suspiciously, he looked down briefly into her flushed face. "Never mind, Devina."

"What do you mean, 'never mind'? This man has accosted me, insulted me!"

"It was all a misunderstanding, wasn't it, Bart?"

Bart's horrified expression responded with silent eloquence, but Charles pressed insistently, "Wasn't it, Bart?"

Bart nodded his head. "It sure as hell was." Turning abruptly, he pushed his way back into the saloon, exiting the scene as quickly as he had appeared.

Doing her best to ignore the snickers of witnesses to her humiliating encounter, Devina pulled herself rigidly erect. Suddenly realizing the abbreviated brim of her saucy little hat was sitting almost on her brow, she raised her hand with great dignity and gave it an effective shove. Refusing to acknowledge its uncertain sway as she turned once more in Charles's direction, Devina raised her chin a notch higher.

"I am most grateful for your timely assistance, Charles. I cannot comprehend how that—that foul character could have been so confused as to think that I . . . that he . . ." She paused, at a loss for words, only to continue a moment later with greater emphasis, "That ignoramus wouldn't know a lady if he tripped over one . . . and he almost did!"

Devina's annoyance flared anew at the deepening of the lines at the corners of Charles's mouth, and her eyes narrowed into angry slits. "Charles, I repeat: I do not find this situation at all amusing."

Making an admirable attempt at solemnity, Charles nodded. "You're right, Devina, of course. But now I suggest that we—"

"We?" Her brows rising with haughty disdain, Devina shook her head imperiously. "I don't know what *you* intend doing, but *I'm* going to the Wells Fargo office."

"I don't think that's a good idea, Devina."

Devina's smile turned to pure acid. "Does it surprise you to hear me say I don't care what you think, Charles?"

Charles's lips stretched into a smile. "No, it honestly doesn't, Devina. But in any case, it would be a mistake."

"Mistake?" Pushed beyond the limits of her control, Devina walked stiffly toward her original destination. Her head high, she ignored the stares that followed her. She lifted her chin higher as Charles's step sounded beside her, then turned with a haughty stare as Charles politely took her arm.

"If you please, Charles. I like to make my own mistakes. And now that I realize what I'm up against in this uncivilized outpost, you may rest assured I will be more careful in the future."

Refusing to relinquish her arm, Charles conformed to her pace while carefully tucking her arm under his. His expression sober at last, he responded, "All the care in the world won't protect you from a similar situation if you stay on this side of the street, Devina."

Devina hesitated.

"Of course, you couldn't be expected to know," Charles went on, "but respectable women don't walk on this side of the street."

A small sound of agreement came from Lai Hua, who was a few steps behind them. Devina shot a glance at her obviously shaken young maid.

"You must be joking, Charles."

"I couldn't be more serious, Devina." A hint of his previous humor returning, Charles shook his head. "Poor Bart, I suppose he walked out of the Alhambra and thought he had stepped into paradise when he saw you waiting for him."

"I was not waiting for him!"

"I think he thought you were. You really should have some

sympathy for the poor fellow, Devina. Consider how disappointed he must be.''

"Sympathy! He insulted me! He said I dressed like a . . . like a . . . He said I wiggled my sweet little—''

"You can't fault the man for his taste."

"Charles!''

Shock bringing her to an abrupt halt, Devina stared at Charles Carter for long moments before the humor of the situation began to take hold. Oh, Lord, could this whole humiliating situation truly have happened to her? The broadening of Charles's smile was infectious, and Devina was suddenly laughing. Charles's low laughter joined hers, effectively relieving both her embarrassment and her tension.

Sober at last, Devina turned toward Lai Hua. "I apologize, Lai Hua. I should have given you a chance to explain. You may rest assured I will never make so foolish a mistake again. And I'll offer a proper explanation to my father—if he finds out what happened.''

"You may rest assured he'll hear about it, Devina. That was too good a show not to bear repeating.''

Charles's soft comment turned Devina back in his direction. Her expression was pained. "You think so?"

"I know so.''

"Oh, dear.''

Charles's face creased with concern. "If you're afraid your father will be angry, I'll be happy to—''

"Me? Afraid of my father?'' Devina took a deep breath and attempted to retain her smile. "Charles, I do most sincerely appreciate your help today, but please, don't say another word about that.''

His smile suddenly returning, Charles nodded. "In that case, since you seem determined to visit the Wells Fargo office, would you mind my accompanying you? I would feel much safer . . .''

Devina's smile softened. "Actually, now that I understand the circumstances, I would feel much safer, too, Charles. I would be happy to have you accompany me, even though I intend to speak to John Henry Thomas in any case.''

"I'm sure you do.''

Tucking her arm more firmly under his, Charles urged Devina along at his side. Leaning toward her confidentially, he whis-

pered in a tone meant for her ears alone, "Actually, I disagree
with Bart, Devina. I rather like your ensemble. I don't think you
look like a—"

"Charles!"

Realizing her cheeks were just a shade short of the color of her
gown, Devina avoided Charles's amused smile and maintained a
wise silence.

A moment later she entered the Wells Fargo office and approached the fellow at the desk.

"I would like to speak to John Henry Thomas."

Devina accepted Charles's proferred arm once more as she
emerged from the Wells Fargo office a short time later. Although
she was dissatisfied with the outcome of her errand, she made no
comment as he guided her across the busy intersection of Fifth
and Allen. When she finally spoke, her voice was as dejected as
her thoughts: "Well, that was a complete waste of time."

"I'm sorry, Devina, but it's obvious John Henry hasn't the
slightest idea who the men were who robbed the stage."

"I was so sure he would be able to remember something about
the man that might furnish a clue to his identity."

His expression devoid of its previous mirth, Charles directed a
strangely intense gaze into her eyes. "What about you, Devina?"

"Me?"

"You're the one who was closest to the fellow. You gave the
marshal a description, but was there anything special about the
man that might set him apart or something that might ring a bell
in someone's mind? What do you remember most about him?"

Charles's dark eyes were searching her face, and Devina felt
herself pale. What did she remember about the man? She remembered everything, the husky timbre of his voice and the
threat it contained, the relentless strength of his arm as it crushed
her ribs, the hard wall of his chest against her back, the sweet
scent of his breath against her cheek. But most of all she
remembered his eyes, their darkly mysterious, penetrating quality. They were menacing, merciless, impossible to dismiss from
her mind.

You wouldn't be worth the trouble . . .

"Devina?"

Snapping back to the present, Devina attempted a smile.

"What do I remember most? He was filthy. He smelled of whiskey and the trail. His clothes were old and baggy, giving the impression that the fellow was nothing but a drunkard and a derelict. I later realized he was neither of those things, Charles. It was all an act, but his disguise was too complete for me to tell you what he actually looked like. He had a full straggly beard and long hair that curled inside the collar of his shirt. He wore his hat pulled down over his face so I had no opportunity to scrutinize his features, even if I'd been inclined to do so. All I can tell you is what I've told others before, that he was tall and that his hair and eyes were black. And he was strong, Charles, very strong. His arm was like steel when he held me prisoner, and he lifted me out of the coach without the slightest effort. And he was ruthless. I . . . I have no doubt he would have killed me if I had challenged him."

A shudder moved down her spine as Devina uttered those last words. She immediately regretted having allowed her fear to regain control when she saw concern replace the intensity in Charles Carter's eyes. Wondering how she could ever have thought Charles's eyes similar to those that haunted her, she gave a short laugh. "I'm not much more help than John Henry, am I?"

Smiling without comment, Charles wisely changed the subject. "Well, it seems you've seen the worst of Tombstone since your arrival, Devina. I'd say it's time for you to be introduced to the more civilized aspects of town. If you have no other plans, I'd like to take you to lunch."

Surprised at the genuine regret that accompanied her refusal, Devina shook her head. "I'm sorry, Charles. I'm meeting Father for lunch at the Can-Can at twelve."

Charles checked his watch. "In that case we'd better walk faster. If I remember correctly, Harvey Dale doesn't like to be kept waiting."

Startled that the hours of the morning had passed so quickly, Devina followed Charles's lead. At the door of the restaurant a few minutes later, Devina turned to face Charles. "I'm truly sorry I can't accept your invitation this afternoon. I find your company very enjoyable, Charles."

"So enjoyable that you'll agree to accompany me to Schieffelin Hall for the performance of—"

"—of Sardou's Divorçons?" Devina gave a short laugh. "I'd be delighted."

The warmth of Charles's smile lingered as Devina made her way through the crowded restaurant toward her father's table, and she experienced the surprising realization that she liked Charles Carter. She liked him immensely.

His gaze lingering on Devina's slender, curved figure as she made her way between the tables, Charles waited at the doorway until she had joined her father. With a smile he acknowledged Harvey Dale's wave and turned away.

His expression suddenly intense, Charles started back in the direction from which he had come. He was disappointed. He had begun to hope more would come of Devina's unexpected predicament that morning, but it appeared Devina could give him no more information about the men who had stolen the payroll than she had already given the marshal. Damn! He had been hoping that once she had overcome her initial fright, she would remember something more helpful about the man in the coach, the unacknowledged leader of the thieves.

Feeling discouraged, Charles took a deep breath. Well, one good thing had come about from their meeting. He would see Devina tomorrow night on a social level. That was a step in the right direction. He had been intrigued with Devina Dale from the moment he had seen her standing in his office doorway. Their unexpected meeting today had only served to heighten that fascination. Devina Dale was a beautiful young woman who grew more interesting with each encounter.

His expression still intensely serious, Charles increased his pace. He definitely enjoyed Devina's company, and he believed she enjoyed his. A closer association with her would be beneficial in more ways than one.

Hudson's Drugstore was only a few feet away when Charles again checked his watch. Old Maggie Whitmore would be arriving at his office soon, expecting more of her powders to be ready and waiting. She didn't trust the pharmacist. She would take medication only if Charles gave it to her personally, but he didn't mind making that small concession to the woman's eccentricity. He could do little else to relieve the incurable disease that swelled her joints. He had just enough time to pick up the powders and return.

• • • •

As soon as Charles disappeared into Hudson's Drugstore,
Camille DuPree stepped out of the doorway in which she had
concealed herself. She ran a quick hand over the upward sweep
of her fiery tresses and straightened her back as she stepped out
onto the board sidewalk. She was well aware that she was
unusually tall compared with the rest of Blond Marie's girls, but
she was proud of her height. She was also conscious of the fact
that her height offset the rather generous proportions of her
voluptuous body.

Camille had never gone through the scrawny phase most
women experienced in adolescence. She had always been full-
breasted. At the age of twelve she had reached her present height
of eight inches over the mark of five feet, and was fully developed to almost her present size. It had been that early maturity
which had set her on the road she had eventually taken to relieve
the poverty of a home with an ailing mother, too many children,
and a father who worked relentlessly to support them on a small
farm on the outskirts of Paris until it put him in his grave.

When there had been no food in the house to feed her brothers
and sisters, and when Mama no longer had the strength to pull
herself out of bed, Camille had taken to a bed of another kind. It
had not been difficult to find men who would pay to make love
to her, despite the fact that she was not truly beautiful. The
brilliance of her red hair and laughing brown eyes had always
caught the male eye. The advent of physical maturity had changed
the tenor of those glances, but Camille knew that men found her
interesting in more ways than the most obvious. She supposed it
was her outlook on life that drew them to her; at least, that was
what she had been told countless times.

"Camille, you're always ready with a smile . . . Camille, you
never let anything get you down." And what was it Charles had
said to her countless times? "Camille, you can make me smile
when I think I haven't a smile left in me. You're good for me,
lady. You make me feel good, real good."

And that was what she wanted to do, make Charles feel good.
She wanted that more than anything else in the world, and she
had been satisfied knowing that she was the only one who
performed that service for the handsome doctor.

She remembered well the first time Charles had come to Blond

Marie's house. Not at all the common brothel, Blond Marie's was one of two houses in Tombstone that were run by the French syndicate which had brought Camille from her homeland to this new country. Having become bored with Paris, she had been only too happy to begin an adventure in a new land, especially since her contract with the syndicate included a generous payment with which she was able to provide doweries for sisters. Camille herself had cast aside the thought of marriage. Her life had taken a different route, and she was not one to bemoan the force of circumstance.

She had had little fear of coming to this new land, for she had spoken to several of Le Comte's girls who had since returned. A procedure had been established in which the girls were transported to a house in the American West and returned to Paris after two years to have others take their place. It was a system Le Comte had devised and with which no one argued, not even Blond Marie.

Camille was justly proud to be the one exception to that procedure. She stayed in Tombstone far beyond the normal term, because she was unusually popular. As the mistress of the house of pleasure for Tombstone's gentry, Blond Marie refused to have an open bar on the premises so as to avoid the drunken brawls that were so common in the other houses, and she set a price so high as to eliminate the common men of the town from her clientele. But although the house was filled with beautiful Frenchwomen, many of whom were far lovelier than she, Camille DuPree was everyone's favorite. When the time had come for her to return to Paris, the protests of Blond Marie's wealthy clients had been so vociferous that Le Comte had decided to allow Camille to remain in Tombstone indefinitely.

Maintaining her brisk step down the busy sidewalk, Camille nodded in reply to the effusive greetings of the men she passed. Her broad smile, revealing well-shaped, perfect teeth, flashed as a host of memories assaulted her mind.

Camille had been pleased beyond words when Charles Carter had entered her life. She remembered the first time he had come to Blond Marie's. He had been called to examine Simone, who had fallen downstairs. The moment he walked through the door, Camille had reacted to his male presence. Her own unusual height had always led her to prefer tall, well-built men whose size made her feel feminine and small. She preferred dark-haired men as well, and she had warmed spontaneously to the concern in his gaze, his gentleness and capability in treating Simone's injury.

Comfortable with no one other than her, Simone had insisted that Camille remain in the room while Charles treated her. She had worked closely at his side, her concern for Simone tempered by her extreme physical reaction to Charles's masculinity. Her response to his soft-spoken air of command and competency had been overwhelming.

Charles had returned several times to check Simone's progress, and when his obligation to her was done he had continued to come to see Camille. Simone had since returned to Paris, but Charles's visits had only increased in frequency.

Although Camille had never spoken aloud her feelings, Charles's entrance into her life had changed it beyond measure. For the very first time, Camille was in love.

With a long history of varied experience with men behind her, Camille had not thought that the act of love could hold any more surprises. But she had been wrong. In Charles's arms, passions never before experienced had come to life inside her. While still maintaining the interest of her other regular customers, she had found there was a part of her that belonged to Charles alone. That he requested her exclusively, no matter the arrival of newer, prettier girls who occasionally drew her other customers, if only temporarily, made her heart sing. It was only she who satisfied Charles's deep and moving passion. That was just, for it was only he who satisfied hers.

Swallowing the lump that had risen in her throat, Camille took a deep breath and crossed the hustle of Fifth Street with caution. Yes, she had given Charles all she could, but there was one thing she could never give him. Respectability had been beyond her reach since she was a child, and she was only too aware that when the time came for Charles to choose the woman with whom he would share his life, it would not be she.

It was for that reason her heart had stopped when she saw Charles face the gun of Bart Wheeler to protect Harvey Dale's beautiful daughter. She had watched the play of emotions on his face—his concern, his deference to the young woman's wishes, his eventual amusement. She had seen the interest in his eyes.

She had seen him accompany the beautiful young woman into an office farther up the street, and she had dallied as long as possible in the small boutique in which she had been shopping, waiting for them to emerge. Having finally given up, she had stepped out onto the street at the same moment as Charles and the lovely Mademoiselle Dale. They had not seen her, and she had been relieved. She knew her emotions were reflected only too clearly in her eyes for Charles not to read them.

She had drawn back into a nearby doorway, unable to look away from the sight of Charles's protective posture and Devina Dale's thoughtless acceptance of it. Camille's pain had increased when Charles leaned down to speak to the young woman in a confidential manner, his eyes searching her upturned face. Camille had seen Charles with other women on the street before, but this time there was a subtle difference in his manner—a heartbreakingly revealing difference. The knowledge that she could not compete with Devina Dale's beauty and respectability was a bitter pill indeed.

As she neared Sixth Street and the neat structure of Blond Marie's house came into view, Camille paused. A familiar figure was emerging from the front door.

The man paused as he saw her approach. His lined aristocratic face creased into a smile, and his well-groomed white mustache moved expressively as he spoke. "Camille, I had given up on you. Marie tried to talk me into allowing Danielle to entertain me, but I told her I'd come back later when you had returned."

Accepting the hand Willard Kingston held out to her, Camille responded to the wealthy rancher with a smile. "So you waited for me, my dear Willie, when Danielle, who is so much prettier than I, was willing to serve you. Why is that, my dear fellow?"

Tucking her hand under his arm, Willard Kingston whispered softly into her ear as he drew her to his side and urged her through the doorway from which he had just emerged. "I waited for you because Danielle's beauty is only on the surface. I enjoy talking to you as much as I like occupying your bed. You warm me in more ways than one, Camille, and I don't mind admitting I've become very attached to you. Neither do I mind waiting or paying the high price for your favors. You're worth it."

Camille reached up and patted Willard Kingston's weather-beaten cheek. Charles had said something similar to her just a few nights ago, and now . . .

Her unfailing optimism returning, it suddenly occurred to Camille that she could not compete with the very beautiful Devina Dale, but Charles would still continue to come to her, at least for a while. She would not give him up easily, not easily at all.

Feeling the heat of tears under her eyelids, Camille whispered huskily, "Willie, now, you see, you have brought tears to my eyes. That will never do, my good fellow."

Camille turned toward the nearby staircase. It was time to go back to work. "Come, Willie, you have been very patient, and it is time for your patience to be rewarded."

Willard Kingston smiled, allowing Camille to lead the way.

CHAPTER V

"DAMN IT ALL, where is he?"

Scowling, Ross walked to the doorway of the cabin and paused to scan the encroaching darkness. A sound from behind made him turn to the disgusted expression of the bearded man sprawled in the lone upholstered chair in the room.

"You goin' to keep doin' that all night, Ross? I don't mind tellin' you, you're makin' me damned nervous with all that pacin'. Pacin' ain't goin' to bring Jake back here a minute sooner."

"What in hell could've happened to him? I told him to keep out of sight while he was watching the Dale house. There's no reason for him to be so late."

"Oh, ain't there?" The unexpected question came from a second man who was seated at the table with a tattered pack of cards spread before him. "Jake's close-mouthed, but it don't take much to tell that he's got a woman stashed in that town somewhere. Hell, a man don't usually go ridin' off until all hours of the night for any other reason. For the life of me, I can't see why he's keepin' her a secret."

Mack's low snicker broke into Harry's speculation, and his toothless grin flashed as he spoke. "Maybe he's afraid of competition."

Casting a deprecating glance toward Mack's bearded face and gaping smile, Harry shook his head. "He ain't afraid of competition from you."

"Well, who would he be afraid of . . . you, by any chance?"

Once more the deprecating glance from Harry, and Mack drew himself erect in his chair. "Watch yourself, Wilson. I ain't takin' that kind of look from nobody, much less a worthless piece of lard like yourself."

Unable to stand any more of the harmless bickering that masked the real affection his two unlikely henchmen had for each other, Ross walked out into the yard. He had been lucky to run into both Harry and Mack soon after they had been robbed of their claims by the same technicalities of law that had allowed Harvey Dale to take over his father's claim. They had been bitter, too tired to start over from scratch, and it had suited them fine to take an easier route for a while. Despite their slow talk and harmless appearance, Ross knew that Mack and Henry were quick with their guns and dependable in any situation. He also knew he'd be unable to handle the robberies without their help.

As Ross turned onto the narrow path that led to the pond, Harry's low comment carried into the yard, penetrating the twilight and interrupting his thoughts.

"See what you did, Mack? You got Ross so disgusted with your troublemakin' and smart talk that he walked out. Hell, you keep arguin' with me that way over everythin' I say and drivin' him to the pond to cool off, Ross is goin' to end up waterlogged. Hell, the way things've been goin' lately, he might even start to shrink!"

At any other time the raucous laughter that erupted would have had Ross grinning as well, but he was long past the point of amusement.

Walking down the narrow trail, he strode to the edge of the pool and stared at its mirrorlike surface. The sounds of night were growing louder, and he frowned at the shadowed beauty of dusk. An expression of pure disgust moved across his face, and he took a deep breath. What in hell was wrong with him, anyway? He didn't need Mack and Harry to tell him the reason Jake was so long in returning. They weren't in Jake's confidence, but he was, and he knew far better than they why Jake had been detained.

Ross turned, his eye catching the towel he had thrown over a bush after emerging from the pool earlier in the evening. A small snicker escaped his lips. Hell, Mack was right. He had been using the pool to cure a multitude of ills lately—his frustrations, tension, the anger that would not cease, and the unnamed driving emotion which had tied him in knots from the moment he had set eyes on Devina Dale.

If he had been able to travel more freely, he would have found a more enjoyable way of stilling his inner turmoil. Rosie and Jenny Lee always welcomed him warmly enough as long as the price was right. Hell, maybe then he'd be successful in exorcising the memory of hair as light and fragrant as an angel's wing brushing his face, and a soft, feminine warmth that had tantalized him even while he pressed the barrel of his gun against that softness.

Ross felt a familiar tug in his groin, and he did not have to glance down to realize that the agitation now assailing him was of another source entirely. A nice long session with Rosie was truly in order.

The realization that he could not continue at his present level of disquiet much longer accompanied Ross up the dark trail a few minutes later. The stirring, conflicting emotions his encounter with Devina Dale had stimulated were drawing hatred and need for vengeance to a head inside him. Continuing back toward the cabin, Ross grimaced at the thought of facing Mack and Harry's scrutiny. He knew they were not as obsessed as he with retribution, that the monetary gain they continued to receive from Till-Dale payrolls provided all the satisfaction they needed to salve their sense of loss. And he also knew that if it had not been for their loyalty to him, they would probably be just as happy at this point to forget the whole thing. They did not understand that he was close to having Harvey Dale exactly where he wanted him.

Devina Dale was the key. Once he had that key . . .

Slowing to a stop as he reached the yard, Ross squinted into the darkening distance. No sign of Jake yet, dammit.

His expression grim, Ross turned toward the cabin, an unconscious decision made. One way or the other, he'd have Harvey Dale where he wanted him before the month was out, or he'd die trying.

Jake Walsh drew his horse to a halt behind the deserted miner's shack. The onset of twilight limited his vision as he scanned the area, and he hesitated a moment longer.

Satisfied that there was no immediate threat, Jake dismounted silently and tethered his horse. Drawing his gun, he walked carefully around the north side of the building, scrutinizing the growing shadows with great caution. He approached the door with a silent step, his light brows drawing together in an uncharacteristic frown as he grasped the handle. In a lightning-quick movement, he pushed the door open and stepped immediately aside to flatten himself against the outside wall of the shack.

Silence was the only response to the slam of the door as it snapped back against its hinges, but Jake paused a moment longer. The sound was still reverberating in the stillness when a high-pitched voice sounded hesitantly from within.

"Who . . . who is it? Who is there?"

A smile turned up the corners of Jake's lips in the moment before he stepped into the doorway of the shack. He did not need to squint into the dimness within when he heard the scramble of footsteps. Instead, he held out his arms to catch the warm body that threw itself against his lean frame.

His heart pounding, he lowered his head to meet the lips raised to his, his mouth covering their fine line with barely suppressed hunger. His hands moved against the petite proportions of the woman in his arms, smoothing the curve of her back through the coarse cotton garment she wore. His kiss deepened, separating her lips even as his hands moved to cup the curve of her delicate buttocks, to fit the warm feminine delta against his aching groin.

A light sound of discomfort sounded against his mouth, registering in the back of his mind even as he crushed her closer, pressed his kiss more deeply. He heard the sound again, belated realization dawning in his mind. He was being too rough; he was hurting her.

Drawing back with reluctance, Jake raised his hand to the smooth cheek so close to his. He stroked the fragile cheekbone, ran his fingers against the curve of the small pointed chin. His voice held a hoarsely apologetic note.

"Did I hurt you, darlin'?" When there was no immediate response, he whispered more softly, "Lai Hua, did I hurt you?"

The dark eyes that met his were bright with emotion.

"No, the sound I uttered did not reflect my pain, Mr. Jake. It reflected only my need."

Her simple response touching him deeply, Jake took a few,

short steps into the shack, carrying her easily with him. Straining
to see the features he knew so well, Jake felt desire flare inside
him. Still holding her securely with his one arm, he turned to
survey the room. His eyes took in the blanket spread on the floor
nearby and the unlit lantern resting beside it.

Releasing Lai Hua, he knelt to light the lantern. He reached
out in a quick movement and pushed the door closed, turning to
curve his arm around Lai Hua's knees to draw her down. He felt
her sweet breath brush his cheek as he lowered her to the blanket
beside him.

"No . . . no, Mr. Jake. You must not light the lantern. It is
for my use alone, so that I may return in safety through the
darkness. We must not use the lantern here. Someone will see
and discover us."

"No one will see the light, Lai Hua. The door is closed and
the windows shuttered."

"But . . ."

"I want to see you, Lai Hua."

Closing his arms around her, Jake stifled Lai Hua's protests
with the driving force of his kiss. Yes, he wanted to see her
when he made love to her.

Pressing her down on the blanket, Jake covered Lai Hua's
mouth with his, a low groan escaping him as her lips parted to
allow him the freedom he sought. His fingers worked quickly,
familiarly at the closure of her jacket. His hand moved hungrily
against her bared flesh, cupping a small breast, a thrill shooting
up his spine as the swollen crest brushed his fingers.

Frustrated by the hindrance of clothing, Jake pulled his mouth
from Lai Hua's and released her long enough to strip away her
coolie jacket and baggy pants. He tossed her clothes to the floor.
Then, kneeling at her side, he paused for long moments to
consume her doll-like beauty with his eyes.

His mouth suddenly dry, Jake was struck by the thought that
his first glimpse of Lai Hua had stirred none of the passion that
now shook him. He had been struck with only one thought when
he had first seen her working behind the counter in the general
store: Another Chinese woman working where she was not wanted.

He had had little use for the people of Lai Hua's race, and he
was uncertain when he had begun to look at Lai Hua in another
way. He supposed it was the moment when she first looked up
into his face and spoke to him. Her unusual beauty, her soft

manner, had touched him in a way no other woman had before. He had never seen a woman so small, so very perfect in every detail. Smooth skin without flaw, almond-shaped eyes that glimmered with intelligence, a round face that enhanced the delicacy of her features. And her mouth . . . He remembered watching her mouth as she spoke, the manner in which her fine lips formed her words. He remembered his pleasure at the clear, bell-like quality of her high-pitched voice, the almost musical tone in which she spoke.

He had held the list of needed supplies in his hand, and she had taken it from him with a small nod. She had turned and removed the articles from the shelves with quiet efficiency. He remembered his surprise that she was able to read English. He remembered watching the lines of her petite body as she stretched to reach the supplies. He remembered the way the light overhead had reflected on the ebony sheen of the hair bound so neatly at the back of her neck. He remembered the first time he had loosened that carefully tended knot and run his fingers through the silk that spilled loose from its confines. It had been only minutes before the shock of his discovery that Lai Hua was a virgin. It had been only minutes before she was a virgin no more.

His heart pounding, his eyes never leaving Lai Hua's, Jake stripped off his shirt and removed the rest of his clothes. Seconds later he was kneeling over Lai Hua, straddling her body. His breathing ragged, he touched her cheek in a gentle caress before sliding his hand into her hair to free it as he had so many times before. He spread the raven strands against the satin glow of her skin. Silk against satin.

But his passion would allow no further delay. He lowered himself upon her, a low groan escaping his throat as white flesh blended with gold. He paused only briefly to probe the warm nest against which his manhood pressed so eagerly. Within seconds he was inside her, her sharp gasp causing him only a moment's distraction as he savored the glory assailing his mind.

Lai Hua . . . Lai Hua . . . His mind sang a litany of her name, a litany that accompanied his thrusts, gave them impetus, brought him all too rapidly to the pinnacle of his soaring emotions. His passion-heavy eyelids lifted momentarily, allowing him a view of Lai Hua's face. Her dark eyes were closed, sharp slashes against the matchless tawny hue of her skin. Her soft lips were parted. He felt her breath against his mouth.

Abruptly the joy of culmination erupted within him. Gloriously, rapturously, he thrust himself deep inside her and brought himself to shuddering rest.

Sated and spent he lay upon Lai Hua's slenderness until a small movement awakened him to her discomfort. He rolled to the blanket beside her, his hand moving to cup her cheek as he turned to face her once more. Lai Hua averted her eyes from his, and momentary anxiety assailed him.

"Lai Hua, is somethin' wrong? Did I hurt you?"

There was a slight pause before her whispered response. "No, Mr. Jake, you did not hurt me."

But Lai Hua's lips were trembling and she refused to meet his gaze. Jake's anxiety increased as a small tear slipped out of the corner of her eye. Damn, he had hurt her.

Remorse sweeping through him, Jake gathered Lai Hua against him. His lips brushed her cheek, the curve of her ear, traced the line of her jaw. His voice was penitent. "I'm sorry if I was too rough, Lai Hua. It's been too long. I wanted you so much. But it won't happen again, I promise you." His lips touched her throat with his earnest whisper. "Let me console you, darlin'."

But Lai Hua was drawing back, searching his face with anxious eyes. "You . . . you do not wish to leave me?"

Jake shook his head, confused. "Not yet, darlin'. I haven't really had a chance to love you."

The dawning of Lai Hua's smile halted Jake's words, and he shook his head, his confusion growing. "Why? What were you thinkin', Lai Hua?"

Embarrassment clouding her expression, Lai Hua lowered her gaze once more. "I . . . I thought you had called me to come to you solely for the purpose of relieving your body, without thought of the woman who received you with love."

Jake swallowed against the emotion Lai Hua's words evoked. He would never become accustomed to her lack of pretense, her candor. "You were wrong, Lai Hua. You were very wrong. It was the thought of you and all you are that drew me to you tonight. You're not just any woman. You're very special to me."

Unable to say the words he knew Lai Hua wanted to hear, Jake again folded her tightly against him. He trailed his lips over the curve of her shoulder and down to the slope of her breasts. He murmured against her warm flesh, "Let me show you how I feel, Lai Hua. Let me prove how very special you are to me."

Jake's mouth closed over the roseate tip that brushed his lips, and he heard Lai Hua's low sigh. Yes, he would prove the words he could not say. He would prove them well.

The heat of passion had faded to a warm afterglow, but Jake still held Lai Hua in his embrace. He knew it would be more difficult this time than the last to let her go. His fascination with her increased at each searing touch, but the hidden reluctance of his passion remained.

Lai Hua was silent in his embrace. Hating himself for his thoughts, for the deep prejudice that would not allow him to say the words he so desired to say, Jake drew her closer still. The warm silk of her hair cascaded over her sweat-slick skin, and he brushed the clinging strands from her shoulder. She was so small, her bones so fragile that there were times that he feared he would injure her with the violence of his lovemaking. Somehow that fear made him want her even more desperately.

Without conscious intention, Jake took the dark silken strands thoughtfully in his hands and held them so they might catch the glow of the lantern, so he might follow the dance of onyx fire there. Unconsciously he compared the untempered blackness with the light golden hairs on the back of his hand. A startling contrast.

Lai Hua began to stir in his arms, and he drew back far enough to see her face. A tender smile flicked across his lips at the love displayed so openly there. Her slender fingers moved against his cheek for a few silent moments before she began to draw herself from his embrace.

"No, not yet, Lai Hua . . ."

But Lai Hau would not allow him to draw her close. She shook her head and reached for the clothes he had discarded so carelessly. "My father will miss me if I do not return soon. I cannot allow that to happen."

Annoyance nudged at his mind, and Jake stiffened. Lai Hua noticed his reaction.

"Mr. Jake, my father must not discover that I am gone."

The irony of the situation struck Jake anew. He berated himself for his own prejudice, when prejudice was just as strong within the Chinese community against people of his own race. He was fully aware Lai Hua would be severely chastised should her liaison with him become known, and he did not want her hurt in any way. But neither could he let her go.

Staying her as Lai Hua sought to rise from the blanket, Jake stared into the dawning of her inquisitive frown. Hesitating a moment longer, he traced her cheek with his finger, trailing it over the pure line of her jaw. He slid it down the fragile column of her throat. Slowly, he dropped it to the rise of her breast and followed the course to circle the soft mounds below.

His eyes on the slowly accelerating rise and fall of her breasts, Jake whispered into the silence, "You say you love me, Lai Hua. Do you really love me?"

Lai Hua's pink tongue moved out to lick her lips. Obviously unable to speak her response, she nodded briefly.

"How much do you love me, Lai Hua?"

Lai Hua's soft voice was hoarse with the weight of emotion. "Very much, Mr. Jake."

"Enough to help me?"

Leaning over her trembling body once more, Jake covered first one rosy crest and then the other with his lips. He drew back at her silent nod to whisper against the soft skin of her cheek.

"I need your help, Lai Hua. I need it very much. It's this lady you're workin' for, Devina Dale."

Lai Hua stiffened, obviously startled that he was aware of her new position in the Dale household.

"I need to know more about her."

"I could do nothing to hurt Miss Dale."

"I don't want to hurt her, darlin'."

"You follow your friend into danger to wreak vengeance on Mr. Dale. Mr. Dale is not a good man, and many of my people enjoy his discomfort. But his daughter is innocent of his crimes."

Lai Hua's words echoed his own statement to Ross of a few days previous, but Jake frowned at hearing them on her lips. Lai Hua's mind was too quick. Not long after they had come together for the first time, she had guessed his involvement in the Till-Dale payroll robberies. In her candid manner, she had stated her suspicions, and he had realized then that he had two choices: He could either explain the situation so Lai Hua might understand the reason he had agreed to help Ross, or he could make the decision never to see her again. Wanting her as he did, he had soon realized he had no choice at all.

But Lai Hua had kept his secret, putting herself at risk each time she answered his signal and met him for a few short hours together. He had had no reason to suspect she might refuse his request this time. Her unexpected response made him angry.

"You said you'd never refuse me anything, Lai Hua."

Lai Hua lowered her eyes. "I will do all I can to help you, Mr. Jake, but I will not harm Miss Devina in doing so."

Jake assessed the firm set of Lai Hua's chin. He had seen that expression before. She would not change her mind, no matter how much pressure he brought to bear; and in truth, he knew he could never bring himself to force her. Abruptly, he was struck with another thought: Lai Hua's new position in the Dale household could be useful in another way . . . but he knew instinctively that now was not the time to press her.

Jake managed a smile. "All right, darlin'. I don't want to make you unhappy. I guess Ross and I can handle things without you."

Appearing startled at his sudden reversal, Lai Hua raised her eyes to study his expression. Her gaze, touched with suspicion, trailed his features slowly: the pale, almost transparent blue of his eyes, the line of his lightly freckled cheek, the firm set of his sometimes stubborn jaw, the warm fullness of his lips. Her gaze lingered there to examine the full, appealing curves of his mouth. She licked her lips unconsciously, remembering the taste of that mouth, the warmth it stirred within her.

Realizing that her perusal was having an erotic effect on the strong body pressed against her, Lai Hua shook her head. "I am pleased that my refusal has not angered you, Mr. Jake, but I must go now. It is late."

Jake's warm breath stirred her hair as he moved quickly and agilely to cover her body with his once more. His voice was low, threaded with a familiar passion as he whispered against her ear. "Just a little longer, darlin'. Just a little while . . ."

The joy of the meeting of their flesh stilled Lai Hua's protest. With a soft sigh she slid her arms around the man she loved. There was no need for words.

The eastern sky had begun to glow with the first light of dawn when the door of the dilapidated miner's shack again opened.

Two shadowed forms paused in the doorway, blending briefly into one before Lai Hua drew back from Jake's embrace. Turning, she snatched up the lantern and the blanket from the floor, and within moments she had disappeared onto the trail back to town.

A flicker of movement in the darkness outside the cabin went unnoted as Jake emerged a few seconds later and moved quickly to the rear of the cabin where his horse was tethered.

The flicker of movement in the darkness of the yard became a shadow as a slight figure rose from concealment. It paused only long enough to allow Jake's horse to begin moving in the opposite direction before turning onto the trail behind Lai Hua.

Concealed, the shadow followed Lai Hua. Silent and unmoving, it watched as she reached her home at last and slipped through the back door. The shadowed figure hesitated. Without a sound, it then turned and slipped off into the darkness, fading into the obscurity from which it had come.

CHAPTER VI

"REALLY, FATHER, THIS time I think you've gone a step too far."

Devina paused in the doorway of the Till-Dale offices. The brilliant sunshine of morning at her back held her features in dark relief, but the exasperation in her voice adequately conveyed her frame of mind. In silent emphasis, she shot a quick glance over her shoulder. It barely grazed the head of Lai Hua before coming to rest meaningfully on the cowboy standing silently behind her, regarding her with a watchful, narrowed gaze.

His gray brows knitting into a frown, Harvey Dale turned fully in her direction. "Come in, Devina. Sharpe, Lai Hua, you can both wait outside. Miss Dale won't be long."

Taking her arm, Harvey drew Devina inside and shut the outer door behind her. Totally ignoring the two clerks who looked expectantly in his daughter's direction, Harvey addressed the short, meticulously dressed gentleman behind him. "George, you remember my daughter Devina."

"Of course I do, Harvey. I'm pleased to see you again, Devina. I hope you'll enjoy your residence in Tombstone. Mrs. Tillson has found living here quite pleasant, now that she's become accustomed to the town's rather rustic charm."

Devina's smile was stiff as she acknowledged her father's partner's greeting. "It's nice to see you again, too, Mr. Tillson. As for enjoying my residence in Tombstone, I'm beginning to have my doubts. Did Mrs. Tillson's acclimation to Tombstone's 'rustic charm' include having a bodyguard follow her when she left the house?''

Hastily interrupting as George Tillson shot a surprised glance in his direction, Harvey again took his daughter's arm. Ushering her firmly toward his office a few feet away, he turned briefly back toward his partner. "George, if you'll excuse us for a few moments. Devina and I obviously have some things to discuss.''

Her perfect lips twitching with anger as her father ushered her into his office, Devina waited until he had shut the door behind them before facing him with the full extent of her anger.

"Father, really! Your insistence on my having a maid accompany me when I wish to do some simple shopping is bad enough, but this fellow I found outside the door this morning, waiting to follow me around town, is beyond reason! I'm actually traveling with an entourage! You're making a fool of me before the whole town!''

"Devina, calm down. There is no need to raise your voice.''

"I am not raising my voice!''

Harvey Dale's well-groomed gray mustache ticked with annoyance. "I will not argue that point with you; neither will I argue any other point with you. I have no intention of seeing a repetition of the incident that came about yesterday. Had Charles Carter not come upon you at the moment he had, you might have suffered far more than embarrassment at the hands of that drunken cowboy.''

"Father, the incident was of little consequence. Charles handled it quite nicely, and I was made to see my error in judgment when I disregarded Lai Hua's advice. Once I am accustomed to Tombstone and become more familiar with the areas that are taboo to the genteel woman, I will not need even her guidance, much less a bodyguard!''

"Devina, I've already told you, I do not intend to discuss the matter.''

The sunshine streaming through the windows to Devina's left illuminated her deepening flush, and Harvey winced inwardly. When would he ever learn his usual autocratic manner was like tinder to a spark when he assumed it with Devina? Well, judging from the heat in Devina's eyes, it was already too late to make amends. Taking the only course left to him, he firmly stood his ground as the fire in Devina's eyes became an all-encompassing blaze.

"That is unfortunate, Father, since I do not intend to spend my life being trailed by that unkempt, unclean, disreputable-looking watchdog you've hired."

"Appearances aside, Sam Sharpe is a very dependable man, Devina. You may rest assured he will defend you with his life, and he—"

"Defend me with his life! Father, that incident yesterday was a simple mistake! The fellow apologized and beat a hasty retreat after Charles explained the situation."

"A mistake, yes. It was a mistake in many ways." His expression assuming an accusing quality, Harvey continued quietly, "It was a mistake on your part when you disregarded my advice and the advice of Lai Hua, whom I had put in charge of your orientation to Tombstone. It was a mistake on your part when you deliberately neglected to tell me of the incident. I am still less than pleased that I had to hear about it secondhand, after the story had been circulating Tombstone for hours. And it was a mistake on my part for having allowed it to happen."

"You did not 'allow' it to happen, Father." Despite her annoyance, Devina was unwilling to have her father assume even part of the blame. She attempted to continue, only to be halted by an impatient wave of her father's hand.

"I suppose whether I allowed it to happen or not is a matter of viewpoint, but the incident did call to my attention the supreme vulnerability of your situation."

"*Am* I vulnerable? Vulnerable to whom?" Her expression tightening revealingly, Devina shook her head. "I fear you are seeing demons where there are none, and I do not expect to suffer for—"

"Devina, please . . ." Interrupting her growing tirade, Harvey reached out to place a gentle hand on Devina's shoulder, his expression changing dramatically as he attempted a smile. "Dear, it will do no good if we continue to rail at each other. I was wrong when I said I did not wish to discuss your objection to Sam Sharpe's presence. Please sit down, dear, and allow me to explain."

Startled by her father's abrupt about-face, Devina hesitated before allowing him to usher her to a chair. Seating himself directly opposite her, he gave a short laugh.

"I suppose you have a right to be suspicious. I've done nothing in the past to make you believe I would consider any viewpoint but my own, but your point is well taken. You're a grown woman now and should not be treated like a child." Abruptly leaning toward her, Harvey took both Devina's hands in his. He held them tightly as he continued.

"I spoke of your vulnerability a few moments ago, Devina, and you objected, but, in truth, it is not your vulnerability I'm worried about as much as my own." Devina's confusion was obvious, but Harvey's smile was patient. "Let me explain, dear. I've already told you about the robberies, six within three months. I've already told you only Till-Dale seems to be under attack, for some unknown reason. Larger payroll shipments from other companies, shipments protected no more heavily than ours, have gone unmolested. I would assume that reason has to do with some sort of twisted vengeance for an imagined wrong, but I haven't bothered to stretch my mind far in that direction at this point in time.

"At the very moment you arrived this morning, George and I were working out a plan with which to entrap these men, or at least fool them long enough to get another payroll shipment through. It is urgent that we pay our miners. Do not misjudge my insistence on this point to be an attempt to convince you of my devotion to my employees. You know me better than that. The men who work in the muck of my mines mean no more to me than the tools with which they work, but they are as necessary to me as those tools are to them.

"I think you are aware, Devina, that a year or so ago water started seeping into the mines in this area. Till-Dale shafts have been particularly affected, requiring expensive pumping in order to allow work to continue. At present I am negotiating with a large San Francisco bank for a loan to finance the purchase of additional pumping equipment. Without it, we will not be able to continue for more than six months.

"In order to comprehend the situation more clearly you must understand the mentality of the men who work in the mines. They are for the most part bachelors who live for the day. There are a few family men who return home to their wives and children after each shift and save their money for a rainy day, but those fellows are definitely in the minority. The majority of our miners work their shifts, sleep, and work again, waiting only to collect their pay at the end of the week, when they'll go abroad in the streets of Tombstone and spend all they've earned

on rotgut whiskey, questionable women, and gambling. There
has been a lot of talk among the Till-Dale miners lately, grumbling and suspicion that might cause trouble if these payrolls
continue to be delayed. These fellows are becoming disgruntled
at the inconvenience of having to wait a few days for their pay.

"To put it bluntly, Devina, there is talk that the men may
walk out to take jobs in nearby mines that are not experiencing
the same difficulty. Till-Dale cannot afford a break in production
at this time, not now, when the bank is considering the viability
of our loan."

Hesitating to survey his daughter's expression and satisfied
that she was following him intently, Harvey continued. "Now,
about our vulnerability. It occurred to me yesterday, when I
heard of your being accosted on the street—"

"But, Father, that was my own fault."

"Devina, kindly allow me to finish. That incident yesterday
caused me to view the situation from another perspective. The
men who have been stealing our payrolls are undoubtedly staging
the robberies as a personal attack against George or me, and
quite frankly, I've reached the conclusion that the attack is most
likely directed at me. Since there have been no attempts to hurt
me physically, I can only assume the thieves wish to hurt me in
another way. With that thought in mind, I assessed the situation
again. Where am I most vulnerable to attack? The answer is
simple, through the finances of my company and through you."

"Father, that is stretching it a bit, don't you think? If those
men had wanted to get to you through me, they would've had the
perfect opportunity the day of my arrival in Tombstone." Doing
her best to ignore the assault of a dark-eyed glance that assailed
her mind in memory, Devina continued, "And if we can believe
the statement of the hoodlum who held me captive on the stage, I
am not considered worth his trouble."

"That was before he realized who you were, Devina."

Devina's only response was a disbelieving laugh.

Contrary to Devina's expectation, her father did not respond
with anger to her disclaiming note. He continued, his voice
dropping a notch lower with the sincerity of his tone. "In any
case, Devina, I have come to the realization that my greatest
vulnerability lies in you. Where you are vulnerable, I am vulnerable. So if you are angry that I am overdoing your protection,
you may satisfy yourself that I am only protecting myself."

"Father, I—"

"Devina . . ." Taking a deep breath, Harvey drew Devina to her feet. Still holding her hands tightly in his, he continued in a hushed voice, "I fear it has become fairly obvious to all but yourself that I cherish you above all things in my life. I could not live with the thought that something happened to you because of me."

Touched and unable to find words to respond, Devina watched as her father's eyes moved assessingly over her face for a few long moments before he slid his hand to her arm and drew her toward the doorway to his office. Pausing with his hand on the knob, he continued softly, "So I ask your indulgence for a little while, dear. I assure you these hoodlums will be either caught and punished or driven from the area within the month."

"And in the meantime I am expected to suffer Sam Sharpe's presence, day and night?"

This time it was Harvey's turn to laugh. "No, dear, only during the day. Wally Smith takes over at night."

"Father!"

"Dear, it's only a precaution."

Devina shook her head. "But I'm to go to Schieffelin Hall with Charles tonight. I don't want this Smith fellow following along at my heels."

"There'll be no need for protection when Charles is with you, dear. I think he's proved he is more than capable of protecting you."

Relief flooded Devina's face. "Well, I'm grateful for that, at least."

Ushering her firmly across the outer office, Harvey smiled in George Tillson's direction. "Devina is leaving now, George. I'll be with you in a moment."

Pausing to open the door, Harvey turned toward his daughter once more. "I appreciate your understanding, dear, and your cooperation. Enjoy your shopping."

Within a few minutes Devina was again on the street.

Her diminutive guide at her side and her villainous-looking watchdog trailing at her heels, Devina gave a low sigh and brought her step to an abrupt halt. Darting a scathing glance toward Sam Sharpe as he almost ran into her back at her unanticipated stop, she turned to Lai Hua.

"I've lost my enthusiasm for shopping, Lai Hua. The morning room will just have to exist in its present state of questionable decoration for a little while longer. In any case, it's getting late, and I would like to take a bath before—"

Suddenly realizing the man behind her was listening to her conversation with Lai Hua, Devina abruptly stopped talking, her small nose twitching with annoyance. Without another word, she turned resolutely back in the direction of Fourth Street and home.

Intent on her own growing irritation, Devina walked briskly. The persistent click of high-heeled cowboy boots against the board sidewalk behind her added to her growing agitation, and she increased her pace without realizing that admiring male glances followed the rhythmic bobbing of her well-endowed female form.

Well, her father had done it again. Her sympathy for her long-suffering mother never stronger than at that moment, Devina closed her eyes briefly with self-disgust. She'd been manipulated just as easily as her mother had been countless times before her. The sincerity, the concern, the love in her father's eyes had been too potent a weapon to fight with simple annoyance. So here she was, as far as the population of Tombstone was concerned, a helpless, frightened female enjoying the protection of an adoring, doting father, when nothing could be further from the truth.

Her mother's blood was strong in her veins, and now more than ever, she had realized that she suffered her mother's weakness. How many times would she have to remind herself that her father's love was limited, that it extended only as far as vocal acknowledgment, and that he would not allow love to discomfort him in any way? Yes, he loved her as he had loved her mother. He was proud of his beautiful daughter, just as he had been proud of his beautiful wife. He wanted what was best for her, but 'what was best' was not open to discussion. She knew he would be satisfied by the fulfillment of his own wishes and his alone. And if 'what was best' did not make her happy, it would make little difference to him.

Why had she not spoken her true thoughts when her father expressed his fears? A nagging voice in the back of her mind demanded that she be honest: Her silence had not merely been the product of her father's mesmerizing and well-practiced skill

in overcoming female resistance. It had also been the product of
the fear that had trickled down her spine as the remembered
dark-eyed gaze she had struggled so desperately to avoid had
again assaulted her mind. It was humiliating to admit, even to
herself, that a man whose identity she did not even know had
managed so thoroughly to insinuate himself in her mind. She
was, even now, at a loss to understand how that unknown man
had managed to instill so much conflicting emotion within her
that the thought of again being in his clutches immobilized her.

And immobilized she had been, like putty in her father's
hands. As a result, she was now saddled with a bodyguard of
dubious value . . . no, *two* bodyguards of dubious value! It was
humiliating, being treated like a lapdog incapable of protecting
herself and incapable of making decisions that would keep her
out of harm's way.

Refusing to turn to see if her bodyguard was still following at
her heels, Devina made a sharp right onto Fremont Street and
breathed a short sigh. A brief glance in her maid's direction
revealed that Lai Hua was disturbed at her unhappiness. Refusing to allow the sweet girl another moment's concern, Devina
flicked her a smile. Father had chosen well indeed in securing
Lai Hua for her personal maid; but something in the back of
Devina's mind refused to allow her to believe her father was
totally responsible for the choice. Father was not terribly skilled
at recognizing the true worth of people. His cavalier treatment of
his wife had been proof of that.

Abruptly grateful that her home was in sight, Devina ignored
the unexpected shiver which ran down her spine. Well, Father
had been successful in another way as well. With his softly
voiced concern and speculation, he had managed to instill a
modicum of doubt in her own mind as to her safety. Certainly
that was the reason that even now, so close to her own home,
she felt the weight of eyes following her. She would not admit
even to herself that she had been pressed by such a feeling before
her father had voiced his fears. Instead, she raised her chin in
unspoken defiance of her own anxiety and continued boldly
forward.

A low expletive escaped Ross's lips with the ferocity of a
snarl. He held the spyglass against his eye and slid closer to the
edge of the overhang on which he lay, seeking a clearer view.

No, there was no mistaking it. Devina Dale was walking down Fremont Street, looking as self-possessed as any young woman who held the world in the palm of her hand. At her side Lai Hua walked nervously, glancing up at her from time to time. And to her rear walked Sam Sharpe.

Sam Sharpe. Ross's cheek began to tick with barely restrained fury. Sam Sharpe would do anything to fill his pockets. . . . It was Sam Sharpe who did most of Harvey Dale's dirty work, but today he'd been given a much more pleasant job. Hell, what man wouldn't enjoy following a woman who looked like Devina Dale?

Ross moved his spyglass to study Sharpe more closely. Maintaining a position close behind Devina Dale, Sharpe let his half-closed eyes moved intimately over Devina Dale's feminine curves. An unknown emotion gnawed at Ross's gut, and he clamped his teeth tightly shut. One thing was certain. Dale had hired the right person to protect his precious daughter. Dale paid well, and Sharpe would kill before he'd let anyone steal his meal ticket.

Damn it all, Ross hadn't expected this complication. He had been shaken from his bad humor early this morning when Jake had arrived back at the cabin and told him that Lai Hua was working as Devina Dale's personal maid. He had been disappointed when Jake had reported that Lai Hua refused to do anything that would endanger her new mistress, but he knew Jake well enough to believe he would be successful in persuading Lai Hua to help them. He had actually begun to relax. After all, from now on they would actually have inside help. So far, the success of their payroll robberies had been due partly to good planning, partly to good luck, and partly to bribes. But their sources of inside information had just about gone dry. Lai Hua's new position appeared to be the perfect solution to that problem.

But Ross's brief feeling of well-being had disappeared with the arrival of Sam Sharpe on the scene. Damn! He hadn't been able to believe his eyes when Sam Sharpe openly took up a position behind Devina Dale as she emerged from her house early that morning. Ross had seen the short conversation that took place between them. He had focused his glass for a clear view of the agitation on Devina Dale's face.

The haughty Miss Dale did not like being trailed by the likes of Sam Sharpe. She had walked directly toward Allen Street, and although Ross had been able to follow her progress only part of the way, he had known very well where she was heading. But it seemed Miss Dale did not have her father wrapped as securely around her finger as she thought, for Sam Sharpe was still close at her heels.

Suffering the same malady as on his previous surveillance, Ross found himself unable to lower his glass, unable to take his eyes from Devina Dale as she continued walking back toward her home. Her stylish green gown fit her lush curves like a second skin, and Ross was well aware that the ridiculous hat which sat on her gleaming hair had probably cost more than the average frontier wife paid for her entire wardrobe. Ross gave a low contemptuous snort. It was obvious Devina Dale accepted all as her due.

Forcing his eyes from her provocative sway, Ross adjusted his glass so he might concentrate more intently on her face. Clear, sparkling blue eyes, flawless white skin, a clarity of feature that was stunning in its perfection. And her lips. Even at his extended distance, he could see that they were full, lush. As much as he thoroughly despised Devina Dale for all she was, he ached to taste that full, warm mouth.

But that inviting mouth was twitching with annoyance. Oh, Miss Dale did not like to meet defeat at her father's hands. She raised the delicate line of her chin with unconscious determination. She turned unexpectedly in his direction, and he saw a glimpse of something else in those breathtaking eyes. What was it?

Damn! The little twit had passed out of his line of vision.

Waiting interminable moments until she was visible once more, Ross watched as Devina approached the house and stepped inside. He shifted his gaze to Sam Sharpe, noting and marking in his mind the position the man took up in surveillance.

Ross lowered his glass at last. The presence of a bodyguard would make his task more difficult, but not impossible. He had long ago determined that if you wanted something badly enough, nothing was impossible. And he wanted Devina Dale.

Ross took a moment to amend that statement in his mind. The truth was that Devina Dale had much to offer him aside from her obvious physical attributes. She could offer him Harvey Dale on a silver platter.

•   •   •   •

Devina turned once more before the mirror in a frustrated effort to obtain a better look at the back of her striking ensemble. Her brow wrinkled with impatience.

"Lai Hua, give me the hand mirror, please."

Snapping to her request, Lai Hua put the elaborately carved mirror in her hand, and Devina adjusted its position so she might get the view she wished. She shook her head. "I don't know, Lai Hua . . . Does this gown make me look large in the rear portion? I should not like to attend my first social function in Tombstone and find out later that the only comment I stirred was related to the size of that particular area of my anatomy."

Lai Hua's face crinkled into a spontaneous smile only partly hidden by the small hand that snapped up to cover her lips. A spot of warmth stirred inside Devina, lightening her frown. Lai Hua seemed to find her very amusing. She had excited varied reactions in people, but she had rarely been considered amusing. Of course, she had rarely felt the need to entertain anyone.

No, the more common emotions she had been known to stir were awe (her presence always seemed to leave some speechless), lust (some men were so easily raised to that primitive emotion by a look or a sassy turn of a hip), and jealousy (so easily read in the eyes of women who envied her beauty as much as they envied her position as Harvey Dale's daughter). She was intensely relieved to find that Lai Hua's reactions appeared to fall into none of these categories. But then, Lai Hua was so sincere, and there seemed to be little that could dampen her good humor. Lai Hua was definitely good to have around, especially in this archaic country.

Devina tried once more.

"Come now, Lai Hua, surely my appearance isn't that amusing."

Her small eyes abruptly filled with concern, Lai Hua shook her head in vigorous denial. "Oh, no, Miss Devina. Your appearance is not at all amusing. In truth, your appearance steals one's breath."

The silver-blue of her eyes taking on a teasing glow, Devina raised her slender brows in mock dismay. "Oh, surely my derriere doesn't look *that* large?"

Lai Hua shook her head even harder. "No, ma'am, it does not! It looks very good, as good as does the rest of you. You are very beautiful, Miss Devina. You must not be upset if Dr. Carter makes no comment at the moment you appear, for I am sure he will be as breathless as I at the sight of your outstanding beauty.''

Devina's smile lost its teasing quality.

''You are extremely generous in your praise, Lai Hua, but I think you're prejudiced in my behalf. Now, seriously, do the fringes on the skirt bring too much emphasis to my posterior portion when I walk? Is it very obvious that the waistline of this dress is a bit loose? I can't imagine how that happened. I had it adjusted just prior to leaving New York. It fit me very well then.''

Realizing she was being called upon to make constructive criticism, Lai Hua tilted her head slightly to the side in an obvious attempt to make an honest response. After a few moments, concern marked Lai Hua's clear forehead and she raised her brows expressively. ''I am sorry, Miss Devina, but I can find nothing amiss with your appearance. You are perfect in all respects.''

Devina's smile flashed, and Lai Hua's head bobbed in further emphasis.

''And now you are breathtaking once more.''

Devina turned away from her servant's scrutiny with a resigned shake of her head. It looked as if she could not depend on Lai Hua for criticism. Well, at least Lai Hua's praise was honest, not inspired by a desire to ingratiate herself or to have her mistress appear a fool because of a misdirected sense of jealousy.

Devina turned back to the mirror with a pensive expression. Well, she supposed she did look beautiful. She had deliberately dressed her hair in casual manner to offset the formal style of her dress, and she supposed it was becoming. Yes, the pale mass she had swept away from her face and coiled atop her head while still damp from washing, did catch the light particularly well, giving her almost a halo effect with its glimmering sheen. She turned her head. The sweep of her hair did accent her perfect profile. She deliberately ignored the few curling wisps at her hairline, which had escaped her coiffure, knowing full well it was useless to try to control them.

As for her dress, blue was definitely her color, and this particular shade was just silvery enough to mimic the color of her eyes. The off-the-shoulder neckline was particularly flattering to her graceful neck and shoulders, even if the décolletage was a bit daring. She eyed the short puff sleeves ornamented with velvet bows in a shade of royal blue. Yes, she liked them very well, and the bodice of the garment fit smoothly against the swell of her breasts, even if the waistline was not as tight as she would have preferred.

Ah, but the skirt—all that flouncing, elaborate draping and swaying fringe. Devina shook her head. A few days before she would not have given the elaborate style a second thought, but her confidence had received a heavy blow when that fellow on the street had said she was dressed like a common strumpet.

Abruptly, Devina was angry. What was wrong with her? Why was she suddenly so self-conscious? Was it because she still had not lost that chilling sensation of being watched? Was it because dark eyes hovered still in the back of her mind, refusing to allow her a minute's peace? Oh, damn, she was behaving like a fool!

Devina turned away from the mirror with an angry step, only to be stopped short by a knock on the door.

From the hallway, Molly said, "Dr. Carter has arrived, Miss Devina. He's waiting in the foyer."

"Tell him I'll be down in a moment, Molly."

Turning toward Lai Hua, Devina raised her shoulders in a small shrug. "Well, that settles that dilemma, Lai Hua. Too much fringe, or not too much fringe, I'm leaving."

Accepting the pale blue silk shawl Lai Hua held out to her, Devina walked toward the hallway with a rapid ·step. Within moments she was descending the staircase to the front foyer, her indecision of a short time before still nagging at her mind. Her eyes touched on Charles's tall, well-muscled frame, outfitted to perfection in a dark suit that emphasized his vibrant good looks. A small flutter moved in the pit of her stomach. There was something about him . . . But her momentary puzzlement was alleviated by the rush of pleasure inspired by Charles's first reaction to her appearance.

Devina suppressed the laugh that rose in her throat. Just as Lai Hua had predicted, Charles had been knocked breathless.

Her smiled widening, Devina gracefully extended a gloved hand toward Charles as she reached the bottom of the staircase. His hand curled slightly around hers as he drew her down the final step.

"Good evening, Charles. You look extremely handsome tonight."

Charles paused in reply. His dark eyes held hers with a stirring warmth. "Devina, I think I can honestly say you are the most beautiful woman I've ever seen, and you've outdone yourself tonight. Without a doubt, you'll set Tombstone society on its ear."

Devina's laugh was genuine and spontaneous. "On its ear! Charles, Tombstone society will never forgive me!"

Leaning forward, Charles startled her by brushing her cheek with a light kiss. "Oh, yes, it will, Devina. It will forgive you anything."

At the sound of an unexpected step, Charles and Devina turned to face Harvey Dale's raised eyebrows. "Charles, if you've finished filling my daughter's head with nonsense, I think it's time for you to start for Schieffelin Hall. Unless it's your specific intention to arrive late for the curtain, you had better not waste time.

"Harvey, I'm not of the opinion that it is a waste of time to tell a beautiful woman just how lovely she truly is."

Harvey Dale's mouth gave a wry twist. "In this case, it is. Devina is well aware that she is beautiful. Blood will tell, you know. I think you will impress my daughter far more by complimenting her on her intelligence."

"But, Harvey, your daughter's intelligence is not particularly obvious at this moment."

At Devina's protest, Charles shook his head. An embarrassed laugh escaped his lips. "Wait, let me rephrase that comment. I meant to say it's not her intelligence that left me speechless as she walked down those steps, and I'm not ashamed to say that I'm going to enjoy escorting the most beautiful woman in Tombstone to the theater tonight."

Appearing genuinely amused, Harvey smiled. "Well, you managed to extricate yourself from that blunder with true dexterity, Charles. But I repeat, you're going to be late."

"Charles, I think Father is trying to get rid of us, so I suggest that we oblige." Turning to her father, Devina paused, her expression sobering. "You *have* called off the watchdog for the night, haven't you, Father?"

"Watchdog?"

Both Harvey and Devina ignored Charles's confused interjection.

"I told you I would, didn't I, dear?"

"What's this about a watchdog?"

Devina smiled. "I'll tell you about it on the way, Charles."

Tucking Devina's arm carefully under his, Charles was halted unexpectedly by Harvey's restraining hand. Devina's eyes rose to her father's face with annoyance, only to be struck by the concern evident there as he addressed Charles briefly.

"If you had not already demonstrated your concern for my daughter's welfare, Charles, I would caution you now most severely. But I know that will not be necessary."

The cutting edge of her voice softened by the visual evidence of her father's honest solicitude, Devina responded levelly, "Yes, Father, you are correct. Your cautioning is not necessary."

Ignoring Charles's confusion, Devina urged him toward the door.

"You heard what my father said, Charles. We're going to be late. We'd make a really noticeable entrance then."

"You'll make a spectacular entrance whenever you arrive, Devina. I have no doubt about that."

Devina's smile warmed, despite the nagging twitch of unease that again assailed her as she stepped onto the porch. "Charles, I think I'm going to like you very much."

Charles's low voice met her ear in a confidential whisper as they stepped down from the last step and turned up the street: "I'm way ahead of you there, dear."

Concealed by the darkness, Ross trained his spyglass on the gaslit street as a handsome couple stepped down from the porch and into the light. Shock held him momentarily immmobile. He followed their rapid pace up the street, a low, incredulous hiss finally escaping his throat.

Charles Carter. A familiar burning hatred swelled inside Ross, and he indulged it for long moments before moving his gaze to the woman who walked at Carter's side. Charles Carter and Devina Dale, as well matched a pair as ever could be.

He would see to it that they weren't together long.

Perversely, Ross was unable to draw his eyes from the couple's laughing progress up Fremont Street. His stomach had twisted into tight knots of disgust by the time he finally lowered his glass, unable to watch any longer.

Drawing himself stiffly to his feet, Ross ignored the semidarkness that shadowed his path as he walked rapidly to where his horse was tied. He had seen enough for this day.

• • •

Harvey remained standing in the foyer as Devina and Charles walked briskly down the street. He noted that they made a very handsome couple, Charles with his tall, darkly handsome good looks, and Devina with her petite, pale beauty. But his mind lingered only briefly on the thought.

As soon as his daughter and the young doctor had disappeared around the corner, Harvey reached for his hat. Stepping out on the porch, he pulled the front door closed behind him.

With great care he placed his high-crowned bowler at the correct angle on his handsomely groomed head and straightened his shoulders. Pausing only briefly to submit to the demands of vanity, Harvey adjusted the fit of his well-tailored jacket before starting down the steps.

With his first step onto the street, all thoughts of Devina and Charles had been thoroughly dismissed from his mind.

"You're certain you don't want to join Wilfred and me for some late refreshments at the Can-Can?" Her slightly protruding brown eyes intent, Sally Lou Keane directed her earnest question toward Devina and Charles, her gaze darting between them.

Thinking that Sally Lou looked for all the world like a wounded fawn, with her narrow face and awkwardly thin frame, Devina took a firm hold of her patience. Sally Lou looked sadly unsophisticated, despite her obvious attempt at chic, and Devina was weary of those soleful, searching eyes.

"Yes, I'm certain, but I do thank both you and Wilfred for your kind invitation."

Devina's look of mute appeal made Charles offer a hasty postcript. "As for myself, Sally Lou, I have early appointments in the morning, but I do thank you for—"

"Remember, Devina, I will be depending upon you to come to my party on Saturday night. I'll be simply devastated if you don't appear." Sally Lou's blatant interruption of Charles's response stiffened Devina's already forced smile.

"I'll certainly make an effort to attend, Sally Lou. Thank you again for your invitation." Turning away from the young woman's anxious expression, Devina urged softly, "Shall we go, Charles?"

His mouth twitching with amusement, Charles briefly tipped his hat in Sally Lou's direction and stepped out into the throng of homeward-bound theatergoers. Waiting only until they were out of earshot, he turned toward Devina. Her obvious annoyance perversely broadened his smile. "It appears you'll be in great demand at social functions now that you've been informally introduced into Tombstone society, Devina. Why aren't you smiling? You were an instant success. You left the men agog and the women simmering in their envy. As expected, you knocked everyone breathless."

Devina's small nose twitched. The heat of annoyance was heavy in her tone, increasing his amusement as she responded stiffly, "Is that so, Charles? I hadn't noticed any shortness of breath on Sally Lou's part. As a matter of fact, she barely stopped talking long enough to come up for air."

Charles's mouth twitched again. "Yes, she is a wonder, isn't she?"

Devina's expression stiffened. "Charles, I am not in the least amused."

"I know. I suppose that's what made the situation all the more humorous." No longer able to restrain his grin, Charles shook his head. "Devina, you should demonstrate more charity. Poor Sally Lou came to Tombstone with her family when she was only a child, when her father was hired as an engineer at the Lucky Cuss mine. She's lived in this town ever since, and except for an occasional shopping jaunt to San Francisco, Tombstone is all she knows of the world. She has recently become engaged to Wilfred Bellows, who is a clerk at the mine. Her marriage to him will guarantee that during her lifetime she will probably never stray far from these treeless hills. She's starved for a glimpse of the world she's never seen, and you represent that world."

"She cannot be starved any longer, Charles, no matter what you say. She was *feeding* on me the entire evening." Her sarcastic barb delivered with a slight flick of her brows, Devina continued without waiting for his response, "How can you ask me to be more charitable? I think I was extremely gracious this evening, even though my ear is actually throbbing from Sally Lou's incessant chatter."

"Beautiful, charming, amusing, exhilarating—I found you to be all those things . . . but gracious to Sally Lou? No, Devina you deliver a powerfully chilling glance."

"To which Sally Lou seemed thoroughly immune."

"Oh, you noticed that?"

"Charles, you're being annoyingly facetious."

"Am I? I thought I was being honest."

"Charles . . ."

"All right, but I have the distinct impression you have no intention of attending Sally Lou's party."

"Oh, heaven forbid!"

Devina's horrified expression stimulated a true bellow of laughter, which Charles found difficult to control. Aware that heads were turning in his direction, Charles tried harder.

"Charles, I told you, I do not find this situation amusing, and I do not intend to subject myself to another night of dodging Sally Lou's incessant barrage of questions and nonstop conversation." Devina paused a moment in obvious consternation, her brows drawing into a frown. "Charles, please stop laughing!"

Charles realized they were approaching the Dale residence. Taking a firm hold on himself, he nodded. "I am sorry, Devina, but if you could've seen your face for the greater part of the evening . . . You looked at Sally Lou as if you could not quite believe what was happening."

"I couldn't!"

"As if she were some strange species you had never before encountered."

"She is!"

"Devina, the girl looks up to you." Charles's voice was touched with amused admonishment. "Charity, please."

"Charles . . ." Devina's expression was pained. Charles Carter was the only person who had ever expected her to discomfort herself for someone else. She was ill at ease with the expectation, but she found herself even more uncomfortable with the thought that Charles Carter might disapprove of her conduct.

Devina shook her head. "Charles, you don't really expect me to go to that party, do you? I can't. I . . . she . . ." Her voice faded away as Charles held her gaze unblinkingly, and her mouth compressed into a straight line for long, silent seconds before she burst out with obvious distaste, "Oh, all right! I'll go to Sally Lou's stupid party!"

Charles's mouth twitched once more. "That's very generous of you, Devina."

Devina's initial response was a suspicious glance. "Charles, are you laughing at me?"

"*With* you, Devina. Never *at* you."

Devina raised her chin. "I'll go to Sally Lou's party on one condition."

"And what is that?"

"That you'll take me and promise not to abandon me to Sally Lou. We can set up some sort of signal, and when I can take no more of her inane conversation you can—"

Drawing her up the steps of the porch as they reached the Dale residence, Charles interrupted Devina's agitated speech with a broad smile and a wave of his hand. Devina's lips snapped closed, and he marveled at the physical perfection of the small woman standing before him. He had been utterly sincere when he stated earlier that Devina Dale was the most beautiful woman he had ever seen.

"Devina, I'll be delighted to take you to Sally Lou's party, and to deliver you from her whenever she threatens to overwhelm you with her idol worship."

Devina frowned once more. "Charles, you make me sound like such a selfish, intolerant twit."

"Do I?"

Devina appeared to consider his response. An unexpected smile suddenly curving her lips, she shook her head. "Yes, you do . . . so why do I like you so much?"

"Because I'm so incredibly likable."

"Oh, I wouldn't go so far as to say that."

Laughter beginning to well inside him once more, Charles reached out to give Devina a spontaneous hug. "You are a dear girl, Devina."

Devina looked startled. "No one has ever said that to me before, Charles."

"No?" Charles was genuinely surprised. "Perhaps that's why you like me, because I have an unusual appreciation for . . . for—"

"For unusual people? Charles, are you calling me 'odd'?"

"Devina, dear . . ." Leaning down, Charles brushed her lips with a kiss. "I'll pick you up on Saturday. And I must honestly say, I avidly anticipate the evening."

Devina found herself nodding, her smile genuine. "I do, too, Charles."

Turning to the door, Devina pushed it open and stepped into the well-lit foyer. Giving Charles a warm parting glance, she closed the door behind her and turned toward Molly with a strong feeling of well-being. She suspected she could become fond of Charles Carter. And perhaps Charles was right. Perhaps she should be more generous, more charitable in her treatment of others. She hesitated a moment. She supposed that included Father.

Realizing Molly was still hovering behind her, she turned abruptly. "Molly, is Father in the den? I should like to let him know I've arrived home safely."

"Your father, ma'am? He's gone out. He left right after you, and I don't know when he'll be back."

Annoyance flashed across Devina's mind. So much for her father's deep concern, and so much for her own generosity and charity. Her head high, Devina turned to the staircase.

Harvey Dale strove to catch his breath. His heart was pounding heavily in his chest, and his skin was covered with a thin veil of perspiration. He attempted to raise himself from the warm body beneath him, but his arms were too weak to support him. Deciding to give himself another few minutes to regain his strength, he turned his cheek, resting it lightly against the satin black of Lily's hair.

Concentrate . . . Concentrate . . . Breathe deeply, Harvey's mind coached him, guiding his actions. His breathing was beginning to return to normal when a thought hit him for the first time: Damn! She had done it again. Lily had all but brought him to his knees.

His strength fast returning, Harvey lifted his chest from Lily's small breasts. Holding himself there, he perused the exotic features of the woman who lay so still beneath him.

She showed none of the signs of the passion he had felt rack her body only minutes before. She was composed, quiet. True, the flawless gold of her complexion bore a light flush, and her lips were parted to allow easier breathing, but she was perfectly composed, showing not a shadow of his own agitation.

Closed, Lily's eyes were dark slashes against the creamy perfection of her skin, and as he watched, the heavily fringed eyelids parted. Deep and glittering black, her eyes were unfathomable as her gaze moved over his face. A strange, unrecognized emotion stirred inside him, conflicting with his anger. He paused to consider it.

Tenderness . . . it was tenderness. It occurred to him that he had taken a beautiful, inexperienced virgin and molded her into a totally exciting, captivating woman. The child that Lily had been when he had first taken her to his bed was gone. The Lily he now held in his arms had used his tutelage well and had progressed far beyond his expectations. For all of her submissiveness and her pleasing ways, Lily had become a truly formidable woman.

How long had Lily been his own private courtesan? He was uncertain. Was it a year? He suspected it was even longer; perhaps his mind refused to acknowledge the extended term of their liaison. In truth, he had not expected his interest in her to exceed a few visits. Instead, he had become a steady visitor to the room at the top of the winding staircase, and his bemusement was complete.

Harvey felt a flicker of annoyance cross his mind. Unfortunately, Lily was beginning to forget her place. She was attempting to step up from her subservience to stand on his level. His beautiful Oriental flower was beginning to develop hidden thorns, but he had no intention of allowing her to turn the tables on him. His own weakened condition at that moment proved he had allowed her to push him past his limits again. Once more she had demonstrated her power over him, and she had done it in a most intimate way.

Strange, how conflicting were his feelings for Lily. She was an enigma, hating him and satisfying his intimate desires so completely. He supposed his fascination for her was of a similar bent. He despised her for the control she had gained over him, but he could no more walk away from her than he could give up the air he breathed.

Separating himself from her at last, Harvey rolled away from Lily's slenderness. He drew himself to a sitting position, aware that her eyes followed his movements. He rose from the bed and stood towering over her for long moments. Lily's eyes roamed his body, and Harvey allowed her heady perusal. He was proud of his physical attributes, aware of his seasoned male beauty.

As he watched, Lily also rose from the bed and drew herself to her feet. She raised her hands to run her long, graceful fingers through the silver-gray of his hair, to touch his face, to tantalize his lips. She slid her soft palms down his neck, across the full width of his shoulders. She moved her fingers over his muscular chest and through the sparse gray mat that covered it. With a single finger she traced the dwindling line of silver that trailed down his chest to the sparse curls at his pelvis. She took his manhood in her hand, fondled it, cooing low in her throat as she held his eyes. His will was fast slipping away, and Harvey was suddenly conscious of his peril. He need make an effort now to gain control, or it would be lost to him forever.

Curling a hand around Lily's narrow wrist, Harvey stayed her erotic caress. He smiled, hoping its forced quality did not show as he whispered smoothly, "You've told me you'll give me anything I desire, haven't you, Lily?"

Lily's smile was full, but Harvey saw the suspicion behind its beauty. "Yes, Mr. Dale, I have always met your desires, have I not?"

"Yes, you have. And you have, at times, exceeded them. But now I have a different request to make of you."

The wariness in Lily's gaze did not match the serenity of her tone. "You have but to ask what you wish of me."

"I want you to talk to me."

"To talk, Mr. Dale?"

"Yes, to tell me how it feels, how it feels to make love to a man you despise."

Lily feigned denial. "But I do not despise you, Mr. Dale. I experience joy in your passion."

Harvey's laugh was harsh, grating. His expression was suddenly mocking. "Joy! Lily, please. Don't take me for a fool. I know your feelings for me. I've known since the first time you met me naked and quaking with fear."

Lily's beautiful smile became stiff. "If that is so, why do you ask a question for which you already have the answer?"

"Because I want to hear you speak the words, Lily. You said you would give me anything I want. Well, I want this. I want you to tell me how you feel when I come at my leisure to your room, when I summon you to service my body."

Lily's eyes narrowed revealingly, and Harvey felt a surge of adrenaline move through him. He was reaching her, getting past her reserve, her calm. He was gaining the advantage, and he pressed her further.

"How does it feel when you realize it was I and I alone who took you from the pedestal on which your mother had raised you out of the muck in which the rest of your people live? Are you filled with bitterness when you realize that the glorious future she had in store for you must be held in abeyance while I use you as my personal whore?''

A dark light flickered in Lily's eyes, and Harvey felt victory within his grasp.

''And how does it feel when you must turn away the man you hoped to love, turn him away and come to me, a man who considers your people beneath him, no more than dirt under his feet?''

Lily was shaking, and Harvey paused for the last supreme thrust. ''How does it make you feel to know that I use your body at my convenience, allow you to pleasure me, when I have no more regard for you as a person than I have for a dog following at my heels, waiting for whatever crumbs I can spare? How does it feel, Lily? Tell me.''

Lily hesitated, and he demanded again, *''Tell me!''*

As Harvey's demand filled the silence of the room, Lily's clear skin colored harshly and she attempted to pull her hand from his grasp. He held it fast, a sneer on his lips. His voice was a low warning hiss, ''Tell me, Lily!''

''Yes! Yes, I will tell you how I feel!'' Her high, clear voice cutting the air like cracks of a silken whip, Lily held Harvey's gaze steadily with her own.

''I hate you, Harvey Dale. I hate you with all the strength in my body. I hate you for the power you hold over my mother, and I hate you for the degrading way you use me. I have hated you since the moment I saw you, and I will despise you, even in memory, until I cease to exist.''

Victory pumped hot and clear through Harvey's veins. One more step and it would be as it should be. He would be in total control.

Still smiling, Harvey looked down into Lily's hate-filled countenance, his mind marveling that she was beautiful, magnificently so, even now. ''So you hate me, Lily . . .''

''With all the strength within me.''

''That is unfortunate, isn't it?''

Harvey released Lily's wrist, then stayed her attempt to snatch her hand away from his body with a softly voiced admonition: ''No . . . no, Lily. I want you to please me.''

Rage flashed in Lily's eyes, and she stepped away from him. ''No!''

"You don't mean that, Lily. You know what your mother will suffer if I turn certain papers over to the authorities."

"No!"

"You *will* please me, Lily, and you will do so *now*. Come, I'll make it easy for you."

Taking Lily's arms, Harvey placed them around his neck. He pulled her slenderness against him, hiding the jolt of hunger that moved through him as her sweet flesh touched his.

"Kiss me, Lily. Remember the repercussions if you refuse. Remember you are a virgin no longer, and you can never return to what you were. Remember you are what I have made of you, and you belong to me for as long as I choose to hold you as my whore. Remember all I have taught you. And then remember the pleasure you feel when I bring you to climax . . . the pleasure you deny so heatedly in your mind but with which your body betrays you. Remember, and give yourself to me. I'm waiting."

The dark eyes so close to his glowed with suppressed emotions as he concluded speaking. He saw fury in their obsidian depths, passion, hatred. And then he saw a brief flicker as Lily began to regain control. He felt the resurgence of her will, its power returning to her body. She saw its reassertion transform her as she slowly raised her mouth toward his. He felt his passion soar at the wonder of this woman, her strength, her determination.

Lily's arms tightened around his neck as her lips covered his. Her tongue stabbed into his mouth and he gasped. Unable to withstand the force of his own emotions any longer, he snapped his arms around her, binding her to him with blinding passion.

She was his again; his matchless Oriental flower, his Lily.

Still smiling, Charles directed a last backward glance toward the door that had just closed behind Devina Dale, then started toward the front steps. His feet touched the street, and he glanced up toward the flickering of the gas streetlamp. He paused, lifting his gaze to a clear night sky filled with stars. His smile slowly dropped away as a vague restlessness began to assail him.

Heading toward Allen Street, he reviewed the long and eventful evening in his mind. His smile returned. Devina Dale was not the average woman. She was as far removed from the average woman of this town as cotton was from satin. Devina Dale was definitely satin, satin and silver.

He was uncertain why Devina called those two symbols of luxury so clearly to his mind. Perhaps it was her attitude, her way of confronting the world. He knew it reflected the manner in which she had been raised, to believe she had far more to offer than the average woman. She was possessed of a keen intelligence, well educated, well traveled, and certainly more beautiful than the average woman. She was completely at ease in any social situation. This evening had been proof of that. She had been as smooth as satin in manner, as clear and flawless in beauty.

As for Devina's reminding him of silver . . . well, he supposed it was because she glittered in every aspect of her personal being; her abundant silver-blond hair, her pale aquamarine eyes, her ruby lips, her opalescent, almost translucent skin. She was a living, breathing symbol of all wealth had to offer, just as silver was a glowing, ever alluring symbol of wealth and success to the men of this wild country. She was as valuable as their silver, and occasionally as cold.

No longer smiling, Charles increased his pace as he reached Allen Street. He turned without conscious thought, the hollow clicking of his boots against the boardwalk resounding in his mind as he continued onward.

But he had sensed from the first an inner self that Devina withheld, denied even to herself. He was certain the facade she chose to present to the world—the hard, sharp-tongued woman intolerant of personal flaws—had been strictly cultivated. He also suspected that in all her dealings with the opposite sex she sought an automatic defense by exerting her unyielding will. It would take a special man to penetrate that facade, to bring her to life, to make her realize the potential of the complete woman she could be.

Charles shook his head. Devina Dale had everything a man could possibly desire in a woman, but was he the man who could crack the shield behind which she hid her softer feelings? He sincerely doubted he was.

He thought of the covert reasons that had first caused him to cultivate Devina Dale's friendship. He reviewed them again in his mind, confirming their viability. However far he intended to pursue his personal intentions with Devina Dale, it behooved him to remain her friend, within her intimate circle. Only through close contact could he possibly hope to achieve his goal . . .

The unexpected expulsion of a whiskey-sodden male from the Alhambra Saloon broke into Charles's thoughts as the fellow slammed through the swinging doors into the street. Landing dangerously close to Charles on the hard-packed dirt surface of Allen Street, the man was abruptly motionless. Long experience made Charles stifle his impulse to hurry to the man's aid. He waited. Within a few seconds, the bearded prospector moved and slowly sat up. Catching Charles's scrutinizing gaze, he flashed a lopsided, toothless grin.

"Damned if I don't think Stan managed to throw me at least two feet farther than he did last night! I'm gonna have to buy that man a drink!"

Pulling himself to his feet, the dust-covered prospector paused a moment to regain his shaky equilibrium before walking in a wavering, uneven step directly back from whence he had come.

Having no curiosity at all about the outcome of the prospector's reentry into the Alhambra, Charles continued down the street. His eyes had touched on a small frame house in the distance before he consciously realized his destination. He began walking faster.

Gauging the flow of male visitors from the neat, familiar structure toward which he walked, Charles slowed his step. He crossed Sixth Street and paused outside the door. It was late. Perhaps it would be best if he came back tomorrow.

Despite his reservations, Charles found himself drawing open the door and stepping into the tastefully furnished foyer. He shot a quick glance into the living room, his eyes surveying the provocatively clad women seated on velvet-upholstered furniture in various postures of casual seduction. A familiar voice turned him toward the woman who approached him noiselessly from her seat of honor just inside the doorway.

"Dr. Carter, I bid you welcome, but the hour is late. I had not expected to see you this evening."

Turning to the even-featured blond woman who greeted him so warmly, Charles nodded. "Thank you for your welcome, Marie. I hadn't intended to stop by this evening, but I found myself with a few hours to spare."

"And with a desire to spend them well, monsieur?" Marie's smile became pleasantly knowing. "Which of our girls will it be tonight? You have not experienced Celeste, have you? The Count has only recently delivered her here from Paris. She is very beautiful. She is also well versed in the ways of pleasing a man, and eager to demonstrate her skills. She has been very busy tonight, but I am sure I will be able to persuade her to find some time for you.''

Charles shook his head, his smile polite. "No, I think not, Marie.''

"Brigitte, then. She has many times expressed the desire to entertain you.''

"No, Marie. I came here expressly to see Camille. If she's busy . . .''

Annoyance flicked across Blond Marie's handsome face. "Dr. Carter, you must not feel obliged to await Camille's availability. She has many patrons and would not feel the least offended if you should choose to spend some time with one of her sisters in this house. Who knows? You might even find you prefer someone younger or prettier than she.''

Charles's smile began to stiffen. "Marie, if you please, I came here to see Camille and Camille alone. I would like to have that message sent up to her room. If she's occupied for the evening, I can return another time.''

Signaling a dark-haired beauty not yet out of her teens from the couch, Marie took Charles's arm and smiled up into his annoyed expression with practiced charm. "Dr. Carter, you are correct. Camille is occupied, but I do think you would enjoy meeting Danielle. She is new and a trifle inexperienced, but so very willing. Perhaps she will suit you better than—''

"Marie!" The deep, harsh sound of her name turned Marie toward the slender, mustached man of medium height who approached her from the doorway of a small office beside the staircase. Marie's pale skin turned paler still as the man came to stand within a few feet of her and continued with an air of cold command. "The gentleman has clearly expressed his preference for Camille this evening. And since his interest lies solely in her, I suggest you send Antoine to inform Camille that she has a special patron waiting.''

"Monsieur Le Comte, you instructed me that I was not to press Camille beyond her limit, did you not?'' Although the words were obviously difficult for Marie to say, she continued tightly, "Camille has seen many patrons this evening. She has sent

Antoine down with the message that she will see no more. She is bathing, and she—''

The Count's small mouth twitched. "I do not care to air our business arrangements before one of our patrons, Marie, so I will repeat what I said before: Send Antoine upstairs to inform Camille that Dr. Carter is waiting."

Charles listened with mixed feelings to the exchange between Blond Marie and the only person whose authority within the house surpassed hers. Marie's jealousy of Camille had caused Charles trouble before, and he was aware that it was only the protection of the Frenchman known as the Count that kept Camille from suffering Marie's vindictiveness. But although he had often benefited from the special privileges the Count granted Camille, he was strangely uncomfortable with the man's special interest in her.

Her fair skin coloring further, Marie signaled a small, dark-skinned boy from his position in the corner. Repeating the Count's instructions, she sent him on his way with a light slap of her hand before turning back to Charles.

"So you see, Dr. Carter, how very hard we attempt to please you. I have no doubt Camille will be with you in a moment. Until then, you may feel free to amuse yourself in whatever way pleases you."

A movement at the top of the staircase a moment later turned the eyes of the small group below toward the woman who moved to the railing. The contours of her lush, obviously wet body clearly outlined through the thin robe she clutched around her, the long red hair streaming past her shoulders, still dripping from her bath, Camille leaned over the rail. Her full lips curved into a smile as her eyes touched Charles's face.

"Charles, I am so happy to see you. You must come up immediately. Surely you know Camille's door is never closed to you."

All other thoughts having been swept from his mind by Camille's appearance, Charles passed his hat to the boy who had returned to his side.

"Watch this for me, Antoine. I'll consider it a special favor for which you'll be rewarded."

"Oui, monsieur."

Turning to the Count with a short salute, Charles nodded.

"Remerciement, monsieur." Pausing in afterthought, Charles

dipped his head politely in Marie's direction. Within moments he was walking up the staircase, his impulse to take the steps two at a time controlled for the sake of appearance.

Charles touched the second floor, only to be immediately engulfed by Camille's lush, damp body as she pressed herself érotically against him. Her arms around his neck, she gave him her mouth in a deep, welcoming kiss. Drawing away at last, she slid her arm through his and urged him toward her room.

"Ah, Charles, I had given up hope of seeing you this evening. I cannot tell you the despair I suffered."

Her bright eyes showing none of the despair of her words, Camille guided Charles through the doorway and closed the door behind them. She turned to face him, her pleasure obvious as he reached out to smooth an errant strand of fiery hair from her cheek.

"Neither had I expected to come here tonight, Camille. To be very honest, I found myself walking in this direction without having made a conscious decision to do so. I don't know what possessed me to come so late, and it looks as if I've put you in a difficult position with Marie because of my insistence on seeing only you."

Camille spoke in a husky whisper.

"You must not worry about Marie, *chéri*. She does not like me, but Pierre . . . the Count does. I am safe from her vindictive behavior through him." Her voice dropping another notch, Camille looked directly into Charles's eyes.

"You say you do not know why you came here tonight, Charles, despite the fact that you obviously have spent what should have been a full evening elsewhere. Shall I tell you why you came to see me, *mon ami*? It was because you wanted to feel good, and I do that so very well for you." Camille paused in her whispered statement. Her voice dropped a notch lower. "I do it so well for you because I do it with my whole heart. You know that, do you not, Charles?"

A low laugh escaped Charles's throat. His body was beginning a responsive swelling to Camille's throaty whispers and the erotic brushing of her near nakedness against him. He shook his head, incredulity in his voice.

"I don't understand how you do it, Camille, but when you look into my eyes, you manage to make me forget the long evening you've already had and the many patrons you've seen. And you convince me for a little while that I'm the only one.''

"Perhaps, Charles, that is because in my mind you truly are the only one." Slowly slipping her arms free of her clinging robe, Camille dropped the damp garment to the floor. She stepped back and raised her hands to him in silent supplication.

"Come. I am fresh and clean and waiting, as I ever am in my heart for you, *mon chèr*. Come to me and we will love."

Touched to the core of his being as he always was when with Camille, Charles took the step forward that brought him into her clinging embrace. With a small sound of acceptance he curved his strong arms around her and lost himself in her once more.

CHAPTER VII

HARVEY TOOK A few moments to reestablish his hold on his patience. He stepped back from his desk, straightened his shoulders, and inhaled deeply, only to be halted by his partner's quiet voice.

"Harvey, it'll do you no good to get angry with me," George Tillson reminded him. "I'm only repeating what the foreman told me this morning. The grumbling in the mines is getting louder, and the miners are getting nervous. I don't know if the few accidents that have occurred are a result of that nervousness or whether they were deliberately caused. All I can tell you is that Jack Higgins said the men are starting to believe they're in danger because of this vendetta that's being waged against Till-Dale. Jack said we're going to start losing men if this whole thing doesn't get cleared up soon."

George paused, intent on Harvey's flushed countenance. "Jack's the best mine manager in these parts, and I respect his opinion. I don't have to tell you a walkout could be disastrous, especially now. Our loan application with San Francisco City Bank is pending, and it'll be viewed with considerable skepticism if our production begins to suffer, along with the other problems we're facing. We need that loan. Harvey, if we're not careful, we could lose our shirts."

Taking the few steps to round the corner of his desk, Harvey walked to the door of his office. He shot a short, suspicious glance at the two clerks working hard at their respective chores.

He frowned and closed the door before turning back to his partner once more.

George's expression registered his incredulity at Harvey's actions. "Harvey, you couldn't possibly suspect Walter Jobe or Larry Watts. They've worked for us for years. They've proved their honesty, and they're completely loyal to Till-Dale."

"Honesty . . . loyalty!" Harvey's tone was derisive. "Don't tell me you truly believe that drivel you're speaking, George! There *are* no honest, loyal men. Anyone can be bought if the price is right, and those two out there are no different!"

Immediately realizing it would be fruitless to debate the point with Harvey in his present mood, George shook his head. "I'm not going to argue with you, Harvey. There are far more important matters for us to take up today. But for the record, I think you're wrong. Those clerks have nothing to do with the robberies, or with leaking information, if that's what you're thinking. I think the men who are out to get us are using other methods of obtaining information."

"Such as?"

"I didn't say I had the answer to that one, Harvey."

"Well, it's about time we got some answers! Dammit, it's been two weeks since Devina arrived. I promised her I'd find the thief who manhandled her on that stagecoach and threatened her life, and I intend to do it!" The thought again bringing him close to rage, Harvey continued with deeper emphasis, "I've demonstrated that I don't intend taking any further chances with my daughter's safety, and I don't intend to take any chances with the safety of our next payroll, either. I've seen to that by personally making arrangements with the president of Wardway Bank in Benson."

" 'Personally'?"

"Yes." Stepping closer to his partner, Harvey continued in a confidential tone, "Yes, I have. I've arranged by direct private correspondence with William Schmitt to have our next payroll shipped here covertly."

"Covertly? Harvey, we've tried that already, and it didn't work."

"I've taken more precautions this time."

George appeared unimpressed. "Just what are you contemplating doing?"

"It is not what I'm contemplating, George. The correspondence has already been exchanged and the matter settled. The plan has been mutually approved and will be put into action with the next shipment.''

George's narrow face slowly stiffened. His resentment was obvious. ''*Mutually* approved . . . without my being consulted? Am I to assume that I'm now included in the group under suspicion? I hope that isn't so, Harvey. I dislike having to remind you that we're partners. *Equal* partners. Somewhere along the line you seem to have forgotten that.''

Harvey Dale's handsome face twitched with annoyance. ''I have no time for your injured feelings, George. What I've done, I've done for the good of the company, and I expect you to accept my decisions in that light.''

''Just as you would accept mine if the situation were reversed?''

Harvey raised his gray eyebrows with undisguised disdain. ''George, we're wasting time.''

George's expression grew cold. ''All right, Harvey, tell me your plan.''

''The plan is simple. The bank will proceed with the usual arrangements to ship the payroll here to Tombstone. Then, at the last moment, the money will be diverted to a supply wagon, which will leave by another route while the bogus strongbox is loaded onto the stagecoach in the usual manner. The supply wagon will come here direct while the stagecoach continues its more circuitous route, diverting attention and any possible action from the true shipment.''

''Is that it?''

''No, not exactly. I've instructed Bill Schmitt to limit the number of people involved to only the most trustworthy of his employees so as to minimize the risk and to narrow the circle of suspects should something go wrong. I've also decided we'll allow Jobe and Watts to handle the arrangements for the payroll in the usual manner so they won't suspect anything.''

''And if your plan doesn't work and the thieves discover your trick in time to go after the supply wagon?''

''Then we'll know the information is leaking from the bank in Benson. Even if we lose the payroll, we'll have our first lead as to where to start asking questions.''

George paused. The lines in his face pulled into a frown as he appeared to study the plan in his mind.

''Well, George, what do you think?''

George stared into Harvey's eyes for long, silent moments. "Does it matter what I think, Harvey?"

"George, let's not be pettish."

A scoffing laugh escaped George's lips. "I think you would do well to remember that remark and repeat it to yourself at the appropriate time," he said. "I'm certain you'll find many instances when it will apply to your behavior far better than it does mine at present." Pausing to allow his jibe to register fully, George ignored the light flush that colored Harvey's face and continued in an even tone, "I also think, Harvey, that I'll go along with your plan because it's too late to do anything else. But I'll take this moment to remind you again that we *are* partners and that I expect to be consulted in all matters of importance to the operation of the mines. I will also state now that I do not intend our partnership to continue under the conditions you seem only too willing to adopt."

Harvey's reply was stiff. "Am I to consider this an ultimatum, George?"

"You may consider it whatever you like, but I advise you to remember my words, because I did not speak them lightly."

Without another word, George turned toward the door. Within moments he had returned to the outer office, retrieved his hat, and was walking out into the midmorning sunshine of Allen Street.

Harvey watched as his partner passed the office windows and walked out of his sight. Damn! What was wrong with George, anyway? He was usually so cooperative. He generally concurred with any business decisions Harvey made and was content to exercise his authority only over the legal aspects of company business. There had been no reason to believe George would take such offense at his secrecy.

Harvey gave an annoyed sniff. Of course, George didn't mean what he said. He would get over his peeve; they had worked together so long . . . In actuality, Harvey supposed he could say that George was his only friend.

Suddenly annoyed at his own train of thought, Harvey raised his chin with a familiar arrogance. Well, if that was the way George wanted it, so be it! In truth, Harvey had done what he deemed necessary, and the end would surely justify the means. When the payroll arrived in Tombstone safe and sound, George would change his tune. Until that time, to hell with his partner's injured feelings. He wouldn't waste his time giving the matter another thought.

Turning back to his desk with a frown, Harvey found himself impatient with the prospect of doing the paperwork that lay before him. Damn. Mired in paper, that's what he was! Well, he'd be damned if he'd spend another moment of this day buried under its deluge!

Snatching his bowler from the rack, Harvey placed it squarely on his head and strode into the outer office. He spoke a few short words of instruction to his clerks and then, ignoring their curious glances, proceeded out onto the board sidewalk. He squinted into the bright sunlight and started forward in a confident step.

Devina darted a short glance over her shoulder as she approached her home. She had no thought for the brilliant late-morning sunlight, which tinted her creamy complexion with a hint of pink and touched the pale silver-blond strands of her upswept coiffure with a shimmering brilliance. Neither did she give a thought to the pleasant breeze that moved the air, occasionally pressing the folds of her yellow batiste gown against her to emphasize the fullness of her firm young breasts and the purity of her body's slender lines.

Instead, her mind was on the relentless watchdog her father had retained, the hired gun who had followed her every step for the past two weeks. But Sam Sharpe was no longer close at her heels. Instead, as was his custom when her home was in sight, he was crossing the narrow street toward the vantage point he usually assumed from which he carefully scrutinized the area.

Devina's nerves were stretched to the breaking point. Closing her eyes briefly, she was grateful to be relieved of her uncomfortably close shadow if only for a little while as she continued toward the front door of her home. How much more could she take? Not only had she been forced to listen to the steady click of Sam Sharpe's boots against the boardwalk behind her the morning long, starting and stopping each time she paused before the shop windows, but she had also been forced to endure the growing familiarity of his gaze and manner as he occasionally drew far closer than she deemed truly necessary.

Damn! How could her father continue to subject her to this? She had not had a moment's peace since she entered this disreputable frontier town. She was sick of being dogged at every step, of never having a moment to herself. So tense had she become that she was unable to shake a sense of being watched even when she was in the privacy of her own room. Had it not been truly frightening, she would have laughed at the number of times she had walked to her window to stare at the nearly barren hills in the distance in an effort to reassure herself that her unreasonable obsession was all in her mind.

But she had ascertained one thing in the past two weeks: She would get no reassurance against her hidden fear from her father. In truth, she was beginning to believe it was her father's repeatedly voiced concern for her safety that had caused this anxiety to develop. Surely, had it not been for the daily reinforcement of that anxiety in the persons of Sam Sharpe and Wally Smith, she would have been able to force her thoughts from the memory of that first day and the man who had held her prisoner so briefly.

Devina paused as she approached her house. That feeling of being watched . . . it was presently so strong that she had to force herself to continue forward in a sedate step. Memories began to flood her mind. Chills raced down her spine despite the heat of the day, and she was suddenly all but running up the front steps of the house.

Stepping onto the porch at last, Devina took a deep breath. Damn, she would never escape those memories if her father's fears continued to feed her own! She reached for the doorknob, only to have it drawn from her grasp as the door opened abruptly to Lai Hua's smile.

"You have finished with your shopping, Miss Devina? I have been awaiting your return. Dr. Carter stopped by to leave word when he would call for you this evening."

"You may tell me what Dr. Carter had to say later, Lai Hua."

Needing a few moments to pull herself together, Devina entered the foyer and placed her purchases on the chair beside the door. She reached up to remove her hat. Realizing that her hands were shaking visibly, she brought them back to her sides. Damn! This could not go on!

A sound made her turn as the library door opened to reveal Harvey Dale's impressive figure. Devina's frown darkened, and her father stopped short. A hesitant smile played at the corners of his lips.

"Devina, such enthusiasm at my unexpected appearance. I came home early with the express intention of taking you to lunch. You have not yet eaten, have you, dear?"

"No, Father, I have not eaten, nor do I wish to eat."

All pretense of a smile vanished from Harvey Dale's face. "Is something wrong, Devina?"

Devina took a deep breath. "Yes something is wrong, Father, very wrong. I will no longer suffer the intrusions on my privacy you are forcing me to bear."

"Intrusions on your privacy?"

"How can I be expected to enjoy even the simplest pleasures with that unsavory character you hired dogging my heels every step of the way?"

"Are you referring to Sam, Devina?"

"Who else?"

Harvey Dale's face was immediately alert. "Has Sam stepped beyond his bounds with you, Devina?"

"In so many ways that I could not begin to count them."

"I would appreciate it if you would be more explicit."

"Father, I am annoyed just by the knowledge that he is there, at my heels."

"Sam's presence is necessary for your own safety."

"My safety, my safety . . . I'm tired of hearing about my safety! I would like to hear a little more about my independence being returned, and my peace of mind. Father, Sam Sharpe would not be at all necessary if the lawmen of Tombstone were not so inept! Has there been no progress at all in catching the men you feel are a threat to my safety? Surely something can be done."

"Devina, dear, please." Conscious of his daughter's truly agitated state, Harvey shot a quick look toward Lai Hua, who stood in silent, anxious observation a few feet away.

"Lai Hua, Miss Devina and I are going into the library. Have Molly make some tea immediately and bring it in to us as soon as it is ready."

Not sparing a glance for Lai Hua as she turned to do his bidding, Harvey ushered Devina into the room across from the staircase and closed the door behind them. He attempted to seat her, but she brushed off his hand and walked to the window, her agitation increasing.

Taking the few steps to his daughter's side, Harvey looked down into her tense expression. His voice was filled with regret. "Devina, dear, I'm so sorry. I would not have put you through this for all the world."

But Devina would not be mollified. "Father, my coming to Tombstone was a mistake from the first. Despite its attempt to present a civilized appearance, this town is little more than a frontier outpost."

"Devina, dear, you're upset."

"Yes, I'm upset, but that has no bearing on what I've said. By what scale do you measure civilization, Father? Do you measure it by the number of stores that line the main street? By the number of theaters or newspapers in town? By the number of prestigious organizations to whose rolls you might add your name?"

"If you're referring to Tombstone's professional organizations—"

"No, I am not referring to any of the things Tombstone has to offer. I'm referring to the thing that Tombstone does *not* have to offer—specifically, safety under the law."

"Devina, Tombstone is not as raw a town as that. The average resident is perfectly safe on the streets."

"Then why the need for Sam Sharpe?"

"Dear, I'm afraid you are not the average resident of Tombstone. You are Harvey Dale's daughter."

Momentarily stunned at her father's response, Devina shook her head. "Father, you fail to realize that 'Harvey Dale's daughter' was perfectly safe walking the streets of New York. I didn't need a watchdog at my heels there."

"Devina, the uncomfortable situation you presently find yourself in while in Tombstone is only temporary, I assure you."

"Father, you must forgive me if I do not accept your reassurances. Unfortunately, little has happened that would lead me to expect the situation to change in the near future." Devina took a deep breath. Her eyes on her father's concerned stare, she continued on a softer, firmer note. "Father, I must repeat that my coming to Tombstone was a mistake. You yourself have stated I have only made you more vulnerable to those men, whoever they are, who are attacking Till-Dale. It would be far better if I returned to Aunt Emily in New York. She was extremely upset at my leaving, and she would take me back gladly."

"Aunt Emily was no more upset than I would be if you left, Devina."

His gray eyebrows knotting with concern, Harvey Dale raised a hand to Devina's cheek. His smile was tight. "I told you when you arrived, dear, you are my only child, and you are extremely important to me. I love you dearly, Devina, and I have no intention of spending the remainder of my life separated from you."

Devina paused, striving to retain her resolve. Her father had been successful once more in touching her heart despite the doubts that nagged at the back of her mind. "Father, I cannot believe—"

"Devina, dear, I'm sorry. Your anxiety is all my fault. If you will listen to me now, I am sure I will be able to set your concerns to rest."

Curving his arm around her shoulders, Harvey drew Devina toward the leather-upholstered couch at one side of the room. He seated her carefully and, sitting beside her, took her hands into his.

Desperately seeking to hold herself aloof from the contrition of her father's face and from his warmly solicitous manner, Devina attempted to pull her hands free. When the hurt that touched his expression became more than she could bear, Devina submitted to his obvious wish to comfort her. The irony of the situation assailed her. As a lonely child in a boarding school far from home, she had longed so often to hear the words her father had just spoken, to see the concern for her now written so clearly in the planes of his handsome face. But he had withheld himself from her then. He had forced her to learn to live without him, to depend only on herself. And now that she was the person his treatment had wrought, when she held herself aloof from him, determined to be sufficient unto herself, he seemed all the more determined to keep her close. Devina paused in her thoughts. There was no denying the love in her father's eyes at this moment. Father, dear Father . . . How she wished she could always depend on his love.

As her father continued speaking, Devina made an effort to concentrate on his words.

"I would have taken you into my confidence sooner, Devina. I apologize for not having realized the true strain this situation has placed upon you, dear. The truth is, I've been so determined to catch these thieves that I've neglected some things . . ."

Obviously preferring to leave the "neglected things" unspoken, Harvey attempted a smile. "But enough said about my mistakes. I'm presently taking steps to right them, and to catch the thieves as well."

"Father, surely you don't intend doing anything foolish. These men are dangerous."

Harvey's small laugh revealed his pleasure at Devina's concern. "I'm not so much a fool as all that, Devina. I have a plan which—"

Harvey turned with annoyance at a soft knock at the door. Lai Hua entered the room. His voice was curt, dismissing.

"Put the tray here."

Waiting only until Lai Hua had closed the door behind her, Harvey resumed speaking.

"I've arranged to have a bogus payroll shipment sent out from the Benson bank via stagecoach while the true payroll travels via a supply wagon by a more direct route to Tombstone. The only people aware of the plan are those directly responsible at the Benson end. That should guarantee the payroll's safety, but if it does not, we'll know where the information has been leaking to the thieves."

"Father, I still think—"

"Devina, dear . . ." Harvey's rich voice was deeply persuasive as he looked into her eyes. Devina could not help but marvel at the earnestness her father displayed, the skill of his plea even as she felt herself succumbing to his coercion.

"You do believe me when I tell you that I will keep you safe here, that you need not fear anything."

"Father, it's not only a matter of my feeling unsafe. I have no freedom here."

"Bear with me a little longer, darling. I promise you, this whole nightmare will soon be a thing of the past. I give you my word."

"Father . . ." Resolution fading in the face of her father's plea, Devina paused in her response. She was no stronger than her mother, for all her professed determination. She would give him one more chance. "All right, Father."

Relief shining clearly in his eyes, Harvey took a deep breath. Turning to the tray Lai Hua had placed on the table, he carefully poured two cups of tea. He watched as Devina lifted her cup to her lips. Then he sipped his own tea, studying her over the rim of his cup. After a few seconds, he placed his cup back on the tray with an air of determination.

"Dear, we've all been a bit tense these last two weeks, and we need something to get our mind off these nagging problems. Now would be the perfect time to have that party I mentioned when you arrived."

"A party!"

"Yes, dear. I had thought to wait until you were able to complete the refurbishing of the house, but I no longer have the patience for it. Besides, I have not had the opportunity to formally introduce my beautiful daughter to Tombstone. It is a pleasure I've delayed long enough. I know your social calendar has not suffered, but I think it's more important than ever to formally announce that Devina Dale has arrived in Tombstone and is here to stay."

Not of a mind to argue the last point with her father, Devina maintained her silence as he continued with growing enthusiasm.

"Of course you may come to me should you need help, but you may feel free to make any arrangements for the affair you deem necessary. And you may set the menu without restrictions. Whatever isn't immediately available in Tombstone can easily be shipped in. How does that sound to you, dear?"

Devina considered the idea. Plan her own welcome party? If circumstances did not change, she was determined that the affair would serve as a farewell party instead. But in the meantime, she would show her father that her education had been far more well rounded than he was aware. She would organize a party the likes of which Tombstone had never seen. Holding her growing enthusiasm in check, Devina questioned cautiously, "I'm to have a totally free hand, Father?"

"Totally. I will depend on you to set Tombstone on its ear!"

"Oh, Father." Devina could not resist a laugh. "What is it about me that causes that phrase to come to people's lips?"

"Perhaps it's that you're the most beautiful woman Tombstone has ever seen, or is ever likely to see. I'm extremely proud of that, and of you. And perhaps it is because I deeply regret that your mother is not here to see you now. I miss her still, you know. But you are her image, dear, and for that reason I am doubly proud."

Strangely, Devina found she was not surprised by the sincerity in her father's eyes as he spoke of her mother. Yes, he had been proud of Mama, just as he was proud of her. She did not question the sincerity of her father's love . . . just its quality.

Devina nodded. "All right, Father, we shall give a party."

"In two weeks' time. That should be long enough for you to also arrange to have a new gown made, something special."

"In two weeks' time." Devina laughed again. "And I prom-

ise you, it'll be a party that Tombstone will talk about for a long
time to come. The idea appeals to me, Father. You know me
well."

"Yes, I know you well, dear, because in so many ways, you
are so much like me."

Not allowing her a moment for response, Harvey picked up
his cup and drained it. Replacing it on the tray, he drew himself
to his feet. Ignoring that Devina's cup was still half full, he took
it from her hand and, setting it down, pulled her up beside him.
"Now that we have all that settled, dear, have you regained your
appetite?"

Realizing the futility of refusing him, Devina offered her
father a smile. "I suppose I'm as hungry as I'll ever be."

Strangely unsettled by his statement of a few moments before,
Devina allowed her father to lead her toward the door. He had
said that she was like him in so many ways. The thought sent a
chill down her spine and returned the echo of words that were
never far from her consciousness. Those words resounded again
within her mind even as she took her father's arm and walked
out into the foyer: *You wouldn't be worth the trouble . . .*

The voices from the library trailed off into silence, and footsteps approached the door against which Lai Hua leaned. Knowing a moment's panic for fear of being discovered, she moved
quickly and silently down the narrow hallway. She had just
turned the corner when the door of the library opened and
Harvey Dale's voice sounded in the hallway: "Molly? . . .
Molly!"

Hesitating only a moment, Lai Hua stepped into her employ-
er's line of vision. Her heart drumming in her breast at her close
call, she nodded politely. "I may be of help, Mr. Dale?"

Harvey Dale's face darkened momentarily, and Lai Hua read
in the flashing glance his distaste for people of her race. It ran
deep in him, and Lai Hua attempted to ignore it.

"Yes, tell Molly that Miss Devina and I will be dining out
for lunch."

"Yes, Mr. Dale."

"Miss Dale won't need you until this evening," he continued.
"Don't sit around. See if you can be of some help in the
kitchen."

"Father!" Miss Devina looked distressed at her father's comment, but Lai Hua maintained her smile in an attempt to dismiss her mistress's discomfort.

"Yes, Mr. Dale."

Within moments Harvey Dale was ushering his daughter out the front door, and Lai Hua turned away. As soon as the click of the door sounded behind her, Lai Hua's smile faded.

Frustration soared anew within Ross as he raised his spyglass and adjusted the focus on Sam Sharpe's slouched form as he stood across the street from the Dale home. Ross gave a low, scornful laugh. So the watchdog was still on duty.

A low fury simmering within him, Ross allowed his gaze to dwell on Sharpe's face. He remembered its oily sheen, its narrow features, the small, close-set eyes. He remembered the amused smile Sharpe adopted when he did work he particularly enjoyed. Ross had seen that look on Sharpe's face, and on the faces of the men backing him up with their fists and guns.

Memory brought a grimace of pain to Ross's lips. He remembered the day well. Pa had had an attack, and Ross had known his father wouldn't last much longer if the whole rotten business with Dale wasn't straightened out quickly. Knowing Dale was at that time in the habit of spending a part of his day at the Till-Dale mill, Ross had gone there with the intention of speaking directly to Dale. He had known that it was Dale who had actually double-talked his father out of his claim. And he had known Dale was the only one who could straighten things out.

But he never got a chance to talk with Dale. All he got was a glimpse of Dale's well-dressed figure at the window of his office as he approached the mill. Dale had turned to speak to someone behind him. The door had opened and Sam Sharpe had been the first one out. Wally Smith and Bart Holt had followed. Ross couldn't remember exactly what Sharpe had said when he had warned him off, but he could remember Sharpe's smile. He had been smiling when he signaled the other two men to grab Ross's arms and hold him. Sharpe's smile had been unwavering, even as he pounded his fists into Ross's helpless body again and again.

Ross's breathing became ragged as bitter memories continued to overwhelm him. He remembered the salty taste of blood filling his mouth as Sharpe's fists slammed into his face. He remembered his gasping attempts to catch his breath as Sharpe's fists pounded his stomach, his ribs, his chest. He remembered his sagging body growing too heavy for the other two men to support. They had let him fall to the ground with Sharpe's last punching blow. And he remembered that he had looked up just before the darkness closed in around him to see Sharpe still smiling.

When Ross had awakened it was dark and he was a considerable distance from the mill. He had made it back to his father's cabin much later that night. He'd checked on his father, nursed his own wounds, and renewed his vow to get his father's claim back for him.

But Dale had been too smart for him. All he had managed to get for himself was three years in Yuma, and a very liberal education. He had come out educated to the hard facts of life.

Ross had changed during those years in prison. Unrelenting physical labor had filled in the already broad contours of his frame with hard muscle, tightened the sinews of his muscular arms and legs, expanded the breadth of his chest. It had added new, harsh lines of maturity to the sharp contours of his face, added a coldly piercing quality to his gaze, and efficiently wiped his smile from his lips.

His spyglass still trained on the bodyguard's face, Ross noted Sam Sharpe's subtle change of expression the moment before he pushed himself away from the wall and started across the street. Shifting his position, Ross turned his glass to the Dale home in time to see Harvey Dale walk down the steps with his daughter at his side. Ross's stomach tensed as Dale turned to his daughter, staying her with a few brief words before he stepped forward to speak to Sharpe.

Ross kept the glass trained on Devina Dale. In the past two weeks, he alone had maintained a surveillance of the Dale household in his effort to ascertain the household's daily routine. Jake, Mack, and Harry had needed time to gather information about Till-Dale's next payroll shipment.

During those two weeks, Ross had become intimately familiar with Devina Dale. He had followed her visually on her daily outings, seldom letting her out of his sight. He had memorized each pure, flawless line of her face. He had studied her erect carriage, the graceful length of her slender neck. He had come to anticipate the determined set of her shoulders when she was angry or annoyed, the manner in which she raised her chin. He had followed the sway of her softly curving hips as she walked, the bobbing of her firm full breasts. He recalled more often than he cared to admit the warmth of her softness against him.

He had also come to recognize Devina Dale's annoyance when Sharpe took up his position behind her; had felt his own annoyance grow each time Sharpe pressed closer to her than his job necessitated. Ross had felt the heat of anger when his close scrutiny revealed the manner in which Sharpe's small eyes followed Devina's provocative sway.

He had also come to anticipate with a growing, puzzling anger the side of Devina Dale that was evident only when she walked at Charles Carter's side. Totally at ease and engrossed in his company, her beautiful face relaxed, her expressions spontaneous, she attained a level of beauty that was startling, incredible.

But she was turning her face away from him now, facing her father as he walked back to her side. Harvey Dale was smiling. Ross memorized his smile. He needed to remember it. The memory would give impetus to his determination to replace that beaming smile with an expression of an entirely different sort.

Harvey Dale took his daughter's arm, and they continued down the street toward the center of town, leaving Sharpe behind. The princess was not presently in need of his protection.

Ross gave a low snort. Well, he would soon snatch the princess from her ivory tower. He had not yet determined the manner in which he would accomplish it, but he knew he would.

Twilight faded into dusk and the sounds of night grew louder outside the abandoned miner's shack. An owl on its nightly foray swooped toward a tempting bit of prey as it scampered across a rotted beam protruding from the structure, only to be startled from its deadly attack by an unexpected flicker of light and the sound of low voices from within. Disappearing into the night, the owl soared off in search of safer prey as the voices from within grew louder.

"No, I may stay no longer without my absence being discovered."

Her soft protest halted by Jake's searching kiss, Lai Hua found herself again being pressed against the worn blanket she had spread a short hour before. She felt its nubby texture against her naked flesh, felt the warm pressure of Jake's muscled body against her softness as he again slid atop her. His hard male organ penetrated her moist womanly core, and a low sound escaped her lips. True wonder assailed her as he came to rest within her, and she sighed, opening herself to him, accepting him fully. Her slender arms curled around his neck, and she ran her hands through the pale gold of his hair.

Gasping as he again plunged deeply, Lai Hua pulled him tight against her. This beautiful man, this golden-haired lover, was one with her as truly as if the spoken word had joined them. She no longer allowed her mind to assail her with recriminations for the deception she practiced on her father. She no longer·allowed herself to think of the future, the time when Jake would leave her for another woman who would share his life, bear his children. She thought only of the present and the incredible, soaring joy they both shared.

Lai Hua reveled in the growing strength of Jake's thrusts. She marveled that his passion was so strong as to come again to the ecstatic culmination they had both experienced only a short time before. She would never have enough of this man.

The heat, the urgency was building, and Lai Hua clutched Jake closer. His labored breaths brushed her cheek, the sound of his hoarse voice calling her name inflamed her. She paused with him, awaiting the final step. The rush to glory was quick, overwhelming, plunging her to deep, shuddering reward.

Jake's slender, muscular body lay heavily on hers. Lai Hua closed her eyes against the supreme pleasure of its weight. If they might only remain thus, together for the rest of their lives . . .

But Jake was slipping from her body, and Lai Hua's short daydream came to an end. Soon he would return to his hidden cabin, and she would return to her own life. They would be separate, with little to join them but the memory of the sweet passion they shared.

Her thoughts were more than she could bear, and Lai Hua felt the heat of tears gathering beneath her eyelids. She attempted to blink them away, only to suffer the final humiliation as a single tear slid from the corner of her eye into the dark hair at her temple.

Jake turned his head toward her. She avoided his gaze only to feel his fingers gently brush the shimmering path from her skin.

"Why are you cryin', Lai Hua?"

"It is only my childish foolishness, my desolation that we will soon part."

Jake lowered his head to caress her lips lightly with his.

"I'm not too happy about lettin' you go right now either, darlin'. Another payroll is comin' through soon, and me, Ross, and the boys expect to hit it about midway between Benson and Tombstone. Ross has the feelin' they won't be expectin' us to try for another one so soon, but just to be safe, I'll have to stay away from town for the next week or so.''

Lai Hua's heart began a slow pounding. She, also, had not expected Jake and his friends to attempt another robbery so soon. Her high-pitched tone betrayed her anxiety when she spoke. ''You must not attempt to take the next payroll!''

Lai Hua felt a gradual tensing of Jake's body as his eyes narrowed. ''Why? What do you know, Lai Hua?''

Lai Hua took a deep breath. ''I was present when Miss Devina returned home today. She seemed distracted, and Mr. Dale was upset by her distraction. In his effort to allay her anger and fear, he confided information about the payroll shipment and the plans he has made.''

''A trap, is that it?'' Jake's voice was suddenly cold. ''Why did you wait so long to tell me Dale was plannin' a trap?''

''No, there is no trap!''

All trace of softness left Jake's face. ''What is it, then?''

''The payroll, it will not be shipped in the Wells Fargo box aboard the stage. The box will leave the bank in Benson as usual, but it will contain nothing of value. The payroll will travel secretly in a supply wagon to Tombstone.''

''When will the supply wagon leave?''

''I am not sure, but I believe the switch will be made at the last minute so it will not be suspected.''

Jake scrutinized her face. ''Is there anythin' else you haven't told me, Lai Hua?''

The coldness in Jake's eyes froze Lai Hua's heart. She had not held back the information because of loyalty to Mr. Dale. She owed no loyalty to a man who despised her and all of her race. Her only true loyalty in that household was to Miss Devina, who was innocent of her father's wrongdoings and prejudice, and who had treated her with respect. Lai Hua had kept silent out of fear of reprisal on her family if anyone learned that she functioned as China Mary's spy. That same fear also kept her from telling Jake she had given the information about the payroll to China Mary only hours before.

Lai Hua took another deep breath. ''No, nothing.''

Jake's eyes were filled with suspicion as he stared into her stiff face, and Lai Hua felt the pain of his distrust.

''You're sure?''

Lai Hua fought the inclination to turn away from Jake's keen appraisal. She swallowed against her sense of betrayal. "Yes, I am sure."

Once more his intense perusal and then the strong arms, which had grown lax in their embrace, tightened to draw her to her feet. Sensing his withdrawal, Lai Hua dressed herself in silence as he dressed beside her. Her heart breaking, she crouched down and rolled up the blanket. She slipped it under her arm and leaned over to lift the lamp from the floor, only to feel Jake's arms slip around her once more. He turned her toward him and crushed her against him. His mouth was harsh against hers, his kiss angry, but she welcomed it. She warmed to its assault, gave in to it, banished his anger with her tender, loving response.

Jake drew his mouth from hers. His breathing ragged, he clasped her painfully close. His tone was rasping as he drew back enough to view her face. "Let me hear you say you love me, Lai Hua."

"I love you, Mr. Jake."

"And because you love me, you would never lie to me."

Lai Hua's response caught in her throat. Unable to speak, she could do no more than nod. Despair touched her as doubt chased itself across the face of the man she loved, and unable to bear more, Lai Hua raised herself on tiptoe and pressed her lips tightly to his. With a quick movement, she turned from his grasp, picked up the lantern, and passed through the doorway. Her softly whispered "Forgive me" trailed on the night air behind her as she fled.

Even as she slipped into the darkness, Lai Hua knew she could not face Jake's response to her whispered plea. Brushing a wayward tear from her cheek, Lai Hua turned her attention to the shadowed trail on which she walked. Fear was strong in her heart that she would never be called on to walk it again.

The fleeting shadow listened at the window of the miner's shack. Abruptly it turned, slipping into the darkness to blend with the surrounding shadows as Lai Hua hurried out of the cabin and along the trail. There was no sign of movement from within, and the figure paused. It twitched with impatience, turning with anxiety toward Lai Hua's quickly disappearing form. It darted a brief, hesitant glance back toward the cabin, realizing little more time could be wasted.

In a soundless flurry of movement, the shadowed figure turned onto the trail. It kept to the darkness, silent, unobserved, not allowing Lai Hua to lengthen the distance between them.

CHAPTER VIII

"AH, *MA CHÉRIE*, I had almost forgotten the smooth, incomparable texture of your skin." Le Comte's well-manicured fingers trailed over Camille's cheek as he continued in a lower tone, "There are times when I miss the beautiful golden days, the times when we were together. Do you remember them, Camille?"

The Count held her gaze as he and Camille stood within the confines of his small office. He had called her there a few minutes before, and she had entered, pleased as always to be summoned to this man. Her pleasure warmed the rich chocolate-brown of her eyes, and the smile that curved her generous lips was sincere.

"*Oui*, I remember them, Pierre. I remember them well."

"We met for the first time in that small, undesirable inn on the outskirts of Paris where I was forced to spend the night when my conveyance lost a wheel. I had just left my room when I encountered you arguing in the hallway with a client who had not entered into your bargain with as much honesty as had you. He was attempting to leave, and you detained him with a sharp admonition. He struck you."

"And you defended me. You struck him and he fell. You then persuaded him to fulfill his part of the bargain to which he and I had agreed. He was not very happy to be called to task for his dishonesty, but he paid the stipulated price. I was very grateful."

"I was struck with your beauty even then, Camille. I had never before seen such vibrant coloring. Your hair was a wild, brilliant hue, a color unmatched to this day in my experience. I remember thinking it was similar to the flames that licked the logs in the great fireplace of my home. It appeared to generate as much life and heat as well. And your eyes were startling in your anger, a warm brown that complemented the color of your hair. Your skin was golden, touched by the sun, but not hardened or lined like that of many country-bred women. And your body, *ma petite*—"

"Pierre, I have never, *never* been petite."

Le Comte's soft laugh was spontaneous. "*Oui*, Camille, never petite, but so very womanly. Even now the memory of your soft flesh brings a flush of warmth. But do you remember what happened then, Camille?"

"I remember very well, Pierre. You took me to your room and talked to me. We talked for a very long time. You persuaded me to come with you to one of the houses you had established in Paris. You gave me money to support my family while I was away and promised to send a similar sum to aid in their support every week while I remained in your employ. It was more money than I had ever seen at one time in my life, Pierre."

"I was aware of that, Camille."

"You took me to Paris. You bought me beautiful new clothes. You introduced me to Madame Le Claire, to whose house you brought me, and you instructed her to teach me all I did not know. That encompassed many things, Pierre, and madame was a very good teacher. Through her I learned of the ballet, art, and music. I was enthralled. And where her teaching ended, yours began."

"It was my pleasure, Camille. The pleasure remains with me in memory still. Your joy, your love of life was infectious. It breathed into me a new zest for living at a time when I believed joy was forever beyond my reach. Prior to meeting you, *chérie*, I had never considered taking to my bed a woman who worked for me. It had been my policy not to mix business with pleasure, but my convictions fell by the wayside the moment we met. No other woman has or ever will take your place, either in my bed or in my heart. Had it not been for the unexpected return to good health of my beloved wife, and her expressed desire to make our marriage full and complete once more, I would be with you still."

Camille smiled. She sincerely doubted that statement, but she was deeply grateful to Pierre for his desire to have her believe that it was so.

Pierre's caressing touch slipped to Camille's softly rounded shoulders, framed so beautifully by the ruffles of her pale blue sprigged muslin gown. His eyes remained on her face, regarding her intently, and Camille studied him in return.

Only a few years had passed since their first meeting, but Le Comte had changed much. The lines in his narrow face were deeper, harder. His hair was now an iron gray, his hairline greatly receded. His small, neat mustache was lightly flecked with gray. The wariness about his eyes, which had impressed her upon their first meeting, was with him once more. He was concerned about something. Pierre's wife was well, and Camille knew he was deeply devoted to her. She also knew he had taken no other mistresses since the months they had spent together those years ago.

Looking at him, Camille found it hard to believe that he was indeed the man who inspired such awe and fear in some hearts. She was well aware that he headed a vast organization with a chain of luxurious bordellos throughout France. She was also aware that the chain now extended to this side of the Atlantic with houses stretching from New York to San Francisco. This house of Blond Marie's was just one of very many.

But Pierre had never flaunted his power with her or demonstrated any sign of threat. His manner had always been so gentle, so patient, that she found it difficult to reconcile one side of his personality with the other. She supposed Marie's manner, her obvious respect for and fear of Pierre, demonstrated only too clearly that a darker side of his personality existed, but this man had always been good to her. He had made her chosen path in life smoother, more filled with roses, and a part of her heart would always be his.

The Count spoke again, and Camille put aside her wandering thoughts.

"I sought to stir your memory tonight, *ma chérie*, so that you might realize that my words to you now are spoken with deep concern for your welfare. You are unhappy, Camille, and because you are unhappy, I am unhappy."

Camille shook her head in vehement denial. "No, Pierre, I am quite content with my life. You know how very much I appreciate all your intercession has allowed me to do for my family.

And you know that I enjóy giving happiness to others in my small way."

"Of first importance is bringing happiness to yourself."

"I *am* happy, Pierre."

"Camille . . .." Le Comte interrupted Camille's protest.

After remaining silent for a few moments, Camille gave a short, rueful laugh. "I had not realized I was so obvious."

"Only to me, *ma chérie*, only to me. It is your friend, the doctor, is it not?"

"Charles is one of my clients, nothing more."

"Camille, there are those you serve from your head and those you serve from your heart. Your heart is hopelessly bound to Charles Carter, is it not?"

Realizing the futility of denying her true feelings to this man, Camille responded in a soft whisper, "Pierre, you know me too well."

"And love you too well, Camille. So you must allow me to help you. What may I do to bring the sparkle back to your eyes?"

"There is nothing you can do." Abandoning all pretense in the face of Pierre's honest concern, Camille shook her head. "Charles has met another woman, one who suits him far better than I."

"You are speaking of the Dale woman, the daughter of Harvey Dale." Le Comte's disapproval was obvious. "Indeed she is very beautiful, but she is a spoiled, haughty girl, the daughter of a spoiled and haughty father. All the warmth has been bred out of her."

"Perhaps that is true in her treatment of some, but I have seen Charles and her together several times. I have seen her face, and there is no hauteur there when she is with Charles. She is smiling and happy then, as is Charles."

"Then how may I help you, *ma petite*? Not too many weeks from now I shall return to Paris. Would you like to return with me? You could spend some time with your family in the country and renew yourself. And when you are totally bored and unable to bear the inactivity any longer, you may return to Paris. Madame Le Claire and I would await your return with eagerness."

"No, no, Pierre, I have no wish to leave this country, not yet."

"*Chérie* . . ."

Reaching out unexpectedly, Le Comte closed his arms around her and drew her against him so she might rest her head on his shoulder. His broad palm stroked her back for long moments before he stepped back far enough that he might view her face. Reaching up, he smoothed the tears from her cheeks. It was not until that moment that Camille realized she had been crying.

"Why will you not leave, Camille? By staying, you only cause yourself unnecessary pain."

Pierre's concern touched her deeply and Camille responded with candor. "Pierre, the answer is simple. Even though Charles has met another, he is not through with me yet. And I am not through with him. I will continue to enjoy the love for him, which I hold secret within my heart. When the time comes that Charles is no longer available to me, I will accept your offer to return to Paris, for I will have nothing to hold me here."

"Camille, *ma chérie* . . ."

"Until that time, I will put my sorrow to the back of my mind and concentrate on my blessings. I have many, you know, Pierre. You are one of them."

Pierre's hand again caressed her cheek, and Camille smiled at his whisper.

"And the sparkle in your eyes?" he said.

"I will rekindle its glow."

Stepping back from his arms in a quick, graceful movement, Camille took a deep breath, pushed away her sadness, and tucked her arm lightly under his. Raising her chin, she walked with him to the door of his office and stepped back as he opened it.

"I have an appointment with Madame Beauchamps, Pierre. She is making a very special garment for me. It is a trifle daring, and I am uncertain about it. I would greatly appreciate your advice if you would accompany me to her shop today. I should not like to shock the good people of Tombstone."

"There is little you could do that would shock the good people in this wicked town, *ma chérie*."

"Then you must come with me and make certain that I do not disappoint them."

Le Comte's spontaneous laugh echoed in the foyer as they stepped through the doorway.

Turning toward him with a flutter of her long eyelashes, Camille moved closer to whisper into his ear, "I will refresh myself and return within moments with my hat, ready for our outing. Will you be waiting for me?"

"Always, *ma chérie*, always . . ."

Turning, Camille took a few steps, then turned and shot Le Comte a broad wink. Waiting only until he winked just as broadly in return, Camille ascended the staircase rapidly, a true smile on her face. The higher she climbed, the higher her spirits rose.

Pierre was right, she realized. The somber mood that had assailed her of late was uncharacteristic. She was Camille. Camille did not allow life to overwhelm her. She overwhelmed life! She would push her sorrow to the back of her mind. There was still much left for her here. Charles would visit her again, and she would enjoy him. She would enjoy him for as long and as well as she might. And, in silence, she would love him. Oh, how well she would love him . . .

From her position inside the entrance to the sitting room, Marie watched Camille ascend the staircase toward her room and disappear from sight.

Meticulously dressed, her bright blond hair perfectly groomed, her features carefully composed, Marie looked toward Le Comte, who stood unmoving at the foot of the staircase. Her pale complexion, suddenly flushed with color.

Le Comte, this man of importance who was feared for the power he wielded both on this continent and abroad, waited like a well-behaved poodle for the country harlot to reappear.

Fury transfused her, and Marie fought to restrain an urge to do violence. She had worked hard and long in the cribs of Paris to attain her present position. It had taken all she had—her beauty, her intelligence, and her considerable skill in more intimate contact—to get her there. A keen sense of organization, a firm will, and supreme determination kept her house the best in Tombstone, and had made her justly proud. She would not allow a farm-grown bitch from the outskirts of Paris to undermine either her position or her authority.

The sound of a closing door drew Marie's eyes to the second floor in time to see Camille take her first step down the staircase. She watched as the hussy descended, brilliant red curls bobbing against her white shoulders, the full curves of her body keeping time with her step. Le Comte, at the foot of the staircase, was enjoying *la grande putain*'s every bouncing jiggle.

Barely suppressing the fury surging through her veins, Marie took a deep breath and turned away with slow deliberation. She did not wait to see Camille's feet touch the foyer, to see the Count take her arm, or to see them walk through the front doorway and out into the street together for all the world to see. The sound of their laughter drifted behind them as they closed the front door, and Marie renewed her silent vow with a vengeance: She would be rid of Camille. She would see to it that the woman was banished from her house forever.

"Lai Hua, look over here! These lanterns will be perfect!"

Her exuberance spilling over into a small laugh, Devina held up one of the colorful Oriental lanterns so that the sun might reflect through its interior. "Oh, yes, it will look lovely once it's lit. How many do you think we'll need?"

Devina turned toward Lai Hua, who stood behind her on the narrow street. Her smile faded at her servant's troubled expression. Devina took a deep, impatient breath.

"Lai Hua, really. You don't believe I'm in danger in this part of town, do you? You live only a short distance from here. If it's safe enough for you, it's surely safe enough for me." Devina shot a short glance toward Sam Sharpe, who followed not far behind her. Her smile became sugar sweet as she continued in a sarcastic tone. "In any case, my watchdog will guarantee my safety wherever I am."

Lai Hua shook her shining head. "I do not worry for your safety, Miss Devina, for indeed, no danger threatens you here. I fear only your father's anger."

"Father's anger?"

"He will not approve of your presence on these streets."

Devina turned a thoughtful, appraising glance around her. The streets she and Lai Hua had been walking for the past half-hour appeared to be narrower than the streets in the other part of town. Devina amended that thought. Perhaps that was not so. Perhaps it was merely the congestion that seemed to abound, the variety of signs of all sizes and shapes that protruded into walkways, their Chinese figures boldly proclaiming a message she could not read, which contributed to the illusion of less space. The buildings were not well constructed; some were mere shacks. But the variety of small stores that lined the cramped avenue, their exotic products colorfully displayed, appealed to

her immensely. The pedestrians walking around her were pre-
dominantly Chinese, and she was suddenly aware she was the
object of many curious glances, but she was not ill at ease.

She glanced back toward Lai Hua, who leaned toward her to
repeat her adamant statement in a low whisper: "Your father will
not approve."

Devina's patience was abruptly exhausted. She took a deep
breath. "Lai Hua, my father said I was to buy whatever I needed
to make this party a success. I have determined that lanterns—
dozens and dozens of them to light the way of our guests and to
line the garden—will add the perfect touch of spectacle needed
to guarantee the success of this party. Certainly there's no better ·
place than the Chinese section of town to find them."

"Most non-Orientals, Miss Devina, refer to this section as
Hop Town. They do not consider it suitable for a young woman
such as yourself to be here."

"Not suitable! We're not going to bring up that old chestnut
again, are we?" Devina shook her head, unwilling to pursue that
particular line of conversation any further. "In any case, we're
wasting time, Lai Hua. Since we're here now, we might as well
do what we came for." Devina raised another lantern for Lai
Hua's inspection. "What do you think of this one?"

Lai Hua sent a short glance toward Sam Sharpe, her frown
tightening at his low snicker. "I think it is very nice, Miss
Devina."

"Lai Hua, please, an honest opinion."

"My opinion is that you should not be here."

"Lai Hua, really!"

Devina truly did not understand Lai Hua's reluctance. Father
could not possibly be as narrow-minded as Lai Hua believed.
Granted, he had been less than civil to Lai Hua several times
. . . Devina amended that thought: He had actually been insult-
ing, and he had not escaped his daughter's anger on those
occasions. But, in truth, he tended to treat all servants with a
certain contempt, regardless of the color of their skin. Even his
social acquaintances did not escape his scorn, she had noticed.
But that was just his way. If you were not a Dale, you were not
on his level.

Devina shook her head. She had despaired of her father's
attitude countless times, as had her mother before her. She could
still remember the countless apologies Mother had offered in his

stead, the excuses she made for him. Her mother had convinced herself that her excuses were justified, but even as a child, Devina had known that her mother made them because of her desire not to have anyone think poorly of the man she loved so dearly.

She supposed, while she was facing facts, she would have to consider the possibility that there might be more to this vendetta than her father had led her to believe. Perhaps someone had good cause to seek revenge on her father. If her father would not discuss matters with her, it was up to her to look into things herself.

A flashing image of the stagecoach gunman's face returned to her mind. The man's features had been all but unrecognizable behind his beard and beneath the brim of his hat, but she could still feel his intensity, and she would never forget the chill of those eyes. Perhaps, for her own peace of mind, she should find out more about her father's activities here in Tombstone. For all his faults, she could not bear the thought of losing him to the hatred in that unknown man's gaze.

Devina's brow furrowed in a worried frown as she examined her concern for her father. Was she beginning to disregard his faults, just as her mother had always done? Was she wrong to rationalize his prejudice? Well, right or wrong, she resolved to apologize to Lai Hua. Father probably *would* be angry when he found out she had come to Hop Town. But she would not allow Lai Hua to suffer for something over which she had no control. In any case, whatever the cost, she did not intend to allow her father's prejudices to become her own. Neither would she let them stop her from any reasonable activity and buying lanterns was reasonable activity.

Devina stopped in her thoughts, the absurdity of the situation sudddenly striking her. All this concern about lanterns, about a ridiculous party, while the man who had threatened her life, had actually held a gun to her ribs, was riding free and probably planning more such attacks.

Reprimanded by her own thoughts, Devina turned to Lai Hua with an apologetic smile. "Lai Hua, I'm sorry if you're uncomfortable, but I give you my word, I won't allow you to suffer for my stubbornness in insisting that you bring me here. Now, please, which lantern do you think will be better?"

Holding two lanterns up to the light, Devina watched Lai

Hua's eyes move from one to the other as she studied the merits of both.

Indicating the lantern Devina held in her left hand, Lai Hua bobbed her head. "This one, Miss Devina. It is constructed of a material that will allow the light to penetrate it far more easily. And I believe it is available in more colors than the other as well."

Knowing she would have agreed with Lai Hua's selection even if it had conflicted with her own, only because Lai Hua had so sincerely put aside her objections in order to be of help, Devina nodded. She turned to the slight Oriental man who appeared at her side. "I would like fifty of these lanterns, in assorted colors." Devina continued briskly, "Have them delivered to the Dale residence as soon as possible. I'll pay you now."

The man turned to Lai Hua and addressed her in Chinese, obviously asking her a question, to which Lai Hua replied with a short statement. The man went inside the store and returned a moment later. Handing Devina a ticket on which he had written several Chinese characters, he waited in silence.

Politely taking the ticket from Devina's hand, Lai Hua examined it carefully and translated the price.

Reaching into her reticule, Devina counted out the specified amount. She could tell that the sale pleased the storekeeper very much.

After speaking quickly to Lai Hua in his native tongue, he returned to his store.

"May we return home now, Miss Devina?" Lai Hua said.

Her annoyance returning at her maid's persistence, Devina turned to survey the stores around her. A laundry, a dry goods store, a grocery store . . . but what was that store over there? Devina took a step forward only to be halted by Lai Hua's touch on her arm.

"Please, Miss Devina, where do you go?"

Devina's annoyance grew. She disliked being questioned by anyone. "I'm going to that store over there." Realizing the sharpness of her tone, she continued more softly, "It occurs to me that an establishment such as that might carry a type of cookie I ate on one occasion in New York. I believe it was considered Oriental. It was rather large and very crisp, and it had a distinct almond flavor. I would enjoy having them available to my guests at the party, as an alternative to the rather heavy desserts I'm planning.''

Devina paused. Was she wrong, or had panic momentarily touched Lai Hua's expression?

''I do not believe you will find the cookies you seek there.''

Restraining her impatience only because of Lai Hua's obvious discomfort, Devina replied quietly, ''I intend to check and make sure.''

Nodding her obedience, Lai Hua walked slightly behind her as Devina started forward. The pale blue hem of Devina's gown brushed the dusty street as she crossed, and she stepped with care onto the boardwalk in an effort to avoid a pile of rubbish discarded casually in the gutter.

An uneasiness crawled up Devina's spine as she walked through the doorway of the store, and her annoyance grew. Damn, was she never to have a free mind in this dreadful town? First, her father's concern had fostered the notion that she was being watched, and now Lai Hua's uneasiness had fostered a new uneasiness within herself. Determined not to submit to it, Devina glanced around the store as she entered. She paused, choosing to walk through the short rows of delicacies.

Suddenly her attention was distracted. What was that fragrance? She could not be certain . . . Some sort of spice, certainly. Her eyes were drawn to a display, but she had taken only a few steps when a curtain to the rear of the store parted to allow entrance to a short but well-rounded gray-haired Oriental woman of indeterminate age. The woman's silent step carried her closer even as Devina unconsciously assessed her rather interesting apparel.

The woman's limited height and excess poundage did little justice to the exquisite garment she wore. Obviously a rich silk, the color was lovely. It was embroidered by an expert hand in a delicate floral design that was breathtaking; but the quality of the material and workmanship was all but lost on the middle-aged woman who paused at her side. The woman smiled broadly, her eyes appearing to appraise Devina keenly even as she addressed her in excellent English.

''Miss Dale, I bid you welcome to my humble establishment. What may I do for you today?''

Startled to be addressed by her name, Devina replied politely, ''I appreciate your welcome, but I admit I'm at a loss. If we've met, I apologize for not remembering the occasion.''

"We have not met, Miss Dale, but your reputation precedes you, even in this humble area of town."

"My reputation?"

"Ah, yes. Even here we have heard of Mr. Harvey Dale's lovely daughter. The reports of your beauty have not been exaggerated."

"Thank you. Thank you very much." Devina felt herself flush lightly at the unexpected compliment. "May I ask your name as well?"

The woman smiled and bowed her head. "I am known as China Mary."

"I'm very pleased to meet you. As for what you may help me with, I'm interested in finding a type of Oriental cookie, made with almonds."

"Ah, yes, we carry such cookies. They are back there, at the rear of the store."

Leading Devina through the crowded rows of merchandise, China Mary brought her to a short counter. At the same moment, the sound of a step raised Devina's eyes toward a younger Oriental woman descending a curved staircase just beyond them. The young woman's eyes held hers, and Devina caught a flicker of an intense emotion in the moment before she stepped onto the main floor.

Devina's first thought was that this young woman was all that China Mary was not. Tall, slender, exceedingly graceful, she suited the exquisite garment she wore to perfection. The subtle blue of the embroidered silk accented the delicacy of her features and the incredible sheen of her coiled hair. She smiled, fleeting dimples and even white teeth adding the final touch to a picture that was exotic perfection.

China Mary's lined face glowed with pride as she motioned the young woman forward.

"And now you must meet my daughter, Lily, who is your age. She is well educated and is also beautiful. In these ways you have much in common. Perhaps someday you may meet and talk. I am sure you two would find you have some mutual interests."

"And just what might they be, Mary?"

A deep, familiar voice caused Devina to whirl around with a start as Harvey Dale stepped to her side. Not awaiting Mary's response, he turned toward Devina, his countenance flushed.

"You are here against my explicit instructions, Devina." He tossed a sharp glance toward Lai Hua, his voice growing harsher. "You were hired to guide my daughter into areas that are acceptable for her. You have not fulfilled that requirement by allowing her to come to this establishment."

"Father!" Looking at China Mary and her silent daughter, Devina offered quietly, "I apologize for my father. He's upset."

"Don't apologize for me, Devina. Had you not come here, this scene would not have occurred. Since you are here, and Lai Hua has failed in her duties once more, I have no other choice but to—"

"Father, please, say no more."

Devina turned toward China Mary and her daughter, only to be startled at their composure. Rather than being insulted by her father's attitude, they appeared almost to be enjoying the confrontation. Nevertheless, her words were short and filled with regret. "If you will forgive me, China Mary, Lily, I think it would be best if I returned home with my father now."

Taking her arm in a restrictive grip, Harvey turned Devina toward the door. His step rapid, he propelled her out of the store and down Third Street without a word. Slowing his pace only when their home came into sight, Harvey continued on in silence. Ushering her up the front steps, he paused to catch his breath.

In total control moments later, he faced her squarely. "Devina, I will not ask what took you into that section of town today."

"Lanterns, Father. I went to buy lanterns for the party."

Harvey's flushed face was unyielding. "I do not care to know. There is no reason that will suffice. I will not tolerate your presence there."

Her anger beginning to rise at her father's autocratic tone, Devina raised her chin. "And what took *you* there today, Father? I cannot believe you went there for the express reason of coming to my rescue when I was not in need of rescue at all."

"It is none of your concern why or how I happened upon you in that portion of town, Devina, but I warn you now: This had better never happen again. If you value your privacy, your independence, your freedom, you will not abuse it!"

"Father—"

"That is all I have to say on the subject!" Taking another deep breath, Harvey continued in a slightly lower tone. "As for Lai Hua—"

"She had nothing to do with this, Father. She tried to stop me from going."

Harvey's pale eyes flicked over Lai Hua's shuddering form with contempt. "I will not argue with you about the girl. You may keep her if you wish." His gaze returning to Devina, Harvey continued in a level tone completely devoid of emotion. "But you will never return to Hop Town again, is that understood?"

"Father . . ."

"Devina, is that understood?"

Devina hesitated, her own anger flaring. She was about to respond with the full heat of her emotions when she noted the abnormal flush that had flooded her father's face, the pounding of the veins in his temple and neck. Suddenly unwilling to further raise her father's ire, she took a deep breath. "Yes, that's understood, Father."

Pausing, her father held her gaze for long moments as he sought to rein in his emotions. Nodding at last, he continued in a strained voice, "You will now go inside, Devina, and I will return to work. We will never discuss this again."

"Yes, Father."

Turning abruptly, her father walked stiffly down the steps to the street. It was only when his tall erect form turned the corner that Devina realized she was shaking. Her expression stiff, she turned to Lai Hua.

"I suppose it would be best for Father if this afternoon was never discussed again; and right now, I think it would be best for me. But we will discuss it later, Lai Hua, and I shall offer you my apologies. But for now, I think I'll go inside. I've quite lost my taste for shopping."

Turning, Devina opened the door and stepped into the coolness of the foyer. She was grateful to be home. She needed time to think.

Harvey strode angrily into the small shop he had left only a short time before. Standing just where he had left her was China Mary. Her smile was broad.

"What in hell did you think you were doing?"

"I, Mr. Dale? I was doing nothing. I did not summon your daughter to my establishment."

"Damn you! What was all that talk about Devina and Lily

having so much in common? I warn you, Mary, if you're up to any tricks, you'll lose everything you have. You'll leave this town even more penniless than you were when you came here, and your precious daughter will have to peddle her wares to the highest bidder to support herself.''

A soft step from behind made Harvey turn toward Lily's tall, graceful form as she stepped into his line of vision.

"And would you like that, Mr. Dale?"

Harvey's eyes moved over Lily's beautiful face as she stepped closer. Despite himself, Harvey hesitated.

Taking her opportunity, Lily questioned in a softer tone, "Would you like the thought of another man's hands on my body, touching me as you have touched me? Would you enjoy the thought of another man making—"

"Enough! That is enough!" Harvey's voice was a hoarse croak.

Turning back to China Mary once more, Harvey hissed through lips stiff with tension, "I did not come back to discuss this matter with you. I came back to issue an ultimatum. You are never, under any circumstances, to go near my daughter again, do you hear?"

China Mary nodded. "I hear you, Mr. Dale."

Harvey turned to walk away when he heard Lily's soft, musical voice. He steeled himself against it.

"You are leaving so soon, Mr. Dale? Do you not wish to visit with me for a little while in the room at the top of the stairs? That is the reason you came here this day, is it not? But unfortunately, you found instead your daughter speaking to your lover." Lily paused in silent emphasis of her words. When she began speaking again, her voice was a purr. "Come, Mr. Dale. I will dispel your anger. I will cause it and all else to cease to exist for you."

Not daring to turn in her direction, Harvey took a shallow, choking breath. Exerting supreme control, he forced himself forward as Lily's voice drifted over his shoulder in a soft siren call, "Do you really wish to leave, Mr. Dale?"

Not daring to answer, Harvey straightened his shoulders and continued forward. It was the hardest thing he had ever done.

Ross turned slowly. Incredulity widened his eyes, displacing the dark, fanatical light that had glowed within them too often of late. A smile grew on his lips, broadening to expose strong white teeth in startling contrast with his sun-darkened skin. Creases in mid-cheek deepened with his smile, and dimples seldom seen during the dark moods that had become his natural state, lifted the planes of his face. His face shed years in that moment, revealing the youthful side of his obvious maturity, lightening his handsome features to reveal a glimpse of the man he had once been. He laughed, the deep warmth of the sound echoing in the cabin to bring the two men outside briefly to the doorway.

Waiting until Mack and Harry had returned to their chores, Ross clamped his hand on Jake's shoulder and gave it a hearty shake. His low voice was filled with enjoyment.

"Damn, why did you wait so long to tell me this, Jake? It's about the best news I've heard in a long time! So Harvey Dale has gone to great trouble to arrange a covert shipment of his payroll. A dummy box, a supply wagon carrying the real thing . . . No doubt he hopes to use the process of elimination to trap the person who's leaking the information to us. He'd have no way of suspecting Lai Hua. No one knows you've been seeing her, not even Harry and Mack. There'd be no way of tying her to the robberies. Oh, this is good!"

But Jake was not smiling. His expression sober, he continued in a confidential tone, "Lai Hua thinks they'll make the switch at the last minute, so there'll be less chance of anybody suspectin' anythin'."

"That makes sense. Did she say when the shipment will go out?"

"No. She said the payroll would be shipped as usual, so I guess we can expect it to go in about a week."

"That'll be perfect." Ross took a deep, steadying breath. His amusement had faded, and his mind was surging ahead to the details of interception. "If they're trying not to stir up suspicion about the supply wagon, I guess that means we can expect it to be traveling without additional guard." Ross laughed again. "Nothing could be better. That makes it easier for us and eliminates the possibility of innocent men getting hurt. Enough innocent men have already suffered from Dale's twisted schemes."

Suddenly aware of his friend's preoccupation, Ross asked, "Is something wrong, Jake? Is there a reason you didn't mention this whole thing to me before this? It's been a couple of days since you saw Lai Hua, hasn't it?"

Jake nodded, maintaining his silence, and Ross was struck by his own thoughtlessness. Damn, he should've realized something was wrong when Jake returned a few nights before. He had been moody and uncommunicative in the days since, and nothing could be farther from Jake's normal behavior than that. If he hadn't been so tied up in his own thoughts, he would have noticed that something was bothering his friend.

But Ross hadn't thought about much besides the woman who had been filling the sights of his spyglass for the past week. During that time he had memorized every detail of Devina Dale's flawless countenance. He could anticipate the vanity in her expression each time she stepped onto the street and caught the eyes of passersby, the haughty lift of her brow when Sam Sharpe assumed his place behind her, and the manner in which she managed to hide her instinctive air of superiority when she emerged on the arm of Charles Carter. Oh, yes, she was all sweetness and light then. If he didn't despise Carter so thoroughly, he would almost feel sorry for the fool.

Ross was suddenly disgusted with himself. Once again thoughts of Devina Dale were distracting him from more immediate matters. He was allowing her to become almost as deep an obsession as his hatred for her father.

His eyes returning to Jake's face, Ross winced inwardly at the torment in his friend's light eyes. Why hadn't he seen it there before? He probed again. "Jake, what's wrong?"

"I had a lot of thinkin' to do before I told you about what Lai Hua said, Ross. One of the reasons was that for the first time since I've known her, I doubted what Lai Hua told me."

"Doubted? You think she was lying about the shipment, trying to get us to go after the wrong one?"

"To be honest, Ross, at first I wasn't sure. I spent a couple of long sleepless nights comin' to the decision that Lai Hua was tellin' me the truth, about the shipment, at least." Jake continued in a softer tone. "I wouldn't have said anythin' if I wasn't pretty positive what I told you is true."

Ross continued to peruse his friend's disturbed expression. "That's not all that's wrong, is it?"

Jake attempted a smile. "I guess you could say that. I'm thinkin' we'd better make good use of the information we got this time from Lai Hua, 'cause we won't be gettin' any more."

"And it's not because she won't be employed by the Dales any longer," Ross said.

"No. It's because I won't be seein' Lai Hua again." Jake's eyes held a suspicious brightness. "She told me about the payroll, but she was holdin' something back. I don't know what it was, but I could see it in her eyes. I gave her a last chance to tell me, but . . ." Jake gave a small shrug. "I've had my fill of people lettin' me down, Ross. I went against my instincts once before and trusted somebody when I shouldn't have. I ended up in Yuma for that. I'm not lettin' Lai Hua put me back in that place, no matter how often she tells me she—" Jake stopped talking abruptly and gave a short laugh. " 'Once burned, twice shy' . . . that describes me real well."

Ross shared his friend's pain. It was damned hard to be betrayed, especially by someone you trusted.

His high spirits of a few minutes before gone in the face of this new complication, Ross said, "We did all right without Lai Hua before, and we can again. We'll get that payroll, and we'll get every Till-Dale payroll after it until that Dale girl puts herself into a spot where we can get her instead. After that, we'll have Dale right in the palm of our hands. When this whole business is done, we'll get out of this territory and blow the red dust of this country out of our hair. Hell, I've had just about enough of it gritting between my teeth for a lifetime."

Abruptly realizing Jake was no longer listening, Ross walked óver to the fire and picked up the coffeepot. He listened to the sound of retreating footsteps behind him, turning just as Jake walked into the yard. Ross poured a cup of the steaming coffee and replaced the pot over the fire. He lifted the mug to his lips, seeing not the dark, steaming liquid, but a pair of incredibly blue, incredibly beautiful eyes.

CHAPTER IX

CHARLES HAD AWAKENED an hour earlier to the sunlit silence of his orderly room. The quarters he maintained to the rear of his office were not luxurious, but they were clean and adequate. For the past few years, since his arrival in Tombstone, he had occupied the former offices of Dr. Henry Harlow, who had been driven from town by the relatives of some of his former patients. The patients themselves had been in no condition to register their complaints.

It had taken Charles almost a week, with the help of two hardworking Orientals, to clean the office and private quarters, but he had been more than satisfied with the results. Instinctively neat, he had maintained his quarters at that level of cleanliness without the fastidious need for perfection that was the mark of the obsessive.

His well-muscled chest bared to the warmth of early morning, Charles walked across the room, unconsciously stretching the stiffness from his broad shoulders and strong arms. The stiffness was due to physical inactivity. He made a mental note to reserve some time before sunset for a ride into the countryside. He needed exercise. Perhaps it would be a good idea to invite Devina to join him. He had never asked Devina if she enjoyed riding, but he was certain she rode well. Her father would have seen to it that she received lessons whether she had wanted them or not. Harvey Dale would not have neglected that aspect of her social education.

Charles walked to the window, pushed the shade aside, and looked out onto Fourth Street. It was still early and little moved past his line of vision. He turned an assessing glance back to the room. He was pleased with what he saw. He had managed to find a very comfortable bed in Tombstone's only furniture store, as well as a table and chairs, a desk, and a leather couch. Just a few months before, he had purchased an elaborately carved wardrobe, which now filled the only remaining space in the room, and he was well satisfied with his selection.

He had also purchased several photographs from Camilus Fly, Tombstone's photographer. He was certain Fly's work would one day be regarded as a pictorial history of the area, and Charles was pleased to own copies of some of his best work. He had had the photographs framed, and they occupied the wall space over his couch.

A smile curved Charles's lips. These Spartan living accommodations were a far cry from the life he had led back east. A large mansion overlooking the Hudson had been the home of his boyhood memories, and he had grown up taking for granted the luxuries made available to him by the railroad fortune of his father, J. Oliver Carter. But J. Oliver Carter was dead now, as was Charles's mother. The company was in good hands, and the mansion had been sold. The proceeds from the sale, as well as Charles's inherited wealth, lay in an account in the family bank. He had not bothered to have the funds transferred to the Arizona Territory, and he had not missed them. These simple living conditions suited him very well. He had other matters on his mind—matters which took precedence and which had not yet been settled to his satisfaction.

His pleasant boyhood memories of New York seemed so far removed from the life he lived now that he almost looked back on the child he had been as someone else.

An unconscious smile again curved Charles's lips. He supposed the fact that Devina Dale and he had both spent a good part of their lives in New York was responsible for the easy familiarity that had sprung up between them. He had exercised great care not to allow a stronger emotion to develop. He didn't want that, not yet. He had cultivated Devina's friendship for a far different reason.

Not that he wasn't truly attracted to Devina. For all her stiff posture, unrelenting self-possession, and rigid sophistication,

Devina was really a dear girl. He was not immune to her beauty or her stimulating intelligence. Nor was he immune to the warm, human side of her nature, which he suspected she concealed from most of her other acquaintances.

He had noticed with considerable surprise that Devina maintained her reserve even with her father. Charles wondered why. Harvey Dale's pride in and love for his daughter were glaringly obvious. It was also obvious that he would do anything to make her happy. Charles supposed this ridiculous party that Devina was planning was further demonstration of Harvey's desire to please her. But if for some reason Harvey sought to buy his daughter's love and acceptance, Charles knew instinctively Harvey's efforts were for naught. Devina Dale was not the type of woman who could be bought.

Charles had cautiously guided his relationship with Devina. He did not want to get so close to her that he might unconsciously reveal himself. He was beginning to think that this reluctance was a true hindrance in gaining Devina's confidence, and gaining Devina's confidence was essential to him.

Charles was suddenly aware that he was frowning. He had attempted to avoid doing so in Devina's presence. For all her spontaneous nature, he had noticed a distinct change in her reaction to him, a definite withdrawal, when his manner became too intense. He had noticed an actual paling of her skin, a frantic look in her eye, if he looked at her severely. Her reactions had made him all the more certain that his instinctive suspicions were true.

His position as Devina's unofficial escort had earned him an important dividend. Harvey Dale appeared to believe Devina's social life was in good hands when she was with him. Harvey also trusted him to guarantee his daughter's safety. He had worked hard to be accepted by Harvey Dale. It was time to make good use of that acceptance. He had already found out that a new payroll was due to be shipped in a little less than a week.

Charles cast a quick look toward the clock on his dresser. He had approximately two hours until his first appointment of the day. Mrs. Rigger, pregnant with her third child, was in an extremely run-down condition. He worried for her. He had prescribed medication to build her up. He hoped it had produced results since her last visit.

Charles walked to the washstand. He did not have time for a

visit to the baths this morning. A quick shave and a fast sponge-down would have to do.

Minutes later Charles opened his wardrobe and scanned the garments hanging neatly within. He realized his insistence on finely tailored garments was a carryover from his moneyed youth, but that was not the only reason for the wide variety of fashionable clothing hanging before him. He was an extremely good customer of Bart Hattisch's tailor shop and of Tombstone's clothier, Glover & Company. He knew his patronage in both those establishments was probably surpassed only by that of Harvey Dale himself. Charles had deliberately cultivated that aspect of Harvey Dale's regard.

With that thought in mind, he carefully selected an inconspicuous but well-tailored coat and matching trousers in blue serge. Choosing a contrasting necktie in shades of gray, he turned to the fine lawn shirts he had picked up from Lum Chee's laundry the day before. Within minutes he was fully dressed and walking through his outer office. His concessions to the more informal style of his new frontier home were the hand-tooled boots he wore and the handsome dark Stetson he took from the rack as he opened the door and stepped outside.

Without a trace of vanity, Charles realized he presented an excellent appearance. It suited his purpose to do so at this time.

No sign of the sense of purpose that had dominated his mind since awakening that morning was evident in his expression as Charles walked up Fourth Street and turned onto Allen. He shot a quick glance toward the offices of Till-Dale Enterprises, a twitch of annoyance moving his brow as he viewed Walter Jobe unlocking the front door. So Harvey had not yet arrived. Damn! It would be just his luck that Harvey would be detained today, of all days.

Annoyance made Charles increase his pace as he crossed Allen Street and turned down toward the Maison Doree. He'd have a leisurely breakfast, very leisurely. He'd maintain his vigil from the window of the restaurant, which just happened to be directly across from Till-Dale's offices. He'd wait until Harvey Dale arrived..He had two hours at his disposal.

He was making himself comfortable at a small linen-covered table when Harvey Dale's impressive figure came into sight. Charles glanced up at the white-aproned, heavily mustached waiter who appeared at his side:

"Just coffee, Nate. I'm in a rush today."

Nate nodded and walked away, but Charles had no eyes for the fellow's silent acknowledgment.

"Lai Hua, hand me that other list, please."

The fine line of her brows drawn into a frown of concentration, Devina stared at the sheet of paper in her hand. She looked up as Lai Hua handed her a second sheet.

"Thank you, Lai Hua. Would you call Molly, please?"

Devina was uneasy. Almost a week had passed since Father had suggested the party, and it had been several days since he had encountered her in the Oriental section of town. True to his word, her father had not mentioned the incident again; but, perversely, Devina almost wished that he had. She had so many questions. Why had he been so infuriated when he found her in China Mary's store? Why was his hatred of Orientals so deep? Or was it a dislike of China Mary herself rather than a dislike of her entire race? Did it have anything to do with the tension the robberies had evoked? Did it have anything to do with the robberies themselves?

No, that was a foolish thought. The man who had held her prisoner was obviously the leader of the thieves, and he was not an Oriental. She was off on the wrong track, again.

Father's stiffness after their meeting in China Mary's store had finally faded, and his enthusiasm for the party had returned. It had, in fact, grown stronger. She was uncertain of the feelings his sudden enthusiasm raised inside her. It was as if he sought to prove a point with the affair, a point that escaped her.

She had finally obtained a rather extensive guest list from him. She had carefully scanned the list and found the balance of guests acceptable—more men than women, but that was usually the case. She had composed a formal invitation and had it printed at Henry Hasselgren's Commercial Printing Shop. The result had been extremely pleasing, and the invitations had already been sent.

In the meantime, she had drawn up a tentative menu for her guests. Her greatest difficulty had been with Molly, who had resisted any attempt at other than the most commonplace dishes. As a result, Devina had insisted on hiring a cook for this special occasion. Her father had thought the idea an excellent one, and he had insisted she pull out all the stops in the composition of their guests' repast.

Devina checked the paper Lai Hua had just placed in her hands. Yes, she had enjoyed following her father's orders in regard to the menu: chicken gumbo, one of her personal favorites; fillet of sole amandine; lamb à la milanaise; pâté financière; French peas and corn; roast suckling pig with applesauce; celery hearts and lettuce à la vinaigrette; vanilla cream puffs and queen cakes a' l'israélite; fruit, walnuts, and almonds.

Devina smiled. Perhaps not the lightest of menus, but it was surely varied enough to suit the rather unpredictable tastes of this frontier society. The Continental touch was her own attempt at culture, which she was certain would go completely unappreciated.

She had arranged to have music for dancing and listening, additional tables for the votaries of whist. The lanterns had arrived and been ignored by her father, but she had been very pleased with them.

She had, of course, visited the seamstress and ordered her gown. Devina's smile widened with true enjoyment for the first time. She was well aware that she was usually considered the best dressed woman at any affair she attended. This affair would be no different. She had even gone to the trouble of swearing Mrs. Lotts to secrecy about the unusual styling of the garment she had promised to have ready with days to spare. Yes, Devina was sure she would truly set this town on its ear.

Now she needed to organize the responses so as to get an idea of the number of guests she could expect. She secretly believed that only a major tragedy or act of God would keep her invited guests from attending—there had been that much talk about the party in town.

Hearing a footstep at her side, Devina turned to see Molly's somber expression. Devina took a deep breath and a firmer hold on her patience. Her one holdout was Molly. Even with a cook hired especially for the occasion, she needed Molly's willing cooperation. There just were not that many good maids to spare in this godforsaken town.

What was it Lai Hua had said about Molly's talent for baking? Devina raised her eyes with a smile.

"Molly, I would like to enlist your aid."

Molly was unimpressed. "Yes, ma'am."

"I'm having a bit of trouble with the cook I've hired for the party."

A spark of interest flickered in Molly's eyes. "Yes, ma'am?"

"Monsieur LeFleur has agreed to arrive from San Francisco two days prior to the party to prepare the feast. He has wired that the menu is satisfactory, but my one problem is the desserts. Monsieur LeFleur has had no experience in making the traditional American desserts, which will be in great demand. He has refused to make either mince or apple pie for fear of embarrassing himself."

Molly was beginning to smile. "Yes, ma'am. Folks around here have come to expect good wholesome desserts at their parties."

"Your pies are legend, Molly. If you would consent to bake for the affair, I would be very obliged. Do you think you could handle it in addition to your regular duties? I will, of course, compensate you generously, and I'll be glad to get you help if you need it." Devina raised her blue eyes in a plea that broke the last flicker of Molly's resistance.

"Yes, ma'am, I think I can. As a matter of fact, I know I can. My hands just fly through that kind of work."

"Oh, that is a relief. I can't thank you enough." Turning from Molly's smile long enough to pick up her pencil, Devina ran her delicate finger down the menu. "Here they are." She added the desserts to the menu with an elaborate flourish: "Apple pie and mince pie."

Following Molly's ample form with her gaze as the pleased woman walked back to the kitchen, Devina was abruptly turned back to the table by a soft giggle at her side. She glanced into Lai Hua's bright expression.

"Miss Devina, that was very clever. You have soothed Molly's hurt feelings and added immeasurably to the party as well."

Strangely, Devina felt little pride in her small victory. "I wouldn't have had the problem in the first place if I hadn't ignored Molly's feelings so blatantly." Devina raised her shoulders in a shrug. "There are times when I feel I am too much like my father, Lai Hua. Sometimes my own deviousness saddens me."

Lai Hua shook her head in violent protest. "Oh, no, Miss Devina, you are not at all like Mr. Dale. You are a good person. You—"

Her small hand snapping up to cover her lips, Lai Hua halted her sentence abruptly. She lowered her eyes. "I apologize for the unthinking words I have spoken."

Unable to stand her earnest young servant's discomfort, Devina rose to her feet and slid her arm around Lai Hua's shoulders. "Please, don't apologize, Lai Hua, or I'll have to apologize to you again for my father's unforgivable behavior. We'll attempt to forget both. I think that would be the best way to solve the problem."

Lai Hua's eyes rose gratefully to hers, and Devina smiled. She walked back to her chair and sat down, suddenly dispirited. She had been burying herself in plans for the party, but she had been unsuccessful in overcoming the unrest that continued to plague her. She had not been able to shake the sensation of being watched, even after Sam Sharpe and Wally Smith were dismissed. In that aspect, her father's plans had gone awry. The party had not totally distracted her.

Devina raised her gaze to Lai Hua's scrutiny. "There has to be more to this vendetta being waged against Till-Dale than Father is letting on, Lai Hua. What is it all about? Do you know?"

Her questions caught Lai Hua unaware. An emotion that resembled fear flickered momentarily in Lai Hua's eyes before she again dropped her gaze and shook her shining dark head emphatically from side to side. "No, I am sorry, Miss Devina. I—I know nothing."

Lai Hua's eyes were still averted when Devina realized that the maid's slender frame was trembling. Moving immediately to her feet, Devina again slid her arm around Lai Hua's shoulders.

"No, please, Lai Hua. It is I who should apologize. I wasn't accusing you of anything, you know. It's just that I feel so helpless against this undercurrent I'm being forced to live with. If I could only make my father talk to me honestly, without subterfuge."

"I . . . I know nothing, Miss Devina," Lai Hua said once more.

"Lai Hua, please, forget I asked. Let's return to the party plans." Devina picked up a list. "Lai Hua, if you'll read the responses, I'll check them off against this list."

Waiting only until Lai Hua had stepped to the table and picked up the pile of replies, Devina seated herself and again picked up her pencil. She glanced at her servant as Lai Hua finally broke the uneasy silence of the room.

"Mr. and Mrs. Parsons will come."

Devina made the appropriate check, her eyes continuing down the list even as her mind wandered once more. Yes, there was more to this vendetta than was immediately apparent, and Lai Hua knew more than she was presently willing to say. Her father refused to let her into his confidence, and Charles appeared to know less than she about the whole affair. At least that was what she had gathered from the tone of his curious questions of late.

Only one alternative remained: She would have to gain the information by herself. A sudden thought occurred to Devina, returning the smile to her lips. And what better time to converse freely than at a party? Yes, this party might prove useful after all.

Her enthusiasm suddenly returning, Devina looked up and smiled, breaking into Lai Hua's careful recitation.

"You know, I think this party is going to be a very good idea after all, Lai Hua. Very good, indeed."

For the first time, Devina meant it sincerely.

CHAPTER X

ROSS WAS PERSPIRING profusely. Sweat was pouring from under the brim of his battered Stetson, running in shining rivulets down his temples and cheeks as he lay in the hot sun watching for the Till-Dale supply wagon. Unconsciously brushing away the damp paths with the back of his arm, he looked toward Jake, who was lying on a rise directly across the road, surveying the approach from town.

Agitation beginning to temper his concentration, Ross darted a quick glance toward the man beside him. Mack was silent and uncomplaining, but he wasn't faring much better in this damned heat. Sweat glistened on Mack's face and neck, forming a damp pool in the hollow at the base of his throat. His shirt was ringed with perspiration.

Ross twitched with annoyance. If that supply wagon didn't show up soon, the damned payroll guards wouldn't have to see them to know they were lying in wait. They'd smell them.

Squinting against the glare of the brilliant afternoon sun, Ross looked toward the other side of the road where Harry waited, also concealed. Hell, Harry was the lucky one. The rise of ground behind which he was hiding served to shield him from the intense sun.

Ross glanced back toward Jake. The hope that he would signal the approach of the supply wagon grew dimmer by the minute. Ross had been all but certain Jake's Chinese mistress had been truthful about the switch to be made in Benson, but his conclusion had not been based on faith; he had removed that particular word from his vocabulary long ago.

Instead, he had sent Harry into Benson earlier in the day. It hadn't been hard to choose the best man for the job of pretending to be a drunken cowboy recovering from an all-night spree in the alley behind the bank. Harry had that kind of face, sagging and heavily jowled, and his slow, casual manner of speaking was vastly deceiving; no one would suspect he was a quick hand with a gun.

That had been proved by the manner in which Harry had been mentally dismissed by the men dressed in freighters' garb who had pulled their supply wagon to the rear door of the bank just after the first rush of the business day had begun. Had Harry not been alerted to their activities, he had said he doubted he would have given a second thought to the innocent-looking crate those men had carried out of the bank and loaded on the back of the wagon. Those fellows had been smart, all right. They had further backed up their innocuous appearance by making other stops along the street after they left the bank.

But Harry's keen eye had also noted that the guns strapped to those fellows' sides were well tended, polished to a sheen that glinted in the early-morning sunlight, and that the inordinate amount of attention they paid to their surroundings did not quite fit the behavior of casual laborers.

Also, it was too coincidental under the circumstances that while the supply wagon was being unloaded in the rear, Wells Fargo agents were entering the bank through the front entrance. The attention they called to themselves and to the payroll they would collect "to be shipped early the next morning" was also a bit difficult to swallow.

When Harry had related all he had witnessed, Ross had been certain that Jake's information was correct. But several hours had passed since the supply wagon had left the bank. He was damned hot and getting more tired by the minute, and the wagon still had not appeared on the road. He was beginning to believe Harvey Dale had managed to outsmart him.

His mount, tethered in the shade below the crest of the hill, let out a low, nervous snort, breaking into Ross's thoughts. Soothing the horse with a few soft words, he glanced at Jake in time to see him stiffen. Turning with a barely discernible smile, Jake made a hand signal. Ross leaped to his feet and hurried toward his gelding. The supply wagon had come into sight.

Jake was scrambling down the side of the rise toward the position where Harry waited with his horse as Ross mounted and turned a quick, assessing glance toward the surrounding countryside. From his position, it would be easy to see any trap that might be sprung from the opposite direction. No, he and his men were quite alone on this portion of the trail.

Ross's mount made another nervous movement, and a surge of adrenaline moved through Ross's veins. His gelding had sensed the wagon's approach. It would only be a little longer.

Holding himself stiffly erect, Ross pulled his neckerchief up over his face so that it concealed all but his eyes. A quick glance revealed the others had done the same. He turned toward the trail, waiting tensely for the supply wagon to round the curve of the rise, which temporarily hid it from view.

Abruptly, the wagon was within sight.

Ross raised his hand. He paused for long moments until the wagon neared the narrowest portion of the road, where no choice would remain for the driver except to halt or attempt a bolting escape, which would be doomed to failure. Ross brought his hand down in a sudden signal, which started Jake and Harry moving toward the wagon from the opposite side of the trail at the same moment as he.

The man seated beside the driver of the wagon spotted their approach and reached for his rifle. Ross immediately drew his gun and fired a warning shot, which was echoed by Jake's gun. Ross spurred his gelding to a faster pace as the guard glanced toward the guns raised at him from either side.

Relief touched Ross's senses as the driver began reining in his horses and the guard threw his gun into the dust of the trail. He had not yet shot a man in the execution of a robbery. He did not want this to be the first time.

Drawing up alongside the wagon as it pulled to a shuddering halt, Ross issued a gruff command as Jake and Harry drew up on the other side.

"Get down off the wagon, both of you."

As the men scrambled to his bidding, Jake and Harry dismounted and ran to the back of the wagon. In seconds they had discarded the tarp and were working feverishly to unstrap the wooden crate.

His heart pounding, Ross leveled his gun on the two men as Mack dismounted, took several strips of rawhide from his saddle, and secured the wrists and ankles of one of the men.

Suddenly a short exclamation sounded at the rear of the wagon. Ross glanced in Jake's direction. Jubilation sent a hot flush rushing through his veins as he read in Jake's pale eyes exactly the message he had hoped to read. ·

The payroll was theirs!

The guard made a sudden furtive movement toward Mack, and Ross issued a sharp admonition: "Don't try it! You don't have a chance."

Breathing easily only after the second fellow's wrists and ankles were also bound, Ross turned his attention back toward Jake. "Ready?"

"Ready."

Darting a glance toward the two men who lay bound and gagged on the trail beside the wagon, Ross could not suppress a smirk. Now it was their turn to wait in the sun.

When his men had mounted, Ross turned his gelding and spurred him toward a nearby rise of ground, which would conceal the direction of their escape. He did not bother to look back.

His rage barely controlled, Harvey Dale delivered a parting sally as the marshal started to close the front door of the Dale residence behind him. "And you needn't worry that I will come to you for help in catching the payroll thieves in the future. The exercise would be futile. I would not waste my time."

The reverberating slam of the door reflected the lawman's anger as he walked down the front steps without a backward glance. It was a fitting end to the violent exchange that had followed the marshal's solemn announcement only minutes before that another Till-Dale payroll had been lost.

Devina turned toward her father, facing him incredulously in the soundless living room. "Father, whatever possessed you to talk to the marshal that way? That man represents the law in the Arizona Territory. How can you expect to find the men who are robbing—"

"I don't need that damned marshal, Devina! The man is totally incompetent! For all that was said about Marshal Earp, when he rode shotgun on a Wells Fargo box, it got through. Things haven't been the same since he left.''

"Father! You didn't inform the marshal of the covert shipment. You know he had no way to protect—''

"I'll tell you what I know, Devina. I know I don't need a marshal who has the audacity to come here and accuse me of being at fault when he is unable to maintain law and order in his territory! If I need the protection of the law in business matters, I will operate in my usual manner. I'll go to the sheriff. I have him in my pocket. I always have.''

"Father!''

"As for recourse to a higher level, I need only call a few friends in Washington, just as I told that fool a few minutes ago. I have hesitated to do so thus far only because I . . .''

The sound of a step at the doorway made Harvey turn toward Charles's unexpected appearance. The sudden silence was too exaggerated to be natural, and Charles hesitated in obvious discomfort.

"I'm sorry if I've interrupted something. I knocked, and Molly let me in. I assumed she had your permission.''

Not able to bear Charles's discomfort, Devina moved quickly to his side.

"Please, don't apologize, Charles. Father's upset. We're both upset. The marshal just told us that the thieves have stolen another payroll.''

"Another payroll?'' Charles's eyes became instantly intent. His expression changed him in a way that sent chills of discomfort down Devina's spine, and she took a spontaneous step backward. His eyes were so different without their friendly warmth.

But Charles was no longer addressing her in friendly interest. His next statement was unhesitant, directed to her father: "The payroll wasn't supposed to arrive until tomorrow . . . on the stage.''

Harvey's eyes narrowed into a surprised, assessing squint.

"I hadn't realized you kept such close tabs on the timing of my payroll shipments, Charles.''

Charles shrugged. "Everyone in town keeps tabs on the dates of your shipments now, Harvey. It's gotten to the point where wagers are being made as to whether or not the next payroll will get through.''

Harvey's nostrils flared in suppressed anger. "Well, this time it appears I fooled everyone except the thieves. The payroll was shipped today, covertly, in a supply wagon. The ploy obviously did not work."

"Was it the same men? Did anyone get a description?"

Harvey frowned. "I dislike being questioned, Charles, especially by someone who does not have a legitimate interest in my affairs."

"Father!" Her anger rising, Devina shot Charles a short apologetic glance. "Charles does have a legitimate interest in your affairs. It is the interest of a friend."

"Devina, Charles and I were merely acquaintances before your arrival in this town. We did not maintain anything other than a casual, passing relationship."

"Well, Father, if you will not claim Charles as a friend, I certainly shall." Slipping her arm through Charles's, Devina faced her father stiffly. "And as my friend, Charles has a natural interest in our problems."

Her challenge not having the effect she expected, Devina watched as Harvey paused. His eyes moved from her to Charles and back again. "I suppose you're right, Devina." Harvey turned to Charles, his glance direct. "I'm pleased to hear that Devina considers you her friend, Charles. She needs friends. But if you'll excuse me, I'd like to go and speak to George now. I think it's time we developed a different tack in fighting these thieves."

"So it *was* the same men."

Annoyance flicked once more across Harvey's brow. "Yes, it appears it was the same men. The marshal said there were four of them. They fit the description of the men who committed the other robberies. Does that satisfy your curiosity?"

Charles gave a short laugh. "Yes, it does."

Suffering a strange sense of anxiety at her father's words, Devina questioned hesitantly, "What do you mean by a different tack? Were you serious about employing the Pinkerton Detective Agency, Father?"

"The Pinkertons!" Charles's exclamation was sharp. "Do you think that's necessary?"

Charles's question appearing to push him to full anger once more, Harvey answered sharply, "Whether it is necessary or not, I will be the judge of that, Charles. And I will suffer neither your inquisition nor your advice. I hope that is understood.''

Charles's expression tightened. ''Perfectly, sir.''

''And now, if you'll both excuse me.''

Pausing as he was about to step away, Harvey cast a short glance toward the sheets of paper lying on the table beside his cup. He frowned, obviously remembering that prior to the marshal's arrival, he and Devina had been discussing the seating of their guests for the party scheduled to take place in less than a week.

''As for the party, whatever you decide will be all right with me, Devina. I trust your judgment implicitly.''

The absurdity of continuing with the affair at a time when her father's business was suffering severe losses brought a spontaneous objection from Devina's lips. ''Oh, Father, let's forget the party, shall we?''

Harvey's expression tightened to severity. ''Definitely not! I will not allow common thieves to intimidate or discomfort me in any way. We will have the party, Devina, and it'll be the most extravagant and memorable party Tombstone has ever seen!''

Turning without another word, Havey walked rigidly from the room. Staring after her father in silence, Devina finally raised her gaze to see Charles staring at her with concern.

Silently, she stepped into the comfort of his arms.

Camille stood unmoving in the middle of her room. She paused, listening to the silence, then gave a short laugh. This room was as quiet as it had ever been, but it was not truly silent at all. Sounds seemed to penetrate the walls in a way they never did when she was busy entertaining a client. She heart Giselle's low giggle, Yvonne's coaxing coo. Now and again she heard masculine voices in response, but they were muffled.

She wondered what sounds Giselle and Yvonne heard when she entertained. But she wondered only briefly. That part of her life was separate and apart from the person she truly was. She had long ago rationalized her vocation in her mind. She performed a service just as a chef cooked a meal, a doctor healed the sick, a maid cleaned a room. Except that she truly strove to impart a measure of happiness. For the most part, she felt she was successful in her efforts. Many had told her so. The only problem was, she no longer received happiness in return.

The day was warm, portending a long, uncomfortable night, and Camille took a step closer to the window and looked outside. Her favored position in Marie's establishment had given her the option of choosing the room she wanted from those vacated when the last group of girls had returned to Paris. Le Comte had told her she had earned that privilege, and she had been extremely flattered.

Camille rotated slowly on her heel, allowing her eyes to survey the room she had decorated so carefully so that it might reflect a part of herself. Bright flowered curtains hung at the windows. A matching comforter lay folded at the foot of her broad, comfortable bed, and a fine hemmed cloth of a contrasting hue covered the table beside it. The lamp on that table was hand-painted with delicate flowers on the base and on the glass chimney that shielded the flame; when the lamp was lit, the flowers appeared to move in a gay lilting dance. Lovely, ruffled pillows in pastel shades lay in careful disarray on the chaise beside the bed, and on the fine dresser in the corner were carefully displayed the likenesses of her five sisters and two brothers.

The room she had chosen was on the second floor, with a view of Allen Street. The reason for her choice had been simple: this room allowed her to watch for Charles when he emerged onto Allen after walking from his quarters on Fourth Street. His schedule was a trifle erratic, but she knew the approximate time he was free at night and when he was most likely to be walking in her direction.

She loved watching Charles walk. He was so handsome with his black, thick hair, his very masculine face, and dark, caring eyes. He was so tall, and he carried himself so well. He walked with an easy stride that bespoke fine coordination and a healthy body. Camille could speak from experience that his was truly an unusually beautiful body. It was by far the most beautiful she had ever seen. He was magnificent, and she loved the love that flowed from his magnificent body into hers. It made her feel beautiful. She did not always feel beautiful, and as many times as she had been told that she was, she knew it was not really true.

Pierre had told her many times that her zest for life made those around her feel more alive. She supposed the innate happiness that was a part of her makeup, the instinctive delight with which she started each day, endowed her with beauty in the eyes of others. If that was true, that beauty was rapidly fading, for in recent days, her instinctive capacity for joy appeared to have eluded her.

The reason for her despair was simple. She had not seen Charles in more than a week.

Camille amended that thought with a small unhappy laugh. She had *seen* Charles several times. She had seen him walking on the street with a friend. She had seen him going into the general store, and she had seen him with Devina Dale . . . which was worse than not having seen him at all.

Camille turned abruptly from the window and walked to the mirror over the dresser. She stood before it and appraised herself critically . . . very pretty hair, but not as pretty as Devina Dale's. Pleasant features, but not classically beautiful like Miss Dale's. As for the rest of her, she was too tall, too full breasted, too voluptuous beside Devina Dale's petite proportions.

Camille continued to stare at her reflection, her despair seeping away as a new thought began to take shape in her mind. Devina Dale was far more beautiful than she, but she had something that Miss Dale did not. She possessed a heart full of love to give Charles Carter.

A spark lit the depths of her eyes, and Camille's full lips began to curve into a smile. Taking only a moment to tuck a flaming errant curl back into her upswept coiffure and to assess the acceptability of her pale yellow cotton gown, she turned and stepped rapidly toward the door of her room. Within moments she was walking down the staircase toward the first floor and Marie's large bedroom at the rear of the house.

Camille emerged from Marie's room minutes later, her cheeks flushed with anger. She pulled the door tightly shut behind her and took a deep breath. With a measured step, she walked directly to the small office beside the staircase. She paused only a moment to gain full control of her emotions before raising her hand and knocking lightly.

The Count's voice responded from within, and Camille opened the door and entered. She emerged a short time later, her smile genuine, her manner relaxed. She turned to bid Le Comte good-bye with true affection and then stepped into the

hallway, halting sharply as she unexpectedly came face to face
with Marie.

Refusing to flinch under the hatred displayed so openly in
Marie's livid expression, Camille returned her stare.

Pierre's voice sounded over her shoulder, causing Marie's
cheek to tic revealingly. "Marie, you will come in here for a
moment, *s'il vous plaît*."

Camille remained still as Marie walked past her into the office
and closed the door behind her. Dismissing Marie's venomous
stare from her mind, Camille ascended the staircase in a light,
eager step.

Life was good again! She had been given permission to bring
a gift to a friend.

Lai Hua ran along the winding, narrow trail, her small feet all
but flying. The lantern she clutched in her hand was lit against
the darkness that swirled around her, but Lai Hua had little fear.
In her hand she carried the strip of red ribbon she had found tied
to a bush beside the path she took each morning on her way to
the Dale home.

She always took the long, circuitous route around the back of
the Oriental section of town where she made her home, past the
outlying buildings of Tombstone. She had traveled that path each
day for the past year.

Her reasons for traveling that path were twofold. She took to
an old woman who lived near that point a portion of the bounty
from her family's table. The old woman depended on her daily
visit for sustenance. The second reason had brought her joys far
more rewarding than an old woman's grateful smile. But for the
past few weeks, those joys had been nil, and she had experienced
only sadness.

Lai Hua clutched the red ribbon tighter as the dilapidated
miner's shack came into view in the darkness. Not taking time
for her usual caution, she ran directly toward it. Her eagerness
did not allow her to see the shadow that hovered at the side of
the building, waiting for her to walk past. She was about to run
to the door when arms reached out, snatching her off her feet.

Gasping, Lai Hua fought the arms that held her captive. She
struggled, twisting and turning, attempting to strike at her captor's shadowed face. She had all but broken free in her frenzy

when a warmly familiar voice sounded in her ear, shocking her into stillness.

"Lai Hua, stop! It's me . . . Jake."

"Mr. Jake . . ." Lai Hua was suddenly motionless. "But why did you frighten me so? Why did you not wait inside the cabin?"

"I thought it would be better to wait outside."

Lai Hua strained to assess Jake's expression. "And now that I am here?"

"Now that you're here, we'll go inside, Lai Hua."

Lai Hua's heart thundered with happiness as Jake led her inside the shack they had shared many times before. A small gasp escaped her lips as he drew her roughly into his arms. She felt the pressure of his lips against hers, the hard strength of his body, the firm rise of his aroused passion, and she gloried in it. She allowed Jake to unfold the light blanket she had hidden under her short jacket and to lay it on the floor. Moments later she was lying beside him. She gasped for breath as he worked feverishly to free the buttons on her cotton garment. She met him eagerly, so very eagerly.

A short time later, silence reigned in the wake of shared passion. Her true love's body had been sated, and he still held her close. But there was no peace in his embrace. Jake's uneasiness transmitted itself to her so strongly that Lai Hua drew back to pose a soft question. "You are not happy, Mr. Jake. Did I not please you tonight?"

The pale eyes returning her questioning stare moved over her face, lingering on her cheek, the line of her chin, resting so warmly on her lips that she almost felt their touch. But Jake continued to frown.

"Oh, yes, you pleased me tonight, Lai Hua. Until this night, I didn't realize how much you please me."

Lai Hua shook her head in obvious confusion. "Mr. Jake, I do not understand."

His frown darkened.

"I've asked you not to call me Mr. Jake, Lai Hua. Now I'm askin' you again. My name is Jake . . . just Jake."

"Oh, but I could not . . ."

"Why? We've just finished making love. You're lying here naked in my arms, and you're tellin' me you can't call me by my given name?"

Lai Hua hesitated. Her eyes held his for silent seconds before she responded with a brief nod. "Yes, that is so."

The pale-complexioned face so close to hers reddened and stiffened with anger. "That doesn't make any sense, Lai Hua." His anger still apparent, Jake was about to speak again when Lai Hua pressed gentle fingers over his lips in a plea for silence.

"Please, Mr. Jake. You must try to understand. My father and I . . . my people are foreigners in your land. We came here as poor immigrants, and as such we do menial work that many of your own people would not deign to do."

"That doesn't mean anythin', Lai Hua. That—"

"Please . . ." Waiting until Jake was silent once more, Lai Hua continued softly. "Here, in this place where we live, you would be looked upon poorly if our association were known. Men would ridicule you, and women would turn away from you. You would suffer in their eyes because you find enjoyment in my body."

Jake's protest was spontaneous. "Lai Hua, it's not only your body I enjoy."

"Please, Mr. Jake. Allow me to continue." Waiting only until Jake was again silent, Lai Hua continued intently. "This harshness, this separation marked by the color of our skin is not confined to your people alone. My people are poor, but their pride is great. They would see in my love for you a betrayal of all that I am. My father would look upon me with anger, and he would feel great shame."

Unable to dispute the truth in Lai Hua's candid statement, Jake attempted a smile.

"But there's no one here to hear you when you say my name, Lai Hua. You're not my servant. If a separation exists between us outside this cabin, I want there to be none when you're in my arms."

A bittersweet pain touched her heart as Lai Hua looked into the face of the man she loved, but she could not relent in the face of a truth so deeply ingrained within her. Her response was a soft plea. "You must allow me this formality, Mr. Jake. It is a small concession I make to the world outside this place. It allows me to maintain my touch with the person I am, and to acknowledge your superior position in the world in which we live. My feelings for you are such that I would not demean you, even in our most private moments by treating you as less than you are."

A low scoffing sound escaped the lips so close to hers. "Less than I am. I'm an ex-convict, Lai Hua, and no matter how much I rationalize the payroll robberies in my mind, I'm a thief."

Raising her hand, Lai Hua traced the fine freckles that dusted the clear skin of Jake's cheek. "You are the man I love."

Lai Hua's simple declaration was met with silence, and she continued with an instinctive insight. "But it is not my manner of addressing you that is the true source of your discomfort this night, Mr. Jake. Although our bodies have responded to the joy we experience in each other, I can sense your tension. Something is wrong."

"Yes, somethin's wrong."

Lai Hua's heart fluttered as Jake slid his fingers through the silky hair at her temples. How very much she loved his touch. It made her heart sing. But he was frowning. His light brows were drawn together in a straight line, and his lips were tight as he continued to speak.

"I didn't want to come here tonight, Lai Hua. I had made up my mind I wasn't goin' to see you again. But the truth was, I couldn't make myself stay away any longer."

The pain Jake's words caused Lai Hua was intense. She had known he did not intend to see her again.

Jake gave a low, self-contemptuous laugh. "After I left you the last time, I was afraid to trust you. Somethin' seemed wrong, like you were hidin' somethin' from me. You made me doubt you, and I kept rememberin' the last time I trusted a woman who said she loved me."

Lai Hua's eyes grew moist as she read the torment on his face. "You still doubt me, do you not, Mr. Jake? Even as you tied the red ribbon to the bush, calling me to you again, you did not trust me. You would not enter this place to wait for me for fear of being overwhelmed by those I might have brought with me, is that not true?"

"Yes."

Lai Hua took a deep breath, realizing all she stood to lose in losing this man. "And now, Mr. Jake?"

"Now, Lai Hua? Now I realize it makes little difference how I think, because it's how I feel that rules my mind. I feel bad . . . real bad without you, Lai Hua, and when I'm with you I feel real good. I made a choice before I tied that ribbon. I decided that if I risked my life by askin' you to meet me here tonight, it would be worth it.''

Tears choked Lai Hua's throat. Mr. Jake refused to speak the words she so wished to hear, but his heart was in his eyes. Her own heart bursting with her love for this man, Lai Hua slid her arms around his neck.

"I will teach you to trust me again, Mr. Jake. I will show you that I will never put another before you in my mind or in my heart.''

Jake made no response except to pull Lai Hua again into his embrace. A soft sigh of joy escaped her lips as their flesh met, and Lai Hua gave herself to him, striving to erase with their joining the doubts that lay between them and the pain of the knowledge, silently confirmed within her mind, that this was all there would ever be.

Within the hour they parted, and Lai Hua drew herself from Jake's embrace with reluctance. His reluctance to part as strong as hers, Jake touched her arm, staying her as she attempted to move toward the door of the cabin. "Saturday, Lai Hua . . . I'll be here as soon as it's dark.''

Lai Hua turned with a frown. "No, I cannot meet you.''

Jake's instinctive stiffening was all too revealing.

"No, Mr. Jake. You must not think I do not wish to meet you. There is no place I would rather be than in your arms.''

Jake was not appeased. "What is it, then?''

"A party. Mr. Dale and Miss Devina are giving a party. It is to be a very big affair, and many people will attend. Miss Devina has hired others to help serve, but she has put me in charge of directing those who are new to the house and unfamiliar with her plans.''

"A party?'' Jake gave a sudden incredulous laugh. "That's a real joke. Ross had the feelin' he was gettin' Dale worried, especially with this last robbery, but it looks like that damned fool Dale is celebratin' losin' another payroll!''

Lai Hua shook her head. "No, Mr. Dale was very angry about this most recent robbery, but he said he would not allow the thieves to think that they had intimidated him.''

Jake's youthful face broke into a full smile. "Well, that's more like it.'' He reached out, his hand cupping Lai Hua's slender neck to draw her mouth up to his. "We'll let Mr. Dale have his party, then. He'd better enjoy it, 'cause if Ross has anythin' to say about things, it'll be the only enjoyment Dale will have for a while.''

His expression suddenly serious, Jake brushed Lai Hua's mouth lightly with his. "All right, Lai Hua." Taking the red ribbon Lai Hua had returned to him from his pocket, he held it close to her cheek. "Be on the lookout for this. You'll be seein' it soon."

"And I will be waiting, Mr. Jake."

Turning, Lai Hua moved quickly through the doorway toward the trail. A sudden movement in the darkness caused her to miss her step, and she gasped. At her side in moments, Jake drew his gun. Taking the lantern from Lai Hua with his other hand, he held it high to scan the surrounding shadows.

Lai Hua stood beside him in silence. She was trembling. She was not certain what she had seen, but she had seen something. She was still trembling when Jake again turned in her direction.

"I don't see anythin', Lai Hua. I'm thinkin' it was some small animal out on a night prowl."

A chill moved down Lai Hua's spine, and she swallowed tightly. Unwilling to show her sudden, inexplicable fear, Lai Hua attempted a smile.

"Perhaps, Mr. Jake."

Lai Hua attempted to take the lantern from Jake's hand, but he refused to relinquish it as he slipped his arm around her shoulders.

"No, darlin'. I'll walk part of the way back with you." Lai Hua's protest was spontaneous. "No, you must not. It is too dangerous."

Jake's eyes flamed in the spill of light from the lantern. "I told you, Lai Hua. I've made up my mind that you're worth the risk . . . any risk."

Lai Hua's throat was too choked to allow response. She could do no more than lean lightly against Jake's side as he tightened his arm around her narrow shoulders and urged her onto the trail.

Only after Jake and Lai Hua had slipped out of sight on the trail did the shadow concealed in the darkness again chance a move. They did not see the tense frustration that marked the dark figure's posture as it paused in indecision. They did not hear the angry hiss that escaped its lips when it turned at last to slip into the darkness from whence it had come.

• • • •

Charles had been writing for an hour, and his hand was getting cramped. Sitting back abruptly in his chair, he took a deep breath and stretched both arms over his head, clenching and unclenching his right hand in an effort to restore its mobility. Damn, that's what he got for putting off his paperwork for so long. But he had been too preoccupied of late to attend to details.

Charles checked the folders on his desk. He had updated eight of his patients' files, and he was caught up for now. At least that was one concern off his mind.

His preoccupation of the last week was dangerous. Realizing the need to stay close to the Dale household if he was to learn anything new about the payroll thieves, Charles had made certain to see Devina at least once a day. The combination of their new familiarity and his strange unrest had found him close, in far too many occasions, to an unwise word or action, which could have caused Devina to become suspicious of his true reason for cultivating her interest.

As far as he had been able to ascertain, however, Harvey Dale had not yet hired the Pinkerton Detective Agency, as he had threatened. Damn, that would be a disaster. He had to find a way to discourage that move, to make sure that Harvey . . .

An unexpected knock at the door interrupted Charles's train of thought, and he frowned. His eyes darted to the clock on his desk, and his frown darkened. It was too late for a casual caller. He hurried to the door. It could not be Charlie Rigger. It wasn't Lucille's time yet.

His anxiety escalating as he slipped the latch, Charles pulled open the door. His breath escaped his lips in surprise. "Camille, what are you doing here this time of night?"

"Charles, I have come to see you, of course."

Charles gave a short laugh, his spirits greatly revived by the sight of Camille's full-blown charms. His eyes lingered for a moment on the brilliance of her hair, alive in the subdued glow of gas streetlamps; the teasing flicker in her warm brown eyes; the incredible glow of her smile. His gaze surveyed the sheer black gown she wore as she allowed her shawl to slip from her shoulders. The dress was lined in a soft peach that almost matched the womanly flesh exposed above the daring neckline.

"Camille, you look enticingly lovely . . . and very healthy. I hope this visit does not mean you feel unwell."

Camille's low laugh was as heady as a kiss, and Charles fought to subdue the instinctive reaction of his body. His eyes dropped to Camille's lips as a familiar hunger came alive inside him.

"*Non, mon cher*, my visit here tonight is not of a professional nature, for either you or myself." Charles stepped back to allow her entrance, and Camille walked past him, pausing as Charles closed the door behind them. She turned to look up into his eyes. Her smile was direct.

"I hope you do not have plans, Charles, because I came here with the intention of spending the evening with you."

Charles's response reflected his surprise. "Marie . . . she doesn't object to your being here? It's not like her to be generous with her girls' time."

In a few silent steps Camille was standing very close. Charles could feel the heat emanating from her warm flesh, and his heart began an escalated beat. In a few more minutes he would no longer be interested in talking.

Camille's voice was a low purr, calculated to raise his already considerable level of physical agitation.

"*Oui, mon coeur*, Marie will face many disappointed clients, but I care little. I have gained special permission from Le Comte to absent myself. I told him I wished to bring you your birthday gift."

Charles's fleeting discomfort at the mention of the Count slipped from his mind. He hesitated. "It isn't my birthday, Camille."

Camille's eyes widened in exaggerated surprise. "Ah, so! *Pardonnez-moi*. I have made an error!" Raising her arms, she slid them around his neck, her voice breathy against his parted lips. "But perhaps, *mon cher*, since I am already here . . . perhaps we can pretend that it is."

Camille's lips were moving persuasively against his, and Charles submitted to their erotic coercion. His heart began pounding, the familiar taste of Camille filling him with a desire for more. His arms slipped around her, crushing her loving warmth against him. His hand moved to cup her firm buttocks, fitting her intimately against the responsive swell of his body. When he spoke at last, his voice was a husky whisper. "Yes, Camille, we'll pretend, and we'll enjoy."

Within moments Charles was no longer thinking. He was just feeling and enjoying. And it felt very good.

The lights from the street shone through a corner of the window shade, allowing a narrow strip of light to penetrate the darkness. Camille lay quietly beside Charles, the man to whom she had given her heart as well as her body. She listened to his slow, even breathing in sleep, delighting in the knowledge that this night, at least, she would sleep beside him and awaken in his arms.

Contentment . . . no, happiness sang within her heart, and she turned toward him, lifting herself on her elbow so she could see his face. She stared at the outline of his strong features, memorizing the lines shadowed by the darkness of the room. She pressed her lips lightly against his and whispered into his unhearing ear.

"*Bon anniversaire* . . . happy birthday, *ma vie*, with all my love."

Charles turned toward her in his sleep, and Camille lowered her head to the pillow once more. She shifted her position, curling her body into the hard, muscular curve of his. Charles's arm moved around her, drawing her against him tightly, even in sleep, and Camille's joy knew no bounds. Charles's hand touched her breast, and she covered it with her own.

"And happy birthday to me . . . a very, very happy birthday."

The light of morning was bright against Charles's eyelids as the last veils of sleep slipped away. He fought awakening momentarily, unwilling to stir from the pale nether world of contentment in which he languished. He reached out, a frown touching his handsome face. The bed beside him was empty, and his eyes snapped abruptly open to scan the room. Disappointment rang hollowly inside him. Where had she gone? The bed linens were still warm from her body, rich with her scent. She could not have left more than a few minutes ago.

Charles's hand moved to the pillow beside him, encountering a slip of paper protruding from beneath its plump softness. He read the words, precisely written with a foreign flavor so reminiscent of Camille herself:

Charles,

As I write this letter, you are sleeping with such contentment that I have not the heart to awaken you. Do I
presume too much, *mon cher*, to believe I am much responsible for the smile which hovers about your mouth,
even in sleep? I do not believe so, for the same smile curves
my lips as well.

I must leave now and begin the work of a new day, but
my thoughts remain with you, as always.

Au revoir for now, *ma vie*.

Camille

Still holding the note, Charles stared at the careful script. He
could almost hear Camille's low, throaty voice speaking the
words. His body, so completely sated during the long night,
reacted predictably, and he gave a low snort. He raised the paper
to his nostrils and breathed in its fragrance. How was it possible
that this sheet, taken from his own desk, carried Camille's
distinctive scent? Or was it just that his heart and mind were still
so filled with the beauty of all that was Camille that he just
believed it to be so?

Slowly lowering the note to the bed beside him, Charles
reluctantly stood up. The smile, which had indeed been hovering
about his mouth, broadened as Charles stretched his naked length.
God, he felt good! He felt warm, happy, satisfied in so many
ways. It was always that way when he was with Camille.

Charles's smile slowly vanished. He walked to the washstand
and met his own reflection in the mirror. It was when he was
apart from Camille that his unrest began.

He was uncertain just when the thought of Camille's other
"clients" had begun to bother him. In his own mind, he no
longer classed himself in that category. It was with considerable
joy the previous night that he had realized Camille's appearance
at his door was proof that she, also, did not think of him entirely
in that way. He remembered her whispered declaration that she
had missed him. The heat of that memory tugged insistently at
his groin. He had missed her as well, but a strange resentment
had been growing inside him.

Abruptly shrugging aside his uncomfortable thoughts, Charles
reached for the pitcher and splashed water into the washbowl. He

glanced at the clock on his desk. It was still early. He doubted Camille had yet had time for breakfast. He would shave quickly and dress, and then he would go to Blond Marie's and pick up Camille. They'd go to the Maison Doree for breakfast, and they'd talk. He suddenly realized how very much he wanted to say to her.

A few minutes later, Charles stepped out onto the sidewalk. He took a deep breath, savoring the sweet, warm air of morning, and headed for Allen Street. The sun shone on the broad brim of his Stetson and warmed the shoulders of his well-tailored suit as he quickened his pace. He was anxious to talk to Camille, to feel the warmth of those loving brown eyes on his face. He wanted to hold her full, lush body in his arms, to hear her husky whisper against his lips.

Charles turned onto the main thoroughfare, only to have his warm thoughts brought to an abrupt halt by the sight that met his eyes. Standing unseen behind a large sidewalk sign, Charles felt all joy and life drain out of him at the sight of the happy, laughing couple walking briskly on the opposite side of the street. Camille and the Count. Camille was a vibrant splash of color against the backdrop of the commercial establishments as she walked happily on the arm of the procurer who had brought her to Tombstone, dressed in a gown and hat of startling pink. She was speaking rapidly in her native tongue, looking up into the Count's smiling face, and Charles saw in her expression a true, undeniable warmth.

A hot, searing emotion flushed through Charles, turning his hard body rigid, balling his hands into fists. He was suddenly shaking, filled with a desire to pound the leering gaze from the Count's aristocratic face, to rip his hands from Camille's soft flesh, to drag Camille back with him to his quarters where he would have her to himself. Breathing heavily, he took a step forward, only to bring his angry advance to a premature halt as full realization struck him for the first time.

Jealous . . . he was jealous of the Count! That had been the reason behind his unacknowledged decision to stay away from her during the past week. He had unconsciously realized the growing depth of his feelings for Camille, and the danger of such feelings. Was that the reason he felt no more than a friendly

affection for Devina Dale, despite her beauty and obviously
warm regard for him?

Unable to draw his eyes from the sway of Camille's generous
curves as she continued a gay conversation with the Count,
Charles felt the knot in his stomach squeeze into pain. What was
the true nature of his feelings for the generous, warmhearted
woman who made his heart sing?

Suddenly unable to face the answer to that question, Charles
turned and walked back toward his office. Whatever those feelings were, they were unwise, crazy, and they needed to be
controlled. He would control them. He did not need this problem
added to the many already crowding his mind.

Within minutes, Charles was back in his office, determined to
begin his workday early. He no longer had the slightest desire
for breakfast. The raging appetite with which he had awakened
had been banished by the sight of the happy couple striding
down Allen Street, by the Count's indulgent expression, but
most of all by Camille's radiant smile.

Ross spurred his gelding to a faster pace. He was hot and
tired. He had spent the long day with his spyglass, lying on his
stomach on a hill outside Tombstone, as he had almost every day
for three weeks. Or was it longer? He was uncertain at this point
in time. The only thing of which he was certain was that he
would not have patience to continue this surveillance of Devina
Dale much longer.

Ross lifted his hat and ran his hand through his hair. It was
damp with sweat like the rest of him, but the cool air of evening
felt good against his scalp. Replacing his hat, Ross felt a strange
desolation begin to overwhelm him.

Damn, what was wrong with him? He had been successful in
taking a large Till-Dale payroll just a few days ago. There was
no doubt that Dale was approaching financial difficulty now. He
had heard Dale's miners were tense and accidents were beginning to happen.

He had also heard water was pouring into the mines at a far
more rapid pace than Dale's pumps could remove it. It appeared
Dale's luck was beginning to turn, and he was extremely glad
that he had had a hand in turning it.

Ross's lips tightened into a firm, hard line. But the pinch Dale was feeling wasn't enough to satisfy him. Nothing seemed to satisfy him now, and he knew nothing would until he managed to turn the tide completely against Dale. He knew how to manage that, but Dale had been one step ahead of him there. In the three weeks he had been watching Devina Dale, he had been unable to ascertain any particular time of day when she was consistently vulnerable . . . consistently enough so that he could form a definite plan for her abduction.

A familiar tension tightened the back of his neck, and Ross's frown deepened. There had to be a way. He was so close.

Ross took a deep breath and attempted to draw his emotions under control. He realized fully that the haughty little witch with the face of an angel was fast becoming an obsession with him. He was at the point now where his thoughts were seldom free of her. It occurred to him that he would not be free until he finished what he had started that first day in the stagecoach, when his initial glimpse of her had so unsettled him.

Turning his mount sharply, Ross guided him onto the narrow trail to his hideout. He flexed the tight muscles in his shoulders and back. He was tired, tired of everything, and most of all, he was tired of the man he had become. But Harvey Dale had had a very strong hand in helping him to become that man, and it was only fair that he should be the one to suffer for it.

His mount was lagging, and Ross pressed his spurs lightly into the animal's sides. The cabin was coming into sight and Ross was anxious to get the dust of the trail off his body and a warm meal in his stomach.

Ross was dismounting at last when a sound made him turn toward the cabin. He gave a short laugh.

"So, you made it back, Jake." Ross eyed his friend with an assessing gaze. "I don't have to ask you where you've been. This is the first time I've seen you without a frown on your face for a week."

"That so, Ross? When it comes to frownin', I kinda think that's the pot callin' the kettle black."

Ross chose to ignore Jake's retort. "I thought you said you weren't going to see that girl anymore."

"Yeah, I suppose I said that."

Ross gave a low snort. "Well, I guess there's no use in making yourself suffer. Everything she told you was true."

"I suppose."

Ross took only a moment to judge his friend's response. Jake still had reservations about the girl, but he couldn't stay away from her. Hell, the poor bastard was really in a fix.

Ross walked into the cabin, straight toward the fire and the coffeepot that hung over it. Damn, it had been a long day. He poured himself a cup, grateful that Harry and Mack had had the foresight to fill it before they took off. He drank deep and long before he spoke again. "Well, I'm glad to see that little girl took care of you, Jake."

"Yeah, that she did. And she told me somethin' that'll give you a good laugh, too."

"A good laugh?"

"Yeah. She told me about the party Dale's plannin'."

Startled, Ross slowly lowered his cup. "Dale's planning a party?"

"Yeah, on Saturday night. Can you beat that? Lai Hua says it's really just for show. He doesn't want to give us the satisfaction of thinkin' he's worried about the robberies. She says it's goin' to be the biggest damned party Tombstone has ever seen. Dale's hired all kinds of help, and just about everybody who means anythin' in Tombstone is goin'."

Ross could feel the adrenaline pulsing through his veins. His heart was beginning to pound.

"I suppose that means there'll be all kinds of commotion, with people walking in and out of the house, and strolling in that big, beautiful garden he went to such pains to put in."

"I suppose . . ."

"And do you suppose Charles Carter is invited to the party?"

Jake was beginning to frown again. "Yeah, I suppose Carter'll be there. You know damned well he's sweet on the Dale girl. You told me yourself he's been there almost every day for the last week."

"So I suppose we can depend on him being there . . ."

Jake took an anxious step forward. "Ross, you aren't thinkin' what I think you're thinkin' . . ."

Suddenly Ross was no longer frowning. The harsh lines of his face were lifting into a smile, the creases deepening into the incongruous dimples that erased years from the sharp contours of his face. He was laughing. Damn, he hadn't felt this good in a long time.

"Ross . . ."

Bringing his laughter under control, Ross clamped a strong hand on Jake's shoulder. "How would you like to go to a party, Jake?"

"Ross, you're crazy! You'll never get away with it!"

But Ross wasn't listening. His mind was moving far ahead to Saturday night and the fun he was going to have. Damn, he could hardly wait.

CHAPTER XI

HARVEY STOOD STARING out the window of his office. His expression was livid, his body was rigid, and his hands were clenched into tight fists. He would not take much more of this.

He stared intently at the tall, slender Oriental woman walking gracefully along the street. He watched as she carefully made her way past the men who lounged outside Hafford's Saloon, the Maison Doree, the Occidental Saloon. He saw the way the men looked at her, their eyes following the delicate lines of her body. He could not hear what they said, but he saw their snickers as Lily walked, her exotically beautiful face averted from their stares. She continued on past Hatch Bill's Saloon, the Alhambra. The comments continued, and Harvey felt the blood rushing to his face. Damn the bitch, she was pushing him too far!

Harvey turned away from the window and took two angry steps toward the door of his office before halting. No, that was what she wanted. She knew how possessive he was of her, how parading herself in front of those lascivious men would drive him wild. She wanted to push him into unwise behavior so that she might smile so delicately and pretend innocence when he confronted her. Oh, she was a clever bitch, all right.

He had deliberately stayed away from Lily since the day he had found Devina in China Mary's store. He knew nothing had been revealed to Devina—neither China Mary nor Lily would dare go that far—but he had not forgotten the knowing look on Lily's face just before he walked away. She knew how hard it

182

had been for him to walk away from her, despite his fury. And she was not content to let matters lie.

It was a subtle war Lily waged. He had no doubt she was coached in her strategy by her clever mother. He had thought to teach both women a lesson by pretending to ignore Lily for a while before he returned unexpectedly and casually climbed that curved staircase once more, but his strategy had obviously been as ineffective as his plans to catch the payroll thieves.

Lily was so clever. In her subtle way she had proved to him that he was not so much the master of the situation as he would prefer to believe. Each day for the past week she had taunted him with her beauty by parading past his window and by exposing herself to the remarks of saddle tramps not fit to touch the hem of her magnificent silk garments.

It galled him to realize that his own weakness for Lily gave her power over him. It galled him even more that Lily was so aware of his weakness. But he ached to hold her. If he did not know it would give Lily the satisfaction she sought, he would stride across the street and tear her away from the lecherous gazes following her. He would then march her to the room they had shared so many times before and take her with all the passion now flooding through his trembling limbs.

Yes, it was a subtle war, and Lily was fast winning the battles. Damn, he had not truly realized what he was doing when he had taken her as his secret mistress. He had not realized she would get into his blood so completely that he would be forced to remind himself at each encounter between them that she was of a race inferior to his, that to declare his relationship to her openly would be to demean himself and all he stood for.

He knew Lily did not want him to openly claim her. She just wanted him to know that the tables were beginning to turn, that the master was being mastered, and being mastered so very well.

Harvey took a deep, shuddering breath. Lily . . . Lily . . . In his unending struggle to subdue her will, he seemed to take one step forward and two steps back. In the back of his mind was the growing doubt he would emerge the victor.

Taking care to avoid glancing out the window, which he knew would only increase his torment, he returned to his desk and sat down heavily. With a shaking hand he reached for the folders in the basket and opened the top one. Yes, the newest diagrams of the flooded shafts. He needed to review them and make a

decision. A decision . . . when his mind was presently filled
with one thought and one alone.

Lily.

On the day of the party the weather was perfect. Devina took a
last glimpse out the window of her room as the setting sun
tempered the misty blue of the Dragoons with reflected color. The
air was clear and pleasantly warm. It would be ideal for the
casual outdoor buffet she had finally decided upon. A formal
table setting, considering the size of the guest list, would have
become too complicated. Instead, the small tables she had set up
on the porches and patio and the house would be ideal. The
buffet would also allow her to have an outdoor area cleared after
dinner, should her guests be inclined to dance.

Devina mentally checked her arrangements.

The chef was putting the finishing touches on dishes that
promised to surpass even her expectations for culinary excellence.

The sounds emanating from the living room below told her
that the musicians had arrived on time. They were tuning their
instruments so they might greet her guests with musical selec-
tions she herself had chosen.

Lai Hua had informed her that the pièce de résistance had
secretly been set up on the vacant patch of land beyond the
garden, according to her instructions. Later in the evening, when
her guests were beginning to believe they had seen the best of
the party, fireworks including an aerial display of rockets, which
Lai Hua had assured her would keep her guests talking for
months, would be set off at her command. It would be breathtaking, spectacular, a tribute to her organizational genius.

Yes, it was going to be perfect.

Devina's smile faltered. Well, perhaps that was an overstate-
ment. Father's mental state of late appeared to preclude that
possibility. Her father's disposition had deteriorated markedly
over the last few days. Had she had not felt that to cancel the
party would only agitate him further, she certainly would have
done so.

It had been several days since the last robbery, and she could
only assume that things were not going well at the mines or with
the investigation of the robberies. Her father had not confided in
her, but a few days ago he had returned home so sorely agitated
that she had been unable to speak a word without eliciting from
him a sharp reply.

Devina gave a short sigh. Never one to accept her father's displays of temper passively, as her mother had, she had flared up at him in return, and the result had been a row that had kept them at odds until this very morning. But the need to put on a good face for the guests had obviously altered her father's behavior, and he had appeared at the breakfast table a changed man this morning. Her relief had been boundless.

Devina walked to the mirror in the corner of her room for a last-minute check of her appearance. She paused to scrutinize the breathtaking apparition that met her eye.

Silver, glittering and dazzling, sparkled from the top of her glorious upswept coiffure, to the toes of her dainty high-heeled slippers.

Devina raised a delicate hand to her hair and touched the silken strands lightly. No, she could not improve upon perfection. As for her gown, the bolt of white lace shot with silver thread, which she had found buried under a pile of less exotic fabrics in the dry goods store, had been a perfect choice. The off-the-shoulder neckline of the exquisite garment was trimmed in delicate silver beading and fashioned so as to expose the flawless line of her neck and shoulders. Short puffed sleeves trimmed with sparkling silver ribbon accented the graceful movements of her arms; the cuirass bodice hugged the generous curves of her breasts and emphasized her tiny waist. The satin skirt was trained and flounced, while the lace overskirt, also flounced, was drawn up at the sides *en tablier* and fell in alternating layers of silver braid and lace ruffles.

The moonlight silver of her hair was piled atop her head in an elaborate mass of glimmering swirls and waves capped with a high chignon that allowed just a few dancing ringlets to fall against her neck. In a touch that was pure inspiration, she had set into each gleaming wave a small faceted silver clip, which caught and reflected the gaslight in a dazzling display. The effect was a glowing halo matched only by the splendor of the total picture she presented.

Yes, this was perfection, Devina acknowledged. She was beauty itself, a living, glittering manifestation of her father's wealth.

Blood will tell . . .

You wouldn't be worth the trouble . . .

Devina was disconcerted. Why had her memory chosen that moment to return those two haunting phrases to her mind?

Annoyed, Devina took a deep breath and forced away the unsettling memory again attempting to invade her mind. She'd show her true worth to that damned outlaw whose memory hounded her. She'd be successful where all others had failed. She'd find out who he was somehow, and she'd laugh in his face when he was secure behind bars.

Realizing with increasing annoyance that she was trembling, Devina raised her chin with determination. Tonight she'd do just as Charles and Father had predicted. She would set Tombstone on its ear.

She gave a short, harsh laugh. Admittedly, she had assigned herself the easier task for this evening. Tombstone would be in her thrall from the moment it set eyes on her. And she would play that moment for all it was worth.

Seconds later Devina descended the staircase toward the bustle below. Determined to ignore the haunting gaze that followed her in her mind, Devina forced a smile.

The first strains of the waltz filled the foyer as Devina continued her graceful descent, and an unexpected sense of anticipation accelerated her heartbeat. She was suddenly, inexplicably sure that this would be *her* night . . .

Harvey emerged from his bedroom and paused to take a deep, appreciative breath. The aroma wafting up from the kitchen was divine. Roasting pork and apples.

As the first few bars of a lilting waltz reached his ears, Harvey's spirits began to lift. Perhaps it would be a pleasant evening after all.

He adjusted the collar of his suit, which he had worn only twice before. He was particularly fond of its lines. The square-cut coat was close-fitting in compliance with fashion, and the narrow, low-rolled collar was the latest thing in style. Harvey knew that his freshly trimmed gray hair and recently cultivated side whiskers were the perfect foil for the dark severity of his dress.

He was not especially at ease in the high collar and stiff front of his fashionable shirt, or with the narrow cambric bow tie, which he'd had difficulty in tying. But he could bear the discomfort for the opportunity to wear his diamond cuff links and shirt studs—symbols of affluence that would not go unnoticed in this society.

Grateful the guests had not yet arrived, Harvey was halfway down the steps when Devina walked into the hallway. He stopped in his tracks, momentarily overwhelmed, as she smiled at him. Devina was a glittering, silver vision. She was her mother, Regina Dale, incarnate, with her extremely delicate, matchless, almost angelic beauty.

Sadness overwhelmed Harvey. Regina, his beautiful wife whom he had treated so badly. With the recent stress in his own intimate affairs, he was only now beginning to realize how she must have suffered because of his dalliances. But he was determined he would not treat Devina badly. She would have only the best, whatever her heart desired.

Harvey covered the distance between Devina and himself in a few paces. Momentarily unable to speak, he raised his daughter's slender hand to his lips.

"Devina, you are exquisite. You make me very, very proud."

Devina's brilliant eyes misted, and Harvey forcibly restrained his desire to draw her into his arms as he had often done when she was a child. But Devina was a child no longer, and her momentary discomfiture was quickly subdued.

"Thank you, Father." Harvey felt a swell of pleasure as she added with obvious sincerity, "And you are quite handsome tonight."

"Then we make a good pair, do we not, dear?"

Not waiting for her response, Harvey tucked her arm under his. He urged Devina along with him as he strolled outside to look around. Small tables covered with white tablecloths, a floral centerpiece on each, followed the line of the curving veranda where the colorful lanterns blinked appealingly in the twilight. Servants were placing gently flickering candles on each table. Large bouquets of flowers were tucked into every corner, scenting the air with their fragrant perfume. He smiled his appreciation of the scene.

"Yes, it looks lovely, doesn't it, Father? I've seen to it that the patio is similarly set, as well as the dining room and the morning room. When the evening has worn on and our guests have eaten their fill, the servants have orders to clear the tables and to provide cards to those who would like them. It is my hope, however, that the majority of our guests will prefer to dance."

Devina paused and added with a smile, "And should a night

of vigorous dancing stir our guests' appetites once more, I've instructed that a light repast be served at midnight, along with a special surprise."

Harvey's curiosity was piqued. "A special surprise?"

"Yes, a surprise even from you."

Harvey led her back toward the foyer. "I look forward to your surprise with great anticipation, dear. Now let me see what you've done to my living room. I understand you've had the rugs rolled back, the furniture removed, and the floor polished."

Devina gave a short, lilting laugh. "That's right, Father. The living room is vacant except for the musicians, bouquets of flowers in each corner, and a few chairs. We need all the space possible if our guests are to enjoy the dancing, as I hope they will."

"Devina, dear, one look at you and every man present will line up for a dance. So, you see, you are guaranteed avid participation. As a matter of fact, I think—"

Harvey stepped into the living room, his words coming to an abrupt halt, his breath strangling in his throat. Temporarily unable to speak, he continued to stare, not believing his eyes as Lily turned a casual glance in his direction. Her smile was brief, her gaze speaking volumes. Gracefully, without speaking, she turned back to arranging the bouquet of flowers in the corner of the room.

"Father, what's wrong?"

Abruptly aware that Devina's hand was clutching his arm, that her beautiful face was tense with anxiety, Harvey fought to overcome his shock.

"What is China Mary's daughter doing here?"

His shock was fast turning to rage as Lily looked at him once more, raising sober, innocent eyes in his direction. Harvey swung back toward Devina in time to see her confused glance move between Lily, Lai Hua, and himself before she responded.

"We . . . we had a problem with help, Father. Someone died in the Mexican neighborhood, and many of the women were unable to work tonight. Lai Hua managed to find some servants to replace them."

Harvey made an effort to control his raging emotions. "That woman is not a servant!"

Stepping forward, Lai Hua bowed. Her tone was apologetic. "I accepted those who volunteered their services. I am sorry, Mr. Dale. I did not realize you would object to her presence."

Harvey swallowed with considerable difficulty. Devina was beginning to look decidedly suspicious. He could not afford to behave in a manner that would allow her to guess the truth.

Damn the crafty Oriental bitch!

Forcing a smile, Harvey apologized to Devina. "I'm sorry, darling. Seeing that young woman here brought to mind the time I found you in her mother's store in that undesirable section of town. I know neither China Mary nor she had anything to do with your straying into that area, but I could not help but associate her with that particularly unpleasant memory."

Turning back to Lai Hua with supreme control, Harvey said cooly, "Of course, I have no objection to the woman's presence, Lai Hua. We need servants tonight, and this young woman is obviously well suited to such a menial task."

"Father!"

Out of the corner of his eye, Harvey saw Lily's clear cheek tic spasmodically at his vindictive remark. It made him feel considerably better, and he scoffed at Devina's shock. "Devina, you worry too much about the feelings of those who are inferior to you. These people know they're suited to menial tasks. They have accepted that position in life."

"Father, please." Taking his arm more firmly, Devina turned him toward the dining room.

His daughter was making a firm effort to avoid harsh words, but Harvey could feel her displeasure. He frowned. Lily had forced this stiffness between Devina and himself when all had been going so well. He would see that she paid for her deviousness.

He would deal with Lily later; but for now, this night was his and Devina's. With that thought in mind, Harvey turned toward Devina with an appealing twist to his smile, which had never failed him.

"Come, show me the rest of your handiwork, Devina. I'm particularly interested in the buffet table. The aromas have been tempting me for hours, and now is the time for me to sample."

"Oh, no, not yet." A reluctant smile breaking through, Devina shook her head. "You're going to have to wait until the guests arrive."

Harvey's smile broadened coaxingly. "Just a bite?"

"No."

Harvey shook his head, relieved at the way the game was resuming. "You are a truly difficult woman, Devina."

Devina's smile dimmed in momentary thoughtfulness. "Perhaps that's because I was raised by a truly difficult man."

Charles's smile belied his inner turmoil. He did not need to look at his watch to see that it was getting late. He would soon be expected at Devina's party, and still Miranda Randolph sat and talked.

A spinster, crippled from birth with a twisted leg and burdened with an overbearing mother who was now bedridden, Miranda was a quiet, selfless woman whose problems were occasionally too much to bear. Medication for her mother's aching joints had brought her to his office shortly after he had assumed practice, and his sympathetic ear had brought her back periodically on one pretext or another. But it was time to bring Miranda's spontaneous recitation to a halt.

Taking her hand, Charles interrupted her gently. "Miranda, it's getting late. I don't think it would be wise for you to travel in the dark."

"Oh, I only have a little way to go."

Charles felt a surge of compassion. He had treated Bessie Randolph several times. He could not blame Miranda for not wanting to return to her sharp-tongued mother's bedside.

"Just the same, I wouldn't feel right if I knew you were on the road alone after dark. Come on, I'll walk with you to your wagon."

Drawing himself to his feet, Charles extended his hand to help Miranda rise. The thought touched his mind that careful treatment at birth could have eliminated the handicap she had suffered with all her life, but Bessie Randolph was not the kind of woman to "tamper with the will of God." He truly sympathized with Miranda's unhappy situation.

Waiting only until Miranda's wagon turned the corner of the street a few minutes later, Charles returned to his office. He cast a glance toward the position of the sun where it dropped rapidly toward the horizon and grimaced. Devina had specifically asked him to arrive early for the party to lend her his support, and it was later than he wished. With a low agitated grunt, he gathered a few necessities and headed for the public baths.

Charles walked back toward his quarters almost an hour later, decidedly tense. Damn! Saturday night and the line at the baths had been endless. It was times like these that he missed the luxury of his home back east with its full bevy of servants and private bathing facilities.

His patience all but expired, Charles crossed his office in a few quick strides and he walked directly toward his darkened living quarters in the rear. A sliver of yellow lamplight from the street slanted through the corner of the window shade, and Charles allowed it to guide him toward the lamp. Damn it all, he disliked the way things were going. He would be late in arriving at Devina's party.

Within a moment a small flicker of light lit the darkened interior of the room and Charles adjusted the flame. He walked to the mirror on his washstand and surveyed the image that stared back at him. His hair was looking a little shaggy. He had been intending to step out for a haircut when Miranda arrived. Well, it was too late for that now, but he was going to have to take the time to shave, whether he liked it or not.

Turning, Charles reached for the razor that lay beside the washbowl, his hand freezing midway as an unexpected voice cut the silence of the room.

"Don't bother to shave, Carter. I shaved for you."

Whirling around, Charles stared at the shadow stepping out of the corner of the room, gun drawn. Charles's words were a spontaneous gasp: "I knew it was you! It couldn't have been anyone else."

Harvey's smile was stiff as he greeted the seemingly endless stream of guests who passed through his front door. He extended his hand toward a large, barrel-chested man. "Walter, I'm so glad you could make it tonight." Turning toward the heavy, plain woman at Walter Sherkraut's side, Harvey attempted to brighten his smile. He raised her hand to his lips. "And Hilda, you look lovely tonight."

The woman's bovine eyes all but bulged at the compliment, and it was all Harvey could do not to snatch his hand back from her clammy palm. He gritted his teeth as his smile stiffened further. Damn! How had an intelligent man like Walter Sherkraut gotten saddled with such a homely wife? In deference to a possible need for Walter's bank in the future, Harvey subdued his desire to shake off the dowdy woman with distaste. Instead, he broadened his smile.

"Walter, I don't believe you and Hilda have met my daughter, Devina."

Quick to seize his opportunity, Walter Sherkraut took Devina's hand, and Harvey winced inwardly at the flicker of discomfort that moved across his daughter's flawless face. It appeared Walter's grip was as deadly as his wife's, and Harvey had the distinct desire to crack the lecherous banker across his large, knobby knuckles. He took a firmer hold on his patience as Walter spoke in a low, almost throbbing tone.

"No, I haven't had the pleasure of meeting Devina, Harvey, but I admit to having seen your lovely daughter around town. How could I have missed her? She stood out like a flower among thorns." Walter bent closer to Devina. "I am so pleased to meet you, my dear."

Devina's reply was unhesitant. "And I'm pleased to meet both of you, Mr. Sherkraut, Mrs. Sherkraut."

"Oh, please call me Walter, Devina." The banker was almost leering into Devina's face, and Hilda was becoming visibly agitated. Damn the old fool! Devina was young enough to be his daughter!

"I would enjoy that, Walter." Devina's smooth tone cut into the growing heat of Harvey's thoughts. He felt a surge of pride as Devina turned gracefully to the ungainly Mrs. Sherkraut. "And if I may call you Hilda . . . ?" Waiting only for Mrs. Sherkraut's stiff nod, Devina brought a smile to the woman's thick lips as she continued softly, "I would enjoy that far better than the formality of 'Mrs. Sherkraut.' After all, there aren't that many years' difference between our ages, are there? I wouldn't want formality to inhibit our conversation, because I'm sure we have very much in common."

Appearing flustered under Devina's attention, Hilda shrugged fleshy shoulders exposed by her outdated brown gown. "Oh, there are a few more years between us than you think . . . Devina."

"I don't believe it."

Taking Hilda Sherkraut's arm, Devina smoothly urged the older woman into the living room with a spontaneous flow of conversation that brought a most becoming flush to Hilda's cheeks. Harvey was speechless. He had never seen this side of Devina, this thoroughly gracious and considerate side. She had put the old dowd perfectly at ease with just a few short words, and was now making her feel like an honored guest. He suspected Hilda had not gotten preferred treatment like this since

she was sixteen and being courted, probably for her money, by
Walter himself. Perhaps there was more of her mother in Devina
than he realized.

Walter still stood silently at his side, and Harvey turned to see
the burly banker staring intently after Devina.

"Walter?"

"Yes?"

"I thought you might want a drink."

"A drink? Yes, I do." His expression distinctly relieved,
Walter waited while Harvey beckoned to a passing waiter.

The banker helped himself to a glass from the waiter's tray
and took a deep swallow. "You must excuse me for staring,
Harvey, but your daughter is one of the most beautiful women
I've ever seen."

"Yes, I believe she is." Realizing he had no desire to discuss
Devina with the lecherous old sot at his side, Harvey motioned
to a well-dressed man who stood in a far corner of the room.
"The fellow approaching is Harry Wiggins, someone you might
be interested in meeting, Walter. He's fresh from the East, a
friend of my partner's, and an investor of some type. He's
looking for financial guidance, and I've been telling him about
your bank."

Walter's beady eyes finally strayed from Devina's gently
swaying rear, and Harvey felt a flash of triumph. If there was
one thing Walter Sherkraut liked more than the taste of young
female flesh, it was the scent of money.

Within a few minutes, Harvey was making his way through
the crowded living room. The party was going very well. Most
of the guests had arrived on time, their promptness doubtless
spurred by both their curiosity and the music that traveled on the
evening air. Several couples had already begun dancing.

Harvey glanced into the dining room. The locusts had not yet
hit the buffet table, but he could see they were lined up for the
attack. He gave a low snort. Doubtless some of them had never
seen such a sumptuous display in their deprived lives.

Harvey cast a glance around the room. It occurred to him that
within the crowd already assembled were perhaps three, maybe
four, men he felt to be on his level. The others he tolerated for
the same reason he tolerated Walter Sherkraut. But there was one
person in the house whose presence he would tolerate no longer.

Maintaining a steady forward motion that allowed no one

more than a quick, passing exchange of words, Harvey made his way to the kitchen. The person he sought had walked in that direction only moments before.

Harvey watched in silence from the doorway of the kitchen as Lily surveyed a tray of artistically arranged candied fruits. Lily was the antithesis of Devina, with her black, shining hair, cream-colored skin, unfathomable dark eyes. So tall and slender in the glowing golden silk of her foreign attire, she was the only woman present who was a match for Devina's beauty.

It occurred to him that perhaps Lily had managed to be present in his house this evening because she especially wished to call his attention to that fact. But if that was so, he knew it was not Lily's main reason for being present. She was in his house this evening for the same reason she had walked the street across from his office—she wanted to torment him.

Harvey took a deep breath. Torment him she did. How long had it been since he had held Lily's naked flesh against his own? He dared not count the days, but he knew it had been too long. She would have her victory this night, because he doubted he would be able to spend another night deprived of her. She was indeed controlling him, and he would allow her that control. But only until he could sate the lust that burned his body.

As if sensing his perusal, Lily looked up, and Harvey's anger surged anew. He would allow Lily in his bed, but he'd be damned before he would allow her in his house.

Motioning her outside into the yard, Harvey waited only until Lily had disappeared through the rear door before making a circuitous path in that direction. Once in the yard, he strode directly to the shadows of the back entrance, where she awaited him. His grip on her arm elicited a gasp of pain, but he ignored the breathless sound as his fingers closed more tightly on her delicate flesh. He spoke in a soft, venomous tone.

"Out! I want you out of my house now, do you understand?"

Holding his gaze even as she moved an almost indiscernable step closer, Lily whispered in her soft, melodic voice, "You are angry, Mr. Dale, but it is my wish only to serve you."

Harvey's laugh was harsh. "Serve me! There's only one way I want you to serve me, and it's not in my house and at my table. Now get out and don't come back! Go back to your gutter where you belong; and wait for me, because I'll be coming to see you tonight when this party is over. I'll teach you then what torment is."

Lily's lips curved into a hard smile. "You will come to me later . . . to join me in my 'gutter'? Ah, Mr. Dale, that a man as great as you should stoop so low. What would your beautiful daughter think of you if she knew?"

His urge to tighten his hands around Lily's graceful neck was almost as strong as the urge to consume her warm, tempting lips. Harvey laughed.

"Your scheme won't work, Lily, because I'm wise to your strategy. You're trying to drive me away from you with your tormenting, to make me suffer with the realization that need has made me as subservient to you as you are forced to be subservient to me. But all you accomplish with your efforts, dear Lily, is your own humiliation, and the stirring of passions within me that will be sated on your body, whether you are willing or unwilling."

Taking a moment to gain control of his heated emotions, Harvey curled a trembling hand around Lily's slender neck.

"Go home now and wait for me. Think of me and allow your passions to rise . . . hatred if it must be, but let it seethe. Because I'll come to you, Lily, and I'll sate those passions. I'll sate them thoroughly, in any and every way that will bring relief to the lust you have so deliberately raised within me, the same lust that I see mirrored in the shadowed depths of your eyes."

Pulling her against him with a rough hand, Harvey covered Lily's lips with his own in a cruel, punishing kiss that all but destroyed the last of his composure. Infuriated by his own weakness, Harvey thrust her roughly from him. His voice was rasping.

"Go now, damn you, and don't come back!"

Waiting only until Lily's slender figure had disappeared into the darkness, Harvey took a deep breath and drew himself stiffly erect.

She was gone, the cunning Oriental bitch was gone, and now he could return to his party and his guests. He could strike Lily from his mind with the knowledge that she would be waiting for him. He could consign her to the part of his life where he wished her to remain, hidden and apart, as was her due.

The two men stood eye to eye in a dead silence. The breadth of their shoulders was evenly matched, Ross's well developed chest and shoulder muscles only slightly more tightly hewn than Charles's. Thick midnight-black hair, slightly disheveled from the heat of the day, fell over the brow of each. Large dark eyes, black and fathomless, set at an upward slant above bold cheekbones, exchanged stares. Well-defined arched brows moved into simultaneous frowns, strong features tightened, firm jaws became more stubborn. Exact replicas of each other, they stared in further appraisal.

Ross, his heart pounding, abruptly motioned Jake forward. He felt he had been waiting forever for this moment, but he knew he'd been waiting only three years.

Ross's hand tightened on his gun. It was difficult hating a man who wore his own face, no matter how valid the reason for that hatred, and Ross despised his own weakness. But reason prevailed, reminding him that this man had put aside the bonds of blood three years before. Carter had earned his hatred.

Ross broke the strained silence with a low laugh. "So you knew all along that I was stealing Till-Dale payrolls."

"Yes. Everyone else thinks you're still in Yuma with two more years to serve on your sentence, but I kept close track of you. I knew you were released, and when the payroll robberies started shortly afterward—"

"Tie him up, Jake."

"Ross . . ."

Ross halted Carter's instinctive step forward. "Don't try anything, Carter. Sit down in that chair and be quiet. You haven't done me a damned bit of good in the past, but tonight you're going to serve a very useful purpose."

"What purpose?"

His eyes watchful, Ross waited as Jake slammed Carter into the chair and pulled his hands behind him. Jake was looping the coils of a rope around Carter's wrists when Ross responded to his question. "Use your imagination, Carter. What do you think I have in mind for tonight?"

Charles paused, his eyes growing slowly incredulous. "Don't be stupid, Ross. You'll never get away with it!"

"Oh, won't I? We're identical twins, remember? I admit there are a few differences, noticeable when you look real close, but nobody's going to be looking for those differences tonight when I show up at Dale's party in your place. Just as you said, everyone thinks I'm still in prison. They'll see only the person they expect to see . . . Charles Carter."

"Ross, you're making a mistake! Someone will catch on and you'll be caught. They'll send you back to prison."

"Oh, no, Carter, I won't get caught. My brother won't be able to lead the sheriff to me, like he did the last time."

"Ross, I didn't lead the sheriff to you. I didn't realize he was following me. He—"

"Save your breath, Carter."

Unwilling to listen to more, Ross stared at the black, concerned eyes so similar to his own. He remembered that concerned expression very well. It had looked at him from outside the cell where the sheriff had thrown him after Carter had betrayed him. And he remembered that Carter had said, "It's all for the best, Ross." He'd never forget it.

"Ross, give me a chance to explain."

Memory sharpened the whiplike crack of Ross's reply. "I'm not interested in explanations, Carter. As far as I'm concerned, we did all our talking three years ago."

Carter resisted Jake's attempt to bind his feet, finally turning to Ross with an earnest plea. "Ross, for God's sake, we're brothers!"

Ross was tempted to laugh, but it occurred to him that the situation wasn't funny. He shook his head. "No, Carter, you've got it wrong. We came from the same womb just about twenty minutes apart, or so Pa said, but that doesn't make us brothers. You did a real good job of cutting that tie."

"That isn't true."

"Save your protests. I was there, remember?"

"Ross, I came to Tombstone looking for you and our father. I had no idea what your problems with Dale were all about. I didn't lead the sheriff to you knowingly, but once you were in jail, I figured it was all for the best. Half the town was out looking for you. You could've gotten killed. Everyone thought you caused that accident at the mine."

"Including you."

"I didn't know what to think."

"And so you accepted everything you were told as fact. You believed everyone but me."

"Ross, I asked you if you were responsible for the accident, and you wouldn't answer me."

Ross gave a short laugh. The pain of that memory was with him still. "I didn't think I needed to answer you. You were my brother. But then I found out what having a brother really means. Hell, it doesn't mean a thing."

"Ross, I—"

"And in case you're thinking you'll be able to convince me that you had a good excuse for what you did, let me set one thing straight. Because of you, I was in jail when Pa died. Pa died poor, and he died alone. I'll never forgive you for that, or forget."

"Ross—"

"Gag him, Jake. I'm tired of hearing him talk."

Jake slipped a gag around Carter's mouth and knotted it tightly behind his head, and Ross stifled his instinctive response to the plea in Carter's eyes. Damn, would he never learn that his brother, his long-lost brother, could not be trusted?

Ross turned and opened the wardrobe in the corner of the room.

Minutes later Ross adjusted the collar of the fine lawn shirt he wore, and casually knotted his tie. The dark blue serge trousers felt unnaturally smooth against his legs as he slipped on a conservative waistcoat. With no pause in his movements, he donned the suit coat and within seconds was adjusting its fit across his shoulders. He frowned as he walked to the mirror. The suit coat was a trifle tight in the arms and chest, but that was to be expected. It had been fitted to Charles Carter's exact measurements, and Carter had not done the heavy physical labor that had been Ross's lot in life for three long years.

Conscious of the lateness of the hour, Ross walked to the mirror and stopped, momentarily stunned. He gave a short laugh, incredulous at the reflection that stared back at him. Charles Carter. Damn! He looked more like Charles Carter than he looked like himself!

Ross studied his reflection a little longer. There were traces of Ross Morrison still remaining. If he looked hard, he could see the harshness of expression that was totally absent from Carter's face. The squint lines at the corners of his eyes were deeper, and his skin was tinted a shade darker than Carter's. But the differences were negligible. He knew they could be easily erased.

With great deliberation, Ross smiled. He watched the upward movement of the lines of his face as the creases in his cheeks moved into the appealing expression so seldom visible. He saw his lips part to expose teeth so similar in size and shape to Carter's that he could not help but marvel. It was Charles Carter who smiled back at him, and an eerie chill moved down Ross's spine. Yes, this disguise would do. It would do very well.

Taking only a moment to pick up his brother's Stetson, Ross adjusted it on his head and turned to face Carter.

A low, amazed grunt escaped Jake's lips, and he shook his head. "If I didn't know who I was lookin' at, Ross, I'd swear you were Carter. I didn't realize how much you two really look alike until this minute." He laughed. "Hell, it gives me a real strange feelin' seein' you like that."

'Don't worry, Jake, the change is only temporary. I won't be Charles Carter for one minute longer than necessary."

Quickly rolling up his own discarded clothes, Ross handed them to Jake. "Here, put these in my saddlebags. Wait until it's a little darker, and then bring the horses around and wait for me. I'll meet you as soon as I can."

Responding with a short nod, Jake started toward the door, and Ross walked toward Carter. He leaned down and briefly checked the ropes on Carter's hands and feet. Carter attempted to speak through the gag, and Ross lifted his eyes to his brother's muffled appeal. His response was completely devoid of feeling. "I told you, Carter, I'm through talking. I'm going to Dale's party now. When I leave that party, I'll have Dale in the position I've been waiting three long years to see him in." Ross paused, his lips moving into a sinister smile. "Don't worry, I'll take real good care of your lady friend. It'll be my pleasure."

Charles tried to speak and thrashed unsuccessfully at the bonds on his hands and feet.

Ross touched the brim of his hat in a short salute. His voice was low, and harsh emotion filled his words. "Good-bye, brother. I hope I'll never have to see you again."

Turning, Ross walked to the door and out into the street beyond.

The sound of laughter almost overwhelmed the lilting waltz as Devina moved to the halting lead of her partner. She cast a quick look to the edge of the dance floor where a small group stood involved in a conversation that was obviously enjoyable. Her glance swept the floor where numerous couples danced with various degrees of proficiency, and she smiled her satisfaction. The party was going very well.

Turning her attention back to her partner, Devina attempted to hide her distaste. Walter Sherkraut leered down into her face, and she tried harder. Her stomach temporarily revolted as a bead of perspiration rolled down the banker's shiny face and disappeared into his high, stiff collar. She was intensely aware that the beefy hand which held hers was uncomfortably moist, and she could feel a similar moistness soaking the waistline of her dress where his other hand gripped her so tenaciously.

Noting her scrutiny, and placing an entirely different meaning on it, Walter Sherkraut leered more broadly. Simultaneously adjusting his hold to pull her closer than she felt she could bear, he lowered his head with a breathless whisper. "Devina, dear, you must excuse me for repeating myself, but you are by far the most beautiful woman I've ever seen. I can't tell you the effect you've had on me tonight. You are exquisite, glittering, breathtaking."

Devina managed a short laugh.

"Since my father's fortune is presently tied up in silver, I thought this gown would be appropriate. And I can certainly understand its appeal to you, Walter. After all, I expect I have all the glitter and dazzle of the silver bullion you hold in your bank's vault."

Devina's frankness had no affect on Walter's amorous bent.

"Perhaps so, Devina, but you're more than beautiful. You're warm and appealing. You're not at all as cold and lifeless and unresponsive as a silver bar."

So Walter would like to believe. Devina's delicate nose twitched.

Devina responded lightly, "But people are so often taken in by glitter and dazzle. They so often overlook the good, the honest, the loving qualities of those whose physical attraction is somewhat muted by shyness or hesitation. I'm so pleased that you're not one of those men, Walter. I admire you immensely for having the sensitivity to see beyond Hilda's natural reticence and her inability to project the true warmth of her personality in casual conversation. You are a very perceptive person for having been able to see through to the true beauty beneath Hilda's demure exterior."

Walter's leer became sheepish. His face took on a flush she was sure was unrelated to the stress of the dance. His smile was weak. "Yes, Hilda is a very lovely woman . . . underneath. She has given me many happy years of marriage."

The fine line of Devina's nose twitched once more. Happy, indeed. Hilda Sherkraut no doubt silently suffered her husband's countless flirtations and any seductions he was successful in conducting with his dubious charm.

Her smile undaunted, Devina continued with a deepening sincerity of tone, "Hilda is so fortunate to have a husband as faithful and loving as you obviously are, Walter. I know you won't be able to believe it, but there are many men who are willing to toss aside the commitment of their wedding vows for casual flirtations and brief, meaningless affairs that break their wives' hearts. I have no use for such men myself. I consider them selfish, cruel, little more than spoiled children who desire to have the best of both worlds at the expense of the women who love them."

Walter was beginning to look decidedly uncomfortable. A nervous tic jumped in his cheek, and Devina hid her satisfaction as her veiled barbs again struck home. Perhaps Hilda Sherkraut was not as beautiful as Devina's mother, but she had probably suffered in the same way because of her husband's infidelity. Well, tonight, Hilda Sherkraut had someone on her side.

The music drew to a sweeping halt, and Walter dropped his hands as if they had been burned. As soon as he had escorted Devina to the edge of the dance floor as etiquette demanded, he bobbed his head and said, "Thank you for the dance, Devina. You are extremely lovely, but now I must . . . ah . . . find my wife. She does love to dance."

Her smile considerably more comfortable than before, Devina nodded. She followed Walter Sherkraut's bulky form as he made his way through the couples around them and disappeared through the living room doorway.

Well, so much for him and his lascivious manner, Devina thought. Mr. Walter Sherkraut, banker and lecher!

But her satisfaction quickly faded as she again scanned the crowded room. Damn, where was Charles? She had specifically told him she would appreciate his early appearance. He was late.

The fine line of Devina's brow furrowed into a frown as yet another of her father's overweight business associates began to bear down on her. Drat! Where was Charles? She could not suffer another assault on her poorly protected toes.

Undecided whether to brave out Albert Wallace's steady approach or to run for her life, Devina was distracted from her dilemma by Molly's quick steps across the foyer as she responded to a summons at the front door. Her father turned from a casual exchange near the staircase as Molly opened the door.

His hand extended in greeting, he walked toward the doorway as Charles stepped into sight.

A relief not unmixed with annoyance flooded Devina's senses. Charles had arrived at last . . . but not soon enough. He shook her father's hand warmly at the same moment that she turned in response to a light tap on her shoulder. Her smile was weak as she glanced up into Albert Wallace's admiring gaze.

"Devina, I've been waiting to find you free. If I might have the pleasure of dancing with the most beautiful woman in the room . . . no, the most beautiful woman in Tombstone . . . it would be the highlight of my night."

"Albert, such flagrant flattery!"

"No, Devina, it's nothing more than a statement of fact, I assure you. Shall we dance?"

Devina looked up into her prospective partner's face just as history repeated itself: A bead of perspiration ran down Albert Wallace's cheek and disappeared into his high collar, following the same route taken by the moisture on Walter Scherkraut's face only moments ago. She suppressed a silent groan. Without a word she accepted the hand Albert proffered. It was moist and clammy. The hand he placed at her waist as she preceded him out onto the floor efficiently adhered to the waistline of her dress with its dampness. Her silent groan grew louder as she anticipated what the next few minutes would bring. Once out on the floor, she turned to face her partner as he stepped out with a firm, hard step.

"Oh, my dear, excuse me!"

Managing to subdue her instinctive cry of pain, Devina withdrew her small foot from beneath the large sole of Albert Wallace's shoe. She glanced down at her battered satin slipper, the thought entering her mind that she might never walk again. Bravely she raised her eyes in Albert's direction.

"It's quite all right, Albert. Let's dance, shall we?"

Allowing Albert to swing her out onto the floor, Devina leaned heavily on his arm, her eyes moving back to the doorway. Father was back in his conversation, and Charles was standing silently in a corner of the living room. What was he waiting for? A reluctant concession to her fear of crushed toes, Devina returned her attention to Albert in time to dodge his heavy foot once more. Damn Charles for playing the gentleman and waiting until the dance was over to come to her side!

Devina gritted her teeth in a determined smile. How much longer would this dance last? More importantly, how much longer would her poor feet last? At this point in time, she was uncertain which would meet an end first.

Ross smiled Charles's smile in return to the many greetings extended to him as he worked his way through the crowded room and into a secluded corner. It occurred to him that following his plan this evening was not going to be as easy as he thought.

Without his realizing it, Ross's smile turned into a frown. Damn, he had not thought Devina Dale would light up the whole house and surrounding countryside with her party! A quick visual sweep of the house as he had approached it had revealed that lanterns were strung the entire length of the veranda and out onto the patio. Every room in the house appeared to be lit, and people moved around the premises with a freedom that would allow him little privacy. Jake's little mistress had surely not exaggerated. Everyone who was anyone in Tombstone was here.

The warmth of the greetings he had been receiving since he had entered amused him to no end. No one had cause to suspect he was anyone other than Charles Carter, and it was obvious Carter had made himself very popular in the three years since he had come to town. It seemed the other man with Carter's face, the man the town had once sworn to hang, had been forgotten along with the countless other felons who had passed through the Tombstone court since. But that was all right. Ross would soon refresh everyone's memory.

His line of thought coming to an abrupt halt, Ross stared awestruck at the vision whirling around the floor in the arms of Albert Wallace. It was Devina Dale—startlingly beautiful, lovelier than he had ever seen her in a sparkling silver gown that caught the flickering lights of the room and reflected them a thousand times. Her pale hair, soft and shining, gleamed with a mirroring hue, framing her face in a luminous, almost ethereal halo.

An angel . . . she was an angel floating on a cloud of glittering silver. But he knew there was deceit in that illusion. The celestial glow of that angel was tarnished by the sense of superiority she had exhibited that first day on the stage, by hauteur, and by conceit. The surface was shining silver. The interior, the heart beneath her beautiful breasts, was cold, unfeeling. Yet he was enthralled, unable to take his eyes off her. He was fascinated by this magnificent, tarnished angel, although he knew full well the stain of selfishness ran deep.

Their glances met and Ross felt the impact of that contact down to his toes. Her glorious eyes appealed to him, asked him to come to her, and in that moment Ross wanted to respond to her summons more than he had ever wanted anything in his life. It took a few minutes for him to get the situation into perspective. Devina Dale was not calling him. She was calling Charles Carter.

With a supreme effort, Ross controlled the angry heat that realization evoked. A smile of bitter amusement touched his lips. What more could he ask? Tonight he *was* Charles Carter. And tonight Devina Dale would belong to him.

Devina managed a smile through her silent sigh of relief. She had thought that dance would never end. The soft curve of her lips stiffened into a grimace as she turned with distaste from the sight of the perspiration trailing down Albert Wallace's puffy face. She had had enough of overweight, laboring dance partners to last a lifetime. As far as she was concerned, her duty dances were done.

Mumbling a few polite words to Albert as he escorted her to the edge of the dance floor, Devina excused herself and took a few steps, seeking Charles's face. Her eyes darted to the far corner where she had last seen him standing. He was not there. Damn, where was he? When she caught up with him she would give him a piece of her mind!

"Looking for someone, Devina?"

Whirling around, Devina started to scold him, but the first deafening chord of another waltz drowned out her tirade. Charles's grin broadened, and she felt its warmth chip away at her annoyance. Only Charles could smile like that, dispel her anger without a word. He slipped his arm under hers and walked her to a quiet corner that would provide them a minimum of privacy. Smoothly but firmly, he backed her up against the wall, blocking her view of the crowded room with his broad chest. He looked down into her face, and Devina's heart jumped and set to racing.

"Now, is there something you want to say to me, Devina?"

Breathless, Devina shook her head. Charles's familiar face was suddenly disconcerting. Strange, she had not realized how very black his hair was, or did it only seem darker because of the way his sun-darkened complexion caught the candlelight? And his eyes . . . she was not accustomed to the intensity she saw in them just now. Why wasn't Charles's smile reflected in their shadowed depths? Why did his gaze make her feel strange, insecure?

Devina hesitated, and Charles broke into her silence. "Well, this is a surprise. I've never known you to be at a loss for words before, Devina."

Devina managed a small laugh. "You've never backed me into a corner before, Charles. Your unexpected tactic took me off guard."

Charles's eyes continued to hold hers as his smile dropped away. "Maybe that was my mistake."

Devina's discomfort was increasing. This side of Charles was new, disturbing. No man had ever knocked her off balance in this way. No man except . . .

A sudden tremor of fear shuddered down Devina's spine, and she took a short step back. A memory of haunting eyes returned sharply to her mind, merging with those of the man standing before her, and Devina attempted to retreat farther, only to feel the wall against her back. She tried to speak, but the words would not emerge past the lump in her throat.

"Devina, what's wrong?"

Charles was frowning, but it was a worried frown. She felt his hand on her arm, heard his familiar voice fill with concern.

"Devina, are you all right? It's hot in here, and you've probably been dancing nonstop since the music began. You need some fresh air. We'll go for a short walk . . . Devina dear, answer me."

Charles . . . it was the old Charles . . . Devina felt strength beginning to return to her limbs. What was wrong with her? Was she having hallucinations? Perhaps Charles was right . . . too much dancing and too little air.

As if to reassure herself that this was really Charles, Devina reached up and touched the lines of his smile with her fingertips. Yes, there was no smile quite like his.

"I'm sorry, Charles. Perhaps you're right. I do need some air, but let's go out on the patio. I can't be seen leaving my own party. Father would have a fit."

Charles took her hand and pressed it to his lips. "We wouldn't want to do anything to make your father angry, would we?"

The warmth of his lips scorched the palm of her hand, and

Devina shook her head. Still holding her hand captive, Charles urged softly, "Would we?"

Devina's response was distracted. "Would we . . . ?"

Charles's smile faded as Devina continued to stare up into his face. His breathing, she noticed, was almost as ragged as her own, and Devina found it difficult to tear her eyes from his lips . . . those full, generous lips that smiled so easily. She wondered how they would feel . . .

"Devina, there you are!"

A familiar gushing voice broke into Devina's distracted state as Sally Lou Keane approached. Her animated expression matched her eager pace, and Devina suppressed a silent groan. Her eyes darted to Sally Lou's side to see the ever-constant Wilfred Bellows in attendance, and she attempted a smile.

"Yes, here I am, Sally Lou. Hello, Wilfred. Are you both enjoying the party?"

"Enjoying the party! Of course Willie and I are enjoying it! It's the most fabulous party I've ever attended!" Poking the silent Willie with her elbow, she urged anxiously, "Isn't it, Willie?"

"It's a lovely party, Devina."

"And your gown!" Sally Lou's eyes devoured Devina's silver dress. "It's just magnificent! I've never seen anything like it. Where did you get it? In San Francisco? New York?" Sally Lou paused as another thought suddenly struck her. Her eyes widened. "Not Paris? You didn't get it in Paris!"

Devina took a firm hold on her patience. "No, not Paris, Sally Lou. I had it made right here in Tombstone."

"Here in Tombstone?"

Devina suppressed a groan. "Yes, here in Tombstone."

Sally Lou shook her head unbelievingly. "*Here?* . . . In *Tombstone?*"

Devina gritted her teeth with irritation. She could just as easily have had this conversation with a parrot. Charles's sudden interruption was as timely as it was unexpected.

"If you'll excuse us, Sally Lou, Devina and I were just about to go out on the patio for some air."

"Some air?"

A smile curled the corners of Devina's lips. Had she actually seen Charles's mouth twitch?

"Yes, some air. We'll see you later, Sally Lou, Wilfred."

Taking her arm in a firm grip, Charles urged her forward. His rapid step did not slow until they had reached the patio. Halting abruptly, Charles acknowledged Judge Walsh's greeting before turning back toward Devina. "If that girl had uttered one more foolish word . . ."

Devina's mouth dropped open with surprise. "Charles, aren't you the one who told me to be kinder to Sally Lou because she admired me so?"

Charles's brows drew together in an uncharacteristic frown. A sudden chill moved up Devina's spine as Charles hesitated, his eyes roaming her face and then settling on her mouth. His voice was low, intense. "Maybe I've decided it's time to put other, more important considerations forward. Maybe I think we—"

"Devina? Where are you, my dear?"

Devina turned spontaneously at the sound of her father's voice, only to feel Charles's hand tighten on her arm.

Harvey Dale appeared beside them, his eyes dropping to Charles's possessive grip. "You're going to have to part with my daughter for a little while, Charles. There is a horde of hungry vultures waiting to devour our buffet, and custom demands that Devina and I lead them to the table." Not waiting for Charles's response, Harvey held out his arm to Devina.

"Are you ready, dear? I hope you are wearing shoes that will enable you to run. If not, I fear we'll both be trampled in the rush to the table."

Devina was suddenly intensely aware that Charles's eyes had not left her face. A responsive tingle moved up her spine, which Devina had time neither to fully comprehend nor indulge as her father urged her toward the dining room.

She was in the midst of her official chore when she looked up again. Charles's eyes met hers, and her heart leaped. Inexplicably confused, Devina turned back to the task at hand.

Ross whirled Devina around the floor to the swaying rhythm of another waltz. Aware that they had captured the eyes of many of the guests, he whirled her faster. Ross was truly surprised that people were talking. He had not expected so many of those present to find his attentions to Devina interesting. He was also puzzled that his charming, smooth-talking brother had not ingratiated himself in a more personal way with the beautiful Miss Dale.

Taking a firmer hold on Devina's waist, Ross danced her toward the patio door. He would make up for Charles Carter's deficiency, and it would be no strain on him at all. He was well aware that although Devina doubtless found his ardor startling, she definitely did not find him repulsive. The attraction was more than mutual.

Noting his change in direction, Devina glanced up curiously. The luminous blue of her eyes touched and held his, and a deeper, more powerful emotion surged to life inside him. Her heavily lashed eyelids flickered only briefly as he returned her stare, and he took a firm hold on his feelings, struggling to suppress his instinctive response to her gaze.

Be careful, fool, his mind cautioned. *It isn't Ross Morrison she sees when she looks at you. If the haughty Miss Dale knew she was dancing in the arms of a penniless ex-convict with a bleak future, she would scream her protest. It's Charles Carter she sees, a respected young physician and heir to the railroad fortune of Oliver Carter, a man she obviously considers her social equal.*

Suppressing a frown in response to his thoughts, Ross pulled Devina Dale's delicate frame a trifle closer. His pulse jumped as her lips parted in a spontaneous gasp. Oh, yes, tonight was the night he had been waiting for. With a quickened step, Ross danced Devina out onto the patio and into the surrounding shadows.

Breathless under Charles's searing gaze, Devina found herself all but swept from her feet as Charles whirled her out onto the patio and into the cool evening breeze. Her short protest went totally ignored as he danced her to a halt in the shadows cast by the flickering lanterns.

For long moments he held her gaze in silence before raising his eyes in a quick assessing glance around them. His frown reflected his annoyance at the interested stares of other guests, and Devina's heart thundered anew.

What was it about Charles that stirred this unexpected heightening of her senses? She had enjoyed his company immensely these past few weeks. She had occasionally been annoyed by his persistent good nature, but she had found that he could stir a deeply buried sense of humor within her, which had previously gone undiscovered. But in all the time she had spent in Charles's company, she had never experienced this breathless reaction to his masculine appeal, this stirring deep in the inner core of herself that marked their meeting this night. She was confused, and a bit shaken by her confusion.

But Charles was turning her to his side, tucking her arm under his, urging her into a quick step toward a less brightly lit corner of the garden. She could imagine the reaction of her curious guests, but in truth, she cared little. It was her own reaction she was concerned about, and it alarmed her. Her heart pounding, her breathing almost ragged, she knew this breathlessness was not due to the strain of the dance. This was all going too fast. This new, intense Charles was not the man she had become accustomed to during their acquaintance. He was not the same man who had inspired the easy camaraderie that had been the mark of their association. This new Charles had an entirely different effect on her . . . an effect that was almost frightening in its intensity.

In her confusion, Devina took a backward step. Charles halted, turning toward her with a small frown as she struggled to regain her composure. She gave a short, breathless laugh in an attempt to lighten the moment.

"Charles, we'll stir no end of gossip tonight. What will people think if we go walking off into the shadows?"

Charles's dark eyes were barely discernible in the half-light. "They'll think I want to be alone with you, and they'll be right."

Devina fought to control her reaction to Charles's throbbing tone. "Perhaps I don't want to be alone with you, Charles."

His gaze narrowed, capturing hers with its burning heat. "Don't you want to be alone with me, Devina, for just a little while?" He took a step closer. She could feel the masculine heat of his body drawing her even as his voice sent little shivers of anticipation up her spine. "Don't you?"

Charles raised a hand to her cheek. He caressed her skin, trailing his fingertips to her mouth to trace the line of her lips with a gentle touch. "I want to hold you in my arms, Devina. I want to taste these lips that have been tantalizing me since the moment I saw you. I want to feel your mouth come alive under mine. I want to know what it's like to taste an angel's kiss."

"You know me better than that, Charles. I'm no angel. I've never pretended to be one."

Charles's fingertips followed the line of Devina's chin, the curve of her throat. His hand cradled the nape of her neck, and he drew her face closer to his.

"You're an angel tonight. No flaws are visible in moonlight, and the moon is very bright right now. Walk with me, Devina. Tonight we're two people we've never been before. Let's find out who we really are."

Devina wanted to be alone with Charles, but a strange, incomprehensible reluctance held her back.

"I . . . I can't leave my own party, Charles."

"Yes, you can. And you will."

The hand cupping the back of her neck drew her closer. Charles's mouth grazed hers, tantalizing her. She could feel his sweet breath against her lips. She could feel the trembling that shook his strong frame as his grating whisper caressed her skin.

"Devina . . . Devina, I've waited so long to hold you close to my heart. Just for a few minutes, darling."

Charles's lips brushed hers with light, fleeting kisses, and Devina gasped at their butterfly touch, at the sweet, promised ecstasy denied by their dancing flight. She was drawn inexorably toward him by the heat of their mutual desire, and she swayed uncertainly.

But Charles drew back. Her heavy eyelids opened wide at his withdrawal, and a spontaneous protest escaped her lips. Her protest was clearly reflected in the obsidian darkness of his eyes as he glanced around them with obvious discomfort.

"Devina, dammit, there's no privacy here. I want to hold you, darling."

They were drawing the attention of the guests at a small table adjacent to them. They would cause a scandal if they remained standing where they were, and they would cause a scandal if they disappeared into the surrounding shadows. Truly, there was no choice to make.

Charles's arm slipped around her waist as he urged her along with him. He pulled her close against his side, and she could feel the smooth movement of his tightly muscled body. She wanted to be held in those strong arms. She wanted to feel Charles's strength envelop her. She wanted to know Charles's mouth completely . . .

They had moved beyond the ring of light cast by the lanterns. Only a shadow of Charles's face remained visible as he suddenly

pulled her to a stop and turned her full into his arms. His arms
slipped around her, and she heard a soft expletive as his mouth
descended in a hard, crushing kiss that echoed with the passion
of his tight embrace. His kiss deepened, forcing aside the temporary barrier of her teeth. He was drawing, drinking from her lips.
He was tasting, savoring, consuming her. He was clutching her
closer, tighter, as Devina's arms slipped around his neck. She
was melting into him, becoming a part of his strength, a part of
his weakness, a part of the emotion that fused them into one.

The heady assault of Charles's lovemaking continued as his
lips searched her face, touching and tasting the curve of her
brow, her fluttering eyelids, the graceful hollows of her cheeks,
before moving to cover her parted lips once more. He drew her
deeper into the shadows, all but lifting her from her feet with the
passion of his breathtaking embrace.

Charles was breathing raggedly when he abruptly separated
himself from her. He stared into her face for a long second, his
expression unreadable in the semidarkness. Unexpectedly, he
released her, raising his hands to disengage her arms from
around his neck. Devina's short gasp of protest was halted by a
movement behind her. She turned in time to catch a glimpse of a
slight, fair-haired man as Charles twisted her arms roughly behind her back and the other man slipped a gag over her mouth.

Devina began to struggle against Charles's restrictive grip on
her wrists, the gag around her mouth. A paralyzing fear overwhelmed her as another pair of hands aided in the struggle to
subdue her, attempting to slip a bond around her wrists as she
squirmed and twisted in an attempt to break free. Not quite
understanding what was happening, she knew only that she was
in danger, grave danger, from the man she had trusted most!

Rage renewed her struggles. Just when her frantic bid for
freedom appeared to be succeeding, Charles's arms suddenly
enveloped her, crushing her helplessly against him. But now
there was no passion in Charles's embrace. Instead, his arms
were cruelly rough, demanding obedience as he rasped harshly,
"Damn you, hold still or I'll have to—"

A muffled gasp escaped Devina's lips. Their struggle had
shifted their position so that a shaft of moonlight lit the harsh
planes of Charles's face. He was looking down at her, all traces
of his ardor erased by the fury in his gaze.

Those eyes! Oh, God, she remembered them. She recognized

the hatred, the menace in them. It was he! The man from the stagecoach! He had Charles's face, but not his eyes.

Horror and a deep, soul-chilling fear endowing her with a new strength, Devina burst into a frenzy of movement. She was twisting, squirming, and pulling at Charles's restrictive embrace in a wild effort to break free, kicking and thrashing at the hands that were attempting to bind her ankles.

She heard Charles issue a soft command—a warning, which registered somewhere in the back her mind—but she dismissed it as she fought his imprisoning grip with an almost maniacal fervor. She felt a fleeting moment's triumph as Charles momentarily let go of her wrists, but it was gone all too soon as his hand descended rapidly toward her face.

A blinding explosion of pain blacked out the rasp of her own labored breathing, the echo of music floating on the night air, the sharp, metallic taste of her fear, and the regretful sound of Charles's low, pained exclamation.

"Damn, you, Devina Dale. Damn you!"

Harvey was beginning to get annoyed. Damn, where had Devina gone?

Making certain not to allow any trace of concern to become apparent in his expression, Harvey slipped his fingers into the pocket of his waistcoat and removed his watch. With a casual flick of his finger, he opened the lid and slanted a brief glance downward.

An hour! She had been gone an hour! An inquiry from Lai Hua earlier had sent him in search of Devina, only to be informed by Albert Wallace, of all people, that his daughter had disappeared into the shadows of the yard with Charles Carter. He had, of course, laughed off Albert's sly smile and its irritating innuendo. He knew Devina better than that. His daughter would not humiliate either herself or him by behaving in such a manner. He had been certain he would find her busily entertaining in another part of the house. But he had been wrong.

Well, he had waited long enough for her to return to the party. If his daughter had been foolish enough to put herself in an embarrassing position, she would get what she deserved.

Aware that Lai Hua's eyes had been following him intently for the past hour, Harvey beckoned her toward him. "Lai Hua, send the servants onto the grounds to find Miss Devina. Tell them I want the search conducted quietly, so it will not draw the attention of our guests. But I want them to find her at once. Have them tell her I wish to see her immediately.''

His annoyance flaring anew at the disapproval obvious in Lai Hua's expression, Harvey asked tightly, ''Do you understand?''

''Yes, I understand, Mr. Dale.''

Turning quickly, Lai Hua disappeared among the guests, and Harvey returned to the living room. The party was beginning to wane. It needed Devina's direction, her enthusiasm to pick it up. Devina would get more than a talking-to when he saw her again.

Harvey stood in the well-lit foyer of his home, an army of servants around him. Music wafted in from the living room behind him, but his guests were no longer dancing. Instead, they stood in small, whispering groups, slanting nervous glances toward him, which he totally ignored.

No longer attempting to hide his anxiety, Harvey turned to Lai Hua. ''You're sure, Lai Hua?'' Ignoring the stress obvious on the young Oriental's face, he pressed sharply, ''You've questioned every one of the servants? They've searched the grounds in all directions?''

''Yes, Mr. Dale. Miss Devina cannot be found.''

Where could she be? Panic touched Harvey's senses. A thorough search of the house and grounds had turned up no sign of either Devina or Charles, but Harvey refused to accept the implications of that fact. He had appraised the tenor of the relationship between Charles and Devina. As surprising as it had seemed to him, it had been obvious to his discerning eye that although a deep friendship seemed to have developed, there was no feeling of a stronger nature between them. This situation was not as it would seem. Something was very wrong.

Not yet ready to face the questions and the speculative glances of his guests, Harvey walked into an isolated portion of the foyer. He needed to think.

He had been ill at ease most of the night, what with Lily showing up unexpectedly and the stress of arriving guests. He had managed the guests and sent Lily away, but there was something else, something his preoccupation had caused him to miss, but that continued to nag at the back of his mind . . .

He had begun to feel uncomfortable again just after Charles

entered the house, although he was still uncertain as to the reason why . . .

With a suddenness that stole his breath, realization struck his mind. Charles's hand! Harvey had extended his hand in greeting, and Charles had accepted it warmly, as he had many times before. But tonight Charles's handshake had been different . . .

How could he have been so stupid? How could he have failed to recognize that difference? The hand that had gripped his in greeting had been hard, callused, the hand of a laborer. It had not been the hand of a doctor! Charles Carter's hands were as smooth, as unused to physical labor as his own. But the face had been the same, the smile, the voice . . .

No!

The color draining from his face, Harvey paused only a moment before striding into the living room to face the guests assembled there. With great urgency, he signaled the musicians to silence. He raised a trembling hand toward his guests. In a voice that quaked with emotion, he spoke into the expectant silence, "I should like to request . . . no, to beg the aid of each and every man in this room. I desperately need your help. My daughter has been abducted."

CHAPTER XII

CHARLES HAD ABANDONED his struggle to break free of his bonds. The chair to which he was bound was too solidly built, and his bonds were too tight to allow him to slip free. He had accepted the realization that he would have to wait to be discovered, wait until someone came pounding at his door.

Frustrated, his agitation growing stronger by the minute, Charles went over the situation again in his mind.

Charles's brow furrowed into a worried frown. He did not want to see Devina hurt, and he did not know what to expect from a brother who was a virtual stranger to him. What were Ross's intentions toward Devina? To kidnap her? To hold her for ransom? Was that all? Would he return her safe and sound if Harvey met his demands? He supposed Ross's veiled threats in regard to Devina were made for his benefit in the hope that he would urge Harvey to meet Ross's demands. He hoped that was so, but there had been something about the light in Ross's eyes at the mention of Devina's name that made Charles uneasy.

Damn, if only he could free himself, get to the party in time to stop Ross from making a dire mistake. If only he could persuade Ross to stop his dangerous attempt at vengeance. If only he could persuade Ross to attack the matter legally. If only . . .

The sound of running footsteps on the board sidewalk outside his window broke into Charles's thoughts. He responded to the sudden pounding on the side door of his living quarters with a muffled shout for help. Within moments the door burst open to reveal, among others, a panic-stricken Harvey Dale.

Charles's eyes closed in dreaded realization. Oh, God, it was too late.

As the sheriff's deputy untied him, Charles met Harvey Dale's enraged gaze.

"Where's my daughter? Tell me now, or I'll see you in a cell next to that criminal brother of yours! Where is she?"

Charles struggled to his feet, which had been numbed by the bonds. He faced Harvey Dale unsteadily. "I don't know what's happened to Devina, Harvey."

Grabbing him by the shirt, Harvey gave him a rough shake. "Don't pretend innocence with me, Charles Carter! Damn, I don't know how I could have been such a fool! I knew you were Brad Morrison's son, but you appeared to be a sensible man, well educated and raised in affluence. You weren't a common ruffian like your brother. I trusted you! But you were just playing me along, weren't you?"

Charles dislodged Harvey's grip on his shirt with carefully controlled anger. "Harvey, I don't know anything about this."

"Your brother received an early release from prison, didn't he? Either that or he broke out. You took advantage of my trust. You used both Devina and me to help him conduct this vendetta against me."

Sympathy welled up within Charles at the sight of the man's distress. It was obvious Harvey was almost beside himself with fear for Devina's safety.

"Harvey, I was busy with a patient and late getting ready for the party. When I returned here from the baths, Ross was waiting with a gun. Until this minute, I wasn't certain what he was going to do."

"Liar . . . liar!" Harvey's face flushed blood red. "I welcomed you into my home as a companion for my daughter, and you betrayed both of us."

"Harvey, calm down, please." Charles's eyes assessed the purple tint flushing Harvey's face. He frowned. "It'll do you no good to push yourself to this level of agitation."

Push myself to this level of agitation! My daughter has been abducted, damn you! Now tell me where she is and how I may get her back. Tell me or I swear I'll—" Turning swiftly, Harvey tried to seize the gun from the holster of the man standing at his side, but did not succeed.

Compassion surged anew inside Charles as he realized the true depth of Harvey Dale's agitation. The man was an arrogant, self-centered bigot, but he loved his daughter and he was suffering. Charles stared into Harvey's pain-filled eyes. "Harvey, please believe me. I had nothing to do with the abduction of your daughter. I'm extremely fond of Devina. I would never do anything to hurt her. And if I had maintained any hope for vengeance against you for the injustices my brother claimed, I certainly wouldn't have waited this long to get my satisfaction. Now, please, tell me what happened."

Harvey was still straining for control when George Tillson stepped forward to respond in his stead. His narrow, lined face reflected his incredulity. "Charles, it's still difficult for me to believe the man who attended the party this evening wasn't you. But now that I look at you more closely . . . perhaps there is a severity to your brother's features that is absent from yours, a look about the eyes, a hint of menace in the gaze. Perhaps we should have realized . . ." His voice trailing away, George shook his head. "But none of us had reason to suspect your brother had been released, or that he would attempt such an unexpected way of striking back at Harvey. We all spoke to him and never suspected for a moment that it wasn't you. Devina was obviously taken in, also. She was last seen walking in the garden with you . . . I mean with your brother."

Uncertain whether he was more deeply concerned for Ross or Devina, Charles turned back to Harvey, his expression sober. "Harvey, I give you my word that I'll do my best to find Devina and bring her back."

Harvey stared into his face in silence before suddenly giving a short, harsh laugh. "This whole situation is my fault, isn't it? I was a damned fool to trust anyone with the tainted Morrison blood, no matter where or how he was raised. But I've learned my lesson in the most difficult way possible, and you may rest assured I'll never make the same mistake again."

Harvey's aristocratic face twitched with emotion as he continued in a low, quaking voice, "I want you to know something, Carter . . . if that's what you still call yourself. I'm going to find your brother and get my daughter back. Then I'm going to see your brother back in prison where he belongs. And just for the record, you're no longer welcome in my home. When this is all over, I hope I'll never have to look at your face again."

Turning on his heel, Harvey Dale walked stiffly through the

crowd that had gathered at Charles's doorstep and out onto the street. The rigidity of his posture and the determination in his face portended poorly for Ross's future, and the future of Charles Carter as well.

Harvey was trembling with rage as he eyed the two Oriental women standing a few feet from him. They were so distinctly different in appearance. One was short, broad in girth, her small nondescript features lost in her round face. The other was tall, slender, as exquisitely beautiful and graceful as the lily for which she was named. The only similarity between the two was in the expression of bland innocence they wore so blatantly.

He took a firm hold on his emotions. "Do you expect me to believe you know nothing about my daughter's abduction?"

China Mary's singsong voice was pleasant. Her lips curved into a smile. "That is correct, Mr. Dale."

Harvey's handsome face grew stiffer. He had left Charles Carter's quarters and come directly to the establishment of China Mary. He had demanded that Lily join China Mary and him in the back room, and Lily had responded immediately to his summons. Despising himself for his own spontaneous reaction to the beauty of his mistress, Harvey had immediately begun his attack. He was still pursuing it to his end.

"So it was merely a coincidence that Lily showed up at my home tonight. It was merely a coincidence that she distracted me with her presence, enraged me with her gall in coming to my home. It was merely a coincidence that she managed to keep me so thoroughly off balance that Ross Morrison was successful in entering my home masquerading as his brother without my realization!"

Lily nodded, her expression serene. "Yes, it was a coincidence, Mr. Dale."

Her calmness pushed Harvey over the edge of rage. He gripped Lily's slender shoulders and shook her roughly. "Tell me the truth, damn you! I want to know why you came to my house. It was a ploy to distract me, wasn't it? You're in league with Ross Morrison. You're using him to seek revenge on me."

"Revenge, Mr. Dale? I seek no revenge."

Harvey dropped his hands as if he had been burned. "You lie, Lily. How very well you lie! You know you despise me . . . just as I despise you."

"You despise me, Mr. Dale?" Lily's thin eyebrows rose in a delicate expression of feigned surprise. "You demonstrate your hatred in a very unusual way."

Harvey could feel the blood rushing to his face. He fought the urge to force the smile from Lily's finely drawn lips. "Bitch! Lying Hop Town slut!"

The light tic in Lily's smooth cheek was the only indication of her reaction to Harvey's harsh words. She ignored the stiffening of her mother's smile as she responded in a light, even tone, "As you say, Mr. Dale."

Fury pounding through his veins, Harvey roughly gripped Lily's chin with his hand. The contact with her smooth skin sent a chill down his spine despite the heat of the moment. He whispered into her upturned face, his voice a low venomous threat. "Lily, you will tell me what you had to do with Devina's disappearance, and you will tell me now, or you will bear the weight of the consequences on your shoulders. *Tell me!*"

Aware of China Mary's nervous twitching behind him, Harvey continued to concentrate his attention on the beautiful woman whose doelike eyes looked up without fear into his, her gaze moving over his flushed, tense expression. When she spoke, her words were soft but unyielding, "I can tell you only what I have told you before. I had no part in Miss Devina's disappearance. I came to your house because Lai Hua was hiring servants for your party."

"Servants! You've never worked a day in your pampered life, much less as a servant!"

"Oh, yes." Lily's eyes moved to his lips. "I have worked as a very personal servant indeed."

Her openly provocative gaze was beginning to weave its usual spell, and Harvey dropped his hand from her chin. He stepped back, a sneer twisting his mouth.

"Whore! You cannot forget your training, can you? I have no time now for your services. I came here for the truth, but it appears you are incapable of speaking it."

Interrupting unexpectedly, China Mary spoke with an uncommon sobriety. "We have told you the truth, Mr. Dale, but you refuse to accept it. We can do no more."

Harvey took a short step backward. "All right, all right. I'll accept what you say for now, because there is nothing else I can do. But I will find my daughter, and I will bring her abductor to justice. And when I do, I will find out the extent of your involvement.''

"And if you find out we have no involvement, Mr. Dale?" Lily murmured.

Harvey was well aware that a part of his rage stemmed from his desire for her. As incredible as it seemed even to him, in the depth of his despair over the loss of his darling Devina, he still wanted the beautiful Chinese tart who had helped to turn his life upside down.

Harvey turned without another word and walked out the door. He was on the street and walking rapidly out of Hop Town a few minutes later. Uncertain where to go from this most recent defeat, he was closer to despair than he had ever been in his life.

Lai Hua stood on the veranda of the Dale residence as the last lanterns were extinguished. The final guests had departed a short time before, and she had taken it upon herself to dismiss the musicians. The party had ended the moment Harvey Dale learned that his daughter was missing.

Issuing quick, precise instructions in her native tongue Lai Hua directed the silent army of servants to finish setting the house in order.

She quickly inspected the premises. The dining room buffet had been cleared. The food was now stored and the room returned to its former appearance. As she watched, the last remaining signs of the party were systematically removed from the living room. The floor had been swept and the rug replaced. The furniture was presently being rearranged. Within minutes the house would be as it was before, with one very large exception. The light, the excitement that was Miss Devina, was missing.

Sadness pressed at Lai Hua's heart, and she fought to swallow against the thickness that choked her throat. The memory of Mr. Jake's beautiful laughing face returned to her mind and lingered there. She saw yellow hair, thick and heavy, curling appealingly around her fingers as she ran her hand through its glossy weight. She saw pale blue eyes, eyes that stirred in her a warmth of spirit previously unknown. She saw light skin peppered with freckles, freckles as she had seen before only on the faces of the children of Mr. Jake's race.

She remembered running her fingertip over the fine dusting of freckles along his cheekbones and his short nose. She remem-

Thrill to the most sensual, adventure-filled Historical Romances on the market today...

FROM 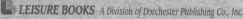 LEISURE BOOKS

As a home subscriber to Leisure Romance Book Club, you'll enjoy the best in today's BRAND-NEW Historical Romance fiction. For over twenty-five years, Leisure Books has brought you the award-winning, high-quality authors you know and love to read. Each Leisure Historical Romance will sweep you away to a world of high adventure...and intimate romance. Discover for yourself all the passion and excitement millions of readers thrill to each and every month.

Save $5.⁰⁰ Each Time You Buy!

Each month, the Leisure Romance Book Club brings you four brand-new titles from Leisure Books, America's foremost publisher of Historical Romances. EACH PACKAGE WILL SAVE YOU $5.00 FROM THE BOOKSTORE PRICE! And you'll never miss a new title with our convenient home delivery service.

Here's how we do it. Each package will carry a FREE 10-DAY EXAMINATION privilege. At the end of that time, if you decide to keep your books, simply pay the low invoice price of $16.96, no shipping or handling charges added. HOME DELIVERY IS ALWAYS FREE. With today's top Historical Romance novels selling for $5.99 and higher, our price SAVES YOU $5.00 with each shipment.

AND YOUR FIRST FOUR-BOOK SHIPMENT IS TOTALLY FREE!

IT'S A BARGAIN YOU CAN'T BEAT! A Super $21.96 Value!

 LEISURE BOOKS *A Division of Dorchester Publishing Co., Inc.*

GET YOUR 4 FREE BOOKS
NOW — A $21.96 Value!

Mail the Free Book Certificate Today!

Get Four Books Totally
FREE – A $21.96 Value!

▼ Tear Here and Mail Your FREE Book Card Today! ▼

PLEASE RUSH
MY FOUR FREE
BOOKS TO ME
RIGHT AWAY!

Leisure Romance Book Club
P.O. Box 6613
Edison, NJ 08818-6613

AFFIX
STAMP
HERE

bered stroking the lines of his boyish face, the outline of his full, warm lips. She remembered the subtle change that came about in that boyish face as the laughter left his mouth and the light in his eyes changed to the light of another, more powerful emotion. She remembered the warmth of the strong, tightly muscled body that moved to cover hers, his pale skin pressing against her golden-hued flesh. She remembered the joy of their many joinings, growing deeper, fuller, as her love for Mr. Jake expanded within her.

She remembered her commitment to Mr. Jake. It had been complete, and although that commitment had not been voiced in return, and never would be, her words had bound her to him as strongly as a vow. He was the dawn to which she had first awakened; the warmth that had gently brought her to life; the sun that had caused her to bloom. The petals of her heart had opened to absorb the glow, the brilliance of life and love that was Mr. Jake. As with the flower, she knew the beauty within her would die without the sun that was Mr. Jake, and her life would ebb away.

Betray him? Never.

But her heart ached with another unwitting betrayal. Because of her love for this man, she had allowed her mistress, who had respected and trusted her, to fall into the hands of her enemies. Why had she not realized that in speaking to Mr. Jake of the plans for the party, of the anticipated excitement and confusion, she herself had planted the seed for the abduction that had taken place?

Lai Hua bowed her head. She was responsible for her mistress's distress. She did not blame Mr. Jake, who had taken the information to his friend. She knew his friendship with this man had grown during the years he had spent in prison in pain and disgrace. She knew it was that friendship which had allowed Mr. Jake to survive the horror of those years. For that reason, her lover's friend was also her own, although she had never met him And for that reason her dilemma was even greater.

Tears filled Lai Hua's eyes. She blinked them away as a step sounded in the doorway behind her. She turned to Mr. Dale's flushed, angry face. She did not need to ask if any trace of Miss Devina had been found.

Dismissing her greeting, Mr. Dale addressed her tensely, "Get all of these servants out of here. I don't ever want to see them back here again, do you understand?"

Lai Hua nodded.

"And you . . ." Obviously unwilling to allow her to escape
unscathed, Harvey Dale lashed out at her. "You were brought in
this house to be of help to me as well as to my daughter. It
appears you have failed miserably in both respects." Harvey
Dale's lips curled into a harsh sneer. "If it were up to me I'd
dismiss you from my service and see that you never worked for a
respectable family in Tombstone again. But I hope to have my
daughter back with me soon, very soon. When she returns, she
will need someone to help her. Although I cannot fathom the
reason why, my daughter likes and trusts you, and you will be
here for her when she returns."

Lai Hua nodded her understanding.

Harvey Dale's face was gray and lined. A peculiar twitching
developed in his cheek as he continued in a low, tight voice,
"Now, get out of this house. I expect you to come back in the
morning and to report every day until Miss Dale returns. But do
not let me see your face. I am sick to death of your wily, devious
race, and I wish to be spared the sight of your discolored foreign
skin. Get out!"

Turning, Lai Hua spoke a few words of swift command to the
servants who were frozen into stillness in the living room by
Harvey Dale's malevolent tirade. She waited only until they had
hurried from the room in a silent line before following behind
them.

Only minutes later, Lai Hua raised her eyes to the dark night
sky as she hurried away from the Dale residence. The darkness
would soon be streaked with the first light of dawn. Where and
how would that dawn find her mistress, and what would the new
day bring? Lai Hua's guilt was a heavy burden. Visions of Miss
Devina and Mr. Jake warred in her mind, and her step faltered.
She knew she must search her inner self and come to terms with
her guilt, but she knew not where her search would lead. Fear
touched her heart.

CHAPTER XIII

DEVINA AWOKE WITH a start to the darkness of the night sky, the rhythm of a horse moving at a steady, moderate pace beneath her, and the sensation of strong arms holding her upright. Then came the pain, throbbing and persistent. She attempted to touch her jaw, the source of her pain, but was unable to lift her hand. Something was wrong.

Disoriented and shaken, Devina was struggling to clear her mind when, suddenly, total recall snapped her eyes wide open, and she glanced around, determinedly ignoring the pain in her head. The horse was traveling over a stark landscape lit solely by a yellow half-moon. Looking down she saw that her wrists were tied in front of her as if she were a common criminal!

Her heart pounding, Devina twisted around toward the man whose arms supported her. His features were shadowed by the wide brim of his hat, but she could see him clearly enough to know that it was the man with Charles's face.

Rage and fear blended into instinctive resistance, and she was suddenly thrashing and twisting in her captor's grip. Unsure who the man was or where he was taking her, she was certain of only one thing: She had to escape.

The strong arms tightened around her. A deep, angry curse was followed by a low grunt as she jammed her elbows into her captor's sides with as much force as she could muster, almost dislodging his hold. For the briefest moment she swayed uncertainly in the saddle, her bound hands reaching for the saddle horn, only to feel her captor's arms clamp even more strongly around her. Her struggles continued even as her captor reined the horse to a halt.

"Sit still, dammit! You almost fell!"

"Let me go! You'll never get away with this. My father will come after us. He won't stop until he catches up and then he'll—"

"Your father!" The deep voice, now chillingly familiar, was filled with scorn. "Your father probably doesn't even realize you're gone."

Suddenly remembering the second man, the blond fellow who had helped subdue her in the garden, Devina glanced frantically around them.

"No use looking for help. We've been on this trail for over an hour, and there's no sign of our being followed. And if someone should start after us tonight, I've left a lookout back a few miles who'll signal in time for me to hide us both without a trace. But don't get your hopes up. No one's coming. No one has any idea where to look for you, and that's the way it's going to stay."

Abruptly, Devina was struggling again, twisting and turning, swinging her bound arms in a desperate attempt to free herself from her captor's grip.

Suddenly the iron grip of her captor tightened, crushing her against the wall of his chest, so tight that she was not only helpless but breathless as well. His warm breath fanned her cheek as he held her motionless in a deliberate silence aimed at allowing the true helplessness of her position to register fully in her mind.

When he spoke at last, his voice was low with a menace that rang frighteningly familiar. "You're wasting your time. You can't break free. But it'll be dawn soon, and I can't afford to be on this trail in the full light of day. You'll either travel seated, as you are now, or you'll travel gagged, tied hand and foot, and slung over the saddle like a sack of grain. Now, what's your preference, Miss Dale?"

Overwhelmed by the sheer size and power of the man, Devina fought to catch her breath. The hard muscular wall of his chest felt like steel against her back, his sinewy arms a cage from which she could not break free. Why had she not realized when she danced in this fellow's arms that his muscular body was broader and harder than Charles's?

Her silence caused the man's arms to tighten, restricting her breathing even more. He did not need to demonstrate further. He was right. He totally overpowered her.

"All right!"

The words burst from Devina's lips as she strained to breathe, but her captor's response was a slight relaxation of his hold. Devina made a desperate attempt to fill her aching lungs with air, finally realizing she would have to satisfy herself with small, gulping breaths. Having no choice but to submit to his superior strength, Devina gritted her teeth as her captor adjusted her posture to fit her more securely into the curve of his body.

Her buttocks were now tucked firmly against the unrelenting stranger's groin, her legs flat against his hard male thighs. Her head was pressed securely against the strong column of his throat, and she could feel his chin brushing her hair. She did not like being held so closely against the warmth of this man's body, almost in a lover's embrace.

"You didn't seem to mind being in my arms in the garden a few hours ago, Miss Dale. As a matter of fact, you seemed to enjoy it."

The man's ability to read her thoughts startled her into a spontaneous response. "I was enjoying the embrace of the man I *thought* you were. Had I known you were a low thief, a stage-coach robber—"

A sound of surprise escaped her captor's lips. "So you recognize me."

"I recognize your tactics. Only a coward like you would get satisfaction from forcing a woman to submit to his will." Devina sensed the cutting edge of her words piercing deep as her captor instinctively stiffened.

"Since you recognize me from my unmanly qualities, Miss Dale, you probably realize I don't make idle threats. Now, do I have your word that you'll stop fighting me or shall I tie you up?"

Devina raised her chin defiantly. "I've already agreed."

"You haven't given me your word."

"And I don't intend to!"

Her captor immediately reached for the rope on the saddle.

"All right!" Devina cried. "I give you my word, damn you!"

He did not release the coiled rope. "Can I trust you to *keep* your word, Miss Dale?"

Devina gave a short, bitter laugh. "You'll soon find out, won't you?"

Devina's captor abruptly spurred his horse forward, thrusting her back against his chest even more solidly than before. But as he did, he loosened his grip and let his arm slip down to circle her waist in an almost casual manner. Devina restrained an urge to laugh.

So the big, bold payroll thief thought he could trust her to keep her word. Well, that was his first mistake! Only a fool would keep a promise that had been coerced from her, and only a fool would believe that she would.

An unexpected howl in the distance penetrated the silence of the night, and Devina cast an apprehensive glance at the eerie shadows of the deserted hills. A chill moved down her spine as the helplessness of her situation registered fully in her mind. Her captor's reaction was to pull her closer against him, and Devina was again reminded of the power in the arms that had so easily subdued her.

Devina summoned the last residue of strength within her. She would not let this land intimidate her. As for this man, whoever he was, he was no match for her, as he would soon see.

The sun was rising, a great golden globe that set the morning sky afire with vibrant hues, but Devina felt little joy in the beginning of this new day. It had been a long and exhausting night during which the tireless animal beneath her had continued onward, bearing the weight of her captor and herself without protest. What little sleep she had been able to manage had been broken by the throbbing ache in her jaw, the chafing of the bonds on her wrists, and her awareness of the hard male body against which she rested.

It had done her little good to attempt to hold herself erect, free of her captor's support. Her spirit had been willing, but her body had been weak, and she had awakened on several occasions only to find herself leaning full back against his strong chest, her head tucked into the curve of his neck. She had finally submitted to her exhaustion, telling herself that she would take advantage of this man's strength until she felt strong enough to escape him.

Hundreds of questions whirled in her mind. Who was this man with Charles's face? Was Charles a party to this masquerade or a victim of it? What did this man intend to do to her?

Unexpectedly Devina's captor turned his mount off the trail and down a sloping pathway to the right. To the best of her knowledge, it was the first time they had left the main trail, and Devina's heart began a ragged beat. Did that mean that they were soon to reach their destination?

Her silent question was answered when a crude cabin came into view amid the uneven terrain. The wood was old, colored by exposure to the elements into a shade that blended so well with the surrounding countryside that the shack was rendered almost invisible. A perfect hideout. A search party could wander for weeks in this area without locating it. Damn, how would anyone ever find her?

Within minutes the horse drew to a halt, and her captor dismounted. Turning toward her the moment his feet touched the ground, he reached up to lift her down, exposing his face to her in the clear light of morning. A short gasp escaped Devina's lips. The handsome, sharply chiseled features, the strong jaw, the full, well-shaped lips . . . Charles . . . Was this man really Charles, or was he not?

Unable to take her eyes off his face, Devina allowed him to lift her to her feet without protest. Her knees were strangely weak, and she swayed slightly, only to feel his hands tighten around her waist. His dark brows furrowed into a frown, and suddenly he was no longer Charles, but the man on the stage, the thief, the villain who had threatened her life.

"Who are you? You're not Charles!" Devina shook her head, thoroughly confused. "But you're his image, except . . ."

"Except for what, Miss Dale? Or should I call you Devina?" Her captor's voice held a sinister note. "Yes, I think I will. All right, Devina, get into the cabin."

Devina raised her chin in open defiance. "I'm not going into that hovel until you tell me who you are and what you intend to do to me!"

"Look at me, Devina." Towering over her, her captor grasped her chin, forcing her to meet his eyes. "I said look at me. Now tell me who you think I am."

Anger flared inside Devina and she attempted to free herself. The throbbing in her jaw flared once more, and she responded heatedly, "I don't know who you are. I just know who you aren't, and you aren't Charles. You look so much like him that I find myself sometimes . . . But Charles is gentle, considerate, well bred. You are the antithesis of all he is."

Her captor's harsh laugh sounded once more. "Thank you, Devina. You've just given me a great compliment."

"Only a fool would take that as a compliment."

"And only a fool would refuse to obey my orders. Now do as I said and get into that cabin."

"Cabin? Is that what you call that place? It's a shack, a dilapidated—"

"I said get inside!"

"I will not go into that cabin unless—"

But Devina did not get the opportunity to finish her statement as her captor lifted her from the ground. Tossing her over his shoulder, he started toward the cabin as she screamed in protest.

"Bastard! Put me down! Damn you, put me down!"

Her protests to no avail, Devina caught a glimpse of a wide fireplace, a crude table and chairs, and rough wooden floors before she was unceremoniously dumped on her back on a broad bunk in one corner of the room. Leaning over her, her captor pinned her against the lumpy surface of the bunk, supporting himself by bracing his hands on either side of her head. He spoke in a very un-Charles-like rasp.

"Let's get one thing straight, Miss High-and-Mighty Devina Dale. I'm the one who gives the orders here. Your future is in my hands, and what I do with it will depend on your father. Save your questions, because I intend to tell you only one thing: In the next few weeks we're going to find out just how important Harvey Dale's daughter is to him, and just what he's willing to do to get her back."

Devina's response reflected no sign of the fear that all but incapacitated her. "Bastard. My father will never submit to your demands!"

The black eyes staring into hers were suddenly cold. "You had better hope he does."

Suddenly drawing back, her captor turned toward the door. Before Devina could frame a reply, the door had closed behind him, and a lock had been engaged from the outside. She did not have to test the door to know that she was this man's prisoner and that he had meant every word he had said.

Devina's eyes slowly opened to the semilight of the cabin, only to abruptly widen at the sight of the tall, broad-shouldered figure standing over her. Fear and anger battled inside her, and she attempted to sit up. Her movements impeded by her bound hands and the throbbing pain in her chin, she flopped back down on the lumpy cot, her face flaming.

The tall man made no move toward her, and she tried once more to rise. This time she succeeded, finally managing to stand beside the bunk as she stared into the eyes of the man with Charles's face. Those eyes were hot, burning with an emotion she could not define, and Devina raised her chin against the quaking that was beginning to assume control of her arrogant stance.

"What do you intend to do with me?"

"Put out your hands."

"What?"

"I said put out your hands, unless you've gotten attached to those bracelets you're wearing."

Not waiting for her to comply, her captor grasped her wrists. The coarse rope cut sharply into her tender flesh, and she uttered a gasp of pain that darkened the frown on her captor's face. She attempted to jerk her hands free of his grasp.

"Stay still if you want me to untie you."

Realizing she had no recourse, Devina remained silent as her captor's long fingers worked deftly at her bonds. She released a short spontaneous breath as her wrists were freed, then attempted to withdraw her hands, only to have her captor hold them fast, his eyes intent on the raw and bleeding skin. Abruptly, and without a word, he dropped her hands and disappeared through the doorway, returning a few moments later with a small tin. Opening it, he placed it on the table and again took her arm. Devina snatched it back with a frown.

"What do you think you're doing?"

Her captor's gaze rose to hers.

"What do you think I'm doing? Your wrists are raw. If they go unattended, they may become infected, and I have no time for such problems. Give me your hand."

Her captor's autocratic tone raised the edge of her anger, and Devina kept her hands firmly at her sides. With a small twitch of his lips, her captor grasped her wrist firmly while he applied a cooling ointment to the abraded flesh. She was intensely aware of the strength of his hands and the surprising gentleness of his touch as he smoothed the salve on her skin. She remembered the caress of those strong hands, the callused palms moving warmly against her back, pressing her closer, closer . . .

As annoyed with herself for her unsought recollection as she was at the manner in which her captor carelessly dropped her hand when he was finished, she resisted when he sought to take her other wrist. With a penetrating look, he grasped her forearm firmly, holding it fast as he applied ointment to her other wrist.

Finished with his ministrations, he coolly dropped her hand and closed the tin. Her skin still tingling from his touch, Devina broke the silence between them with an angry snap. "I hope you don't expect me to thank you."

The man with Charles's face gave her a short glance. "The thought never occurred to me. Truthfully, I couldn't care less."

Devina stiffened, her face flaming. "Well, what *do* you care about? Money? Is that why you kidnapped me? For ransom, because my father is wealthy?"

Even as she asked the questions, Devina knew this was more than an attempt to extort money from a rich man. There were too many other loose ends, the most startling of which was the handsome face staring coldly back into hers.

"You're not Charles, I know you're not, but who *are* you? Are you his brother, his twin? But you hate my father. Charles doesn't, and Charles isn't devious. I would've seen it in his face, read it in his eyes if he was in league with you."

"You know Charles so well." Her captor's tone was mocking. Deliberately broadening his smile until it transformed his face in a way that sent a chill down Devina's spine, he stepped closer. His voice dropped to a husky tone that set her heart to racing as it had done so efficiently once before. "You know Charles so well, yet you didn't realize that it wasn't Charles who was holding you in his arms in the garden, kissing you."

"I . . . I had no reason to suspect—"

"No reason, Devina? You know Charles so well, and you couldn't sense that it wasn't Charles who was making love to you?"

Devina's mouth turned dry as her captor loomed closer, as Charles's smile changed in a way that added a familiar menace to its curve. She attempted to step back, only to feel the edge of the bunk block her retreat. Her spontaneous words of defense were halting, but vehement. "I . . . I did sense a difference! It's just that . . ."

Realizing she could not complete her statement without revealing herself too completely, Devina found her voice trailing away. But her captor was quick to pick up her thought.

"It's just that what, Devina? It's just that you were enjoying the difference? So Charles is an inadequate lover . . ." Her captor gave a short laugh. His point made, he stepped back from his intimidating stance, even as Devina's fury surged anew.

"No, damn you, Charles is *not* an inadequate lover. Quite the contrary, he's a stirring, virile man, thoroughly exciting in every aspect of his lovemaking." Not giving a care to the erroneous impression she was creating, Devina ignored the tightening of his expression as she continued with considerable heat, "*That* was the difference I noticed—the lack of feeling when you took me into your arms, the coldness."

"Devina, you were anything but cold in my arms."

"I told you, I had no reason to suspect you weren't Charles. I knew what to expect of Charles, and I expected the best was yet to come. Charles isn't devious."

"No, Charles Carter isn't devious. He's everything you respect in a man, and he's everything I'm not. Isn't that what you said, Devina?"

Devina returned the gaze of the man staring down at her. The intensity in his eyes shook her deeply. With supreme power of will she managed a short, triumphant laugh. "You've answered one question for me. Charles isn't in on this with you. I knew I couldn't be wrong about him."

Her captor's cheek ticked revealingly. "I'm no longer interested in discussing Charles Carter."

Flushing as her captor rudely turned his back and walked away, Devina demanded harshly, "What *are* you interested in? Tell me what this all about, dammit!"

Rigid with anger, Devina felt her flush darken as her captor dismissed her question with a brief shrug of his broad shoulders. When he glanced back toward her, his face was devoid of the livid emotion of a few moments before, and Devina was struck momentarily speechless by the man's bewildering vacillations.

"Right now I'm interested in eating. Your party was really impressive Devina, but I spent very little time at the buffet. I had other things on my mind."

"But I want to know—"

Her captor's expression turned abruptly hard once again. "I thought I had made the situation clear to you this morning, Miss Dale, but it's obvious that you didn't quite comprehend what I said. So I'll explain it one more time: *I'm* in control here. *I* ask the questions, and *I* get the answers."

"Damn you, I want to know who you are! I . . . I don't even know what to call you."

The dark brows rose in an expression of feigned surprise. "Oh? I thought you had decided on a name. Bastard, wasn't it?"

More intimidated by her captor's menace than she dared admit to herself, Devina fought to control her trembling. "Damn you! You *are* a bastard!"

Her captor's eyes assessed her briefly. "Get hold of yourself, Devina. If you keep trembling like that, you're going to lose what's left of your dignity. And if you're hoping to play on my sympathy, you're wasting your time. All the sympathy has been burned out of me. Just do what you're told and you'll have no problems."

Coldly dismissing her anger, he turned to the fireplace. "I'm hungry. I'll start a fire so you can cook us something to eat."

Devina's burst of laughter made him turn back to face her.

"Me? Cook? That'll be the day."

"Suit yourself. If you don't cook, you don't eat."

Devina's response was a low, haughty laugh.

Devina was no longer laughing. The fragrance of sizzling bacon filled the small cabin, combining with the tantalizing smell wafting from the pot of beans warming over the fire. Devina cursed the loud rumble of her stomach, which she was certain carried only too well in the limited confines of the one-room structure.

Seated resolutely on the bunk in the corner of the room, Devina glanced quickly toward the table where her captor sat enjoying his evening meal. Seconds later she abruptly averted her face. Oh, the humiliation of it! She was actually salivating!

Damn him, whoever he was! She had not thought he would actually sit there and allow her to watch him eat three meals in a row without offering her a bite! It was not that he didn't have enough or that he needed her help in cooking the food. He had prepared the rather primitive meals far more efficiently than she could possibly have done. It was all just another excuse to exert his authority over her. Well, she would not allow him his victory. She was not hungry . . . *She was not hungry* . . .

The low rumble of Devina's stomach sounded once more in contradiction of her mental statement, and Devina felt tears of frustration fill her eyes. She blinked them back with angry determination. Damn! She was starving.

She had been able to haughtily dismiss breakfast and lunch. The bucket in the corner filled with fresh water had quenched her thirst. But she was so hungry right now, despite her disclaimers, that she could barely control the urge to rush to the table and snatch the plate out of her gluttonous captor's greedy hands.

Unconsciously, Devina plucked at the voluminous garment she had viewed in the mirror with such joy only the night before. She thoroughly despised it now. It was wrinkled and marked with perspiration from the long hours she had spent locked inside this poorly ventilated hovel. It was only when her captor was present that the door was left open to allow the entrance of fresh air. She was silently and intensely grateful for the small comfort.

She lifted her arms with an unconscious grimace, feeling the sticky discomfort of the bodice, which adhered to her body like a second skin. She fussed at the neckline yet again in an attempt to adjust the fine lace striped with silver threads, each and every one of which now scratched her skin unrelentingly. Her shoulders and arms glistened with perspiration, and she was certain her face was covered with the same oily sheen. How she longed to strip away the long silk stockings, which had not been off her legs for twenty-four hours. Damn, she was suffocating in her former magnificence!

An annoying, tickling sensation persisted at the back of her neck, and Devina raised a hand to brush it away. Oh, Lord . . . Her elaborately coiffed hair was hanging in straggly curls against her neck, her extravagant silver clips riding in a steady downward path on the drooping silver-blond waves. She had not bathed since the previous night; and, horror of horrors, she actually was beginning to sense an odor arising from under her arms! Oh, the humiliation of it all!

And now the final mortification: She so desperately had to piddle!

Devina stole a sly glance at her captor who was ignoring her debasement. It was easy for him to sit there enjoying his meal! He had abandoned the fine clothes he had worn to the party—one of Charles's suits, no doubt. His gun belt was now slung low over trousers that showed the signs of many launderings, and he was wearing a soft cotton shirt, which apparently was well suited to the heat of the cabin. He had obviously shaved and bathed while he was absent from the cabin a short time before. He was comfortable, clean, and would soon be very well fed.

Unable to stand the inactivity any longer, Devina stood up abruptly. Ross glanced briefly in her direction, then resumed eating. Damn him, he had actually gone to the fire to refill his plate with those enticingly fragrant beans, and he was now spooning them casually into his mouth, enjoying each and every bite.

If only he would choke.

Devina turned her back on the unbearable sight of her captor's gluttony and took a step toward the doorway. She took another, sneaking a glance at her silent captor. He was still eating and ignoring her. She took another. The door was open wide, and she could see her captor's horse grazing on the sparse vegetation.

Devina's heart began an accelerated pounding as a plan took rapid shape in her mind. Her captor was so sure of her, so sure she was no threat. He did not even look at her as she took another step, and another.

She remembered the sound of the slide lock on the outside of the door. If she could just manage to slip through the doorway before the damned villain realized her intention, she could slam the door and slip the lock into place. Surely it would hold even against his strength, at least until she had time to mount that horse.

Quietly, Devina continued her slow progress toward the doorway. When she was within a few feet of it she made a dash for the outside. At her first burst of movement she heard the sound of a chair scraping the floor behind her, its crash as it hit the wooden floor, the pounding of heavy steps coming up behind her.

But her captor was too late! She was through the doorway and slamming the door closed behind her! She was sliding the lock! She was almost free.

But no! Slowly, steadily, the door was opening, the superior strength of her captor coming to bear even as she put all her weight into her attempt to slip the lock the final measure.

The door flew abruptly open and a deep, paralyzing fear held Devina immobile for long moments as her captor's furious face came into view. Abruptly, she flew into motion, at the same moment her captor reached out and snatched her off her feet. Kicking and scratching, she fought him as he pulled her back inside the cabin and slammed the door behind her. She was still kicking and pounding her fists against his chest, his face, his

arms, when he slowly and efficiently grasped her burning wrists
and twisted them behind her. He crushed her against the hard
wall of his chest, effectively subduing her with the same procedure he had used the night before. She was breathless against his
grip even as he crushed her tighter, closer.

All her strength suddenly devoted to pulling a few lifesaving
breaths into her lungs, Devina went motionless in her captor's
arms. She winced at the fury in the harsh whisper that brushed
her temple.

"So you can't be trusted to keep your word."

Devina looked up to her captor's face, realizing belatedly that
it brought her mouth only inches from his. "Did you really
expect me to keep my word to *you?*"

Her captor's response appeared to be directed more to himself
than to her, even as he stared coldly into her eyes. "Sometimes I
amaze myself with my own gullibility."

"Well, if you believed me, you were more than gullible. You
were a fool!"

Devina was suddenly swung off her feet and into his arms.
Within seconds she was descending just as unexpectedly, her
body hitting the bunk with a loud, jarring thump. Her captor
snatched a coil of rope off the wall and held it near her face.

Fatigue, discomfort, hunger, and fear combined within Devina
as she caught sight of the rope that had bound her the night
before. Her captor's gaze lingered on her white face even as his
dark eyes sparkled with anger.

"You don't want to be tied, do you, Devina? Yet you've
already called me a fool for giving you the freedom you just
threw back in my face. And you can save your tears. Do you
really think you can gain my sympathy now?"

Devina's hands trembled nervously against her tender wrists.

"You're not talking, Devina. What's the matter?"

Devina struggled to sit up on the bed, but he would not allow
her the luxury. Abruptly leaning over her, he braced his palms
on either side of her head and peered hotly into her eyes. She
was only too aware that he still held the coiled rope in one hand
and that it lay on the bed close beside her. She shuddered
instinctively at the thought of its harshness again cutting into her
skin.

"I'm waiting, Devina."

Devina looked up into his hard face. Oh, how had she ever
mistaken this cruel stranger for Charles?

"Devina . . ."

When she answered, her voice came out in a shaky whisper. "No, I . . . I don't want to be tied up again."

Her captor greeted her shaken response with silence. His gaze moved slowly over her face. It dwelled for long moments on her tear-filled eyes, and Devina felt the humiliation of those tears. He continued looking at her face, gazing at her cheeks, her chin, her trembling lips. He was breathing heavily—from exertion or anger, she was not sure which—and she saw a muscle jump in his cheek.

"Get up!"

Abruptly standing beside the bed, her captor stared sternly in her direction. "Get up, I said!"

Drawing herself to her feet, aware that she was trembling uncontrollably, Devina stood in silence as her captor uncoiled the rope. A low sob escaped her throat as he took a step toward her. She flicked her eyes closed, only to hear her captor's low command.

"Open your eyes, Devina. Look at me!"

Devina's eyes snapped wide open in response to the fury in his tone.

"That's right, Devina, look at me when I talk. I want to be sure you understand what I'm saying to you now, because this is your last chance. You don't like being bound, do you?"

Devina swallowed with determined effort and shook her head.

"Answer me!"

Devina swallowed again. Her response was a rasp: "No . . . I don't."

"And you don't like being hungry either, do you?"

"No."

"You realize that your comfort is in my hands?"

"Ye . . . yes."

Her captor's dark eyes devoured hers. She felt the heat of his gaze sink into her mind, all but consuming her strength of will as his voice dropped a notch lower.

"So now I'm telling you for the last time, you'll pull your full weight in this cabin. You'll cook the meals. You'll wash the dishes. You'll do whatever I decide you should do. You'll also remember that I'm in control here. And you'll never, never again try anything like that little trick you pulled a few minutes ago. Do you understand, Devina?"

Devina's trembling lips would not allow her to respond, but her captor was not impressed with her distress. Clamping his hand roughly on her upper arm, he gave a hard shake.

"Do you understand?"

Devina's soft affirmative response was almost inaudible, but it was sufficient to make her captor drop the rope to the floor. Still grasping her upper arm, he turned her toward the door and pushed her into motion. Leaning down, he snatched up some things from the bench near the door, then tugged her roughly outside into the lengthening shadows of evening. He pulled her along a narrow trail that led behind the cabin and down a short incline. Within minutes they were standing beside a small pool.

Dropping her arm, her captor thrust the bundle into her hands. She glanced down to see a shirt and trousers similar to those he wore.

Her puzzled glance was met with a low response. "Do you remember when we met the first time, Devina? You were at your nasty, arrogant worst that day. You made it plain that you could not abide being on the same stage with a foul-smelling drunk. Well, you don't smell very pleasant right now, either, and I have no intention of sharing a cabin with someone who smells worse than my horse.

"So you have a choice. Get out of that gown, bathe in that pool, and put on those clean clothes—or you'll share the same accommodations as my horse. You'll be less comfortable than he is, though. He's free; you'll be tied hand and foot."

Her captor paused, making certain his statement had registered clearly in her mind, before he pressed relentlessly. "What's your decision?"

Devina's hands tightened slowly on the bundle of clothes. Her slight frame stiffened, her chin rising as her captor's insult registered fully within her mind.

How dare he say she stank!

Her paralyzing fear of a few minutes before eliminated by the surge of pure fury suffusing her, Devina managed a tight, stiff smile.

"My decision? I have no problem with the thought of bathing here or anywhere else. I find it personally rewarding to feel clean at all times, and I remind you that it is only due to your inhuman treatment that I am less than pleasant to be near right now."

Her captor's gaze was onyx ice. "I don't care how or why you do what I tell you, just as long as you do it and do it now. I don't intend to wait here all night."

Devina's short intake of breath sounded sharply on the still twilight air. "Wait . . . here?"

"That's right."

Devina's small frame was rigid as she gave a short glance around the barren terrain.

"But . . . but . . ."

"Is there a problem, Devina?"

Devina's small chin rose higher. "You certainly don't expect me to . . . There's no privacy here! How can I bathe?"

"Unless I misunderstand the process, all you need to bathe is water, the willingness to get wet, and the piece of soap that's rolled up in that bundle you're holding."

"But . . . but . . ."

Grasping her arm, her captor started to drag her back toward the trail they had just descended.

"All right!"

Wrenching her arm free, Devina took a short backward step. "Stay there and watch, if that's what you want! I don't care!"

Anger flared in his dark eyes. "You have no one to blame but yourself. If you hadn't already proved that your word is meaningless, you'd have as much privacy as you want right now. Instead, you've got company."

Her fine lips twitching with the heated response she suppressed, Devina turned her back on her captor's hated face. She was intensely conscious of the silence behind her as she attempted to unfasten the back of her gown. Her fingers worked laboriously at the closure even as she waited hopefully for the sound of a retreating step. Damn him! He *was* going to stay and watch!

Abruptly a step sounded behind her, but it was approaching, not retreating. He was coming closer! Devina felt familiar hands brush her fumbling fingers away from her dress. Whirling around, she faced her captor.

"What are you doing?"

"If you think I'm going to wait all night while you fumble with the buttons on your dress, you're wrong," he said disgustedly. "I said stand still, dammit!"

With an agility that spoke of considerable experience with feminine garments, her captor worked efficiently at the back of her dress until Devina felt her bodice hanging loosely against her shoulders. Her heart fluttering in her breast, she held the dress in place until she heard the retreating steps she had been waiting for. But they did not retreat far enough. A short, surreptitious glance over her shoulder told her he had returned to his former position a few feet from the edge of the pool.

Muttering a low, inaudible epithet, Devina allowed her gown to fall to the ground. She kicked it aside to remove the overskirt on her crinoline. When the overskirt and her crinoline were lying in a circle around her feet, her hands moved to the silk stockings that had caused her so much discomfort. She was stripping them off when she heard a low, choking sound behind her. Not bothering to turn around, Devina gave a short snort. Damn him, she hoped he *did* choke.

When she was down to her chemise and underdrawers, she straightened her shoulders. Her hand moved to one delicate lace strap, and her eyes briefly closed. Her trembling fingers gripped the narrow strip of material, but at that point her courage faltered. She could go no further.

Still trembling, she bent down to search through the bundle of clothing until she found a drying cloth and a ball of soap.

Then, resolutely and without a backward glance, Devina walked into the pond.

Ross walked stiffly up the incline toward the cabin, his eyes on the slender woman walking in front of him. He took a short, shaky breath, grateful that the twilight had deepened, that the shadows had worked to partially obscure the figure that had emerged from the pool a few short minutes before. Damn, he'd had just about all he could take.

His control had been sorely tested as Devina Dale peeled off her clothes, but that was nothing at all compared to the supreme test of his will that had followed. Submerging herself in the water, she had arisen from the shadowed depths, the intimate curves of her body glistening through her water-soaked undergarments. Unable to turn away, he had watched with supreme fascination as she let down her hair and lathered it liberally before submerging again. Then had come the torturous visual experience of watching the caress of soap against her smooth limbs and his silent acknowledgment of his own driving desire to join in that caress.

He was grateful that she had kept her bathing time short, emerged quickly, and wrapped herself in the cloth. He couldn't see her face, and he was uncertain of her reaction to the enforced intimacy they had shared. He knew only that those long moments were burned into his mind.

She had slipped the oversize clothes over her wet undergarments, ignoring the fact that the long spirals of her water-darkened hair lay wetly against the fabric of her shirt. She was presently walking barefoot in front of him, a ridiculous sight in a shirt that dwarfed her meager proportions, in trousers rolled up several times in order to allow her to walk without tripping. She clutched her gown and its accompanying paraphernalia, as well as the white satin high-heeled slippers, even as she struggled to hold up the waist of her oversize trousers.

She stumbled, but he made no move to aid her, and she quickly righted herself. He could not afford to touch her. Not now, not yet.

They were walking on level ground again. The cabin was in sight, and Devina walked faster, drawing farther ahead of him. He was surprised at her haste to return to the cabin.

Devina's slender shoulders tensed almost imperceptibly. He sensed more than felt the sudden alertness that moved through her body as she turned toward the cabin. Only a second later she switched directions in a quick, startling movement and threw her voluminous gown in his face.

The heavy garment caught on his shoulders, temporarily impeding his sight, allowing Devina the head start she needed to dash to the spot where his horse was grazing. She mounted with startling agility, then pressed her bare heels into the gelding's sides.

The startled animal reacted wildly, turning, fighting her, allowing Ross time to reach her side. Fists and feet flying, Devina resisted his attempt to drag her from the horse. She punched and kicked him until, in sheer frustration, he grabbed a fistful of her wet hair and pulled her to the ground beside him.

Fighting to subdue the furious little demon in his arms, Ross raged inwardly at his own stupidity, at the driving force of his aching male organ, which had almost overwhelmed his common sense. In one quick movement, he threw the raging woman over his shoulder, ignoring her frustrated screams, and strode back into the cabin.

He walked stiffly to the corner of the room and roughly dumped Devina onto the bunk. He followed her down, pinning her on the hard surface with the weight of his body. He heard her short startled gasp as she renewed her struggles with added vigor. Determined to see the last of her resistance, Ross grabbed her wrists, wresting them roughly above her head, holding them fast as he grasped her chin with his other hand and forced her to meet his furious gaze.

She was gasping for air, and her eyes were wild with frustration and rage. His own breathing was no less strained as he fought to keep the wildcat in his arms under submission.

"Give it up, Devina. You've lost, and you know it. You took the chance and you lost. Now you have to take the consequences."

A spark of another kind temporarily lit her great silver-blue eyes. Fear . . . had he seen fear reflected there? Her next words thoroughly dismissed that thought from his mind.

"Consequences? Do whatever you want, I don't care. But I'll never, ever submit to your threats. My father will—"

"Shut up!" Ross was nearing the limits of his endurance.

"You can't make me do—"

"I said shut up!"

Intensely aware of the slender, squirming body beneath his, Ross knew he could stand little more. Desperation forcing him to extremes he had hoped to avoid, he increased the pressure of his hold on Devina's delicate wrists to the point of pain. At her low gasp, he whispered against her parted lips, "All right, Devina, are you ready to listen?"

"No, I—"

Ross tightened his grip.

"All right!" She gasped again. "Talk! Go ahead!"

Ross released Devina's chin, and she turned her head away in a weak gesture of defiance. Still gripping her wrists, he relieved her of the full weight of his body and drew her hands down to her waist. Stretching out his free arm, he grasped the coil of rope lying on the floor beside the bed. He looped the coil around her wrists and saw that same flicker of emotion flash in her eyes. Still uncertain whether it was fear or fury, he bound her hands tightly, letting the long end of the coil dangle free. Then, straightening up, he removed a narrow rawhide strip from a wall peg. Taking Devina's bare feet in his hands, he forced her ankles together.

"What are you doing?"

Ross didn't bother to respond.

"Damn you! Don't you dare tie my feet! You can't get away with this."

Ross tied her slender ankles together with a few quick flicks of his wrist. "I can, and I did."

"You'll suffer for this!"

"We'll see."

Devina Dale's defiant blue eyes held his for a moment longer. Then she turned her head with great deliberation and closed her eyes.

A sense of triumph conspicuously eluding him, Ross turned and walked out the door.

He didn't like it. The crafty little witch was too quiet.

Ross squinted through the half-light at the silent, unmoving figure on the bunk. An hour had passed since Devina's aborted escape. If he didn't know better, he'd say she was asleep.

He went to stand beside the bunk. She wasn't acting; she really was asleep.

Ross stood in silence a few moments longer, his eyes moving to the bonds on her wrists and ankles. She was so still.

A sudden thought caused Ross to reach out and touch Devina's forehead. Her skin was warm under his palm, but only pleasantly so. Too pleasantly. Unconsciously he stroked back a curling wisp of hair from her cheek. Her father should see her now. Gone was his sophisticated, fashionable daughter. Harvey Dale would hardly recognize this innocent-looking child-woman dressed in oversize men's clothing. Ross frowned. She did indeed look like a child with her pale hair tumbling across the pillow in splendid disarray, with her anger hidden behind closed eyelids. A beautiful, abused child.

Ross's eyes moved to the thong that held her ankles and to the small feet twitching uncomfortably in her sleep. He had tied the thong too tightly. It was cutting into the delicate skin there, marking her. If he could trust her, he would untie those bonds, at least while she slept.

Ross raised his hand and ran it roughly through his heavy dark hair in an agitated gesture. Damn it, now was not the time to soften. But she was hurting.

Leaning over, Ross freed Devina's ankles. He stared at the

coarse rope binding her wrists. A moment later he untied it even as his mind mocked his actions. He dropped the rope to the floor beside the bed.

Ross vowed that he would not be foolish enough to turn his back on Devina Dale again, or to trust her, but neither would he allow his hatred for Harvey Dale to turn him into a man he had no desire to be.

Taking a last cursory glance around the cabin, Ross satisfied himself that all was set for the night. He unstrapped his gun belt and lowered the flame in the lamp. Then in a slow, measured step, he walked back to the bunk.

Silently, Ross slipped his gun belt out of sight under the bunk before sitting on the edge and removing his boots.

Ross studied Devina's features in the flickering light of the fire for a few seconds longer. He reminded himself that, as innocent as she looked, she hated him and would do anything to escape him. He couldn't really blame her . . . and right now he didn't want to.

Careful lest he disturb her sleep, Ross lay down and gently fit Devina into the circle of his arms. He would keep her from escaping. When she awoke . . . well, then they'd see.

Ross pressed his cheek against the brilliant silk of Devina's hair and breathed deeply of her scent. He had already memorized the sweet fragrance of her skin. It was in his heart and mind. With great reluctance he forced himself to remember that this beautiful woman who lay sleeping in his arms was not the woman she now appeared to be. Tomorrow morning, she would awaken, and the battle would start again. But tomorrow was a long time away.

Content to allow his mind to rest on that last thought, Ross pulled his sleeping hostage closer.

Devina was too warm for comfort. A heavy weight lay across her legs. A similar weight was heavy on her chest, and she pushed at it even as she fought awakening to the light of the new day.

Her first awareness of the sinewy arm draped across her breast snapped her into instantaneous consciousness. Her sharp intake of breath broke the early-morning silence of the cabin as her gaze flew toward the man who lay beside her, his head on her pillow, his face turned toward her.

Charles! No, it wasn't Charles.

Devina drew on all her strength to control her reaction to the man who lay beside her. She lowered her gaze to the muscular arm stretched so casually across her chest, to the long leg flung across her own. Both weighed her down, pinned her as effectively as if she were bound.

Devina jumped as her gaze encountered a dark-eyed stare.

"What's the matter, Devina? Uncomfortable?"

Devina's lips twitched nervously as she attempted to pull away from his intimate embrace. Her reply was short, stiff. "Would it change anything if I told you I was?"

"You're not as uncomfortable as you would have been if I had decided to leave you tied."

Devina's glance darted to her wrists and then to her bare feet. She felt a spark of hope.

"Don't get any ideas. I untied you last night because I didn't want you incapacitated, temporarily or otherwise. I want to keep you healthy for your father."

The arm across her chest tensed, and the wide palm resting close to the full outer curve of her breast twitched. Devina gritted her teeth against the involuntary caress.

"Why do you hate my father so much? And who are you?"

No response.

A frustrated flush flooded Devina's face. "I would like to know your name, at least your first name."

The narrowed dark eyes studied her a moment longer. "There's no reason for me not to tell you my full name. Your father will know it soon enough. It's Ross Morrison."

"Morrison!"

Morrison's gaze hardened. "Surprised? You didn't really expect it to be Carter, did you?"

"But you look exactly like—"

"Carter's the one who changed his name, not me."

"What are you saying?"

The heavy arm lifted from her chest, the leg shifted, and Devina was freed of Morrison's weight as he rolled away and drew himself to his feet.

"Get up."

Devina hesitated.

"I said get up!"

Devina rolled to her side and stood up, intensely conscious of her appearance. Her hair had gone uncombed after bathing and lay in an unruly, curly mass on her shoulders. The rags she had been provided hung limply on her body, and she was certain she had not a spot of color on her face.

"Put out your wrists."

Devina closed her eyes. She could not bear to be tied again. She took a deep breath.

"H-how can I cook if you tie my hands?"

"Cook?"

Devina raised her chin a notch higher. "I'm hungry. If I have to cook to eat, I'll cook."

Morrison squinted suspiciously at her stiff expression for some moments before taking a step toward her. Switching the rope to his other hand, he looped it around her waist, then tied it securely as she watched with a knitted brow.

"I've made all the mistakes I'm going to make with you. You'll stay untied as long as you keep yourself busy, and just to make sure . . ."

Morrison tied the other end of the rope around his own waist. A sinister smile flickered across his lips.

"Now get to work."

Devina suppressed a sharp retort. With supreme control she turned to the fireplace.

CHAPTER XIV

HER BRILLIANT SMILE absent from her face, Camille walked along the gaslit main street in a brisk, angry step. She glanced with unseeing eyes toward the brightly lit saloons. Honky-tonk music, the steady clink of glasses, and shrieking female laughter blending with hearty male tones filled the night air. They were the sounds of Tombstone, as characteristic of the bawdy frontier town as the rhythmic pounding of the stamping mill and the rattle of ore wagons moving through the streets. It was a sound she would always associate with this time and this place.

Camille unconsciously noted that it was apparently a very profitable night for saloons along the gaudy strip. The miners, prospectors, and assorted other patrons of the establishments appeared to have turned out in force in their nightly attempt to forget for a few hours the grueling work underground, the disappointment of played-out claims, and the monotony of long, hot days with little to look forward to other than a willing ear, a warm body, a bottle, and friendly companionship.

Camille was well aware that it would be a similarly busy evening at Blond Marie's establishment, although their clientele was of a different class. But Camille knew from long experience that all men were alike when it came to the needs that drove them. She was well versed in the satisfaction of that need, and the demand for her services tonight would doubtless be very strong. In her heart, Camille knew the true reason for Marie's refusal to grant her a few hours away this evening had nothing to do with that fact.

Camille's anger flared anew. Marie's attitude toward her was no longer one of resentment. Marie's feelings for her had long ago passed that benign stage and moved toward emotions of a far more dangerous tenor: distrust, fear, jealousy, and hatred. Le Comte was the buffer between herself and those emotions, and Camille knew her relationship with him was also the cause of Marie's jealousy.

"Camille, good evenin', darlin'."

"How are you tonight, Camille?"

"You're lookin' mighty fine tonight, Camille. Real fetchin'."

Turning toward the chorus of male voices coming from the doorway of the Oriental Saloon, Camille smiled. Beers in hand, the cowboys responsible for the slurred compliments devoured her with their eyes, and she felt a flash of pity. These poor fellows did not stand a chance of accumulating the sum necessary for even one visit with her, but that did not stop them from wanting her. With a generosity of spirit typical of her nature, Camille broadened her smile without slowing her step.

"*Merci, monsieurs.* You warm the heart of a poor working woman with your kind words."

Camille was not surprised when the three fellows politely tipped their hats in her direction. Unlike many of the other women of her profession, she had always been accorded this kind of courtesy, and she appreciated it, without truly understanding the reason behind it.

Her anger of a few minutes before considerably lightened by the encounter, Camille paused at the intersection of Fourth and Allen, awaiting a break in the traffic. Taking her opportunity, she crossed quickly. Once on Fourth Street, she felt her heart begin an instinctive acceleration. She slowed her pace as she reached Charles's quarters. The window shade was drawn, but a soft light glowed from behind it. Charles was home.

Camille tossed her heavy red curls and raised trembling fingers to the neckline of her gown. She had carefully chosen her attire for this visit. Green was her color, and the soft batiste definitely added an air of fragility to her rather substantial frame. On a woman of less ample proportions, the style of her frock might have been considered demure in its simplicity, but Camille was well aware that she could never look demure. Her vibrant coloring, her stately size, and her very personality precluded that possibility.

Her trembling persisted, and Camille could not resist a short, self-deprecating laugh. Ah, when one loved, one became so insecure, especially when one was not loved in return.

It had been too long since she had had a visit from Charles. He had not come to her since that night of love they had spent together in his quarters. She had encountered him several times on the street, and his manner had been polite, casual, almost preoccupied. She had been hurt, confused.

Only a short time after their last night together, Devina Dale had been abducted, and Camille had noticed Charles's preoccupation the next day. She had heard from several sources that Charles had attempted to join a party setting out in search of the beautiful young woman. She had also heard of his anger when Harvey Dale had refused to allow him to participate in the search.

The town was divided in its opinion of Charles's part in the abduction, but Camille did not need to speculate. She knew Charles had had no part in it. Such an act was too foreign to his character, no matter that it had been his brother who had kidnapped the wealthy young woman.

The ache in Camille's heart had grown with each passing hour. Charles was worried about the wealthy, cultured Devina Dale and obviously missed her. In his misery, he had no time for anything or anyone as unimportant to him as she. The ache of that realization had turned to pain.

But her pain and her overwhelming desire to see Charles were not the only reasons she had again appealed to Pierre for permission to absent herself from the house this night. She would never force her presence upon Charles for such selfish reasons. Information had come to her only a few hours earlier, information that Charles needed.

Ah, Charles, she pleaded silently, *you must not be angry with me for coming here even though you have made it plain you no longer wish to see me. And you must not be angry with my interference in your personal affairs. For you see, whatever threatens you threatens me also. I am a part of you, and always will be a part of you.*

Her brown eyes bright with moisture, Camille smiled and knocked firmly on the door.

The door opened to reveal Charles's frown as he stared at her for a long, silent moment. His hair was ruffled, a dark shock lying on his forehead in unaccustomed disarray. He was in his stocking feet and was clothed only in his trousers and a partially unbuttoned, wrinkled white shirt. Camille's eyes touched on the fine mat of dark hair on Charles's chest, and her heart gave a little lurch. How well she remembered lying beside him, her naked flesh pressed against his as she ran her fingers through that dark, coarse hair. She remembered the sensation of those same coarse hairs brushing her breasts and the erotic tumult that had ensued.

But Charles was squinting in a manner which revealed that her knock had awakened him from sleep, and Camille resisted an urge to reach up and brush the wayward lock of hair from his forehead. Ah, how this man touched her heart.

"Camille, is something wrong?"

"Wrong, *mon ami?* Must something be wrong for me to visit you?"

Charles shot a quick look toward the clock on the desk before stepping back with apparent reluctance to allow her entrance. "This is your busy time of night, isn't it? I thought Marie resented your taking personal time when it conflicted with her schedule."

Camille nodded and walked past him into the room. She turned as he closed the door behind them.

"Marie resents much that I do, Charles, but I do not concern myself with her resentment. It matters little."

Charles's expression stiffened at her response. "Yes . . . The Count protects you from her ill will. I forgot."

Camille gave a short laugh. If she had not known better, she would have thought she heard resentment in Charles's tone when he spoke of Pierre. But she knew she was merely responding to her own desire for Charles's deeper affection. Unable to withstand the temptation a moment longer, Camille stroked the dark hair on his forehead into place. He drew back from her touch, and the glow of her eyes darkened.

"Yes, he protects me, but I did not come here to discuss Pierre." She saw Charles's gaze harden, and her smile faded. "Are you angry with me, Charles?"

"Angry? Why should I be angry with you, Camille?"

Camille attempted a smile. "I do not know, *mon cher,* but I do not enjoy the thought. I would never want you to be angry with me.''

Charles's expression tightened further. "I'm afraid I'm going to have to ask you to be brief, Camille. I promised one of my patients I'd stop back tonight. She's had false labor several times this week, and she's not a well woman. I'm concerned about her and . . .''

Halting in his explanation as Camille's gaze touched his lips, Charles frowned more darkly. "Why are you here, Camille?''

Charles's sharpness cut her deeply. "I have come to warn you, Charles.''

"Warn me? Of what?''

"Walter Sherkraut visited Giselle this evening. He is a very talkative man, very impressed with his own importance. One of Giselle's many talents is that she is a good listener, and this evening she listened very well. When Monsieur Sherkraut left, Giselle came directly to me.''

"What has Walter Sherkraut to do with me, Camille?''

Hiding her pain at Charles's obvious impatience to be free of her, Camille went on, "Walter Sherkraut is a close business ally of Harvey Dale. It appears Monsieur Dale is attempting to gather the influential men of Tombstone together to have you driven from town.''

"Driven from town!''

Charles's handsome face flushed a deep red, and Camille shared his distress. "Yes, Charles. It appears he has convinced a considerable number of these men that you assisted your brother in the abduction of his daughter.''

"That's untrue, and he knows it.''

"I know, *mon cher*, but Monsieur Dale has considerable influence.''

Charles gave a low snort. "And he intends to use that influence against me, even though I'm innocent. He hopes to punish my brother through me, and it makes little difference to him if he ruins my reputation, or even if I'm guilty.''

"That is correct.''

Charles laughed, but the sound was harsh, totally devoid of its usual warmth. "My brother was right all along, and it says little for me that I can see that clearly only now, when I am threatened by Harvey Dale, just as he was.''

"But you could not have known. Harvey Dale has been

successful in fooling many with his cunning. Pierre has told me that even he was once—''

Halted by the stiffening of Charles's expression, Camille shook her head. "*Mon cher,* what is wrong?"

"Don't call me *mon cher,* Camille. My name is Charles. You can save those endearments for 'Le Comte,' or for your other clients. They'll appreciate them more than I."

Charles's harsh words cut her like a whip, and heat flooded her face as she swallowed against the hard, tight ache of realization. It was over between them. In losing the beautiful Devina Dale, Charles had discovered his love for her, and he no longer wanted any part of the common courtesan who adored him.

Camille nodded. Her voice was a low whisper. "As you wish, Charles. I do not want to offend you."

Turning blindly, wanting desperately to escape before she embarrassed both Charles and herself, Camille walked rapidly toward the door, then paused with her hand on the knob. No, she was not a child, and she would not run from the man she loved, however deep his words had cut her. If she must say good-bye to him, she would say it with dignity, and with the memory in her heart of the warmth they had shared and of her enduring love for him.

Camille turned back to Charles. Her eyes caressed him lovingly. "*Au revoir,* Charles. It is my hope that these problems which have come about with Harvey Dale will be settled amicably. It is also my wish that the beautiful Devina Dale will be returned to you unharmed. If you should need me, I will always be available to you. You know that, do you not, *mon cher?*"

Realizing she had unconsciously slipped into the endearment to which Charles had objected only a few moments before, Camille swiftly opened the door and stepped out onto the sidewalk. Within moments she was walking rapidly back in the direction of the house on Sixth Street, which was her home, the only place left to her now that Charles no longer wanted her.

Charles watched, silent and unmoving as Camille closed the door behind her. Unable to hold himself back any longer, he covered the distance to the entrance in a few rapid strides and opened the door. Camille was walking quickly toward Allen Street. He swallowed tightly at the desire that coursed through his veins as he noted her rigid posture, the manner in which she turned her head to avoid the scrutiny of passersby. He had seen the tears in her warm brown eyes, and he regretted having caused them. If it had been up to him, he would have seen to it that a far different emotion was reflected in Camille's beautiful eyes. But he could not afford to indulge his weakness.

Unable to look away, Charles allowed his eyes to sweep the familiar curves of Camille's generous frame. She looked lovely tonight, almost childlike in that simple green dress. Charles gave a short laugh. No, that wasn't true. Camille could never appear childlike. She was too lush, too womanly, with her full breasts, her soft, welcoming body, and her gentle, knowing hands. He remembered the touch of those hands a few minutes before, when she had stroked the hair from his forehead. Her touch had seared his skin, and it was all he could do to maintain his control. Then her eyes had caressed his lips.

Charles closed his eyes briefly, remembering the emotions that had swept his senses at that moment. But Camille herself had snapped him from his momentary weakness by mentioning that all too familiar name: Pierre . . .

Pierre . . . Le Comte. The sound of that name on Camille's lips had the power to unleash in Charles a flush of jealousy so severe that he did not recognize himself while in its throes. He was a stranger to such intense emotions. The affluence in which he had been raised had given him life on a steady, even keel. He had never been a grasping, greedy person, and he had always had everything he wanted.

But now his traitorous body wanted a woman who was committed to a way of life far different from his and utterly foreign to him. He and Camille would forever be a lifetime apart, even when they were in each other's arms. And there was his jealousy to contend with. It had been so easy to accept Camille and all that she was before he had come to love her. He had not realized how possessive love truly was, how he would suffer at the thought of the nights she spent in other men's arms. Each time he thought of her, the gnawing ache in his vitals began again, but he knew that as much as Camille's eyes had adored him during their night together, as often as her lips had spoken loving words, as generously as she had offered her soft body to him during the long, passion-filled hours, she would never be truly his.

Even now he berated himself for his thoughts. Camille had made no attempt to present herself as anything other than what she really was. He had no cause to feel betrayed and angry. But perhaps he was angry at himself for not being able to accept her as she was, a warm, loving, giving woman.

The shortcoming was his, for he wanted Camille to give herself only to him. The strength of his feelings would allow him to have her no other way.

Camille's curving, womanly figure disappeared around the corner, and Charles suffered a supreme sense of loss. He had hurt her, and he had not wanted to do that, for surely, she had never intentionally hurt anyone in her entire life.

He was determined not to allow that loss to spill over into the other aspects of his life. He had let Camille down by refusing to accept her as she was, but he wouldn't let Ross down, not again. He'd find his brother and persuade him to return Devina to her father before it was too late.

So, it was true!

Stepping back into the doorway of Tasker and Pridham's General Store, Harvey Dale flashed a short, venomous smile. It was fate that had brought him to this particular establishment in his campaign to rally the community leaders against Charles Carter. It had brought him there so he might witness for himself Camille DuPree's emergence from Charles Carter's bachelor quarters. Harvey had needed to see for himself the "noble" Charles Carter's involvement with the most talked about whore in Tombstone in order to believe it.

A slow rage transfused Harvey's mind. He had been right in saying that Charles Carter had had a part in Devina's kidnapping. Carter had never had true feelings for Devina. He could not have and still maintained his relationship with a common French tart. He had used Devina to help his criminal brother exact his revenge.

Harvey's aristocratic face twitched revealingly as he followed the practiced sway of Camille DuPree's well-rounded contours. It infuriated him that he was powerless to have the law act against Carter. It had been a stroke of genius on Morrison's part to leave Carter to be found tied in his room after the abduction so it would appear Carter was just another victim in his brother's plot for revenge. Harvey had realized from the first that he would not, under the present circumstances, be able to prove anything against the doctor, but he thought his influence in the community would prevail when he used it to stir public sentiment against Carter. It had frustrated him no end to find that there were some in Tombstone who stood firmly in Carter's defense and refused to believe ill of him.

It hadn't been that way when he had used similar tactics against Carter's brother. It had not been at all difficult to cast suspicion on Morrison for the accident in the Till-Dale mine. Morrison, by that time, had gained the reputation of being a hothead, and relatives of the victims, wild with grief, had been only too happy to place the blame on someone. Morrison had been the perfect scapegoat, and Harvey had also managed to eliminate the only obstacle between himself and the final take-over of Brad Morrison's claim. It had mattered little to him that Morrison was innocent of blame. Morrison had been impeding the growth of Till-Dale's mining operations, and Harvey Dale had removed him.

He had begun to learn that Charles Carter would not be handled so easily.

Harvey drew back farther into the shadowed doorway of the store as Camille DuPree walked stiffly past the door. A bold, cheap tart with flaming hair and jiggling breasts. Well, he would see that Charles Carter no longer found pleasure in her warm flesh. Carter might presently be impervious to his attack, but the foreign whore was not.

A plan forming rapidly in his mind, Harvey felt a blood rage suffuse him at the realization that Charles Carter had played both him and Devina for fools. The lovestruck Carter, unaware of the fate that loomed ahead, was standing in the doorway of his quarters, fondly gazing after his tart as she made her way home.

Pain, frustration, fear, and a devastating sense of loss overwhelmed Harvey in a sudden wave of emotion. Dear Devina. He must find her.

As Harvey watched, Carter stepped back inside his quarters, closing the door behind him. Harvey's heated stare remained intent on the closed door as he made a solemn vow. *You'll not go untouched in this affair, Carter. If I can't get to you directly, I'll get to you through your good-natured little whore.*

The gnawing hunger in Jake Walsh's stomach caused him to

urge his mount to a faster pace. According to plan, he had maintained his position midway between Tombstone and the cabin for a day and a night so that he might watch the trail. He had been vigilant, dozing only occasionally. During that time he had not chanced lighting a fire and had eaten only dried beef and drunk only the lukewarm water from his canteen.

He had awakened from a fitful doze at daybreak and watched the trail for a few hours longer. Then, satisfied that it was perfectly safe, he had mounted and begun riding toward the cabin. He was stiff, exhausted, and hungry. He could almost smell that coffee perking, could almost see that bacon frying, could almost feel that bunk, lumpy or not, under his back.

A physical discomfort of another kind bothered him also, but it would be a while before he would be able to satisfy that ache. Jake shook his head at the realization he had suffered the night of Devina Dale's party.

Hidden, he had watched the party in progress while waiting for Ross to bring Devina Dale into the garden. It had been a fine affair, with no expense spared, that was for sure. He knew that fact would not escape Ross's notice. The upper crust of Tombstone had been well represented, dressed in their best, the women looking as good as they had ever looked in their lives. He had recognized a few: Bart Collins's daughter, with her bright red hair, Maggie Sills, with her buttercup-yellow dress. But none of those women had truly stirred his interest.

He remembered the exact moment his heart had come to life—when Lai Hua appeared in the doorway. She had paused, silhouetted there in her drab servant's garb, and his heart had skipped a beat. She had walked down into the garden and turned to direct one of the other servants. Her small face had been illuminated by the lanterns, and the rush of emotion that had flushed through him had shaken him. How had Lai Hua managed to push thoughts of other women so firmly from his mind?

Stupid question. He knew exactly how Lai Hua had softened the bitterness inside him, how she had brought tender emotions back into his heart. She had done it by giving herself to him without asking anything in return. She had done it by loving him, even when he couldn't make himself say the words she whispered so sincerely to him. She had done it by accepting him as he was, an ex-convict who silently held her race against her even while he held her in his arms. She had done it by telling him he was the most important thing in her life.

Why couldn't he make himself tell her the same thing in return?

Jake took a deep, weary breath and attempted to turn his mind to a more pressing subject: Devina Dale.

He removed his hat and ran his hand through his fair hair. He had not approved of the plan to kidnap Devina Dale, but Ross had been determined. Jake had learned long before that whatever Ross set his mind to do, he did. This time Ross had fooled them all, just as he had said he would. In a few weeks all this would be over, and he and Ross would leave Tombstone and everyone in it behind them.

As for Lai Hua . . .

The cabin came into view, and Jake sighed his relief. With a good meal under his belt and a few hours of uninterrupted sleep, he'd be fine.

Instinctively, Jake surveyed the terrain around the cabin as he approached. Ross's horse was grazing a short distance from the door, and smoke curled in a slender stream from the metal chimney. Jake doubted that smoke would be visible from a distance. The cabin stood in a hollow between rolling hills, and the smoke would travel up for quite a distance before it would be visible from afar.

Jake's tension mounted as he approached the cabin, and he was suddenly aware of the reason why: He had no desire to face Devina Dale. Even if all Ross said about Harvey Dale's rich and spoiled daughter was true, he wasn't comfortable with what they had done. He had been a prisoner for too long not to feel guilty about forcing the same situation on somebody else.

With true reluctance, Jake reined his mount up near the spot where Ross's horse grazed. The sound of his approach brought Ross to the doorway, and Jake took note of the stiffness of his friend's expression. He knew his approach had been sighted long before, that Ross was undoubtedly awaiting his arrival, but he had not expected to be greeted with such a scowl.

As he dismounted, the strong aroma of brewing coffee met his nostrils, and Jake smiled. Damn, that smelled good! Only seconds later the smell of frying bacon joined the assault on his senses, and Jake's stomach growled in eager response. Well, he supposed he could stand a bout with Ross's bad humor in return for a good breakfast. As a matter of fact, right now he'd walk on a bed of hot stones to get a hot meal. He was hungry . . . mighty hungry.

As he neared the cabin, the aroma began to change drastically. He smelled coffee—*burned* coffee. And scorched bacon! His step slowed as a cloud of black smoke billowed out through the doorway, only to be followed by Ross, carrying a smoking frying pan.

Jake blinked. Trailing behind Ross from the other end of a rope secured around his waist was Devina Dale. But this was a Devina Dale he had never seen before. Long, straggly silver-blond hair hung in her face, all but blinding her as she scrambled after Ross. Her feet were bare, and as he watched, one leg of her oversize trousers rolled down and covered her foot, almost tripping her as she hurried to keep up with Ross's long strides. She stumbled, then righted herself awkwardly, only to emit a short cry as her bare foot came down hard on a sharp stone. She brushed back her hair in time for Jake to get a short glimpse of the fury and frustration registered in her face.

Ross stopped abruptly, and Devina Dale's forward motion brought her up smack against his back. A short laugh rose to Jake's lips. He bit it back as Ross turned slowly, sending a deadly look in Devina Dale's direction. Disengaging herself from his back, she shot a glance toward the smoking frying pan in Ross's hand, then looked up at him.

Ross held Devina Dale's gaze with a silent stare for a few meaningful seconds longer before turning to face Jake. "I'd wipe that smile off my face if I was you, Jake. You're looking at all that's left of breakfast."

Jake shot a quick look toward the woman who stood in absolute silence behind his friend. He struggled to control the grin he felt tugging at his mouth. Damn, she was a wreck! Harvey Dale would hardly recognize his daughter if he could see her right now. But the girl's spirit didn't seem to have been hurt any. He could see her reaction to his amusement, and it wasn't good at all.

Ross continued talking, even as he shook the remains of the charred bacon out of the pan and onto the ground. "I suppose your arrival here means the trail is clear."

"You suppose right, Ross." Jake glanced at the blackened

pan. "I guess I can wait a little longer for breakfast. I'll just take a cup of that good strong coffee I smell brewin'."

Ross's glance darkened. "Sure, you do that. Don't bother to pour it, Jake. Just whistle, and that coffee'll walk right over and jump into your cup."

Ross slanted a reproving glance toward the glowering young woman. By way of explanation, he offered stiffly, "Our cook here dumped almost the whole sack of coffee into the pot."

Jake's grimace seemed to be more than the silent young woman was able to bear. Tossing her head in a haughty gesture completely out of keeping with her unkempt appearance, she ignored Jake's presence and directed her comments to Ross. "I am not accustomed to performing menial tasks. I did not claim I could cook, but I *did try*!"

Turning fully toward her with an abruptness that forced her to step back, Ross thrust the handle of the pan into her hands. "Try again!"

Ignoring the woman's furious expression, Ross turned to Jake. There was no doubt in Jake's mind of the note on which this day had begun.

"Come on inside, Jake. We've got things to discuss." Ross headed back to the cabin.

Reluctant to step into the middle of the conflict, Jake watched as Ross's long strides took up the slack in the rope, abruptly jerking Devina forward. Managing to stifle his laughter as Devina struggled to match Ross's long strides, Jake shook his head. It seemed like Ross was in for more than he'd expected with this woman.

Ross disappeared inside the cabin, dragging Devina behind him. Waiting only until they both had cleared the doorway, Jake took a deep breath and followed.

"All right, do you understand exactly what you have to do?"

Jake's brow knit in a frown. "Ross, we've been over this a dozen times. I leave here in the mornin' and go directly to Tombstone. I find out from Mack and Harry exactly what's been happenin' since the party." Jake paused to glance at Devina's back as she worked at the fireplace. He frowned. He wasn't comfortable with the Dale woman's keen eyes watching him and with the tension between her and Ross. Hell, Ross was acting downright queer.

"And then what are you going to do, Jake?" Ross's voice was lacking in patience, and Jake's frown deepened.

"I'm goin' to hang around Tombstone for a couple of days, and when I'm sure Dale is runnin' around in circles, I'm goin' to come back here to report to you."

"Just make sure you don't let those two wastrels lead you astray, Jake." Ross's dour expression softened slightly. "If I know Mack and Harry, they're propping up a bar at the Alhambra or the Oriental, and they're enjoying every minute of it."

But Jake wasn't smiling. "Sure, they're enjoyin' every minute, Ross. They couldn't care less about this whole thing. You know damned well they're only doin' you a favor by stayin' in town and watchin' things until I come back. As soon as I get to Tombstone, they're goin' to take their stake, clear out, and forget the whole thing."

The small woman at the fireplace turned, and Jake caught her glance. Devina Dale wasn't missing a thing, and he had a feeling deep inside that he was going to regret this day.

But Jake's anxious thoughts were interrupted as Devina Dale approached the table carrying a plate. He smiled. "Perfect, ma'am! That bacon is fried up just perfect. You sure are a quick learner."

An unreadable flicker moved across Devina's face at Ross's low snort.

"Finally," Ross said. "Now dish up the leftover beans and pour the coffee."

Devina's sudden panic-stricken expression and her quick turn toward the fireplace brought Ross's instructions to a halt. His eyes followed her as she went back to the fireplace, his brows knitting together even more darkly than before.

Still facing the fire, Devina stated flatly, "I forgot to stir the beans. They're stuck to the pot."

Ross raised his eyes expressively toward the ceiling. "Looks like we're going to have to be satisfied with bacon and hardtack, Jake."

"It doesn't matter much to me, Ross. I wasn't hungry, anyway."

Jake's stomach took that moment to loudly contradict his response, and he smiled sheepishly. "As a matter of fact, I'm thinkin' I won't wait until tomorrow to go back to Tombstone. It doesn't look like you need me around here, and there's no use wastin' time when I can be findin' out how things are goin'. While I'm there, I'll—''

"I don't want you going anywhere near that girl when you get there, Jake." Ross's low command cut sharply into Jake's words. "It's too dangerous."

Resentment creased Jake's fair brow. "If you're thinkin' she isn't to be trusted—"

"It's not a matter of trust. It's too dangerous. Somebody might be watching her."

"Come on, Ross! You know damned well nobody knows about Lai Hua and me."

A low gasp from the fireplace made both men turn toward Devina.

"Lai Hua? She's in on this with you?"

Darting Jake a silent reprimand for his slip of tongue, Ross continued without acknowledging Devina's question. "Like I said, Jake, I don't want you going anywhere near the girl."

Jake stiffened. "I'm thinkin' this isn't the time or the place to discuss Lai Hua, Ross."

"Where and when would you think *is* the right time, Jake?" His voice hot with annoyance, Ross did not bother to acknowledge Devina as she poured coffee into the metal cups beside their plates. Ross leaned intently toward Jake. "I'm telling you to stay away from her for a while. For all we know, Dale could be having her watched."

"Nobody knows about Lai Hua and me," Jake said again.

"As far as you know."

"I'm sure."

Ross's face darkened. "We've waited a long time for this, Jake. A slip now could bring it all down around us."

Jake's pale blue eyes were unrelenting. "You don't need to tell me how much plannin' and all else has gone into this, Ross. I was there from the beginnin', remember? And I'm thinkin' you should've learned by now to trust—"

"Jake, I'm not going to say it again. Stay away from the girl, unless you want to see us both back behind bars in Yuma."

Shock made Devina stiffen and turn toward Ross.

"That's right, Miss Dale. You've been kidnapped by two ex-convicts, one of whom your father sent to prison." The pale blue eyes widened, and Ross squelched his reaction to the extreme beauty of her delicate face. "So you've gotten some of the answers you were looking for. Does it make you feel any better?''

Devina's face continued to whiten, and Ross snapped harshly, ''Sit down before you fall down, Devina.''

Devina sat in silence, and Ross pushed the plate of bacon in front of her with a deprecating glance. ''Eat something. You won't be any use if you faint on me. Besides, I want to keep you in good health.''

Ross's harshness with the Dale girl brought a flush to Jake's face. There was a war going on between them, and Jake didn't want any part of it. He didn't bother to raise his head as Ross again addressed him.

''Jake, about the girl . . . you heard what I said.''

''Yeah, I heard you. I'm goin' to Tombstone right after I finish eatin' and takin' care of a few things here.''

Ross hesitated, his face slipping into a frown. ''There's no rush. I told you, I don't intend to contact Dale for at least a week.''

Jake raised his head briefly.

''I'm thinkin' I'll find more to do with myself in Tombstone than here while we're waitin'. I'm thinkin' I'll be more useful there, too.''

Ross shrugged a broad shoulder in silent assent.

Jake glanced at Devina Dale. It occurred to him she was a bit too quiet. His light brows pulled into a thoughtful frown.

Ross stood in the doorway of the cabin, squinting into the brilliant light of midday. Jake had just turned out of sight on the trail back to Tombstone. During the short time he had remained at the cabin he had left Devina Dale as wide a berth as possible. Jake's discomfort with their beautiful hostage had been obvious, and Ross had no doubt it accounted for his early departure.

Ross's squint turned into a frown. Jake didn't approve of his methods, but then, Jake didn't have a personal stake in this situation. Unlike Ross, he didn't have demons eating at him, driving him. He didn't feel the sense of urgency building inside him, the realization that he had to make this plan work.

At a sound behind him, Ross turned, halting Devina Dale in her step. His eyes touched on the disheveled young woman who was the key to the success of his plans. His heart lurched in his

chest as she held his gaze for a long, silent moment with her
great silver-blue eyes.

When she spoke, her voice emerged in a whisper. "Is it true?"

Annoyed at his conflicting reactions to her and angered by the
agitation they worked within him, Ross frowned. "Is what true?"

"Lai Hua was part of this scheme?"

"I told you, I don't answer questions."

"Damn you! At least tell me that!"

Ross held her gaze a few tantalizing moments longer. "What
do you think?"

Tears filled her eyes, and Ross felt a moment's regret as she
turned and walked back to the table. Abruptly angry with himself
for his weakness, he went to her side. When she raised her
head, his inner struggle was reflected in the fierce frown that
darkened his face as he reached out to untie the rope encircling
her waist.

Devina's reaction was one of surprise. "You're untying me?"

"You have a conveniently short memory, Devina. Last night I
gave you some freedom, and you abused it. Did you think I
would forgive you just because you made a halfhearted effort to
cooperate this morning?"

The rope fell from her waist to the floor, and Ross reached for
the narrow leather thongs on the mantel. In a quick movement he
forced Devina's wrists together and looped the leather strip
around them. She started to speak. Failing in the attempt, she
swallowed and tried once more. Her voice emerged in a low
rasp. "Please . . ."

His desire for this woman growing more overpowering with
each moment those solemn eyes looked into his, Ross responded
with a gruffness that was foreign even to his own ears. "Please
what, Devina? What do you want?"

"Please don't tie me."

"Give me a good reason why I shouldn't."

"I . . . I don't want to be tied."

Steeling himself against her appeal, Ross pulled the thong
tighter. In a quick movement, he lifted her off her feet and
carried her to the bed. Dropping her on the hard mattress, he
snatched her feet together and looped the second thong around
them. Leaning over her, Ross looked into her brimming eyes.

"I realize you don't know what it means to pay the price of

your actions. I also realize that you've never had to earn anything in your life. But you should've remembered how little you liked being tied when you broke your word yesterday. You've got a few hard lessons to learn, Devina. The first one is that you're not your daddy's little darling in this cabin. The second is that I don't make empty threats. You're going to have to earn your freedom, Devina. It might be an unpleasant lesson, but it'll be a valuable one. Almost as valuable as the lesson your father taught me." Ross paused. In answer to her silent question, he responded harshly, "Don't ask what that lesson was. You don't want to know."

Ross looked down at his helpless captive for a moment longer before walking away from the bunk. In a few long strides he was through the doorway of the cabin and had turned out of sight in the brilliant sunlight beyond.

CHAPTER XV

THE THUNDERING HOOFBEATS around him slowed to a moderate pace as the town of Tombstone came into view. Harvey reined his laboring sorrel to a matching gait and glanced at the leader of the small posse with a low grunt of disgust. Sheriff Bond. Damn the man for the inept, blundering fool that he was!

Harvey ignored the dust-laden air and the heavy residue of grit that coated his face and riding attire. Frustrated as he was, he cared little for his appearance or for his discomfort.

It had been a week since Devina was abducted, and he had received no word from the bastard who had taken her, nor had he found a single clue to her whereabouts. He had tried everything. He had hired Sam Sharpe to follow Charles Carter every time he left town. That effort had turned up nothing more than the names of a few patients who had been too ill to come to his office. Harvey had even employed Wally Smith to keep an eye on Camille DuPree, but that effort had been just as unproductive. Finally having given up on those approaches, he had pressed Sheriff Bond all the harder.

The silent group of men around him turned their horses toward Dexter's Livery. It was obvious that they had had enough. That same feeling was only too evident on Chester Bond's narrow, lined face. But Harvey Dale had not had enough, and if Bond thought he was going to give up, Bond was sadly mistaken. The damned fool had been in his pocket for years. He had never done more to earn his money than to lend his lawful presence when it was needed at Till-Dale Enterprises.

The men of the posse dismounted and began to drift away in a disorganized manner that symbolized in Harvey's mind the ineffectiveness of the group. Saddle tramps and trail bums, most of them, willing to spend a day riding around in the wilderness at Sheriff Bond's direction if it would put a few extra dollars in their pockets. The few extra dollars had been supplied by Till-Dale Enterprises.

Ignoring the ache in his bones resulting from his unaccustomed activity, Harvey regarded Sheriff Bond coldly as he dismounted.

"Another long day riding in the sun, Sheriff. Am I to assume that is the most I can expect from you, three or four hours of riding in circles? Who in hell did you think you were fooling? You have no idea where Morrison is holding my daughter, do you?"

Sheriff Bond's mustache twitched as he shot a quick glance toward the curious stares of the men around them. His narrow face stiffened.

"I'm thinkin' this ain't the proper time or place to discuss the matter, Mr. Dale."

"And I'm thinking there's no better place than this, in full view of your constituents. I do think the people who put you in office should be aware of your performance. And your performance is nil, Sheriff, nil!"

Chester Bond's wiry frame stiffened. "You're upset, Mr. Dale, and I can understand that. I can understand that it might bedevil a man that somebody can just kidnap his daughter and disappear off the face of the earth with her like that fella Morrison did. But we caught him once before, Mr. Dale, and we'll catch him again . . . you wait and see."

"I'm tired of waiting, Sheriff." Harvey Dale's aristocratic face began to flood with color at the sheriff's placating assurances. "You have no idea where that swine took my daughter!"

"You're right there, Mr. Dale."

"I'm right! That's little consolation, indeed. What do you intend to do about this whole damned thing?"

Chester Bond took another quick, surveying glance around them. Curious onlookers were beginning to cluster around, and his discomfort increased.

"Like I said, Mr. Dale, this ain't no place to discuss what I intend doin' about this situation."

"You don't want to discuss your plans to find my daughter, Sheriff, because you haven't formulated a plan, isn't that right? Admit it, dammit!"

"Mr. Dale . . ." His squinting gaze assessing the purple tint coloring Harvey Dale's face, Sheriff Bond shook his head. "I ain't discussin' nothin' with you right now. You're out of your head with grief and worry, and I can understand that. If you wasn't, you'd realize that Morrison didn't take your daughter without a reason. I'm thinkin' that reason is money, and if it is, you'll be hearin' from him soon. I know this scoutin' we've been doin' in the last week don't stand nothin' more than an outside chance of turnin' up anythin', but I figured it was a chance you'd want to take. If I was wrong, we'll just forget the whole thing and wait until—"

"Fool, damned stupid fool! He's outsmarted you, hasn't he? A jailbird, an ex-convict straight from Yuma Prison has you running in circles!"

Pausing, Chester Bond fixed his squinting stare on Harvey Dale's enraged expression. "Seems to me that jailbird has outsmarted you, too, Mr. Dale. Else, you'd be leadin' this posse straight to where he's holdin' your daughter."

Harvey went pale but said nothing.

Growing bolder, Sheriff Bond pressed on in his nasal tone, "Ain't that right, Mr. Dale?"

Harvey Dale stared into Sheriff Bond's unrelenting gaze for a few seconds longer before turning abruptly on his heel and striding away.

Harvey was still walking in a brisk, driven stride when he realized he had no idea where he was heading. It came to him then that he had been floundering without a sense of direction from the first moment he had realized that Devina was gone.

Charles paused, his eyes flicking between Harvey Dale and Sheriff Bond in contemplation of the scene being enacted for the curious eyes of Tombstone. It was his feeling that, as well staged as it was, it was entirely impromptu, stimulated by the exhaustion, fear, and despair of Harvey Dale. But somehow, Charles could not feel pity.

It occurred to Charles that Harvey Dale was not the man he had been before Devina disappeared. Certainly that Harvey Dale would never have appeared in public with such a casual disregard for his appearance. Were it not for his posture, his air of privilege, Dale could have been mistaken for any cowboy on the street in his dust-covered trousers and open-neck cotton shirt. Charles was well aware that Dale had been seen this way more often than not during the week Devina had been gone. Dale had participated in almost daily searches in the hope of finding her. The long rides had obviously taken their toll.

As Charles watched, Dale straightened in reaction to something Sheriff Bond had said, then walked away. The man was shaken, badly so. The sheriff and he had been all but shouting, but Charles had been unable to hear their words over the din of the street traffic.

A cold knot of fear clenched tightly in Charles's stomach. Oh, God, it could not be Devina! Dale could not have learned something tragic . . .

Uncertain whether the rapid pounding of his heart was the result of fear for his brother or anxiety about Devina, Charles followed Harvey Dale. His rapid step soon brought him up beside Dale. He halted, startled by Dale's vacant stare as the older man walked past him without recognition. Charles placed a staying hand on his arm. "Harvey . . ."

The aristocratic gray head swung in his direction; the light eyes focused with considerable effort, widening at the moment of recognition. "Get out of my way, Carter!"

"I want to talk to you a moment."

"I have nothing to say to you. You, with your pretended innocence. I know you're in league with that criminal brother of yours. Damn you, I can see the villainous gleam in your eyes! I wonder that I was so blind to it before."

"Perhaps you were blind to that gleam, Harvey, because it wasn't there. Perhaps that gleam you see now is just a product of your imagination and your nervous exhaustion."

"Don't tell me what I see! You're a criminal, just like your brother. Are you gloating, now that you see how ineffective the law is in finding him and my Devina? Do you laugh when you report back to him that we ride out every day and come back empty-handed?"

"You know I've had no contact with my brother, Harvey."

"How would I know that?"

"Because you've had me followed." Charles smiled at Harvey's startled reaction to his statement. "I'm not the fool I was three years ago, Harvey. I watch my back now."

"You were in on this whole thing with your brother right from the start! You think you have this town fooled, but you don't. When I'm done with you, there'll be no place for you in Tombstone, or anywhere else in the West."

"I didn't stop you to listen to your threats, Harvey. I want to know if you've found out anything more about Devina. I'm just as anxious to see her returned as you are."

"Liar! Hypocrite! Don't pretend to me, Carter. I'm not taken in by your acting skills. And don't think you'll escape unscathed, either. You think you're untouchable, don't you? The good and noble doctor. But you're not as untouchable as you think."

Charles assessed Harvey Dale with a professional eye. His complexion was mottled and purplish. This conversation was doing the man no good.

"Harvey, it is not to your advantage to allow yourself to become so agitated."

"Damn you! You've taken my daughter! She's gone, and I don't dare think what that criminal brother of yours has done to her! But I tell you here and now, Carter. If you or your brother has harmed one hair on Devina's head, I'll make you pay. If it takes me to my dying day, I'll make you pay!"

Realizing it was senseless to respond, Charles turned without another word and walked back to his office, leaving Harvey staring at his retreating back.

Jake lifted his glass to his lips and took a deep swallow, but he tasted nothing. His mind was intent on the confrontation taking place outside the saloon.

It had been real considerate of Charles Carter to stop the hard-nosed Harvey Dale right out in front of the saloon door, so that Jake could hear their conversation. It didn't take much to see that Dale was at his wits' end with worry about his precious daughter.

Jake lifted his glass to his lips and took a deep swallow, and then another. He drained the glass and turned toward the back table where Mack and Harry were amusing themselves with a game of poker. The time was ripe. He'd talk to those two boys and turn them loose, and tonight he'd start back toward the cabin. But first, before he took on that long ride, he'd see to it that he went back in a far better frame of mind than he'd been in for the last few days. It had been tough being so close to Lai Hua and staying away from her. Ross didn't know how much he owed him for that.

His hand slipping into his pocket to touch the red ribbon he had toyed with all week long, Jake turned toward the table where Mack and Harry were bickering in their familiar way. His step quickened at the thought of the night to come.

The Count paused in the shadows of the hallway and raised his eyes to the staircase to follow the slow descent of the voluptuous red-haired woman. He carefully appraised the expression on her open, sober face, and his graying brows furrowed into a frown.

Hearing a sound in the foyer he turned to see Marie open the front door to a short, well-dressed gentleman. Marie's pretty features relaxed into a smile of greeting, which faded as the fellow responded almost absentmindedly, his eyes on the staircase. Removing his hat, he handed it to Marie.

"Camille, I was hoping I'd find you available this afternoon." With an embarrassed laugh the fellow proceeded to the foot of the staircase. "It is a bit early in the day for me to visit. I wasn't sure . . ."

Pierre's eyes narrowed as he looked back to Camille. The change in her expression was immediate; her smile was forced as she greeted the anxious gentleman.

"Ah, Monsieur Collier . . . William. How nice to see you. You have not visited for so very long. I thought you had abandoned me."

Reaching up to take her hand, the fellow smiled more earnestly. "Never, never, Camille."

Pierre was amused to see that Camille stood almost an inch taller than her client. The fellow's spare frame seem to shrink in comparison to her well-fleshed proportions. But it was also obvious that her formidable stature in no way intimidated the tense banker. He appeared to relax immeasurably as he took her hand and raised it to his lips.

The fellow's low whisper carried easily to Le Comte's ears.

"Camille, I couldn't wait any longer to come to see you." The fellow reached out a trembling hand to stroke Camille's cheek. "You always help me when things aren't going well."

Camille's concern was obviously sincere. "William, it is your wife, is it not? She has worsened?"

"Yes." William Collier's thin face twisted with pain. He cast an anxious glance around the foyer. "If we could go upstairs to your room, just to talk for a little while."

"I am sorry, Monsieur Collier." Marie's sharp tone cut into the whispered conversation. "But our services do not include extended conversations when one of our girls could be more useful elsewhere."

Collier took a short step back, still holding Camille's hand. "Of course, I intend to pay, Marie. I would not expect to take Camille's time without paying the usual price."

Marie's expression tightened further as Camille's brows furrowed in unspoken objection to her harsh interference.

"Camille, take your place in the parlor with the other girls. I make the policy in this house. Monsieur Collier and I will discuss this matter."

Pierre took a short angry breath. "Marie!" His cheek twitched with suppressed anger. "Marie, *I* make the final decision on policy in this house." Turning toward Camille and her client, he continued politely, "Monsieur Collier, we are pleased we can be of service to you in any way. Camille, if you wish to escort the gentleman upstairs . . ."

Watching as Camille smiled in William Collier's pale face, Pierre was touched by the gratitude in the poor fellow's expression as he clutched Camille's hand and started up the staircase at her side. Waiting only until Camille's bedroom door had closed behind them, Le Comte turned sharply toward Marie.

"That will not happen again, Marie, if you value your position here. *Comprenez-vous?*"

Marie's stiff nod was accompanied by a low *"Oui."*

"And you will inform Camille that I am waiting to speak to her when she is again free."

"Oui."

"Bon."

Turning sharply on his heel, Pierre walked back into his office. He raised his head at a light knock at his office door a short time later.

"Entrez."

The door opened and Camille hesitated in the doorway. "You wish to see me, Pierre?"

"Yes, Camille. Come in."

The spark of warmth Camille always generated within him

blazed to life at her tentative smile. He held out his hand, feeling the warmth of her light touch all the way to his heart as he grasped hers lightly.

"Camille, I have been waiting for you. Have you done your best to help Monsieur Collier?"

Camille nodded, her smile dimming. "Yes, but William's distress was not of the body." Her smile flashed again briefly. "Although he visited me for that purpose when I first arrived in Tombstone, he rarely does more than kiss me with surprising tenderness on his visits now. Mostly, we talk. His wife is very ill, has been for many years, but he loves her dearly."

"He loves you, too, Camille."

Camille appeared startled by Le Comte's words. "He is lonesome. His wife is in too much pain to share his daily life with him."

"He loves you, Camille." Pierre's smile was gentle. "Do you find that so hard to accept?"

Avoiding a direct response, Camille shrugged. "I do not believe he loves me. I fill a temporary emptiness in his life."

"I saw his face, Camille." Pierre was insistent. "He loves you. It is not difficult for me to understand that man's love, for I love you in the same way, *ma chérie*."

Bright tears filled Camille's warm brown eyes, and she swallowed tightly. "Is there so much in me to love, Pierre? I hardly believe so."

Pierre's smile dimmed. He had been correct in his assessment of Camille's state of mind. He had seen the unhappiness grow inside her in the past week. It had been almost imperceptible at first. And then, with startling abruptness, it had swelled to encompass her totally. Her unhappiness would not have been evident to the casual observer, but it was all too evident to him, for he had loved her too well, for too many years, to be fooled. Camille suffered, and when Camille suffered, he suffered.

Pierre's dark eyes rose to hers. "Yes, Camille, there is much to love in you. Very much."

Heavy tears hung precariously in Camille's eyes, but she raised her chin as he drew her toward the settee and urged her to sit. He sat beside her and raised her hand to his lips.

"And now you will tell me why you are unhappy, who has made you so." His eyes darkened, and his lips drew together in a hard line. "I am aware that Marie has made your life difficult. If it is she, I will—"

"No, Pierre, it is not Marie." Camille gave a short laugh. "Marie dislikes me because she sees in me a threat that does not exist. She fears for her position because—"

"Because she knows you are in my heart. Is that not correct?"

"Pierre . . ."

Pierre smiled at Camille's reluctance to confirm his statement. He spoke in her stead. "*Oui*, that is correct."

Camille lowered her eyes. "Marie does not understand that I have no desire to take over her position, that my only true desire . . ."

She hesitated, and Pierre frowned. It was not like her to hold back from him. He pressed her softly. "Your only true desire, *ma chérie* . . . ?"

Camille gave a short shrug and forced a smile to her lips. "It matters little, Pierre. One cannot always have what one desires."

Pierre shook his head. "*Peut-être que non* . . . perhaps not, but I will tell you this. If it is in my power to put the light back in your eyes, to restore the joy to your heart, it will be done."

"It is not in your power, Pierre."

Pierre waited, but Camille did not continue. "Tell me what is making you unhappy, Camille."

Camille averted her face. "Pierre, please . . ."

"Tell me."

He heard her deep sigh, felt it shake her body before she turned to him once more.

"Pierre, this woman who is so lovable is not loved."

Realization flickered across Pierre's mind. Of course. He spoke softly, gently. "Camille, you are loved by so many, and by me in particular, but is it not those loves that concern you, is that correct?"

"*Oui*, Pierre."

"It is the love of Charles Carter."

Camille's face froze into stillness.

"You need not answer, *ma chérie*, except to tell me how I may help you."

A single tear trailed down Camille's flushed cheek, and she brushed it away with impatience. "Pierre, with the best of intentions, you cannot make a man love me. And Charles does not. He loves Devina Dale."

"But the woman is gone. It is possible that she will never be seen again."

"Charles's heart is with her. I went to warn him of Monsieur Dale's plot against him. He despises me, Pierre."

Pierre stiffened. "Was he cruel to you, Camille?"

"No." Camille shook her head in fervent denial. "It is just that the realization of his love for Devina Dale has opened his eyes to all that I am, and he resents the fact that I, a common courtesan, am free while the good woman he loves is gone. He hates me, Pierre. He does not wish to see me again."

"He will change his mind."

"No, he will not."

Pierre was silent while he weighed the words Camille had spoken. His lovely Camille was not hysterical, nor was she angry, but her heart was broken.

"*Ma chérie,* how may I bring the happiness back to your heart? Tell me, and it will be done."

Leaning forward, Camille pressed her damp cheek against his, and Pierre felt the warmth of this woman envelop him. Charles Carter, fool that he was, did not deserve her! Pierre listened as Camille's whispered response met his ears at last.

"Pierre, perhaps my time in this land has come to an end. Perhaps I should return to my family, as you suggested to me once before. Perhaps . . ." Camille took a deep, trembling breath. "But not now, Pierre. I will wait a little longer."

Pierre raised his hands to pull Camille closer. He was prevented from consoling her by Camille's sudden withdrawal from him, by the heartbreakingly brave manner in which she raised her chin and determinedly wiped the last trace of dampness from her cheeks. Her smile tore at his heart.

"But in the meantime, Pierre, I do not intend to inflict my unhappiness on others. And I ask that you strike my poor confession from your mind. It is a problem I must deal with alone."

Abruptly Camille drew herself to her feet. Waiting only until Pierre had arisen to stand beside her, she slipped her arm through his and urged him along with her as she walked toward the door. "I must get back to work. My clients will be clamoring for my attention, and I must not disappoint them."

Quickly she slipped through the doorway and into the hallway. Watching as she closed the door behind her, Pierre felt a new, overwhelming despair . . . the despair one suffered at the torment of those one loved.

• • •

The click of Le Comte's door sounded in the foyer, and Marie's head turned toward the sound. Her heart stopped as *la grande fille* emerged into the hallway, a smile on her common face. She was flushed, no doubt from Pierre's avid attentions, attentions he saved solely for the accommodating country bumpkin.

The time had come for Marie to take steps against this interloper who wished to steal all she had worked so hard to attain. She had heard many things that would help her to rid herself of this threat to her future. She would put them to work for her. And she would do it soon.

Her smile brighter than it had been in many weeks, Marie turned back to the well-tailored client who had just entered the foyer. She greeted him warmly.

Jake fidgeted nervously. He took the two short steps to the window and looked out again into the surrounding darkness. Damn! Where was Lai Hua? It had been dark for over an hour!

Impatience and an annoyance not untouched by anxiety combined to form a tight knot in his stomach. This whole affair with Harvey Dale was drawing swiftly to a conclusion. He'd start back to the cabin tonight, and the next time he returned to Tombstone, he'd be carrying the note that would put the final steps of Ross's plan into action. From that point on, he was certain it would not be long before he would leave this country.

The knot in Jake's stomach tightened. Time was slipping away from him, and he hadn't seen Lai Hua for over a week. He ached for her. But he knew the ache was not just for the physical release the next few hours would bring.

Jake's thoughts halted abruptly as a bobbing light appeared on the path. His heart jumped, and he swallowed against the anticipation building inside him. Lai Hua's small, shadowed form came into view, and a spontaneous joy rushed through him. The door opened and he scooped Lai Hua into his arms.

Not stopping to allow her to lower the lantern she carried, Jake crushed her against him. His mouth found hers, crushing it with the force of his kiss, separating her lips. He kissed her again, his lips finally sliding from their possession of her mouth to press hungry nibbling bites on the curve of her chin, the smooth line of her cheek.

"Lai Hua, you're late. I was beginnin' to think you hadn't seen the ribbon. I've been so damned crazy to see you."

But Lai Hua was not responding. She was standing stiffly in his arms, as stiffly as his searching hands and lips would allow. He felt a moment's trepidation, which turned to alarm as he slowly pulled far enough from her to look down into her face.

He took the lantern from her hand and raised it higher so he could see her more clearly. "What's wrong, Lai Hua?"

The glitter of tears sparkled in Lai Hua's eyes.

"My torment has been great since I saw the red ribbon. I took it from the bush with a trembling hand, knowing I would be forced to make the decision that has torn my heart."

"Decision? What are you talkin' about, Lai Hua? What's tormentin' you?"

"My torment is the pain of realization, Mr. Jake, the realization that in my joy in loving you, I had forced away the thought that I was being used in a very cruel way."

"Used?" Jake shook his head, his hands springing up to her slender shoulders. "Lai Hua, what are you talkin' about?"

"At the first there was honesty between us. Your eyes touched mine and a fire was lit within my heart. A similar fire touched yours, and when you held your arms out to me, I went willingly into them. But that honesty is now gone."

Jake shook his head, bewildered. "This is crazy, Lai Hua! Explain what you're sayin'."

A single tear overflowed Lai Hua's brimming eyes, and she took a short, shaky breath. "I declared my love and my loyalty to you, Mr. Jake, and you knew it to be strong, unyielding. So was my trust. I spoke freely to you, told you of my regard for my mistress, who had treated me with a respect and courtesy I have not received from others of your race. I said I would put no one else before you, and I have kept that promise because of my love. But love cannot take the place of honor in one's heart."

"Damn it, Lai Hua—"

"The last night we were together I told you of Miss Devina's party. I told you of the great number of guests invited and the confusion that was expected. You took my words to your friend so he could use them to satisfy his vengeance."

"Lai Hua, I didn't . . ." Jake started to deny the accusation, then changed his mind. "I mean, I didn't do it on purpose. I mentioned it to Ross and he—"

"My words were the seeds that bore the fruit of my mistress's abduction. It is I who carry the blame, the guilt."

"The guilt doesn't fall on you, Lai Hua. Hell, if there's any guilt to be placed, it should be put on Harvey Dale's shoulders for the lyin' and cheatin' that killed Ross's pa and put Ross in jail!"

"Mr. Dale is an evil man who has earned the hatred of many. I owe such a man no allegiance, but it is not of him I speak now. Miss Devina is blameless of her father's crimes, and I am dishonored by her betrayal."

"Dishonored?"

"I will not be free to take joy in my own life until I am free of that dishonor."

Jake shook his head, his pale eyes incredulous. "You can't be askin' what I think you're askin', Lai Hua."

"I ask only that which will free me from the burden of being dishonored. I ask that you free Miss Devina."

A stillness began to consume Jake. He spoke from the depths of that numbness. "And if I can't do as you ask?"

Lai Hua paused. Her lips trembled, but her eyes were unyielding. "A woman without honor is worthy of no man."

"If anyone isn't worthy, it's me. You know what I am—an ex-convict and a thief!"

Lai Hua did not respond and, filled with despair, Jake reached out and pulled her into his arms. He held her close. He felt her shuddering and her pain as she raised her tear-streaked face to his.

"You have more honor than any woman I've ever known, Lai Hua. And I want you, darlin'. I want you more than I can ever say."

Slowly lowering his head, Jake covered Lai Hua's quivering lips with his own. He tasted the salt of her tears and consumed them hungrily, hoping to erase Lai Hua's sorrow with the warmth of his loving. Her mouth was still unresponsive beneath his, and he crushed her closer, his lips devouring hers. He kissed her again, his desperation growing as she remained still and cold as stone.

Drawing slowly back from her, Jake swallowed with difficulty, his eyes not moving from Lai Hua's sober face. "Lai Hua, you know I can't do what you ask." His low whisper was strained. "Have you stopped lovin' me, darlin'?"

Jake waited for long, anguished seconds as Lai Hua struggled to speak. When she did, her voice held a low note of finality that froze his heart.

"Love is a noble emotion. As a woman without honor, it is beyond my reach."

"Lai Hua . . ."

"Good-bye, Mr. Jake."

Disengaging herself from arms that were suddenly without strength, Lai Hua turned, picked up the lantern, and fled.

Unable to move, Jake stood for a long moment watching as the light of Lai Hua's lantern zigzagged along the trail. It disappeared from sight, and Jake shook his head in bewilderment. It had happened so quickly. In all the times he had been bedeviled with thoughts of the future, of his parting with Lai Hua, he had never thought it would end like this.

The shadow concealed in the darkness started with surprise when Lai Hua emerged from the cabin only minutes after entering. It watched as she fled with great haste, her hand brushing away her tears.

Jake appeared in the doorway a few moments later, and the shadow remained motionless as he ran toward his horse. Waiting only until Jake had ridden out of earshot, the dark figure mounted an animal secured nearby.

Leaning low against the saddle, it spurred its mount forward to follow Jake at a cautious distance, a shadow that was unseen and unheard.

CHAPTER XVI

BLONDE MARIE MADE her way through the early-morning traffic of Allen Street with a quick, purposeful step. She carried herself with pride, her shoulders straight, her chin high. She smiled, dipping her head toward the familiar male faces she passed. Because of the high social position many of her clients enjoyed in Tombstone, it was her policy to exercise caution in her greetings outside her house, allowing her clients the opportunity to acknowledge her first. Her discretion had earned her establishment its excellent reputation, and she was proud of its success.

Slowing her step, Marie cast a careful glance over her shoulder. When she had stepped out of her house a few minutes earlier, Le Comte had been busily involved in a business discussion with a gentleman from San Francisco. Pierre would soon be expanding his chain of houses to smaller towns along the coast. He had brought this potential investor to her house to observe its smooth operation. She knew Le Comte would be busy impressing the gentleman for a few hours longer, at least.

Satisfied that she could proceed unobserved by anyone who mattered, Marie turned abruptly and stepped down off the sidewalk, frowning at the cloud of dust that rose to her nostrils as she crossed the street. She stepped up onto the opposite side and continued walking. Midway down the block of commercial buildings, she turned and entered the offices of Till-Dale Enterprises. She smiled sweetly at the startled clerk as he raised an inquiring glance, then spoke in her most pleasant, melodic tone, *"Bonjour, monsieur. I should like to speak to Mr. Harvey Dale . . ."*

Lily stiffened. Her step faltered, and the amply proportioned woman walking at her side darted a short glance up into her daughter's clear, beautiful countenance. The myriad lines in China Mary's face creased with alarm at the expression she saw there as she followed her daughter's gaze across bustling Allen Street. The same cold fury she had seen reflected in her daughter's eyes stabbed her sharply as she saw the French madam, Blond Marie, boldly enter the offices of Till-Dale Enterprises.

Mary followed her daughter, who had slipped into the shadows of a doorway. The two women watched through the window as Blond Marie spoke to the startled clerk. The fellow disappeared into an office in the rear. Within moments Harvey Dale emerged, his expression unrevealing.

Lily's smooth cheek twitched spasmodically as she suppressed the emotions Mary knew were raging within her. A familiar hatred soared anew inside Mary as she watched Harvey Dale extend his hand toward the Frenchwoman and then graciously lead her into his office. The door closed behind them, and Mary felt its soundless snap reverberate through her daughter's slender frame.

Lily stepped back onto the boardwalk, and Mary resumed her place beside her. Their pace rapid, they walked in silence, finally turning north onto Fifth Street, in the direction of the Safford Hudson Bank. The night's receipts from the fan-tan games conducted in the rear room of Mary's commercial establishment had been especially heavy, and she was pleased to be able to deposit such a hearty sum in her account. She had brought Lily with her as was her usual custom, to make certain that her beautiful daughter would become familiar with the workings of her business and the accounts she maintained. It was all for Lily, after all. The money would guarantee the prosperous future she had planned for her precious jewel, the most valued person in her life.

A familiar tension seized Mary, and she clutched her bag with a strangling grip. It had long been her desire to crush the joy from Harvey Dale's life in the same way. Even now, while he held herself estranged from her daughter, Lily suffered at his hands. Her lovely Lily . . .

"It appears Mr. Dale is searching for another outlet for his passions," Mary said softly.

Lily's dark eyes turned to her mother and Mary felt her daughter's pain. No, it could not be true. Lily could not care for this man who degraded her.

"No, mother, do not fear. The emotion you see in my eyes is not jealousy. It is humiliation and rage."

Mary attempted a reassuring smile. "You are free of him now, daughter."

"No, I am not." Lily smiled, bitterness evident in the curve of her delicately drawn lips. "Mr. Dale still holds secreted somewhere those papers that can destroy you. He knows I will not allow you to sacrifice all you have achieved here for me, and he knows because of that I am still subject to his whims. He seeks a subtle vengeance for the part he feels I played in the abduction of his daughter. He dangles my freedom in front of my eyes, knowing that I know he will call me to him again. He wishes to make certain I am aware that he is in control, and he now bargains to temporarily take a French whore in my place to humiliate me, to make me feel I am no more than she in his eyes."

Lily paused in an attempt to still the trembling that had beset her slender frame. Dark eyes blazing, she continued in a quaking voice, "This passion you see in me is the passion of loathing. I would be free of this man, once and for all!"

Mary gripped her daughter's arm, steadying her as they continued walking. She swallowed against the choking hatred for Harvey Dale that rose within her throat.

"Soon, daughter. Soon."

Lily took a deep breath, the conviction in her mother's tone signaling the return of more stable emotions. She breathed deeply once, twice, seeking the serenity of her inner self. She fixed her mind on the warm sun that beat down on her head, consoling her, and the fresh air that bathed her face. Control began to reestablish itself in her mind.

Mary's hand dropped from her daughter's arm as Lily's expression lost its stiffness. Realizing she had inadvertently caused her mother pain, Lily raised her chin, storing the memory of her mother's torment in her mind. She vowed in silence that for this, too, Harvey Dale would pay.

•   •   •

To Harvey Dale,

If you want your daughter back alive, you will have to pay a price:

1. Stop all work in the Till-Dale mines and give the miners a month's pay in advance.

2. Turn all files on the purchase of my father's mine over to Charles Carter and, with him as a witness, transfer to me the title to my father's mine. The purchase price will be one dollar. Carter will pay it.

3. Turn over the financial records of my father's mine to Carter so he can make an accounting of all profits taken during the last three years. Open an account in my name in the Safford Hudson Bank and deposit that amount.

4. Make a written confession of the way you cheated my father and include the truth about the accident in your mine that sent me to jail. Give the confession to the federal marshal. Have copies printed and posted around town.

Don't get the sheriff or the marshal involved in this except as instructed. You're being watched. Don't try any tricks or your daughter will suffer.

Ross Morrison

A hard smile played around Ross's lips as he gave the ransom note a last cursory glance. He had had a long time to compose that list of demands. Three long years . . .

Ross glanced up from the letter, his smile dimming. Jake had been unnaturally silent since he arrived from Tombstone a short time before.

"What's the matter, Jake?"

Jake shook his head. "Nothin' . . . nothin's the matter."

"You aren't fooling me, Jake. I know that look. You're holding something back."

Jake shook his head, his eyes darting toward Devina, who was tending a bubbling pot at the fireplace. "It's just like I told you. The sheriff's been out almost every day lookin' for her, but he hasn't turned up anythin'. Half the town thinks Carter had a part in the kidnappin', and gossip has it Dale's tryin' to get Carter thrown out of town. He isn't goin' to get his way, though. Too many people are standin' up for the doctor."

Ross gave a low snort. "Yes, I know. The town loves him."

"Anyways, Dale's runnin' around like a crazy damned fool, makin' enemies and accomplishin' nothin'. The whole town's talkin'."

"Bastard."

The muttered expletive from the direction of the fireplace snapped both men's heads toward Devina. Jake's startled expression elicited a caustic comment from Ross. "That's right, Jake. The lady has a surprising vocabulary. As a matter of fact, the lady's not much of a lady at all."

Her eyes blazing, Devina turned back to the fire.

Ross ignored the glance Jake darted between the two of them. "You can rest here a day or so and then start back."

"No, I'll be goin' back to Tombstone tonight, Ross."

"What's the rush? I thought you didn't like Tombstone. Too damn crowded for you, you always said."

"Yeah, well, maybe I changed my mind. Seems to me this cabin's a hell of a lot more crowded than Tombstone right now. Besides, I got some business to take care of."

"Jake, I told you to stay away from that girl."

Jake's boyish face turned suddenly hard. His voice took on an unyielding note. "I don't take your orders when it comes to my personal life, Ross."

"It's not your personal life I'm thinking of, Jake, and you know it. The girl's probably being watched."

"I'm careful."

"Jake . . ."

Abruptly pushing himself away from the table, Jake shot another glance toward Devina, his light brows furrowing at the sight of her venomous stare. He stood up and within seconds was striding toward the door.

Ross stared at his friend's retreating back. Something was wrong, and he'd be damned if he was going to wait another minute to find out what it was.

Catching up with Jake, Ross clamped a hand on his friend's shoulder, slowing him to a halt. "Wait a minute, Jake."

Jake's response was brusque. "What do you want?"

Ross was at a loss. He hadn't seen his friend so unhappy since he had met his Chinese mistress. He didn't have to strain his mind to know what was at the bottom of Jake's misery.

"You saw her, didn't you, Jake? And something's wrong."

Jake hesitated, then gave a short shrug. "Yeah, I saw her."

"So?"

"She put an end to it, just like that." He jerked his head toward the cabin. "Because we kidnapped her."

"You told me she guessed what we were doing a long time ago. Why the sudden objection?"

"I don't know. She blames herself. Somethin' to do with her losin' her honor. I don't understand half of it."

Ross released a short breath. "I'm sorry, Jake."

Jake shrugged again. "Yeah, well, I guess it doesn't make much difference. We're goin' to be done with all of this and out of this part of the country soon, anyway. She just saved me the trouble of findin' the right words."

Ross offered his friend a brief smile.

"So what's the business you're so anxious to take care of in Tombstone?"

Again Jake hesitated. "Well, the truth is, I owe her somethin', Ross. I need to explain things a little better to her so as to get some of that guilt off her shoulders. I need to tell her we would've gotten that girl one way or another even without her help."

Ross's frown darkened. "Jake, it's dangerous seeing her."

"I'll be careful, Ross, real careful."

Ross nodded, realizing nothing he could say would make a difference. Jake's mind was made up. "When are you leaving?"

"Just as soon as I can."

"All right, Jake. Whatever you say."

Devina slipped from her concealed position in the shadow of the doorway, exceedingly glad that she had chanced listening in on the conversation between Ross and Jake. She moved back toward the fireplace, tears of relief threatening to spill down her cheeks.

Lai Hua hadn't betrayed her after all, not knowingly. A choked laugh escaped her. She hadn't realized how much the friendship of the Oriental woman had come to mean to her. Damn that lying Ross Morrison for making her think Lai Hua had been playing her for a fool!

Devina took a firm hold on her emotions. That was just another of the many grievances for which she would eventually make the handsome bastard with Charles's face pay.

But right now her captor and his henchman were walking back

toward the cabin. She shot a quick glance toward the beans bubbling in the pot. She had added bacon and raw sugar, just as Ross had instructed her, and there was no doubt the beans were nearly done. Good! The sooner Jake returned to Tombstone and got the note to her father the better. Then her father would pay the ransom and she would be free.

Her eyes fell on the note still lying on the table where Ross had left it. In her eagerness to listen in on the conversation between the two men, she had almost missed her opportunity to read the letter.

All other thoughts drifting away as her eyes consumed its contents, Devina felt a slow shock overwhelm her. The demands were impossible! There was no chance of their being accepted. George Tillson would never give his consent, and she would be doomed.

"What are you doing, Devina?"

Devina's head snapped up to Ross's dark scrutiny. Her response was spontaneous: "These demands are impossible!"

"Are they?"

"They would require the consent of George Tillson, my father's partner. He'll never give it. The mines are flooding. The pumps barely keep the shafts clear of water when they operate twenty-four hours a day. If my father stops work in the mines, he'll never be able to open some of those shafts again. George won't allow my father to endanger the company."

"It'll be up to your father to convince him, won't it?"

A stab of fear pierced Devina's breast. "You know my father can't afford to pay the miners a month's salary in advance, especially after the way you've been robbing him."

"That's unfortunate."

Rage surged through Devina. "Your demands would break Till-Dale and leave my father with nothing!"

"Then he'll be in the same position my father was in when Harvey Dale was done with him."

Devina was stunned by the hatred reflected in Morrison's eyes.

"My father never . . . My father is a clever businessman, but he isn't dishonest. He would never—"

Ross's short laugh halted Devina's statement. Either you don't know your father very well or you're just as much a liar as he is."

"You can't ask my father to sacrifice his company."

"Can't I?"

Fury flushed Devina's mind, overwhelming caution. She took a quick step toward the table and snatched at the note, but Ross was too fast for her. Grabbing the letter with one hand, he captured her wrist with the other. "Oh, no, you don't!"

"Let me go, damn you!"

Twisting and squirming in an effort to break free, Devina made another grab for the note, forcing Ross to drop it on the table as he grasped her other wrist and twisted them both behind her back.

"Stay still, you damned she-cat!"

Consumed with the desire to scratch his handsome face to ribbons, Devina increased her efforts to break free, hissing her hatred as Ross easily subdued her. Breathless and close to tears, Devina finally admitted she was overpowered. She met his eyes defiantly and tossed her long, wild hair off her face. Her shaking voice carried the full conviction of her words. "You won't get away with this. I'll see you behind bars. I'll see you begging for mercy, crawling . . ."

Ross met her raging gaze with a cold stare. "If your father doesn't meet those demands, you won't be seeing much of anything, Miss Dale."

After allowing the full portent of his words to register in her mind, Ross released Devina so abruptly that she staggered, almost losing her balance. His strong arm steadied her even as he taunted, "What's the matter, Miss Dale? Feeling faint?"

Devina's quick response belied her lack of color. "That'll be the day!"

Ross's laughter was harsh. "Then you might as well make yourself useful. Start dishing out the food. Jake has a long way to go before sundown, don't you, Jake?"

Jake was still standing near the doorway, his expression peculiar.

"Sit down, Jake. Devina will be only too happy to serve us."

Acutely aware of the beautiful, vicious bitch whose full breasts rose and fell with deep, agitated breaths beneath the oversize shirt she wore, Ross pressed relentlessly, "Won't you, Devina?"

Turning with a sharpness that set the pale strands of her hair flying, Devina walked to the fireplace. Her back to them, she hesitated briefly before lifting the steaming pot from the fire. She turned with slow deliberation and approached the table where the

two men had seated themselves. Her eyes not moving from
Ross's face, she paused, her hatred clear and threatening. Her
fingers trembled on the handle.

"I wouldn't do that if I were you," Ross warned softly. "It
would be a big mistake."

Abruptly slamming the pot down on the table, Devina stood
beside him, visibly trembling.

"Get the plates, Devina, and the cups and spoons."

Her smoldering hatred registering clearly in the silence, Devina
suddenly turned and followed his command. Ross looked back at
Jake, then deliberately provoked her by saying, "Hurry up,
Devina. Jake is anxious to get started."

Devina's shoulders stiffened, but she carried the plates and
utensils to the table and put them down with elaborate care. She
then sat down on the bunk, her lips tensed in a straight, furious
line.

Ross ignored the censure in Jake's silence. "You're sure you
don't want to stay the night and start out in the morning, Jake?"

"I'm sure."

Ross picked up the spoon and scooped some beans into his
plate. The aroma wafted up into his nostrils, and his stomach
made an appreciative growl. It seemed he was hungry, after all.

Devina was still sitting on the bunk when Ross and Jake rose
from the table a short time later. Conversation between Ross and
Jake had been stilted, inhibited by the black stare of the woman
seated a few feet away. Ross felt a certain regret for the direction
the afternoon had taken. His friend did not share his deep and
abiding hatred for the Dale name. Jake obviously pitied Devina,
not realizing that behind her angelic face was a woman who
could watch him swing from the branch of a tree without blinking an eye.

Ross's gaze dropped to the note on the table beside him, and
he picked it up to read it carefully once more. It was almost
perfect. Only one thing was lacking.

He pushed his chair back and got to his feet. His eyes on
Devina's face, he started toward her, drawing his knife from the
sheath at his waist as he walked. Devina's eyes flickered only
briefly as he stood over her, knife in hand. He heard the scrape
of Jake's chair against the floor at the moment he reached down
to take a lock of Devina's hair in his hand. She gasped as he

raised his knife and severed a curl, but made no comment as he turned and walked back to the table where Jake stood tensely.

Taking the shimmering lock of hair, Ross carefully folded it inside the ransom note and handed the letter to Jake.

Jake frowned. "Christ, Ross . . ."

"You didn't think Dale was going to accept that letter as genuine without some sort of proof, did you? I don't think there's another person in the territory with hair that color. Dale won't have a doubt in the world that it's his daughter's."

Jake turned toward the door without a response.

They were walking to Jake's horse when Ross tried one last time. "You're sure you don't want to stay the night, relax, get some rest?"

Jake shook his head. "No, thank you. I'm not lookin' to get myself involved in this war you got goin' between you two. I got the feelin' I couldn't win nohow, and I'm not about to stand around watchin' the blood flow. I got better things to do."

Ross shrugged. "Suit yourself."

Watching as his friend mounted, Ross finally smiled. "Take good care of that note, Jake. We've got a lot riding on it. And don't get anxious. Wait at least two days before you deliver it to Dale. The comings and goings in town are probably being watched very carefully. If they see you come back and the note is delivered a little while later, they're going to make some pretty good guesses."

Jake nodded. "Take it easy on the girl, Ross. You're pushin' too hard."

Ross's smile stiffened, and Jake scowled in annoyance.

"Oh, hell, do what you want. You never listen to me, anyway. I'll be back when I have somethin' to tell you."

Slapping the reins against his horse's neck, Jake turned him toward the trail and spurred him into a canter.

Ross watched until his friend turned out of sight and then walked back to the cabin. His mind on the letter Jake carried, Ross hoped he would not be forced to convince Dale that he had meant every word he had written.

Devina fought to control the rage simmering below her surface calm. Ross had been watching her relentlessly since Jake had left for Tombstone an hour before. His brooding gaze followed her every move, and her skin was sensitized, all but burning, from the intensity of his dark-eyed stare. Feeding her anger was her realization that despite her hatred of the despicable stranger, he touched her, raised her awareness of him as a man in a way no other man ever had before.

"What are you thinking, Devina?"

Her shoulders coming abruptly erect, Devina felt her face flame. "What I'm thinking is none of your business!"

Ross moved from the doorway, blocking the light as he walked toward her. While his broad frame was in silhouette, his features were almost indiscernible, and a shudder shook her. He was so big, so overwhelming. She was embarrassingly familiar with the strength of the hard body that dwarfed her and with the cruelty often reflected in those dark eyes. There was power in every movement of his lean, well-honed frame as he approached with slow deliberation. She knew he meant to intimidate her, and she was determined not to allow him to realize how very well he succeeded.

Devina steeled herself as Ross grasped her shoulders, his handsome face illuminated by the fire at her back. "Answer my question."

Ignoring the tremors moving down her spine, the awareness escalating within her at his touch, Devina forced a laugh. "You already know what I'm thinking, don't you? I'm thinking that you're a fool for making demands that you know my father can't meet."

"He'll meet them."

"He can't. George—"

"You're wasting your breath, Devina. I know where the strength lies in that partnership. Once your father gets that letter, he'll do anything he has to do to get you back."

Devina was beginning to shake. "Bastard!"

"Name-calling again, Devina? You're not the lady your father thinks you are. But he doesn't really know you, does he? Not as well as I know you."

"As well as you know me?" Devina was incredulous at his presumption. "All you know about me is that I'm Harvey Dale's daughter and a means for your revenge on him."

A smile played at Ross's lips. "You're wrong. I know you very well. You haven't been out of my sight since you arrived in Tombstone."

A strange fluttering began in the pit of Devina's stomach as

Ross continued staring down into her face. She knew instinctively it was not fear that caused her knees to weaken and her heart to pound when he looked at her that way. "That . . . that's impossible."

Ross's voice dropped to a husky whisper. "You could feel me watching you, couldn't you, Devina?"

"Watching me?"

"From the hills behind your house, with my spyglass. I knew everything about you. I knew the time of day you woke up in the morning, when you dressed, the hours you liked to walk into town, and the hours you stayed at home. I knew exactly where your bodyguard waited for you every day." Ross's voice hardened. "He was getting bolder, wasn't he? And you resented it." His gaze flickered briefly, and his voice dropped a notch lower. "The damned slimy bastard."

"So it was you watching me."

"I got to know you very well, Devina. I knew the way you spoke to Lai Hua when you walked with her, the way you stiffened when your father tried to tell her what to do, the way you tilted your head up to Carter and smiled at him when you walked out together." Ross's expression tightened. "Good old Charles Carter, my well-liked, respectable brother."

Devina felt Ross's hatred. "Liked and respected by everyone but you," she said. "If Charles is as bad as you say he is, why does your letter say to give him the records on the claim my father bought from yours?"

"Carter will do anything to get you back, and I like knowing I have my brother under my thumb."

Ross had raised his hand to Devina's cheek and was stroking it lightly as he spoke. The callused, lightly abrasive touch of his fingertips was strangely erotic. It interfered with her thought processes, and she fought her slow submission to his caress.

"You're wrong about Charles."

"Just as I'm wrong about your father?"

"No . . . Yes. I mean—"

"You mean you don't really know either of them, do you?"

Devina flushed. "I know them better than I know you. All I know about you is that you're an ex-convict and that you enjoy abusing women."

"The way I abused you?" Devina did not respond, and Ross

gave a contemptuous laugh. "You don't know what it is to be abused."

"No, of course not! Only you know what it is to go hungry, to be treated like a slave, to be given less respect than a servant!"

A muscle twitched in Ross's cheek. "You've been so privileged and so spoiled all your life that you don't have a genuine bone in your body. You don't know the truth when you hear it."

"What truth? That my father is a cheat and a thief? That Charles would help send his own brother to jail for something he didn't do?"

"That's right."

"Liar!"

Ross shook his head, disgust evident in his strong, even features. "I haven't decided whether you're loyal, just plain stupid, or a damned good liar."

"How about smart—too smart not to see through an ex-convict, a thief, and a kidnapper?"

"An ex-convict, a thief, and a kidnapper . . . not up to your social caliber or the caliber of my respectable brother."

Devina ignored the growing ferocity of Ross's tone. Elated to have struck a sensitive nerve in his previously impenetrable facade, she continued mercilessly. "Charles is an educated, cultured, and sympathetic human being. He's too good for this uncivilized frontier."

"Too good for Tombstone and everyone in it—just like you. Is that right?"

Devina paused. "I'm not too good for Charles."

His handsome face suddenly looked savage, and Devina gasped as Ross's hands cut painfully into her shoulders. "So you've set your sights on Charles!" he said. "Well, he's not going to get you, damn him! Not him or anybody else!"

Ross's mouth was descending toward hers when Devina realized she had gone too far. Panic endowing her with a strength she did not realize she possessed, she shoved hard at his chest, catching him off balance and making him stumble back against the table, allowing her the edge she needed to race toward the door. Within seconds her bare feet were pounding against the dry earth outside as she headed toward Ross's mount. When she heard running footsteps behind her, she ran faster, plunging into the brush.

"Devina, stop! Watch out!"

The footsteps halted abruptly, even as the tone of Ross's voice caused her a moment's hesitation. She turned to see his hand drop to the gun on his hip. He wouldn't shoot! He couldn't . . .

A sudden rattling sound stopped her in her tracks—too late. A blur of movement whipped along the ground at her feet. She felt a sharp sting in her ankle, heard the bark of a gun. She cried out as the snake, its fangs embedded in her flesh, burst in two with the force of the shot.

Unexpected weakness assailed Devina as pain, hot and intense, pierced her leg. The world wavered around her, and she felt herself sinking slowly to the ground. Strong arms suddenly caught her, cushioning her fall, even as she grimaced against the pain and fought the fear that filled her mind.

She looked up to Ross's face. It was dark and angry as he crouched over her and drew his knife.

Another hot stinging flash of pain stole her breath. Gasping, Devina fought the darkness quickly descending, but her struggle was to no avail. She submitted to the merciful blackness that overwhelmed her, blocking out the pain, the angry accusing eyes, and the glint of a descending blade.

No time to think, no time to feel: Her slender ankle was already beginning to discolor and swell. He pushed up Devina's trouser leg, slipped his bandanna around her calf, and pulled it tight, knowing his best hope was to stop the venom from traveling. He made first one cut and then another across the marks where the fangs had penetrated her skin, then began to suck the blood and venom from the wound.

A few minutes later the blood was no longer flowing freely, and Ross looked up into Devina's face. She was still unconscious, her beautiful face devoid of color.

Lifting her into his arms, he ran toward the cabin. As he clutched her tight against him, Ross was faced with the dawning realization of all he would truly lose if he lost her.

Ross felt the nudge of panic as Devina returned his gaze with wild, unseeing eyes. She mumbled unintelligible words as she sought to brush away his hand. Even in her delirium she fought his touch. It had, in fact, been her wild flight from his kiss that had almost caused her death.

Speaking soft words of comfort, Ross laid his palm against Devina's brow. It was still hot, but her fever was dropping.

Devina's eyes fluttered closed, and Ross's heart froze. His gaze moved to the pulse in her throat and he released a tense breath at its steady, if accelerated, throbbing. Turning to the basin on the table beside the bunk, he squeezed out the cloth and carefully sponged the beads of perspiration from Devina's brow. Damn, she was so pale.

Ross surveyed the wound on her ankle once more. An ugly purple swelling marked the puncture and the cuts he had made with his blade. The wound was no longer bleeding, and he pressed a clean damp cloth to the bruise. He pushed the wide trouser leg farther up her bare leg, and his eyes touched on a second bruise that circled her calf just below the knee. He had removed the bandanna as soon as it was safe to do so, but the damage had been done. Hell, he hadn't even been able to help her without hurting her.

Devina was moaning again, and Ross shot a quick glance to the window. The darkness of night met his eyes, and he was startled by the blackness. How long had she been delirious? How much longer would it be before the fever broke, before he was certain she would be all right?

Ross's throat tightened as he looked into Devina's face. He had been a fool to allow her defense of Carter to push him over the edge of restraint. He still did not fully understand his reaction to her statement about Carter. He had never envied his brother. He had always considered himself the luckier one to have stayed with Pa after his mother left them. Nobody could have had a better father or a happier childhood. His education had been informal, more earned than learned, and it had suited him fine.

When he first emerged from Yuma, he had cared for nothing but revenge. But his thoughts had begun to change subtly the moment Devina Dale entered his life. He was uncertain just when he had begun to desire Devina for herself instead of as an instrument for revenge. But right now he was all too intensely aware of what he wanted. He wanted Devina Dale to look at him the way she had looked at Charles Carter. He wanted to see acceptance of him as a man in her eyes, not hatred and fear. He wanted to see her laugh, to see her smile for him alone. He wanted her to feel his warmth in every bone of her body, just as he felt hers. He wanted her to need his warmth, to crave it the way he craved hers.

Devina made a sudden, spasmodic movement, and Ross's heart jumped erratically. He pressed his hand to her forehead at the same moment she began shuddering, her eyes snapping open in unseeing panic. Her voice was low, quaking.

"It's cold."

Cold. Ross shook his head. The air in the cabin was stagnant and warm, but Devina was shuddering more wildly than before. Ross pulled the blanket up tighter around her, his hand moving to stroke her cheek.

"Devina."

But Devina gave no response. Her teeth were beginning to chatter, and a peculiar blue color began to tint her lips. Reluctant to leave her for a moment, Ross glanced toward the doorway of the cabin. His saddle was outside, and secured on it was another blanket. Turning back, Ross leaned toward her, striving to catch her panicked gaze.

"I'm only leaving you for a minute, Devina. I'll be right back."

Covering the distance to the doorway in a few rapid steps, Ross was soon in the yard and pulling the blanket from the saddle. Returning as fast as his feet could carry him, he leaned over the bunk and tucked the second blanket around her. Her quaking continued, and Ross began to panic. A sheen of perspiration covered Devina's beautiful face despite her shaking, and he wiped her smooth skin clear with the palm of his hand.

It was all his fault. Devina had been safe in Tombstone, safe from this kind of danger. If she didn't recover . . .

Devina's panicked, blue-eyed stare assailed him again. "I'm c-cold. Please . . ."

The realization that she would never appeal to him in such a way if she were in full control of her senses tightened the knot in Ross's throat to the point of pain. He had to do something.

Leaning over, Ross pulled off his boots. He unbuckled his gun belt and dropped it to the floor, then kicked it aside and drew back the blankets on the bed. With extreme care, he slipped into the bunk beside Devina. Emotion tightening his throat, he slid his arms under and around and pulled her close against him.

Devina moaned low in her throat, and Ross winced at her pain as he pulled her closer. He whispered soft, gentle assurances as he fitted her slender softness against his chest, tucked her head into the curve of his neck. He curved his hand around the

contours of her firm buttocks, fitting her softness flush against
the heat of his body. He held her tight, rocking slightly back and
forth until the blankets were tucked firmly around them.

Wrapped in a cocoon of warmth, Ross pressed his cheek
against the dampness at Devina's temple. She began perspiring
profusely, her shuddering slowly subsiding, and Ross felt his
edge of panic begin to drop away.

"Rest, Devina. Close your eyes. I'll take care of you. You're
going to be all right."

Devina was motionless in his arms at last, but Ross's grip did
not loosen. He could not release her. Not yet.

Narrow shafts of light shone through the openings in the
boarded windows, and Ross squinted at his first waking realization that it was dawn. Devina lay still wrapped in his arms, and
he looked down anxiously at her motionless, sleeping face. Her
body's night-long battle against the poison was evident in her
unnatural pallor, her perspiration-soaked hair, and the dark shadows under her closed eyes. But she was breathing evenly, and
she looked more beautiful than he had ever seen her.

Carefully unwrapping the blankets from around them, Ross
withdrew from Devina's clinging warmth. She stirred, her heavy
eyelids flicking open, then dropping closed once more. The cool
morning air of the cabin touched his own perspiration-soaked
clothing, and Ross was immediately alerted to the danger of chill
for Devina. Quickly stripping off his shirt, he flung the clinging
garment onto the floor. Relieved of its dampness, he decided on
his course of action.

He turned and made his way outside. A quick search of his
saddlebags turned up the ragged shirt he had worn the day he
robbed the stage. It would serve the purpose.

Ross hurried back to Devina's side. He uncovered her, and her
eyes flew open. She shuddered.

"It's all right, Devina."

Devina closed her eyes at his soft reassurance, and Ross began
working at the buttons on her shirt. His fingers grew more
clumsy with each button he unfastened, each new patch of
smooth white skin revealed to his eyes. The final button undone,
he removed the shirt and threw it to the floor. He then dispensed
with her delicate chemise, his eyes touching her naked feminine
flesh for the first time.

His heart was racing, but he had no time for the myriad feelings assaulting him. Raising her gently, Ross slipped the clean, dry shirt on her body. He buttoned it with trembling fingers, then released a long, shaky breath. His work was not yet done.

Quickly unbuttoning the closure on her oversize trousers, Ross stripped them away, uncovering her wounded leg with infinite care. His eyes touched on the shadowed triangle barely visible through the sheer fabric of her underdrawers, and he swallowed tightly. With shaking hands Ross dispensed with the flimsy garment. His eyes touched Devina's smooth, unmarked skin, the moist, golden brown curls nestled in the appealing delta between her thighs. His chest heaving, he closed his eyes in an attempt to regain his composure.

A tremor shook Devina's slender frame, and a flush of guilt assailed Ross. Quickly smoothing the oversize shirt down over her bare flesh, Ross pulled up the blankets once more.

Returning his mind to the task at hand, Ross lifted the bottom of the blanket to reveal Devina's injured ankle. He assessed the discolored area, the cuts made by his knife, and elation touched his mind. The swelling had not spread, had, in fact, abated. Devina would recover.

Ross's relief was so profound that he felt a startling desire to laugh as he drew himself to his feet. This woman and the conflicting feelings she aroused in him had efficiently reduced him to a quivering, shaken wreck. He had to get himself in hand.

Devina moved abruptly in her sleep, interrupting his thoughts. Ross frowned as a grimace of pain swept her delicate features and her eyes flicked open once more. She looked searchingly in his direction, straining to penetrate the dim light of the room. Stepping closer, Ross looked down into her pale face. He reached out to stroke her cheek, tenderness welling within him.

Devina attempted to speak, but her voice emerged in an unintelligible croak. Ross crouched beside her and gently stroked a few silver-blond wisps from her temple. She raised her hand weakly to cover his, finally succeeding in a hoarse whisper, "Charles . . ."

Charles!

Ross's shock slowly changed to hot fury. Curling his hand around hers, he held it captive as he leaned toward her with a low whisper, "No, Devina. It isn't Charles."

But she appeared not to hear him. Her eyes drifting closed; her lips moved again to a single, soundless name: *Charles.*

No, dammit, no!

Rage assuming control, Ross slowly raised himself to his feet. He stripped off his pants and dropped them on the floor. Raising one corner of the blanket, he slipped into the bunk and with great gentleness took Devina into his arms. He fitted her against him, gritting his teeth as she muttered the name again: *"Charles."*

Pulling her closer, Ross pressed his lips to Devina's hair. He'd make her forget Charles existed.

CHAPTER XVII

His eyes half closed, his narrow, unshaven face composed in an expression of indifference, the balding piano player banged out another raucous tune. Jake glanced around him, noting that the only reaction the fellow had received from the other patrons of the Crystal Palace Saloon was the raised volume of their voices as they sought to make themselves heard over the din. Jake frowned, unconsciously straining to identify the piece. He thought he had a good ear for music, but in the time he had been spending in Tombstone saloons in the past weeks, he had come to believe he was wrong. All the songs these fellows played sounded alike—lively and loud. He took a long, cool swallow of whiskey. He was getting a headache.

Jake shifted his position at the long polished bar for a better view of the offices of Till-Dale Enterprises. With affected indifference, he pushed back his hat, allowing a shock of wavy wheat-colored hair to fall over his forehead. He had arrived in Tombstone in the early hours of morning, but he had slept only a few hours. It had made little difference that his body ached from fatigue or that the bed in the Occidental Hotel was one of the most comfortable he had slept on in recent memory. A tense agitation had overwhelmed him the moment he opened his eyes, and he had been unable to go back to sleep. He had made only two concessions to his physical exhaustion: a trip to the baths and a hearty breakfast. He had been keeping watch from the various bars up and down the street in the time since.

His ears keenly attuned to the conversations around him, Jake had been able to pick up enough information to convince him that nothing had changed; the general public still knew almost nothing about Devina Dale's kidnapping. He had listened to considerable speculation, but had made few comments on the affair. His observation of the Till-Dale offices had shown that no unusual activity was progressing there. George Tillson had shown up at the usual time, but, as yet, Harvey Dale had not appeared. Jake darted a quick glance at the clock over the bar. Eleven-thirty. Well, he would wait a little longer, and then he'd wander around town and try to find out where Harvey Dale was spending his time.

The emergence of a familiar figure into his line of vision interrupted Jake's thought, and he squinted his pale eyes in tense appraisal. Harvey Dale was walking up the street toward his offices. Jake's lips twitched in a fleeting smile. Ross should be here right now. One glimpse would do him a world of good.

Dale was a changed man. Gone was his characteristically confident step and the conceited tilt of the head. Jake had no personal grievance against Dale, but the man's obvious high opinion of himself had struck a jarring chord inside him from the first.

He scrutinized Harvey Dale's approaching figure more closely. Even from a distance he could see that Dale was tense. It was obvious the man was ripe for the ransom note he had in his pocket. He'd wait one more day, as Ross had instructed, and then he'd deliver it. Things would start happening quickly after that, and if everything went the way Ross planned, they'd be out of the Arizona Territory before another few weeks were over.

Harvey Dale turned into his office, and Jake shifted his position to rest his elbows on the bar. The scent of cheap perfume preceded a light touch on his shoulder from behind, and the sensation of a womanly arm slipping around his waist. Jake turned to look into a brightly painted female face and a heavy-lidded, provocative gaze. He raised his light brows and gave her a tentative smile. "Can I help you, ma'am?"

The reply to his question was low and throaty. "You're stealin' my line, cowboy. I'm the one who usually does the helpin' around here. I help fella's like you to relax, pass a little time. I help them to feel real good. As a matter of fact, I'm an expert at makin' fellas like you feel good.''

Jake laughed. ''Fellas like me?''

''Yeah, fellas with time on their hands. Fellas who look like they got a lot on their minds and need a little fun.''

Jake's smile dimmed.

''So I look like I need a little fun.''

The smiling bar girl inched closer and rubbed her full breasts against his chest. The smell of unwashed flesh mixed with the overwhelming fragrance of her perfume, and Jake fought to suppress his distaste. He remembered Lai Hua's clean, fresh scent; her pretty features, free of paint; the inner beauty that shone in her eyes. A sense of desolation swept over him, and he smiled apologetically.

''You're right, ma'am. I do need a little fun. But you hit the nail right on the head when you said I had a lot on my mind. I'm thinkin' that as much as I'm tempted, right now isn't the time to take advantage of your generous offer.'' Dipping his head politely, Jake continued in a lower tone, ''But I appreciate the offer, ma'am, and I'd like to buy you a drink.'' Not waiting for the woman's reply, Jake signaled the bartender. ''Jack, give the lady a drink.''

Reaching into his pocket, Jake pulled out a coin and put it on the bar with a tip of his hat. Within a few minutes, he was outside, the high heels of his boots clicking hollowly against the board sidewalk as he walked toward the outskirts of town. He adjusted his hat at a rakish angle. Hell, he would have to do better than this if he was going to make people think he was in Tombstone just to pass some time between jobs. He had never thought it would be so hard to do nothing and look as if he was enjoying it.

Jake slid his hand casually into his pocket. His fingers touched the smooth, silky ribbon. He knew for a fact that Lai Hua was still working at the Dale house, that she'd be coming back along the trail in a few hours. When she walked past tonight she'd see the red ribbon tied to the bush. He'd meet her at the shack and he'd explain. Hell, he had to do something.

As Lai Hua walked silently to the door of the kitchen, Molly looked soberly in her direction. Lai Hua bobbed her head and attempted a smile. Smiling was difficult in the Dale household

when every step, every sound, made people look up with apprehension, with anxiety, with slowly diminishing hope. Over a
week had passed and no communication had been received from
those who had abducted Miss Devina.

Lai Hua attempted to swallow her guilt. Her love for Mr. Jake
was still strong even though he was now beyond her. Her vow
never to betray him would remain unbroken. He had told her of
the hatred his friend felt for Harvey Dale, of the strong reasons
behind that hatred, but she did not know if that hatred also
encompassed Miss Devina. She hoped it did not. She would not
be able to live if the price paid for her own unwitting part in the
plan was Miss Devina's life.

Molly's broad face creased in a halfhearted smile. "Leavin'
for tonight, Lai Hua?"

Lai Hua bobbed her head politely. "Yes, my duties are finished. I will return tomorrow."

"Maybe there'll be more for you to be doin' tomorrow if we
hear from them kidnappers. Maybe Miss Devina will be comin'
back."

Lai Hua averted her gaze. "Perhaps."

Within a few minutes, Lai Hua was outside and walking
briskly toward the street. Her mind was racing with sad, confusing thoughts as she headed for the hard-packed trail she traveled
each day. She was worried, and there was no one to share her
fear.

Lai Hua's gaze touched on the bushes that lined the trail in the
distance, and her heart began pounding as a red ribbon caught
her eye. Her mind filled with memories of love, pictures of a
light-skinned, boyish face, pale eyes brimming with unvoiced
emotions, emotions that rang deep within her as well. She
experienced again the pain of sadness at the loss of that love, the
desolation of betrayal. She had betrayed and been betrayed
because of a hopeless love that knew no future but despair.

Lai Hua reached out. Her fingers touched the bright ribbon,
brushed its surface, and she snatched her hand back, ashamed.
Summoning all the strength of will at her command, she turned
slowly, firmly away. Her step, halting at first, gradually became
faster and faster, until she was running in headlong flight from
that which could not be.

Jake restlessly paced the floor of the miner's shack. He slowly opened the door to search the darkness for a sign of movement, a flickering light on the path, but there was none. He glanced up at the clear, heavily starred midnight sky, the brilliant half-moon glowing like a great amber lantern.

He had arrived at the cabin at twilight, hoping that Lai Hua would be waiting and had been disappointed to find the shack empty. His anxiety had deepened with each passing hour, but he had refused to believe that Lai Hua was not coming.

Realizing that it was too late, he continued to stare toward the trail, clinging to quickly diminishing hope. There was no doubt Lai Hua had seen the ribbon. He had waited in town, covering the only other route she might have taken back to Hop Town. He had been both relieved and disappointed when she had not appeared, knowing she had seen the ribbon he had left for her.

The lump in Jake's throat thickened, and he swallowed with difficulty as he sought to retain his hold on his emotions. Lai Hua had never refused him anything. He had not realized how very much he had counted on her limitless love. But now it seemed that her love was not so limitless after all.

A new thought suddenly occurred to Jake: His noble gesture, his attempt to meet with Lai Hua tonight so he might convince her that the guilt she harbored for Devina Dale's abduction was unfounded, had merely been an excuse to hold her in his arms again.

Well, it looked as if Lai Hua meant what she said. Why had he ever doubted it? She had always been straightforward and honest with him. It had been he who held back.

Jake stepped out of the cabin and closed the door. Myriad emotions assaulted him and he mounted his horse in silence and cast a final glance at the abandoned shack.

As he traveled along the dark and silent moonlit path, the last shred of hope within him died. He nudged his horse forward, keeping his eyes trained on the trail ahead for he knew with heartbreaking certainty that there was no use looking back.

A supreme sense of unreality assailed Devina as she opened her eyes to the dim light of early morning. She felt so strange. Her head was swimming. She found it difficult to concentrate. She was warm, uncomfortable. A pain, sharp and breathtaking, stabbed her leg and she gasped.

"Devina, what's the matter?"

She turned toward the low-voiced question to find Ross leaning over the bunk. She gazed into his face, attempting to sort out
her confusion. He looked different somehow. She inhaled sharply
as the pain surged anew. "My leg . . . it hurts."

Ross raised the blanket to uncover the leg. Devina's ankle was
swollen and discolored.

Memory returned: her desperate flight into the brush, Ross's
warning shout, the stinging pain.

Devina closed her eyes as debilitating weakness assailed her.
She felt the touch of a callused hand against her forehead.

"Devina, do you feel sick?"

She forced her eyes open and attempted to ignore the persistent pounding in her leg, to concentrate on the concerned face
above her. "Yes . . . no . . . I feel strange. My ankle is
throbbing. It hurts."

"Do you remember what happened?"

Devina nodded. Her throat was parched. She was finding it
increasingly difficult to speak. "Yes," she said. "A snake."

A strange flicker moved across Ross's face as his dark eyes
trailed over her face. "You were very sick last night, but your
fever's gone now. You'll probably have pain for a few days
longer, but you'll be all right." Sliding his arm under her
shoulders, he gently raised her head and held a cup to her lips.
"Drink slowly."

Devina took a sip. The water was so good. She drank again,
swallowing deeply.

"That's enough for now."

Pain shot up her leg, and Devina bit down on her lower lip
and closed her eyes. She felt so weak.

"Devina . . ." Ross's hand cupped her chin, and she struggled to open her eyes. His face was very close to hers.

"The pain will fade soon. Don't be afraid, Devina. I'll be
close by."

The gentleness in his voice, in his touch, was strangely debilitating. She wanted to consign herself to the strength of his
hands, to feel them stroke her, console her.

Devina felt a deep surge of anger at her weakness. She would
not fall victim to fear. Another pain stabbed her, and she expelled her breath in a rush of harsh words, "Go away. I . . . I
don't want you to take care of me."

Devina felt Ross's responsive stiffening, but pain and the

force of her inner struggle robbed her of her strength. She fought to concentrate on his face, but it was no good. His voice echoed in the distance as she drifted away.

"I'll be here, Devina."

Charles cast a quick glance toward the clock on his desk and attempted a smile as Miranda Randolph's quick eye followed the direction of his gaze.

"I have stayed too long again, Doctor. I'm sorry."

Charles patted the chapped, work-roughened hands that worked nervously in Miranda's lap. What was the matter with him? He had lost his concentration of late. Miranda had been talking for the past five minutes while thoughts of Camille and Devina had alternated in filling his mind. He had heard barely a word Miranda had spoken.

Conscience-stricken, he said sincerely, "Don't apologize, Miranda. Please go on with what you were saying."

"No, I must leave." Miranda drew herself to her feet. "You're a very kind man, Dr. Carter. I want you to know I don't believe any of the things that are being said about you, and I won't let anybody say anything about you in my presence, not ever."

Aware of the rumor that he had been a party to Devina's abduction, Charles was touched by the woman's concern. Taking her arm, he walked her to the door. "I appreciate your confidence in me, Miranda, but I don't want you to get involved in any controversy on my account. I'm certain the truth will come out when Devina Dale is freed. In the meantime, let me know how you're feeling and how things work out with your mother."

Miranda's eyes filled with tears. "I hope you won't let all this trouble force you to leave Tombstone. So many of us would miss you."

Appearing suddenly embarrassed by her words, she nodded a silent farewell and headed toward Allen Street. Weary in heart and mind, Charles watched Miranda's limping gait until she turned out of sight.

As he stood in the doorway, Charles released a tired breath. The warmth of the midmorning sun warmed his skin, but it did little to raise his spirits. No trace of Devina had yet been found, and because of his foolish jealousy, he could not even avail himself of Camille's understanding to lighten his burden of guilt.

He feared for Devina's safety at the hands of his unpredictable brother, and he missed Camille desperately . . .

Charles's thoughts came to a jarring halt as Camille came unexpectedly into view. His heart began a ragged pounding at the sight of her brilliant curls, the familiar sway of her unconsciously provocative walk. But she was not alone.

Jealousy flared at the sight of the Count walking briskly beside Camille, and the unhappiness within him expanded to a deadening ache. Why could he not get it through his head that she was the same woman she had always been, that it was he who had changed?

That thought giving him little consolation, Charles turned, determined to set his mind to solving a problem. He would find some way to bring Devina home. He would devote all his effort and all his thoughts to that end.

Resolved to force Camille from his mind, Charles walked back into his office and firmly closed the door behind him.

Attempting to ignore the steady ache in her leg, Devina stared through the doorway of the cabin into the yard. She shifted her position on the bunk, her eyes following the actions of the tall man working steadily in her direct line of vision.

Ross.

She was uncertain when the change had come about in her mind, when his image had ceased to vacillate between the face of her unnamed captor and the face of her friend, Charles, and when he had become the man named Ross to her. Perhaps the reason for the change was that she no longer confused this irritating, frightening, altogether mysterious man with his brother in any way. She had finally accepted the fact that despite their almost identical appearances, they were two distinctly different men who could not be less alike.

Charles was good-natured almost to a fault. He was not easily stirred to a temper. In the weeks she had known him, he had not once been provoked to anger. Not so this man Ross. Strong, heated emotions appeared always to simmer beneath the surface of his calm, waiting to be brought to a full boil by as little as a word or a glance. His dark eyes spat venom as unexpectedly and effectively as the reptile that had caused her present distress, and his sting was as sharp and painful.

But she had learned in the past few hours that she could not even depend on the bite of his words. The events since her awakening this morning were as good an example of his inconsistency as she could possibly entertain.

Devina winced as the throbbing in her leg began anew. She had finally admitted to her fear when she first opened her eyes. The pain, the weakness, the memory of her flight from Ross, which had resulted in her being bitten, had been overwhelming. She had reacted with anger, and the exchange between Ross and her had been harsh.

She had awakened again a short time ago to find Ross sitting on the side of the bunk. His honest concern had been evident as he touched her forehead, and she'd had neither the inclination nor the desire to withdraw from the consolation she had derived from his touch. He had been extraordinarily gentle as he slid his arm behind her back and supported her while he held a cup of cool water to her lips. The harsh words, the anger had disappeared, and her relief had been overwhelming.

He had later approached her bedside with a bowl of clear aromatic broth and he had fed her cautiously. He had not spoken a word, but his dark, direct gaze had conveyed only too clearly that his silence was meant to eliminate the trap they consistently fell into in their dealings with each other. In his gentle ministrations, there was no challenge, only concern. She had finally accepted the limitations her weakness forced upon her and had not protested the service. She had never tasted anything as good as the broth he offered her. Conscience had forced her to tell him so, and she had been rewarded with a smile that had unaccountably set her heart to pounding.

It was then she had realized that, for the first time, her mind had not automatically converted Ross to Charles. She presently wondered how she could possibly have entertained that confusion for a moment. Ross's slower, gradually broadening smile was so unlike Charles's quick, wide grin. Its rarity somehow made it more rewarding, and she had been inordinately pleased to have brought that smile to his lips.

The memory of that smile and the emotions it had stirred within her brought a frown to Devina's brow. She could not allow her weakened state and her temporary need to endow Ross with qualities he did not possess. She must remember to keep in mind who he was, why she was his captive, and the fact that her father's future and her own depended on him.

Distress, deep and profound, returned with the thought of her circumstances, and Devina closed her eyes as a flash of weakness returned. It would be far better if she put aside these disturbing thoughts temporarily and allowed herself to enjoy the temporary truce that reigned between her handsome, enigmatic captor and herself. When she was well she would be able to think more clearly. Until then, she needed to accept the fact that she was helpless and dependent on his goodwill and care.

Devina gazed out the open doorway at the man who continued to work in the yard. Stripped to the waist, the broad expanse of his shoulders and chest exposed to the brilliant midday sun, Ross was leaning over a tub washing clothes.

A heat not related to her wound abruptly colored her face as the tall, broad, half-naked man carefully wrung out her delicate chemise and hung it beside the other clothes on the line he had strung between the shrubs. Devina was abruptly and embarrassingly conscious of the attire she wore under the light blanket. She had awakened in a shirt and nothing else, and she had been unable to force herself to examine the how and the why of it.

A new wave of heat suffused her cheeks as Ross plunged his hands into the washtub and withdrew her lace-trimmed underdrawers. Devina turned her eyes away from the sight. Was there no end to this humiliation?

Determined not to torment herself any longer, Devina kept her eyes on the wall, but Ross's image remained bright and clear in her mind. In truth, she had never seen a more beautiful man. With each passing minute, the physical differences between the two brothers were becoming as clear as the vast differences in their personalities.

She remembered the incredible stretch of Ross's shoulders, bared in the sun as he performed his tasks; the sheen of his skin and the ripple of the tight, well-honed muscles across his back as he hung the wet clothes on the line. She remembered his expression when he turned back, unaware of her scrutiny. Serious, intent on his chore, he had been squinting against the sun's glare, the strong planes of his face free of the anger often visible there. He had raised his hand to brush back a lock of hair that had fallen onto his forehead, and she had remembered the surprising gentleness of those work-roughened hands. She had been intensely stirred in a way that Charles had never stirred her.

"Devina, are you all right?"

The unexpected sound of Ross's voice at her side made Devina turn to face him with a speed that set her head to spinning. She raised a shaking hand to her temple as a flush of heat colored her cheeks.

When she hesitated to respond, Ross's expression tightened into a frown. He laid his palm against her forehead.

"You're flushed, but you don't seem to have a fever."

Devina was unwilling to allow Ross to speculate further. "I . . . I'm all right. I just felt a little strange, that's all."

The hand resting against her forehead slipped to her cheek. "You're sure?"

"Yes." Devina reluctantly met the dark eyes scrutinizing her so intently. Oh, damn, she was so confused. She wanted to relieve the concern in this man's eyes, to touch his cheek even as he touched hers and tell him that he need not worry. She would be all right. She wanted to make him smile, to see his mouth slowly curve upward, to see his face reflect the warmth of those lips. She wanted to light the spark that would warm his dark eyes. Most of all, she wanted this man to remain as he was now—concerned, tender, almost loving.

Devina's thoughts jarred to a halt. She was incredulous at the direction her wandering mind was taking. All this she wanted from the man who had threatened her life, who held her captive, who sought to destroy her father and possibly her as well.

She was so confused.

Ross was still looking at her intently, and Devina sought to avoid his gaze, only to feel his hand cup her chin and turn her face, forcing her to meet his eyes.

"What's wrong, Devina?"

Her eyes traveled the broad planes of his face. His sun-tinted cheeks were smooth, cleanly shaven. It was obvious that he had made a visit to the pool while she was sleeping; he was clean and refreshed despite his recent exertion. Abruptly she was only too conscious of her own disheveled state. She was warm and uncomfortable. Her hair clung damply to her head, and her skin was moist and sticky. She felt weak, unkempt, sick, confused, miserable. Tears filled her eyes, and she closed them in another attempt to avoid Ross's scrutiny.

The deep voice moved closer, became more concerned. "Devina, are you in pain?"

She shook her head. What was wrong with her?

"Devina." The urgent note in Ross's voice made her look up at last. He searched her face, his frown intense. "If you're feeling worse—"

"No, I'm not feeling worse. I . . . I guess I just feel envious."

"Envious?"

Nodding, Devina was further humiliated by the tear that slipped down her cheek. "Yes. You look so clean and comfortable, and I feel so sticky and hot."

Ross's callused palm smoothed the tear from her cheek. A hint of a smile not untouched with relief played at the corners of his mouth. "Well, that's easy enough to fix."

Without another word, Ross snatched up the bucket and disappeared into the yard. Ashamed and disgusted with herself, Devina again turned her face to the wall. She suddenly realized that where Ross's anger and threats had failed to break her, his gentleness and concern were succeeding. She was a fool for having succumbed to her own weakness, to her desire to see in this man what she wanted to see. She needed to take herself in hand.

At the sound of a step, Devina turned back toward the doorway just as Ross walked in. He carefully placed the bucket on the table beside the bunk.

"Can you bathe yourself, Devina?"

Devina's mind immediately jumped to the alternative, and her face flamed. Her reply was indignant. "Of course I can bathe myself."

Ross shook his head. "I don't know . . ."

Devina summoned up her pride, and a familiar hauteur returned to her tone. "I'm quite capable of taking care of myself if I'm afforded a little privacy."

Ross's lips tightened at her tone, and Devina immediately regretted her words. She could not stand much more of her vacillating feelings. But she realized it was too late for regrets the moment Ross stood and nodded stiffly.

"Of course, Miss Dale. You can have all the privacy you want." Ross stalked angrily to the door and out of sight, and Devina immediately began to berate herself. Now she had ruined everything, of that she was certain. Ross was angry again, and she didn't want him to be angry with her. Would she never learn?

Now that she had provoked him, however, she felt she had to

show him she meant what she'd said. Summoning up her last reservoir of energy, she threw back the blanket and forced herself to sit up in bed, refusing to look at her swollen and bruised ankle. Pain stabbed her leg, almost stealing her breath, and she felt a sheen of perspiration break out on her brow.

Her expression hardened as she stiffened her resolve. She *could* take care of herself. All she needed was a little privacy.

Although the effort exhausted her and increased her pain to an almost unbearable degree, she finally managed to ease her legs over the side of the bed. A wave of exhilaration swept through her at the small victory. Now that she was sitting up, the rest would be easy, she told herself. She dipped one hand into the bucket of cool water. Relief was instantaneous. A bath was all she needed to feel good again. Very soon she'd be all right.

But the soap and cloth were just a little out of her reach. If she could just stand up for a minute and pull the table closer . . .

Placing her bare feet on the floor, she slowly began to shift her weight as a prelude to rising. Her trembling legs resisted the movement, and the rest of her body began to quake with the effort, but she disregarded its pitiful response. She *would* get up, she *would* bathe herself, and she *would* show Ross Morrison that she could take care of herself.

With supreme determination, Devina pulled herself to her feet. She was standing! She gripped the edge of the table and attempted to pull it closer to the bed. The heavy table resisted her weak effort, and Devina felt the heat of exhausted tears burn her eyes. He had done it on purpose! He had put the table just out of her reach to show her that she couldn't manage by herself. The kindness, the gentleness he had shown her had all been an act to break her down. And he had almost succeeded. But she'd show him that he'd never get the best of her!

Taking a deep breath, Devina pulled with all her might. The rasp of the table against the floor as the table lurched closer was simultaneous with the horrendous jolt of pain that shot up her leg, stealing her breath. Devina clutched the table as the room reeled around her. She held on with all her strength as her knees began to give beneath her, as she began sinking toward the floor. She gasped, calling out as her clutching fingers began to lose their hold on the table edge.

Ross paused in his rapid angry step as he attempted to put

some distance between himself and the cabin. He ran a hand through his hair in an agitated gesture. Where in hell was he going? And just what was he doing?

Only this morning he had decided that he would not allow Devina to anger him. Sharp words were her defense against him, and a very effective defense they were! In his mind he went over their angry exchange of a few moments before. He had been doing very well in getting her to trust him. He had read her gradual acceptance of him in her eyes. He had only needed a little more time.

Then suddenly there was anger between them again. It was all his fault. She was ill. He had handled the situation badly. He had embarrassed her, forced her to refuse his help. Now, dammit, he was stuck with the result of his stupidity.

Ross turned abruptly and walked back to the cabin. Devina was too weak to take care of herself, no matter how stubbornly she had declared she could. He'd go back inside and help her. She needed his help. She needed him.

Ross was a few feet from the doorway when he heard the scrape of the table against the floor, heard Devina cry out. He was running through the doorway when her slender body began to crumple toward the floor.

In a moment she was in his arms, and he was clutching her close. She was so very pale. Loathe to release her, he laid her small, limp body on the bunk and pulled the blanket up to her waist. Turning, he reached into the bucket and withdrew the cloth. Squeezing it almost dry, he cautiously, tenderly touched its coolness to her forehead and pale cheeks.

Her heavy eyelids were fluttering open even as he cursed himself for having allowed his anger to again cause her pain. Her dazed eyes met his, and Ross swallowed tightly at the confusion he saw there. She attempted to speak.

"No, Devina. Don't say anything. We both should've known better. You're too weak to help yourself right now. Just lie back and relax."

Determined to ignore any protests she might voice, Ross moistened the cloth and rubbed it briskly against the soap. Working up a lather, he touched the cloth lightly to her face. She closed her eyes as he gently bathed her forehead and cheeks. He rinsed her clear skin free of soap. Then, smoothing back the damp tendrils at her temples, he patted her skin dry. His eyes slipped to the pulse in Devina's throat, and he watched it throb with an accelerated beat for the space of a breathless second, even as the dark fans of her eyelashes fluttered and began to rise.

Ross hesitated, then began to unfasten the buttons on her shirt, his eyes meeting Devina's firmly as hers widened. Her trembling hands moved to his wrists, but he shook his head.

"No, not this time, Devina."

Brushing away her hands, Ross continued to unbutton the shirt until it lay loose over her breasts. Devina's murmur of protest was met with his own low words of reassurance as he lifted her gently and slipped one arm free and then the other. He swallowed against the rush of emotion that suffused him as the perfection of her naked, feminine beauty was exposed to his gaze. Her clear, unmarked skin, her full, round breasts, the crests pink and inviting, tempting him.

With supreme control, Ross smoothed the lathered cloth over the column of her throat, along the slope of her shoulders, and down the length of her graceful, slender arms. His heart thundering in his chest, he bathed her firm, perfectly shaped breasts, circling them gently, lovingly.

His hands trembling, his chest heaving from the strain of emotions held tightly in check, Ross rubbed Devina's damp flesh dry and then raised her to a sitting position in his arms. Supporting her with his chest, intensely aware of the incredible softness of her cheek as it pressed against his throat, he scooped the long, curling spirals of her hair into his hand and swept them over her shoulder. He heard his own sharp intake of breath as Devina leaned full against him, her breasts warm against his bare chest. The sweet, natural scent of her body rose to his nostrils, taunting him.

He soaped the cloth once more and moved it in gentle, caressing circles over the smooth contours of her back. All resistance appearing to have slipped away, Devina sighed, settling herself more comfortably against him, and Ross's heart throbbed to a ragged beat. Uncertain how much more he could stand, he dried her back with a trembling hand.

Devina stirred against him once more. She was beginning to draw back, away from him, and Ross fought the urge to clutch her closer even as she raised heavy-lidded, uncertain eyes to his. Her gaze dropped to his lips as her voice emerged in a low ragged whisper, a single word: "Ross."

And then his mouth was covering hers, lifting his name from her lips, tasting its echo, taking it deep inside him as he kissed her with growing hunger. He cupped her head with his hand, supporting her as his kiss passed the barrier of her teeth to touch the intimate inner reaches of her mouth. His other hand moved down the slope of her naked back, caressing her skin, pressing the fullness of her naked breasts against his chest. He drew deeply from her mouth, loving, consuming.

His breathing ragged, Ross withdrew from her mouth, cupping Devina's head more securely as he trailed his lips across the cool, delicate skin of her cheek to press light, butterfly kisses against her fluttering eyelids, the throbbing pulse in her temple, the fine line of her brow. Intoxicated by the taste of her, he touched his lips to the small intricate shell of Devina's ear to taste and probe the fragile hollows, even as low-voiced, trembling words of endearment fell from his lips.

Devina moved subtly in his arms, arching her back to provide the perfect path for his lips down the slender column of her throat to the warm, throbbing wells at its base. Oh, God, how sweet she was, how warm, how well she fit his mouth, his kiss.

But Devina was trembling. The hand that had rested on his shoulder fell away, and Ross drew back to look at her. She was too pale. Her eyes were closed, and her breathing was uneven. Guilt assailed him. Gently, with utmost care, he pressed her back against the pillow, following her down to touch his lips to her mouth with a concerned whisper. "Devina darling, are you all right?"

Her heavy eyelids lifted slowly, the glorious silver-blue of her gaze bemused, almost bewildered. A swell of tenderness rose within him, and Ross swallowed against the pull of her aura, despising himself for the desire coursing through him, pressing him for more, so much more, despite her weakened state. He raised his palm to her cheek, caressed its velvet softness, his sharp intake of breath again sounding sharply in the silence as Devina turned her head to press her lips against his palm.

Ross's eyes closed briefly against the bittersweet agony that assailed him. He pulled her against him, gasping as Devina's pink, erect nipples teased his chest. His parted lips moved against the curve of her jaw, nibbling and biting in his overwhelming desire to consume her, draw her in, make her a part of him. His voice was a low, shaken whisper against her ear.

"Devina darling . . . I want to love you. I want to hold you in my arms so close that there'll be no one in the world but the two of us. I want you to belong to me, now, Devina . . ."

Devina turned toward him. She was breathless, uncertain, as his mouth trailed along her cheek to brush her mouth once again. Her lips trembled as she sought to speak, but no sound emerged. His passion almost out of control, Ross was seized by a new shuddering.

Devina swallowed, her eyes flicking briefly closed. Her lips trembled once more, and Ross covered them with his, holding them firm under his kiss, lending her his strength and his weakness as he slipped his arms under and around her to enclose her in a crushing embrace. Flesh to flesh, their hearts pounding in ragged unison, Ross kissed her again and again, his hunger growing, consuming him even as a nagging fear tore at his conscience. She was ill, weak . . .

Drawing back, Ross pressed his lips to Devina's temple in an attempt to halt the rapid escalation of his passions. He stroked the fair hair there, marveling at its incandescent glow even as he sought to retain the last of his waning control.

"Devina, you're going to have to tell me to stop. You're going to have to tell me loud and clear that you don't want me to touch you, because I won't be able to stop by myself. Devina, say it now, darling, or don't say it at all, because in a few minutes it'll be too late."

There was no response to his ragged whisper, and Ross drew back slowly. He was overwhelming her, not giving her a chance to speak, even if she wanted him to let her go. He drew back farther, his eyes moving over Devina's supremely beautiful face, the pale hair splayed out in a shimmering halo against the pillow, her graceful shoulders sculpted against the hard surface of the bunk, the full, perfect curves of her breasts. He dared not think of the rest of her soft body, which lay beneath the thin blanket, not if he hoped to retain a last shred of control.

Devina's chest was rising and falling rapidly, and Ross placed his palm against one firm, full breast, caressing the sweet curve, cupping it lovingly. He lowered his head to the sweet flesh and tasted it with his tongue. He heard Devina's low gasp, and he opened his mouth to take in the warm pink peak. He drew on it gently, his heart thundering as his hunger mounted, as he sought to devour the sweet flesh. But he could not be satisfied with just a taste. Hotly, anxiously, he moved his voracious quest to the other mound, his hands cupping its round firmness, caressing it, wanting all he could take and more.

He was not certain of the exact moment he felt Devina's fingers moving sensually in his hair, gripping him to hold him fast against her. Elation surged through him, and he shuddered with the joy of her acceptance. But he needed one thing more . . .

Drawing back from her sweet flesh, Ross slid up to press his lips lightly against Devina's once more. He spoke softly, his voice low and caressing. "Devina, open your eyes, look at me."

Devina's heavy eyelids again fluttered, rising slowly until she met his gaze. He saw wonder in the brilliant eyes meeting his, and he saw her confusion at the emotion that moved between them with a heat so intense that she was helpless against it. The desire reflected there was only a pale shadow of the force that pounded through his body, but it exhilarated him. Still, it was not enough. He had to be sure.

"That's right, darling, look at me. Tell me who you see."

Devina still seemed confused. Anxiety touched his mind as an aching suspicion began to grow inside him. His expression hardened, and his body grew tense. His grip tightened unconsciously as his voice became harsher, more demanding. "Devina, tell me who you see."

A flash of pain moved across Devina's face, and Ross felt another anxiety touch his mind. But he could not relent. "Tell me."

Devina's voice emerged in a confused whisper, "Ross, I . . ."

Ross was suddenly still. "Say that again, Devina."

"Ross."

Ross's mouth closed over the sound, swallowing it, consuming it and the lips through which his name had passed. Then, drawing back, aware that Devina's eyes were following his movements, he shed the rest of his clothes, the last impediment to the intimate meeting of their flesh, and stripped back the coverlet that hid Devina's full naked beauty from his view. Lowering himself slowly, gently upon her, gasping at the first full meeting of their flesh, Ross covered Devina's mouth with his. He drank deeply, seeking to sate the thirst that had raged unabated within him from the first moment of their meeting. Lifting Devina's arms, he slid them around his neck, his joy rising as they closed tighter around him, drew him closer. He

was consuming her, drawing deeply, taking all she had, all she
would give.

Suddenly there was no more time, and another kind of rage
shook him. It was too soon, too soon.

Ross tore his mouth from Devina's, his eyes speaking his
regret in the inadequacy of words. Moving to straddle her hips
with his knees, he brushed Devina's thighs with his callused
palms, pausing to stroke the warm nest nestled there for the
briefest moment before he separated her legs. He saw the surprise on her pale face, the sudden fear reflected there in the
moment before he nudged the moist core of her femininity with
the firm staff of his desire, in the moment before he entered her
tentatively and then thrust full and deep within her.

Devina's low gasp echoed in his mind as her body arched
beneath him, but he held her fast. He felt her shudder, and he
gripped her closer still, his lips moving against her face to find
her mouth. He kissed her again and again, whispering soft words
of love, of need, of consolation even as he plunged repeatedly
within her.

Her slender body was warm under his, moist with perspiration, but he was insensible to all but the growing heat inside
him, the wonder of the intimate warmth that closed around him,
the low whimpers of a responsive passion growing stronger
against his lips.

And then the flaring heat of climax, the wonder of Devina's
small body shuddering, taking him full and deep within it, the
sweet giving of her body as it rose to meet his, as it gave him all
it had to give, all he had ever wanted, all he would ever need.

Jake leaned indolently against the carpenter shop window, but
his casual posture belied the racing of his mind. He pushed back
his hat and raised his face to the midafternoon sun. It had taken
more patience than he thought he possessed, and more time than
he had wanted to spend, to reach this particular spot on Fremont
Street at this particular time of day. He supposed that went to
show how damned desperate he really was.

He had all but worn himself out with caution. About two
hours earlier he had left the Crystal Palace Saloon, making
certain there were enough witnesses to his statement that he had
to go check on his horse. He had turned onto Fifth Street and
walked at a leisurely pace toward Fremont. From there he had

sauntered toward Fourth Street, stopping to pass the time of day
with a few familiar faces along the way. He had taken each
opportunity to restate his reason for his casual jaunt toward
Bullock and Crabtree's Livery Stable.

He had then spent the alloted time at Bullock and Crabtree's,
pestering Jack Crabtree about his horse's condition when he
knew damned well there was not a thing wrong with the animal.
Making sure that he had firmly established the reason for his
presence on Fremont Street, he had then walked farther down
and propped himself against the window of the carpenter's shop,
where he now stood.

He had made certain to be properly obnoxious while eyeing
the women who emerged from Addie Bourland's dressmaking
shop, and had been startled at the smile he had gotten from the
daughter of one of the town's wealthy bankers. Had he been
interested, he was certain he could have made more of that
meeting than just the short wink he had given her.

Jake shifted his posture again, hoping the movement had not
revealed his impatience, then turned and looked toward Third
Street, his eye on the big house near the corner. With annoyance
he noted that he had not seen a sign of life in the Dale household
since he had arrived, and he was getting damned tired of waiting. Where in hell was Lai Hua?

Even as impatience brought a frown to his brow, Jake shook
his head. He was stupid for having come here today. Last night,
as he had traveled that dark trail away from the miner's shack,
he had vowed to stay away, but the dawning of a new morning
and the prospect of another long day stretching ahead of him had
altered his thinking.

He had tortured himself with the thought that maybe Lai Hua
hadn't seen the ribbon. It was possible, after all. He had gone by
the trail that morning and seen it still tied where he had left it.
He had removed it from the bush and stuffed it into his pocket.
He realized belatedly that he was clenching the damned scrap in
his hand right now. In any case, he had determined that he
would try again.

Jake took a deep, weary breath. Damn, he felt like hell. He
had lain awake most of the night going over and over everything Lai Hua had said. He had done a lot of other thinking, too.
He had reached the conclusion that he was not only an ex-
convict and a thief, but a fool as well. The first two things he

could do nothing about, but he definitely intended to work on the third.

But to do that, he had to see Lai Hua. If he wasn't too far off his guess, she should be coming out that back door any time now to go on her afternoon shopping tour. Ward's Butcher Shop was right across the street from where he stood, and he was pretty sure Lai Hua would be taking that route real soon.

Jake squinted into the distance, his eyes focusing on a flutter of movement as the back door of the Dale house opened. He felt his heart leap as Lai Hua walked across the yard and turned onto the street. He started slowly in her direction.

He knew the exact moment Lai Hua spotted him walking toward her. Her small frame stiffened, her chin rising with determination. It was then that he felt the first stab of fear. Watching as she crossed the street farther down, he crossed as well, so they might meet casually, as far as observing eyes might see. She was walking at a steady pace in his direction, her eyes carefully turned to avoid direct contact with his. Under any other circumstances, he would have admired her caution.

With a sinking heart, Jake realized Lai Hua was about to walk past him. His hand snaked out, grasping her narrow wrist, causing her to look up at him. Her dark eyes were cool and that coolness shook him more than he had realized possible. He attempted a smile.

"I waited, Lai Hua. You didn't come. I just wanted to make sure. I thought maybe you didn't see the ribbon."

Making no attempt to avoid his gaze, Lai Hua responded simply, "I saw it, Mr. Jake."

Carefully disengaging her arm from his grasp, Lai Hua turned away and continued down the street. Following her small figure with his gaze until she turned into Ward's Butcher Shop, Jake abruptly turned and forced himself to walk casually toward Third Street and back to Allen.

Hafford's, the Occidental, the Alhambra—any saloon would do, now that he knew it was truly over.

So now Ross knew.

Devina was silent and still, sleeping in his arms in the aftermath of their loving. The sun-drenched landscape outside the door was bright with the light of afternoon, but somehow he had been unable to make himself rise, to separate himself from Devina's slight, clinging warmth.

Guilt touched Ross's mind. He should have known better. He had exhausted Devina with his loving, teased her untutored body until she had used up her small remaining reservoir of strength. His need for this woman had driven him past common sense, and he was angry with himself for his own weakness. But even in the face of his self-directed anger, he was unwilling to separate himself from her, perhaps because everything was suddenly so clear. Now he knew . . .

Ross still felt incredulous. This deep well of emotion was the force behind the driving anger that had left him little peace from the moment his eyes had first touched on Devina Dale. He knew this was not pure lust. He had experienced lust for many women, but he had never known the concern, anxiety, regret, and soul-shaking tenderness this woman inspired in him. This emotion that bound him to Devina—this desire to hold her as a part of him, to keep her safe, to care for her; this melting heat that soared to life deep within him each time his eyes touched her; this tenderness—had no part in so base an emotion as lust.

Devina stirred in his arms, interrupting Ross's train of thought, even as unrelenting tenderness stirred anew. Devina's slender nakedness fitted naturally against his side. Ross drew her closer, turning her against him more fully. His eyes dropped briefly closed with sheer joy as her breasts pressed full and warm against his chest, as he fitted her head into the curve of his throat. He slid his hand down to cup her small, firm buttocks, to fit her securely against the warmth of his groin. He felt the responsive swell of his body and he gave a low, disbelieving snort.

His hand slipping into the silver-blond hair that teased his chin, he held Devina close within his embrace as he lowered his head to cover her mouth lightly with his. Devina stirred, and he drew back from his kiss. She was exhausted. She had to rest.

Guilt forced Ross's gaze down the length of Devina's slender leg, toward the swollen, angry bruise on her ankle. It would be another day, maybe two, before she regained her strength, began to return to herself. He was beset with conflicting emotions at the thought.

When she was stronger and no longer physically dependent on him, would she hate him for pressing his attentions on her while she was so weak? Would she turn away from him? He only knew that he could not, would not allow that to happen.

It no longer mattered to him that Devina's name was Dale, that hatred, contempt, and distrust were waiting to separate them in the world outside this cabin. Devina had no part in the old score he had to settle with her father, and he would hold her separate from it. He would overcome her objections just as firmly as he had overcome her resistance to his lovemaking.

And in the meantime, he would love her. How very well he would love her. He now realized that for him, it could be no other way.

Night had fallen, but Tombstone had come alive with the garish lights of the dance halls, raucous music, shrieking laughter, and rowdy calls and conversations conducted at a shouted pitch as drunken cowboys stumbled from one saloon to another. But Jake had had his fill. Swaying in the doorway of the Alhambra Saloon, he raised his glass and downed the last few swallows of beer. Turning with the slow deliberation of a man finding it difficult to maintain his balance, he slammed his glass down on the nearest table and walked uncertainly out through the swinging doors. He paused, tipping his hat to the gaudily dressed young woman who turned her brightly painted face in his direction.

"Good evenin', ma'am."

He continued walking, hearing her harsh laughter as he tripped on a warped board in the sidewalk, managing at the last minute to save himself from coming down hard on the swaying wooden walk. He took a deep breath and attempted to clear his whirling head.

Damn, he was drunk.

Turning abruptly, Jake steadied himself before stepping down into the street. He looked sharply in both directions, amused at his own caution.

Jake, old friend, you have somethin' to do, he told himself, *and now's the time to do it. Drunk or not, now's the time*.

With great deliberation, Jake walked across the street in a wavering path. It came to him that it had taken most of the day, but he was finally almost numb. A joke, that's what it was, a joke. He wondered just how long this numbness would last.

Grinning with satisfaction, Jake reached the other side. Well, that hadn't been as hard as he had thought. He attempted to step up onto the walk and tripped again. The same harsh female laughter sounded behind him, and he turned with a widening grin to lift his hat in its direction. He was beginning to like the sound of that laugh. He really must be drunk.

Turning back to the task at hand, Jake stared at the floating step as it rose and fell unevenly in front of his eyes. He gave it a hard kick, smiling as it flattened into place. He negotiated it with a new confidence and beamed as he stood at last on the sidewalk.

Straightening his back victoriously, his chest swelling with pride in his achievement, Jake launched himself forward, then recognized his error as the impetus thrust him headlong into a hazy, uncertain direction. Jake caught hold of a doorway as it passed by and pulled himself to a swinging halt. He squinted into the blurry darkness, trying to determine his whereabouts. He grinned. Right, he was going the right way, after all.

But his second launch was not working out favorably. Attempting to draw himself up short, Jake staggered and tripped on the damned weaving walk, attempting to hold it down with his stamping feet, but somehow that didn't work. Instead, he toppled head first and belly down in a full, gliding slide that landed him, dusty and much the worse for wear, in a dark doorway.

Jake looked up around him. A smile stretched across his lips. Pretty good, pretty good . . . He reached into his pocket and withdrew his bandanna. The damned slippery cloth eluded his grasp and fell to the walk beside him, and he was able to retrieve it only after a long, arduous search. He wiped it across his perspiring face. This was damned hard work!

Slowly, laboriously, he stumbled to his feet and fixed his gaze on the Occidental Hotel. Not too far, not too far . . . He'd make it.

When he had finally regained his equilibrium, Jake took a stately step forward. He was quite proud of himself. He took another. He was even more proud. His legs were beginning to obey him, and even if his head wasn't completely clear, he was pretty damned clever.

No, sirree. Nobody, but nobody, could've seen him slip that note under the door of Till-Dale Enterprises, where he had landed so unceremoniously a few minutes before. Tomorrow mornin' that damned clerk would open the door, pick up the note, and within the hour there'd be hell to pay in Harvey Dale's office.

Feeling better than he had in days, Jake navigated the weaving sidewalk with a new satisfaction. Inside a week, or maybe two, he and Ross would be gone from this damned town, and they'd both put everything behind them.

His smile not quite as bright as before, Jake turned into the lobby of the Occidental Hotel. He'd had enough. In a lot of ways, he'd had enough . . .

A slender, shadowed figure walked along Allen Street in the darkness of the overhang. It drew back cautiously as the lurching, weaving figure of Jake Walsh turned into the lobby of the Occidental Hotel. It paused a moment longer, making certain the drunken fool did not decide to turn back and emerge once more onto the street.

Satisfied at last at the safety of its endeavor, the shadowed figure slunk stealthily up the street, coming to an abrupt halt in front of the offices of Till-Dale Enterprises. It turned to peer through the window into the darkened interior of the office. A smile flickered across its lips as its keen gaze fastened on the folded note lying on the floor just inside the doorway. The smile broadened, the hiss of satisfaction that accompanied it going unheard amid the din of the street. The time of waiting was almost over.

The shadowed figure turned abruptly and moved back in the direction from which it had come. It turned quickly into a nearby alley and disappeared from sight, knowing the satisfaction of a mission accomplished, a job almost done.

CHAPTER XVIII

"I'M SORRY, HARVEY, it's out of the question."

Harvey's aristocratic face registered his shock at his partner's softly spoken response. Incredulous, he stared for a few silent moments into George Tillson's sober countenance. He took a step forward, narrowing the distance between them within the already limited confines of his Till-Dale office.

"What do you mean, out of the question?" Tightly clutching the lock of pale silver-blond hair that had fallen out of the ransom note in his hand, Harvey took a deep breath. "There's no doubt the note is genuine. This is my daughter's life we're talking about!"

George Tillson raised a graying eyebrow. "Harvey, if the situation were reversed—"

"This isn't a theoretical situation, George. My daughter's life is at stake here." Harvey's face colored an apoplectic red. His chest began an agitated heaving.

"That's beside the point, Harvey. I have no intention of—"

"George, I warn you . . ." Harvey's rage was instantaneous, reverberating in the stillness of the small room as he took another step forward. Quaking with the force of his fury, he stood threateningly over the smaller man.

George's narrow face tightened, his eyes turning cold.

"Don't threaten me, Harvey. You're in no position to alienate me, you know. You have damned few friends as it is, and you need my goodwill right now, more than you ever have in your life."

"Your goodwill!" Harvey shook the ransom note in his partner's face. "My *friend?* Is that really what you call yourself? You read this ransom note. You know what I have to do."

George Tillson shook his head. "No, I don't. I only know what that note tells you to do. The price you're being asked to pay for your daughter's release is not at all reasonable."

"Reasonable! I don't care if the price is reasonable! I'll pay any price that bastard Morrison asks to get my daughter back safely."

George's gaze did not waver. "Unfortunately, Harvey, *I* will *not.*" Anticipating Harvey's reaction to his words, George attempted a conciliatory smile and patted Harvey's arm reassuringly. "Harvey, I don't mean to be unkind or unreasonable. I know how you feel. I just want you to stop and think a moment."

Harvey jerked his arm free. "No, you don't know how I feel, George. You couldn't, or you wouldn't be arguing with me right now. Your wife is waiting for you at home, and your children are safe in boarding school. You leave this office each night and go to a home where your wife makes you welcome. I haven't had that luxury for many years."

Impatience flicked across George Tillson's face. "Harvey, Harvey, this is George you're talking to, remember? I remember when you had Regina waiting for you at home, and I remember the many nights you *chose* not to go home to her, but to visit one of your many mistresses instead! Regina was a beautiful and loving woman, and I have no doubt you loved her in your way, but you've had no lack of mistresses since her death, and I doubt that you've spent a lonesome day or night without her. So, please, don't expect me to fall for that hogwash you're handing me."

Harvey's flush deepened to a purple hue. "So, my past indiscretions have come home to roost, is that what you're telling me, George?"

"I'm telling you no such thing."

"You're telling me that I'm overreacting, that if I lose my daughter as I lost my wife, I'll go on just as I did before, that my mistresses and the bodily comfort they give me will make me forget that Devina, the child of my body, my own flesh and blood, is lost to me forever. You're telling me that I should accept that eventuality because the price asked to return Devina safely is too high."

George Tillson's lined cheek twitched with discomfort. "Harvey, you are reading entirely different meanings into my words."

"Then tell me, damn you, what you *do* mean!"

George stiffened at the heat of Harvey's attack. He pulled his slight frame up to its full height and raised his chin. Staring Harvey directly in the eye he spoke softly, distinctly.

"I'm telling you that you're wasting your time trying to stir my sympathy with that story about my having a wife and children safe at home. Harvey, I have a wife waiting at home who loves me because I have taken the time to love her back during the many years of our marriage. You never did that for your lovely and unfortunate Regina. In the time since her death, you've been too busy gratifying your ego and your lust to truly mourn her or to cultivate a real relationship with another woman. It's only now when Devina is threatened, that you realize you have no one to turn to for comfort. It's unfortunate that Devina has fallen victim to Ross Morrison's desire for revenge, but you're at fault there also, aren't you? From the beginning, I objected to the methods you used in acquiring Bradford Morrison's mine, but you assured me they were all aboveboard and that the fellow understood the legal technicalities of the contract completely."

Harvey stared in silent fury at his partner's calm expression. "Yes, George, you registered your objections to my conduct of the whole Morrison affair, as you have many times in the past in other situations. But, George, you raised no objection at all to the enormous profits my 'questionable' transactions have reaped."

George Tillson's narrow lips curved into a smile. "That's right, Harvey, I neither objected to nor refused to accept my share of the enormous profits this company has made. And I do not intend that those enormous profits shall cease."

Harvey Dale's tall, well-proportioned body twitched almost convulsively. He shook his head. "George, do you realize what you're saying?"

"Yes, Harvey, I'm saying that I don't intend to pay the ransom."

"You bastard!"

Harvey's angry advance was halted by the expression in his partner's eyes and his sharp admonition.

"Stop where you are, Harvey. Don't do something you'll regret."

Harvey was twitching with the suppressed desire to close the remaining distance between himself and George Tillson and to snap his hands around the man's skinny neck. With a profound effort, he held himself in check. "All right. I'll buy you out, here and now."

"Don't be a damned fool, Harvey. I know your financial position. You can't afford to buy me out."

"Then what are you suggesting, damn you? That I calmly refuse to meet Morrison's demands, that I let him do what he wants with my daughter? You know the man hates me! God knows what Devina's already suffered. I—"

His throat filling with emotion, Harvey fell into a choking silence, bringing the first sign of compassion to George Tillson's thin face.

"Harvey, you got yourself into this spot all by yourself, and you're going to have to get yourself out the same way. Don't ask me to sacrifice my own future and my family's future for your mistakes."

Harvey shook his head. "He'll kill her, George. If I don't submit to his demands, he'll kill Devina."

George remained unshaken. "Then let him think you're doing exactly as he instructed. I have no objection to that."

' Harvey was confused. "What good will that do? When he finds out—"

"You're going to have to outsmart him! Use that conniving brain of yours, Harvey. Stall for time. Call Charles Carter in, as the ransom note demands, give him the files on the Morrison claim, let him make an accounting of the profits of the claim in the past three years. Put an ad in the *Epitaph*, as Morrison instructed and post a full confession, as the note demands. Just don't involve me in any way. You can pay the miners a month's salary at your own expense. I'll even consent to suspending operations at the mines for a short time to give the impression of compliance, but I will not allow the pumping to stop. You can follow through on any other details that will make Morrison think he's getting exactly what he wants. But that's as far as I'll go, Harvey. Do not expect me to sign any papers for the transfer of moneys or title to any part of what's legally mine, or to get involved personally in this fiasco in any way."

"George—"

"That's *all*, Harvey."

"All right!" Shaking with fury, Harvey waved the ransom note in his partner's face. "But you'll pay for this, George!"

Unflinching under Harvey's rage, George smiled. "Harvey, if the situation had been reversed, you wouldn't have given me even as much leeway as I'm giving you."

His breathing so ragged that it was almost painful, Harvey stared into his partner's face in venomous silence for a few moments longer before turning on his heel, striding out of the office, and slamming the door behind him.

As he marched down the street, George's words echoed in his ears despite his fervent attempt to drive them from his mind, despite his desire to deny all George had said, despite his unwillingness to face the realization that every word George had uttered was true.

Jake took a swallow of the steaming coffee and gasped, choking and sputtering as the boiling liquid burned all the way down to his protesting stomach. He gave a low, defeated groan. Hell, this morning there didn't seem to be a part of his body that wasn't aching.

He ignored the curious glances his gasps and groans had elicited from the other patrons of the restaurant as he set his cup down in disgust and stared out the window at the street.

It was not by chance that he had chosen this particular table in the Maison Doree this morning. It was not by chance that his view of the street included the offices of Till-Dale Enterprises.

As he watched the street and awaited his breakfast, Jake attempted to pretend the unrelenting pounding at the top of his head was not echoing all the way to his toes, that the taste in his mouth was not more revolting than poison, that his eyes had not shrunk into permanent burning slits. He was grateful that he could move at all. For the first few minutes after he had awakened this morning, he had doubted he would be able to sit up in bed.

Movement inside the Till-Dale offices interrupted Jake's thought processes, causing him to squint a little harder. Damn, why did there have to be all that sun out there, shining on the glass, blurring his vision?

There it was again. There was no mistaking it this time. Those clerks were taking turns listening at Dale's office door. A smile curved Jake's lips for the first time that morning. He had known there would be hell to pay when Harvey Dale read that note.

Jake raised his head as a steaming plate of steak and eggs was placed in front of him. He nodded, regretting the action a moment later when the pounding in the top of his skull began with a new fervor. He turned back toward the window.

This morning he had dragged his aching body out of bed first thing and sat down on the sidewalk until his stomach had quieted down enough for him to think about breakfast. All the while, he hadn't taken his eyes off Till-Dale's office doors. He had seen one clerk open the door, pick up the note, and then go inside Dale's office.

It was then that Jake had gone into the Maison Doree. A few minutes later, Harvey Dale and George Tillson had met on the street, exchanged a few words, entered the building, and gone into their respective offices. A few minutes later, he had seen the clerks react to what must have been a bellow from Dale, and had seen George Tillson go into Dale's office and close the door behind him.

Jake had been so intent on watching the window that he had burned his mouth on the damned coffee. So far, it had been a hell of a morning, but it looked like it was soon going to pay off.

But something was up. The clerk who'd been listening at the door was running back to his desk. The office door opened, and Harvey Dale stomped out. He marched out to the sidewalk and headed toward Fourth Street.

Jake could not suppress a grin as he watched Dale stride along Fourth and turn down Allen Street. Jake knew where Dale was headed: Charles Carter was about to receive a visitor. It was all going just as Ross had planned.

Jake looked down at his plate. His stomach did a quick flip-flop as the two sunshiny egg yolks looked back at him. He picked up his fork and knife. He'd get himself back in shape, and he wouldn't repeat the mistake he had made last night. The numbness hadn't lasted long, and his heart still jumped every time an Oriental woman walked into view.

Jake forced his train of thought to a halt. He stabbed his steak with his fork and made a savage cut with his knife. He hoped Ross was doing all right with the wildcat he had on his hands. Jake had a feeling both he and Ross were going to be mighty glad to shake the dust of this territory off their boots.

Charles read the note for the third time, his incredulity unabated. He looked up as Harvey Dale's caustic laugh broke the silence of his office.

"You really missed your calling, Carter. You should've gone on the stage. You're a much better actor than any I've seen at Schieffelin Hall. It's no wonder you managed to pull the wool over our eyes. If I didn't know better, I'd be convinced you didn't know anything about that note."

"I didn't, Harvey."

Harvey's expression tightened. "You still deny that you had anything to do with my daughter's disappearance, and you still insist that your brother took your place at my party without your consent."

Charles had no intention of continually denying his guilt. Dale would believe what he wanted to believe. But this note made no sense at all. Ross was trusting him to carry out a very important part in this elaborate scheme.

Charles glanced at Harvey Dale's mottled face. "How do you know this note is authentic, Harvey? Anybody could have sent it. You aren't the most popular man in town right now. Maybe someone's playing a cruel joke."

Dale withdrew a lock of pale hair from his pocket. There could be no mistaking that particular shade.

"That's right, Carter, it's Devina's." Dale's voice choked, and Charles's frown darkened. The man was working himself up to a dangerous point. It didn't take a doctor's eye to see that.

"Harvey, sit down, and let's discuss this whole matter like rational people. Everything's gotten out of hand."

"It's easy for you, isn't it, Carter? You're just as calm as can be, knowing you've got the upper hand. You're a good actor, all right. I could've sworn you had feelings for Devina. And all the while you were using her to get back at me."

"Harvey, sit down, will you?" Taking a step forward, Charles placed a hand on Harvey's shoulder. The fellow was shuddering. His color was heightening, and his lips were tinged with blue. Damn, he had spent the last week thoroughly despising this man for all he had done to his natural father and to Ross, and for trying to get him run out of Tombstone, but the man was obviously beside himself with worry over his daughter.

"Take your hand off me." Harvey shook off his hand. "And don't pretend concern. I know there's nothing you'd like better than to see me dead."

Charles shook his head. "I want no such thing, Harvey."

"Oh, no? Maybe you'll be content to see me ruined financially. That's the idea of these demands, isn't it? You know damned well I'll be ruined once all these stipulations are met."

"The accusations are all true, aren't they, Harvey?" Charles focused intently on Harvey Dale's stiff face, wanting to hear confirmation once and for all, needing it for his peace of mind. "Everything my brother says about you is true. You cheated my father, you had my brother convicted of a crime he didn't commit, you blackened the Morrison name, and you turned the town against Ross by blaming him for that accident at your mine."

"Your father was a fool, and your brother is no better. Neither of them had the sense to see that they were beaten."

Silence.

Charles was assailed by regret, anger, and despair at all that had passed which could never be changed or forgotten. And this man, who had caused his father and brother so much pain, expected Charles to feel guilty.

"I'm not here to talk about the past, Carter." Harvey Dale's rasping voice snapped Charles back to the present as he continued with no lessening of venom. "I'm here to tell you that you can pass the word to your brother that I'll meet his demands—but it will take time. I'll turn over the files to you as soon as I can get all the papers together. I'll stop work in the mines. I'll write up the confession he asked for, damn him. But the legal work will take time. I want you to make sure that he doesn't take out his impatience on Devina."

"Harvey, I've had no contact with my brother; I didn't know anything about this ransom note. I'll follow the instructions, but I don't know any more about them than you do."

"Carter, tell your brother I want some proof that my daughter is safe."

"Dammit, listen to me, will you?" Frustrated, impatient, and angry, Charles heard himself defending his brother. "Ross would never deliberately hurt Devina, and the demands . . . well, they're nothing more than a request for simple justice that has been a long time coming."

"Justice?" Harvey Dale's face twitched alarmingly. "I'll tell you about some justice that's going to prevail in Tombstone within the next few days. There's a whore who works in Blond Marie's establishment who's been getting a little out of hand.

Her clientele includes some of the wealthier married men in town. It appears that someone has done Tombstone the favor of anonymously informing the wives of these men by letter where their husbands have been spending their free hours. Those letters have revealed the exact number of times the husbands have visited this whore, the fees she charged, and the favors the persuasive bitch has asked of these men . . . expensive favors.''

Rage assailed Charles with a sudden, blinding heat. He lunged forward and seized Harvey Dale's lapels.

"You're talking about Camille, aren't you, you bastard? You're going after her to get back at me."

Harvey Dale laughed. "Camille . . . yes, I believe that's the woman's name."

Charles shook Dale roughly, unmindful of the man's unhealthy color, unmindful of all else but Camille and the position she had been forced into by her association with him. He would not see another innocent party suffer because of Harvey Dale . . . especially not Camille.

"Leave Camille alone, Dale, I'm warning you. If you harm her in any way—"

"Carter, I had nothing to do with the whole affair. I'm innocent, just like you." Harvey Dale's expression was suddenly one of mock innocence, his pale eyes wide.

Fury, hot and deep, surged through Charles. In defense against its rampant advance, he released Harvey Dale with a sudden thrust that sent the older man staggering back a few steps. When he spoke, his voice was unrecognizable in its grating vehemence. "Send those files to me so I can follow my brother's instructions. You're getting what you deserve. It's Devina who's the true victim here, and I'll do anything I can to get her returned safely, both for her sake and for Ross's. But I'll tell you one thing: If Camille suffers in any way because of your attempts to get revenge on me, I will personally see to it that you pay."

Satisfaction had crept into Dale's expression, and Charles belatedly realized he had played into Dale's hands by providing the exact reaction he had been seeking. He was barely in control of his rage when Dale nodded his head.

"I'll get those files to you as soon as I can, Carter. I'll expect you to pass my message to your brother, and I want you to know I will hold you responsible for any hardship Devina suffers while she's your brother's prisoner."

"And I'll hold you to account for any hardship Camille suffers."

"Oh, yes, the French whore. I must admit I thought you had better taste."

Carefully concealing his anger, Charles raised his eyebrows, focusing on Dale's triumphant expression. He shrugged. "Well, unlike some men, I've never had a driving obsession for Oriental women."

Harvey Dale jerked abruptly erect, his narrow lips twitching spasmodically, and Charles took his turn to laugh.

"You've taken the trouble to snoop into my private life, Harvey. I suppose it never occurred to you I'd do the same. Devina will be interested to know you have an Oriental mistress who is a year younger than she."

Maintaining his shaken silence, Harvey turned and walked out of the house without another word, his rapid step taking him back in the direction of Allen Street.

Charles's flash of satisfaction was brief. He had meant what he said: He would not allow Dale to hurt Camille. He had also meant what he said about Devina being the true victim of this whole mess. Even now she was subjected to Ross's bitterness and hatred, though she had done nothing to earn them except to be born to the name Dale. Would his brother realize that, or was he at this very minute causing her to suffer?

Devina's eyes moved over Ross's profile, etched against the morning light streaming through the doorway of the cabin. He was so intense as he leaned over her ankle and examined the stubborn swelling there. But her own attention was not so undivided. She found she was far more fascinated by the manner in which Ross's dark hair curved against the shape of his head and lay smoothly against his neck. She remembered the texture of that thick waving hair under her hands as she ran her fingers through it while she clutched him against her.

A hot flood of emotion colored Devina's cheeks, and she closed her eyes. She was still sick from her wound. Her mind was cloudy, refusing to function in a logical manner, but one thing had never been clearer to her: She wanted this man with every fiber in her body.

She was only too conscious of the broad expanse of Ross's shoulders, now covered by one of the shirts he had laundered so carefully the afternoon before. He was fully dressed and proceeding with the chores of the new day. He had approached her from the fire the moment she opened her eyes to the light of morning and had stood over her with a strangely sober expression. She had been momentarily disoriented, uncertain whether she had dreamed the events of the previous night or whether they had truly happened. Her reaction to her uncertainty must have registered on her face, for at that moment Ross had crouched down beside the bed and lovingly covered her mouth with his.

Devina took a deep, shaken breath. That kiss stirred her now, even in memory, as did the echoes of Ross's whispered endearments as his lips had strayed to her cheek, her fluttering eyelids, her ears, the column of her throat. Her heart had begun a rapid beating, her breathing had quickened, and Ross had drawn back. She remembered the hunger in his eyes as he spoke in a throbbing whisper.

"You make it hard for me to listen to my common sense, Devina." He had stroked her cheek and kissed her lips once more before continuing with a small smile, "I should've waited until you were stronger to make love to you, but once I had you in my arms, I was past waiting, past thinking." He had smiled again and leaned closer until his chest rested against the coverlet that shielded her nakedness, his lips touching hers. "But we have time, time for you to grow stronger."

His dark eyes promising more, which went unspoken, Ross had then drawn himself back to his feet. He had turned to the fire and filled a cup and carefully held it to her lips until she had drained the last of the steaming coffee. He had been tending to her ankle ever since.

She knew he was concerned about the swelling. She had seen it in his frown, in the way his eyes snapped back toward hers when he had lightly touched the wound and she gasped. He had been bathing the ankle for the past half-hour, soaking cloths in water as hot as she could bear, and applying them to the wound. Her ankle felt significantly improved, enough for her mind to wander, as it was now.

She realized these new feelings which filled her were an abrupt reversal of her previous attitude toward Ross. She was uncertain whether this sense of time suspended, this strange unreality was due to the complications of the snakebite. Whatever its source, it provided her a welcomed relief from the anxieties she had suffered from the moment at her party when she had realized it was not Charles, but a stranger with Charles's face who held her in his arms.

That man was a stranger no longer. He was Ross. It came to her in a flash of unexpected clarity that this new intimacy between them, this closeness that eliminated all fear and uncertainty, was a desire which had remained undeclared in her mind from the moment she had awakened in Ross's arms.

It had been Ross's eyes that had haunted her, given her no peace after their first meeting on the stagecoach. But she now saw in his eyes none of the threat, the confusing contempt she had first seen there. Instead, she saw all she had unconsciously wanted to see, and an exhilarating joy touched her heart.

Somehow it mattered very little that she was Ross's hostage. He was caring for her, loving her. It mattered little that in the world outside the cabin, Ross Morrison was an ex-convict, a thief, and a kidnapper, that she was his victim. She no longer felt victimized. She felt only cherished, loved wholly and completely, loved more thoroughly than she had ever been loved before. She would not question these feelings. They were right for this time and place, and they would be enough for now.

The water had cooled and Ross had returned the cloth to the bucket. He was examining the swelling again, frowning more intensely. He turned to look at her and his expression changed. He drew himself slowly to his feet and moved to stand near the head of the bunk. He remained looking down at her, the chiseled planes of his face sober before he finally slipped to his knees beside her.

Cupping her face in his hands, he whispered in a low, ragged voice. "Don't look at me that way, Devina. I'm having a hell of a time with myself this morning. I dragged myself out of that bunk before you woke up because I knew what would happen if I stayed there any longer. I kept telling myself that you aren't well, that you need rest. I promised myself I'd behave and give you a chance to regain your strength. But, honey, if you keep looking at me like that . . ."

"Looking at you?"

Ross shook his head. "Dammit, Devina." He lowered his mouth to hers, and Devina surrendered to his hungry kiss. She had no resistance to the drowning sea of emotions that surged within her as he pressed his kiss deeper. She gave herself up to the arms that held her lovingly, to the hands that caressed her, to her own desire to draw him closer, to take him in.

Devina murmured an inaudible word of protest as Ross abruptly withdrew from her. He took a deep, steadying breath, expelling it seconds later in a wry, shaken laugh.

"You're pale, Devina. You look exhausted. Your hair is tangled, your cheeks are drawn, your eyes are two blue mirrors of confusion in your face, and you look lost and forlorn in that bunk all alone. But you're beautiful, more beautiful than any woman I've ever seen, and I've never wanted any woman more than I want you right now."

The spark glowing deep within his eyes flared to flame again, and Ross touched his lips lightly to hers once more. A low groan escaped him as her mouth clung to his.

"You're sick, Devina, dammit! Your ankle is still swollen and you're going to need every bit of your strength in order to get well. I know what I should do and what I shouldn't, but I'm fighting a losing battle with myself, and you're not making it any easier."

"I'm sorry. I didn't realize."

"Your face is an open book, darling, and you're going to have to help me, or I'm going to climb into that bunk right now and make love to you."

The emotions raging inside Devina were suddenly making her head swim, and she closed her eyes in defense against them.

"Devina."

"I . . . I'm all right. I'm just a little tired."

Ross was frowning again. He touched his hand to her forehead. Obviously relieved, he nodded.

"Sleep, then. I'll have something ready for you to eat when you wake up. You'll feel a little stronger after you've eaten."

Devina closed her eyes obediently. She did not feel like sleeping, but sleep was a safe retreat from the chaotic emotions assailing her, from this new, appealing Ross who touched her heart, who made her want to reach out to him, who had turned her hatred of him into a soul-shaking emotion she had never before experienced.

Ross was still beside her. She could feel his sweet breath fanning her face as he brushed a strand of hair from her cheek. She sighed at his gentleness, and relaxed under his touch. She did not want him to leave her.

• • •

Slowly descending the last three steps to the foyer, Camille raised her hand to her hair in a characteristic gesture and tucked a bright, straying wisp back into her upswept coiffure. She had long before given up hope of perfect grooming, acceding to the stubbornness of the curls, which persisted in escaping despite her attempts to subdue them. She had been told by a particularly affectionate client that her wayward curls were a reflection of her personality: bright, energetic, warm, full of life, and so very lovely to touch. That affectionate client had been Charles Carter. Camille had never forgotten those words, and she had never looked at her riotous curls with dismay again.

She released a soft sigh. That particular memory was only one of the many that she cherished.

The annoying thickness in her throat returned, and Camille swallowed hard against it. She felt the familiar prick of tears, and she took a deep, steadying breath. This affliction had been the bane of her existence in the past few weeks, returning at the most inopportune moments to assail her. She feared she would never be free of its rigors.

Charles, I miss you so terribly . . .

Camille gave the foyer a perfunctory glance. Several of the girls were busy entertaining clients in the parlor. It was early in the day, and they had no need to hurry. They would drift upstairs soon.

A knock at the door made Camille turn in its direction. She was surprised to see Giselle respond to the summons. With practiced charm, the lovely brunette guided a well-dressed client toward the parlor, and Camille's brows rose even further. Marie must be slipping to allow one of the younger girls to assume her duties so early in the day. She knew Marie would rather die than turn the house over to one of those potential rivals for her position, even for a minute.

Camille gave a small shrug. She cared little about Marie's insecurities and petty jealousies. She had found during the past few weeks that there was very little she truly cared about. The small spot of desolation that had begun to ache inside her when Charles dismissed her from his rooms had expanded to encompass her heart and her mind, until she had been forced to feign even the most casual friendliness to her faithful clients. She had received several concerned inquiries as to her health, and it was

obvious the change in her had not gone unnoticed. She was well
aware that she could not go on this way.

Camille turned toward the familiar doorway beside the staircase. Pierre had summoned her to his office. She had spent a
considerable amount of time with Pierre in the past weeks, and
she was extremely conscious of his tender regard. The thought
had touched her mind that Pierre's tenderness was beginning to
exceed the bounds of friendship, and she sincerely hoped she
was wrong.

It was one thing for her to please a client; that was a business
matter, and there was no strong personal tie. It was another
matter entirely when a heart was involved. It was especially
difficult when the man so involved was one she loved and
respected as a friend. It complicated matters to no end when a
step taken toward a more intimate relationship by that valued
friend would compromise his avowed commitment to a wife he
loved and cherished. She did not want Pierre's compassion to
lead him to a betrayal for which he would never forgive himself.

Camille's light brows drew into a concerned frown. Pierre had
been so good to her. She did not wish to cause him pain.

At the door to Le Comte's office, Camille paused and took a
firm hold on her composure. She would be honest with Pierre; she
would explain things, so he might view the situation between them
more clearly. He would soon leave for Paris. He would return to
his loving wife, and his self-inflicted celibacy would end. Camille
knocked on the door, suddenly determined that, whatever happened in her personal life, she would not cause Pierre difficulty
in his.

A quick response from within took Camille into the small
office, only to bring her up short. His back to the window, the
light of morning holding his compact frame in dark relief, Camille
saw Le Comte. Beside him, her satisfaction only too visible,
stood Marie. Apprehension touched Camille's senses.

"Camille, *entrez, s'il vous plaît*. Do not stand so hesitantly.
You are in the company of friends."

Her apprehension under control, Camille moved smilingly to
the Count's bidding and closed the door behind her. She was
rewarded when Pierre immediately stepped toward her and raised
her hand to his lips. Marie's instinctive stiffening registered
within Camille's mind, even as her own smile curved with true
affection for the man who looked so warmly into her eyes. But

there was more than warmth in Pierre's eyes. What was it? Caution? Concern?

Camille's reply was characteristically candid. "I apologize for my hesitancy, Pierre. I thought you had summoned me about a personal matter. Marie's presence startled me. Is something wrong?"

Pierre's smile was not untouched by genuine amusement. "Camille, *ma chérie,* you do not waste words on trivialities."

"Only when trivialities are part of the game, Pierre."

"And, of course, you play the game so very well . . ."

At a short sound of impatience from behind him, Pierre turned toward Marie, and his smile faded. He did not like this situation any more than he liked Marie's impatience. Camille's apprehension mounted. The matter to be discussed was obviously very serious, for Pierre would not easily allow Marie to push into this kind of confrontation.

Pierre turned back toward Camille, his displeasure efficiently erased from his face as he addressed her directly. "It is easy to see that you are apprehensive, Camille, and I do not wish to extend your discomfort. Come, sit beside me, and we will talk, will we not, Marie?"

As he led Camille to the small settee, Pierre directed Marie to a chair. When both were comfortably seated, he took a paper from his desk, then sat beside Camille.

"Camille, first, I wish to make it clear to you that I would never allow anyone to hurt the women under my protection in any way. But, *ma favorite*, you do realize my protection extends with a much deeper affection to you."

Le Comte's gaze was intent on hers, and Camille felt the true depth of his regard register sharply within her. It brought the glitter of tears to her eyes, and she blinked them back with practiced firmness.

"*Merci*, Pierre."

"I do not wish your gratitude, *ma chérie*, merely your complete honesty in the matter we are about to discuss."

"I am always honest with you, Pierre. You have been too good to me to deserve any less."

Marie's impatient fidgeting made Pierre turn sharply toward her. "If this conversation moves too slowly for you, Marie, you may leave at any time. I will be only too happy to inform you of any decisions made."

Marie's pale face twitched with discomfort. "No, I will remain."

Le Comte murmured, "I suspected you would," as he turned back to Camille. He watched her face carefully as he handed her the paper. "This arrived at our door this morning, Camille. I do not think it needs explanation."

Realizing her hands were trembling, Camille paused, her unfamiliarity with written English causing her difficulty as she sought to understand the contents of the formal document. After long moments, she raised her eyes to Pierre's for confirmation.

"It is a demand, a petition, is it not, correct, Pierre? It seeks to have me barred from the city because of my disturbing influence on family life in Tombstone. It states that I have sought to better myself by illegal means and at the expense of others, and that I am an undesirable and a detriment to the community."

"What shall we do about this petition?" Marie asked, a satisfied smile playing around her lips. "The signatures on that document are those of very prominent people in Tombstone, people of much influence, people who could force the closing of this establishment."

"Marie! *Cela suffit!* That is enough! It is I who will conduct this inquiry this morning, not you!"

The flaming color that flooded Marie's face brought regret surging to life within Camille. This would not do. She had never wished to have Marie as an enemy, and such an exchange would only cause Marie to hate her more strongly than before. She did not wish to be hated, not by anyone.

Covering Pierre's hand with her own, Camille slanted him a smile. "Pierre, Marie has good reason to be disturbed. This petition is dangerous to the future of the establishment into which she has poured considerable effort. It is easy to see where the problem lies. The signatures are those of women . . . the wives of many of my most faithful clients. It is obvious that they do not like having their husband's activities outside the home revealed for the world to see."

"Camille, *ma petite*, you know as well as I that these men came here seeking you; you did not solicit their favors. They return here to you because you give to them that which has been denied them at home. Aside from the physical aspect of your association with them, you speak to them of their intimate problems, console them when they are distressed, do you not, *ma chérie?*

"So we can put aside the implication that the blame rests with you. You satisfy a need within these men, and if they did not come to you, they would find someone else. You have performed a service and have been paid accordingly. This is solely a business matter. We have just to decide who is behind this vendetta against you and how we are to handle such an attack."

"Handle . . . ?"

"Oui." Le Comte's narrow mustache twitched with anger. "We will fight this."

Pierre's unexpected words made Camille feel intensely worried. If she fought to defend herself, there would be trouble and embarrassment for her and for those men who had sought her out. Charles . . . would he be drawn into this conflict? Would he suffer humiliation because of her? The thought was more than she could bear.

Camille stood up. "No, I have no heart to fight, Pierre." Tears again filling her eyes, Camille sought to avoid Le Comte's concerned gaze as he drew himself to his feet beside her.

"Camille, this is unlike you."

"You are right, Pierre." Struggling to overcome her emotion, Camille tossed her brilliant curls and shrugged her shoulders. "Perhaps the time has come for me to go home, Pierre. I have been here a long time, perhaps too long. It was only the favor and affection of prominent individuals that held me here. It appears that affection has been rescinded. I am no longer wanted, Pierre. And I am no longer happy."

Camille sensed the smile that turned up Marie's lips before she actually saw it. Well, at least someone was happy over this sorry affair. Most assuredly it was not she. She turned to Pierre's disturbed expression.

"Camille, do you want me to find out who initiated this attack?"

"No, it is of little importance."

"And you wish to return to France?"

Camille's smile was pathetically thin. "It appears there is little reason for me to remain here."

A new light appeared in Pierre's gaze, and his voice dropped a notch to intimacy. "I return to Paris at the end of the month. I was to take Simone and two of the other girls, but Simone's tenure here may be extended. It will matter little to her if you go in her stead. I confess, Camille, I would regret having to leave you again."

Marie's movement caused Pierre to turn toward her with irritation. "Marie, you need be impatient no longer. The matter is settled. Repercussions from the petition will not fall on this house. Camille is leaving, at her own request." Pausing, Pierre fixed his gaze on Marie even more firmly than before. "That is understood, is it not—at her own request? I will not have it known any other way. *Comprendez-vous?*"

Marie nodded stiffly, her lips barely parting in her response. *"Oui."*

Le Comte paused again, allowing the full import of his gaze to register in Marie's mind as he continued in a softer, more intense tone. "And I will not suffer talk about this matter in my house."

Marie raised her chin. "I understand."

Pierre's smile was cold.

"We have nothing more to discuss, Marie."

Realizing she had been dismissed, Marie rose to her feet. Her short glance in Camille's direction was met with Pierre's curt response.

"Au revoir, Marie."

Her slender nostrils dilating with suppressed anger, Marie left the office without another word.

Camille followed her silent exit with a frown, only to feel Pierre's hand on her chin, turning her back to meet his gaze.

"Do not waste your sympathy on that one, Camille. Marie is a hard woman who would spare you little compassion in return. And I suspect she is not guiltless in this affair."

Camille shook her head, confused. "I do not understand."

"It is strange, is it not, that the wives of all your most faithful and wealthy clients signed that petition? Surely no casual observer would have known who your clients were."

"Pierre, Marie does not like me, but—"

"She fears you, Camille. She is well aware of my affection for you, and she sees your popularity as an added threat. The petition was aimed at eliminating that threat, and now that you are returning to Paris, she will fear you no longer. If it was not your wish, I would not allow her this triumph, no matter how efficiently she tends to the business matters of this house."

Camille pressed her hand over Pierre's lips. She shook her

head. "No more. You cannot be sure it is Marie who is at the bottom of this persecution, and in truth, it does not matter. I am leaving, Pierre, and all of this will soon be in the past."

Pierre kissed her fingers, then held her hand tightly, searching Camille's eyes as if looking for a deeper meaning.

"You are certain you wish to leave, Camille?"

"As certain as I will ever be."

Unexpectedly, Pierre leaned forward to touch his lips lightly to hers, and Camille felt the love for her this man suppressed. With the openness so much a part of her character, Camille whispered with a responsive emotion of her own, "Pierre, I do not wish to cause you to do anything you will one day regret."

Halting her words with another light kiss, Pierre turned Camille toward the doorway. He urged her forward, his tone purposefully light.

"Then we will see, will we not, Camille? We will see what the future and the voyage home bring to us. We have time . . . much time."

Grateful beyond words for his generosity, his thoughtfulness, Camille slipped through the doorway. She knew there was no response she could give, except to say, yes, she would see.

Lost in thought, Camille made her way to her room and went toward the window. She stared at her reflection in the glass—her tall body with it's abundant proportions, the rowdy color of her hair, her unremarkable features. There was no life in her face in the absence of the smile that made her beautiful. She wondered if she would ever be beautiful again.

She stood and stared down at the street as it pulsed with life. She would miss this place and the desert surrounding it. Its sun, its heat, the raw energy that streamed through its streets, its contrast to the small village where she was born . . .

A familiar figure turned the corner of Fourth onto Allen, and Camille's heart skipped a beat. There was no mistaking that broad-shouldered physique, that self-possessed walk. Charles. He was striding in her direction, and she indulged herself in the brief hope that he was coming to see her. Her heart began to race, and she raised a shaking hand to her hair.

No! She was being a fool. Charles would turn into one of the offices, one of the stores, a restaurant. Camille touched the modest, lace-trimmed neckline of her pale blue gown. Why did she torment herself that she was not looking her best today? Charles would not see her. He was not coming here.

But he did not pause in his approach. He was crossing the intersection of Allen and Fifth, and coming closer. He was striding past the Palace Lodging House, Hudson's Drugstore, the hardware store, Hartman's Jewelry, the tailor shop. Camille caught her breath as Charles hesitated in front of the Bird Cage Theater. No! He would not go in there!

Camille released the breath she had been holding. Charles had stopped in front of the theater in response to a summons from a friend to exchange a few words. The exchange was brief. He was continuing on.

He crossed the intersection of Allen and Sixth and headed directly toward the front door of the house in which she stood. She drew back from the window, from the possibility of catching Charles's eye, and waited in breathless silence.

She heard the front door open and close. She waited for a summons, but heard instead a heavy familiar step on the stairs and a rapid approach to her door, followed by a knock.

Her heart was pounding so furiously that she was unable to respond. She took an involuntary step backward, coming up against the night table. She could not answer, for if it was not Charles . . .

The knock sounded again.

"Camille, are you in there?"

Joy soared to life within her at the sound of his voice, and she ran to the door. He had returned to her.

With a trembling hand she threw the door open. Her rapturous smile died on her lips the moment she saw Charles's tense countenance. This was not a man who had come to make amends. This was not a man who had come to see the woman he loved . . .

Camille's gaze traced the strong planes of Charles's face, lingering on the troubled frown, the angry set of his chin, the firm lips that separated as he prepared to speak.

"Camille, I'm sorry to burst in on you like this. Marie tried to stop me, but I told her I had to see you. If you have someone waiting . . ."

Charles hesitated, and Camille felt a shudder of despair shake her. She forced a smile. "No, Charles, I have no one waiting. I am free for a few hours."

Relief flickered across Charles's face, but his smile was a poor imitation of his usual, warm grin. "It's kind of you to be so generous with your free time. I assure you I wouldn't bother you if it wasn't urgent."

Camille felt tears sting her eyes at Charles's formality, and she forced them back with great determination. He was using this aloof manner to keep distance between them. It caused her no end of pain despite the softness of her reply. "Are we not past 'kindnesses,' Charles? Surely, the time we have spent together assures us of that. Please know that I will always welcome you for whatever reason you visit me."

Stepping back in silent invitation, Camille waited until Charles had walked inside, then closed the door behind him. Not realizing her gaze all but consumed him, she questioned softly, "What is it that is so urgent, Charles?"

Charles looked concerned as his eyes moved over her face. "You're pale, Camille. Are you well? You look thinner."

"I . . . thinner?" She laughed softly. "There is, as there has always been, far too much of me on this womanly frame."

Charles did not laugh. "Too much of you?" He shook his head, his expression intensely serious. "There could never be too much."

Camille maintained her silence as Charles spoke again.

"I came to warn you, Camille."

"Warn me?"

"Harvey Dale visited me this morning."

Camille stiffened. "He brought you news of his beautiful daughter."

"No. He doesn't know where Devina is or how she is faring. That's part of the reason he is seeking to vent his frustration on me."

"On you, Charles! But why?"

"You know the story, Camille; everyone knows it. My brother, Ross, abducted Devina Dale. Harvey believes I had a part in it."

Camille shook her head, her distress deepening. "The man is a fool if he thinks you—"

Charles interrupted Camille's response with the pure force of his anger. "The man is more than a fool, Camille. He is vicious and dishonest. A great many innocent people have suffered because of his dishonesty, and now he seeks to involve the innocent again to get back at me."

"The innocent?"

Charles took a deep breath. "He has been ineffective against me, Camille, so he is presently planning trouble for you."

"But why?"

"Because of our association."

Camille shook her head. "Did you not tell him that you . . . that we—"

Charles took a step forward, then halted. "What I told him is of no consequence. His mind was made up and no threat would have changed his intent."

"Charles, what are you telling me?"

"I'm telling you to beware. The damned bastard is trying to stir people up against you. He wants to have you thrown out of town. He's going to—"

Camille's laughter halted Charles's heated statement, and she spoke softly into the silence, "So Harvey Dale was responsible . . ."

Charles's face whitened. "Then I'm too late."

Camille shrugged her smooth white shoulders. "It is of little consequence."

The sudden flare of anger in Charles's eyes startled Camille even as Charles gripped her upper arms and gave her a small shake. "Little consequence? What did he do, Camille?"

"Do not upset yourself. It is nothing."

"Tell me!"

Camille's heart began to pound. She had never seen Charles so angry.

"Camille . . . ?"

She attempted a smile. "Charles, it was nothing. A petition was delivered this morning. It was signed by the wives of many of my influential and wealthy clients." Her fair complexion colored lightly. "It stated many things, some true and some untrue. The petitioners seek to institute action against me."

Charles stiffened, his fury visible in his handsome face.

"No, Charles, the petition is unimportant. Pierre has taken care of everything."

Camille felt the shock of her words strike Charles's strong body. The intensity of his reaction confused her.

His hands dropped from her arms. "Pierre, of course."

Camille continued, "Pierre will return to Paris within the month, and I will return with him."

Charles replied softly, "France. That's what you want, Camille?"

Camille gave a small shrug. "I have been away from my country for a long time. I have completed the terms of my contract with Pierre. There is no longer any reason for me to stay in Tombstone.''

''Of course. And Pierre is happy to have you return with him?''

''Yes. He feels I will be happier at home.''

Charles's gaze burned hotly into her, and Camille struggled to keep up the pretense. She would not bind Charles to her with guilt. She loved him too much for that. She held his gaze determinedly with hers, concealing her despair as he questioned softly.

''And will you be happier at home, Camille?''

''Happier than I am now? Who knows, Charles? Who knows?''

Charles nodded, and Camille felt the last shreds of happiness slip away as he turned toward the door. He turned back, his eyes sweeping her face.

''That is what I wish for you, you know, Camille . . . happiness. I hope you find it.''

''*Oui.* I wish the same for you, Charles.''

Charles's lips tightened, and Camille longed to reach out and touch him, to stroke away his discomfort and distress. But he no longer wanted her consolation.

''If you ever need me, Camille.''

''*Merci,* Charles.''

Charles hesitated, intensely sober. ''Good-bye, Camille.''

''*Au revoir,* Charles.''

The door closed, and Camille whispered into the pulsating emptiness which surrounded her, ''*Au revoir, mon ami.*''

CHAPTER XIX

FROM HER RECLINING position on the bunk, Devina looked nervously toward the doorway of the cabin. Ross was nowhere in sight and she released a short, relieved breath. She would never have a better opportunity.

As quickly as her stiff muscles would allow, she swung her legs over the side of the bunk. She spared only the quickest glance for the yellowing bruise on her ankle and the puncture marks that were a silent reminder of her close escape from a fate she dared not contemplate. Her feet touched the cool wooden floor, and she allowed them to rest there for a few minutes as she steadied herself.

She cast another apprehensive glance toward the doorway. Myriad feelings assaulted her, increasing the confusion with which she had awakened. Only three days had passed since she had been bitten, but she hardly recognized herself as the person she had once been.

In her weakened state, she had found it so easy to accept Ross's tender ministrations and selfless concern. The memory of his strong body lying beside hers through the night, the rise of his passion hard against her, left little doubt as to his feelings, despite the fact that his earlier attentions had not gone beyond a few stirring kisses.

But with her returning strength had come a renewed awareness of reality and a rush of doubts about her encounter with Ross.

Who was the true Ross Morrison? Was he the cruel, relentless

man filled with hate, determined to wreak vengeance on her
father and his own brother at any cost? Or was he the gentle,
tender man who had loved her so completely, who ministered to
her with endless patience and kindness, the man who was capable of stirring such deep, loving emotions within her?

Filled with a new determination, Devina cast another quick
glance toward the open doorway and the brilliant sunlight beyond.
She needed to get on her feet so she would be independent of
him again, so she could stand back from the Ross Morrison who
had made himself so indispensable to her and see him clearly.
She could not suffer this confusion any longer.

With a supreme effort, Devina shifted her weight and pulled
herself to her feet. Fighting the light-headedness that assailed
her, she took one short step, then another. As strength began to
return to her quaking limbs, she became aware that she was very
thirsty. She looked toward the water bucket by the door.

A few more steps and Devina was steadying herself with the
palm of her hand against the wall as she submerged the dipper
into the cool water. She was raising it to her lips when the sound
of a step startled her. The cold water splashed over her shirt as
Ross's angry voice shattered the silence of the cabin.

"What are you doing out of bed?"

Not waiting for her response, Ross disposed of the dipper and
scooped her up into his arms. With a few long strides he crossed
the room and deposited her on the bunk.

"You haven't been on your feet for three days. Dammit,
Devina, you could've fallen and hurt yourself."

Devina steeled herself against his concern as she sat up. "I'm
all right. I can walk."

"You're not well enough to walk alone yet."

"I have to get back on my feet."

Ross paused, his face stiffening. "Why? You're not going
anywhere."

Devina did not respond and Ross's features tightened further.

"You are feeling better, aren't you?"

Hardening herself against the assault of softer feelings, Devina
attempted to rise. "I have to get up on my own."

Sitting down on the side of the bunk, Ross blocked her
attempt, his dark eyes on her face. "Not yet, Devina. You'll
hurt yourself. Please."

The last of her resistance crumbling at Ross's softly voiced appeal, Devina met his eyes with an appeal of her own. "Ross, I can't be quiet and lie still anymore. There are too many unanswered questions on my mind. Who are you, Ross? Sometimes I look at you and I see a criminal Ross Morrison who kidnapped me. Other times I see another Ross who is more like his brother, Charles."

"Don't compare me with my brother."

Devina was startled into momentary silence by the hatred that flashed in Ross's dark eyes at the mention of his brother's name. Her voice was low with incredulity. "How can you hate him so . . . your own brother, a man who wears your face?"

Ross's gaze narrowed. "Wears my face? Is that the way you see Charles, Devina?"

The import of her own words startled Devina. The situation had reversed itself. Ross was now the dominant man in her mind, and Charles was merely the shadow figure, the man who resembled him. The thought struck her that it had been that way from the first, somehow, without her realization.

Not completely willing to accept that thought, Devina shook her head. "I don't want to discuss Charles with you, Ross."

His eyes hardening, Ross drew her closer. "I don't want to discuss Carter, either, Devina. It would be a waste of time. He'll never get you back."

Ross pulled her closer still. His lips brushed the line of her cheek and trailed along her jaw. A familiar weakness assailed Devina as she attempted a response.

"It was never like that between Charles and me, Ross. We . . ."

Ross's arms tightened possessively. His voice roughened. "There is no 'we' but you and me, Devina."

The warm heat inside Devina reacted to the growing passion in Ross's gaze. It enveloped her senses, holding her breathlessly still as the last of her resistance began slipping away. "Ross, there are so many things I want to know."

His dark gaze intense, Ross drew back with a husky whisper that touched her soul.

"The only thing you have to know is that you belong to me, Devina. You've belonged to me since the first moment I saw you, and no one is going to come between us now."

The last remnants of coherent thought slipped away as Ross claimed her mouth at last. Her questions and confusion disappeared as Devina's eyes fluttered closed, her lips parting to accept the joy of his sweet possession.

• • •

Charles faced Harvey Dale across the narrow expanse of his office at Till-Dale Enterprises. Charles had arrived a few minutes before and he still could not quite believe the change in the man.

Aside from the marked deterioration in Dale's grooming in the short time since he had last seen him, and the fact that he looked as if he had slept in his clothes, Dale looked ill. His color was high, his peculiar squint indicated intense anxiety or pain, and his face was deeply lined. Charles's physician's eye told him this man was on the verge of collapse, and he marveled at the complexity of human nature which could allow him to experience a concern totally devoid of sympathy or regret.

Charles waved a dollar bill in front of Dale's face. "Here it is, Harvey, the purchase price of Bradford Morrison's claim. I'm paying it in my brother's name. The price is inadequate, I know, but you're not in a position to bargain, are you?"

Harvey Dale's stiff face twitched. "You and your brother have seen to that very well, haven't you? Well, I hope you'll keep in mind that although I'm presently standing with my back against the wall, I'm not accustomed to coming in on the losing side of business transactions. There will come a time for reckoning."

Charles's dark brows rose. "Strange, I thought that was exactly what was happening now."

Harvey Dale's facial spasms became more intense. "The papers for transfer of title to your father's mine are not yet ready."

Charles frowned. "I would suggest you hasten the legal procedures, Harvey. I don't pretend to know my brother well, but I'd say he's a very angry and determined man. I don't like to think what will happen to Devina if you—"

"I've had enough of your threats!" Harvey's furious rasp broke into Charles's statement.

"And I've had enough of yours!" Charles struggled to regain his patience. How had he ever been taken in by this man? Mentally railing against his own stupidity, he continued in a lowered tone, "I've been speculating on the reason my brother involved me in this situation since the arrival of the ransom note. I assume it was his way of punishing me for what he considers my betrayal. My observations have brought me to the conclusion that you should take that note very seriously. There's a lot of hate inside my brother."

"I've done everything your brother instructed."

"Everything? Who are you trying to fool, Harvey? The paperwork on the claim can't be that complicated. I've just given you the figure that has to be transferred to my brother's account. I've checked it twice, and it's accurate to the dollar. I've paid the purchase price of the claim. There's no reason for any more delay."

Harvey Dale raised his chin with a touch of his old arrogance. "It's quite obvious you're entirely ignorant of legal matters. These things take time."

"You don't have time, Harvey."

Rounding his desk in a few angry strides, Dale came to stand eye to eye with Charles. He was visibly quaking, as he croaked in a low, uneven tone, "Don't worry, Carter. You can tell your brother he'll get his pound of flesh as soon as I can secure it legally for him. You can also tell him that if he touches a hair on Devina's head—"

"You're wasting your threats on me, Harvey." Charles met Harvey Dale's pale eyes without flinching. "And I repeat, you don't have any time to spare."

Harvey Dale's chest was heaving with agitation, but Charles felt no pity. The hypocritical bastard was getting just what he deserved. Charles would have had no qualms about adding to his distress by telling him his efforts to get Camille thrown out of town had been pointless, since Camille had already been planning to leave, but he knew Dale would believe only what he wanted to believe.

Cheated of that satisfaction, Charles broadened his smile with great deliberation. "I'll say good-bye for now, Harvey. Try to keep in mind that my brother is a very impatient man. Of course, if you value your bank account more than Devina's life . . ."

Turning on that note, Charles walked toward the door, leaving a totally enraged Harvey Dale behind him. He was pulling the door open when the thought occurred to him for the first time that he was not so unlike his brother as he had thought. He, too, was capable of hatred and a desire for vengeance against the man who had hurt someone he loved. And he was not above using the vehicle Ross had provided for wreaking that vengeance.

Charles walked through the outer office, a broader understanding of his brother filling his mind. He stepped out on the street, realizing that this new understanding of Ross had come just a little too late.

• • •

"I'm not here to listen to your denials or your protestations of innocence, Mary."

China Mary's broad face creased into a smile. "Then, Mr. Dale, I would ask why you have come here. On your last visit you expressed only too clearly your distaste for my daughter and myself and your need to separate yourself from us. Have you changed your mind and come to visit Lily again?"

"No!" The vehemence of Harvey's response was as much a denial of his feelings for Lily as it was an answer to Mary's question. "I want no part of your conniving daughter, not while my own daughter's fate lies undetermined. Devina's future appears to rest in your hands."

China Mary's broad smile suddenly stiffened. She tilted her head, fixing her gaze on his countenance with intensifying scrutiny. "I do not quite understand, Mr. Dale."

"Then let me clarify my statement." At the sound of a step, Harvey turned to watch the door slowly swing open. His sharp intake of breath revealed his unconscious reaction to the beauty of the woman who stood there for the space of a moment before entering the room. He steeled himself against the rapid pounding of his heart.

Lily was walking directly toward him, smiling into his eyes. She knew the power she had over his body. She knew the way that damned traitorous part of him came alive at the sight of her, threatening to destroy his credibility in this most important negotiation.

Harvey muttered harshly, "Stay where you are, Lily. Don't come a step closer."

Lily's narrow brows rose in innocent surprise. "Dear Mr. Dale, I was but making ready to welcome you. Did you not come here to see me?"

"You know damned well I didn't." A new wave of color flooding his face, Harvey felt his groin tightening, and his self-loathing increased. "I came here to speak with you and your mother, to make you an offer."

Mary's soft, singsong voice interrupted with unaccustomed boldness. "You have twice mentioned an offer you are to propose. I would hear that offer now, Mr. Dale."

Choosing to ignore the subtle change in Mary's voice, the air of command in her tone, Harvey raised his chin. "I never believed either of you when you denied knowing anything about Devina's abduction.''

China Mary's round face stiffened further. "I will not continue to profess my innocence, Mr. Dale, since you choose not to believe me. Instead, I ask that you approach the point of your visit with more haste. I am impatient with your dallying."

Harvey's fine lips twitched. "You're taking a chance with that attitude toward me, Mary. You are not yet free of my influence."

Mary's inscrutable smile returned. "But I soon will be, is that not so, Mr. Dale?"

"That is entirely up to you."

Waiting only until Lily came to stand at her side, Mary nodded. "We are waiting, Mr. Dale."

"I want to find my daughter, quickly." Harvey swallowed with visible discomfort. His request finally voiced, a tight hand of fear seemed to close around his throat. If they could not help him, if they *would* not help him . . .

"And what will you offer me if I am able to uncover information leading to the whereabouts of your daughter, Mr. Dale?"

His patience expiring at this game of cat and mouse, Harvey released his breath in a low snarl. "You know what I'm offering! The documents I hold, dammit! Lead me to my daughter and I'll put those papers in your hands so you'll be free of my influence forever. That's what you've always wanted, isn't it?"

China Mary paused, her smile widening. She cocked her head to the side once more in the manner that caused him so much distaste and Harvey fought to overcome his revulsion.

"Don't pretend you don't understand me, Mary. I'm not fool enough to believe—"

Harvey's heated harangue was interrupted by Lily, who took a step forward. Her eyes caught and held his, and she smiled. She spoke in the soft musical voice he remembered so well. "I would have your statement clarified so I might better understand your intent, Mr. Dale." Lily's gaze moved to caress his cheek, his lips, as she continued softly, "You are saying that if my mother and I supply you the information you seek, you will no longer visit me at your convenience and demand that I tend to your needs?"

Lily paused, awaiting his response, and Harvey swallowed tightly. His desire for the exotic beauty standing before him raised his agitation to produce a reaction so strong that he was trembling. Lily's hand rose to his cheek.

"What is wrong, Mr. Dale? You are trembling. Your cheek is unshaven, your hair uncombed, your clothing unkempt. Your bodily scent is not fresh. You are unclean, Mr. Dale." Lily's eyes rose to his in exaggerated innocence as her hand slipped to the growing bulge beneath his belt. "And now you have another problem as well. That is unfortunate, Mr. Dale."

Harvey's voice was a harsh rasp. "Lily . . ."

"But you have not answered my question, Mr. Dale. Are you telling me that you will free me of my subservience to you if my mother and I provide the information you seek? You will allow me to pursue my own life, to take a man of my own choosing?"

Lily's smile broadened at Harvey's suddenly heightened color. She continued with her low-voiced questions. "Are you telling me that you will forsake the touch of my body, the warmth that it conveys to you, the consolation it offers? Is that what you are telling me, Mr. Dale?"

A soft, strangled sound escaped Harvey's throat. A violent shudder shook him as Lily raised her hand to his lips, touching her tongue erotically against his palm before placing his hand on the soft swell of her breast.

"Remember, Mr. Dale, remember the sweet comfort of my flesh, the joy you experience in taking me. Remember the wonder of the meeting of our bodies, the pleasure you feel in the intimate taste of mine. Remember the hours in which you indulged yourself in me, sating yourself in any manner that would give you pleasure, and my concurrence with your every wish. Remember that when you asked for more, it was granted to you. You do remember, do you not, Mr. Dale?"

Harvey managed a short, stiff nod.

"I do not hear you, Mr. Dale."

Harvey swallowed. "Yes, I remember."

Lily's narrow brows rose in a delicate expression of incredulity. "And you would give up all this willingly?"

"Yes."

Lily slowly removed Harvey's hand from her breast.

"You would not suffer, knowing that another man would touch this sweet flesh for which you hunger, that I would welcome this other man into my body and I would gasp and whisper soft loving words in his ear, words I have never whispered in yours?" Lily paused, finally urging into the silence that followed, "You have not answered me, Mr. Dale."

A low, choked "No" passed Harvey's lips.

Lily's black velvet eyes appeared to laugh at him. With slow deliberation she pressed his hand against her narrow waist, then moved it steadily downward until it covered the warm delta between her thighs. Of its own accord, Harvey's hand curled to accommodate the curve of her body.

"Tell me, Mr. Dale. You would not suffer that I would offer all this to another man?"

"Yes, yes, I would suffer, Lily." His agitation suddenly more than he could bear, Harvey attempted to draw her closer. "I would free you of your obligation to me, but only your obligation. I still want you, and if you would let—"

Lily's eyes were abruptly cold. A harsh laugh escaped her throat. "Unhand me, Mr. Dale."

Incredulous, Harvey shook his head. "Lily . . ."

"I told you to unhand me, Mr. Dale. You have answered my question. I want nothing more from you."

Stunned, Harvey dropped his hands to his sides. A slow flush transfused his face as a quick downward glance revealed the hard, full rise of his passion. He lifted his gaze to Lily's triumphant expression.

"Bitch. Incredible, conniving bitch."

Lily was again standing at her mother's side. "So you have said before, Mr. Dale."

"You'll pay for this. You'll—"

"I will not suffer your threats against my daughter, Mr. Dale, not while you seek my help."

China Mary's sharp interruption made Harvey turn toward her unsmiling, suddenly ominous expression. He took a deep breath and a tenuous hold on his emotions.

"Then give me your answer."

"I would make one stipulation, Mr. Dale. I would have you put the papers for which we bargain into the hands of a neutral party when the information you seek is delivered to you, with instructions that the neutral party surrender those papers to me immediately upon your daughter's return. Are you agreed?"

Harvey stiffened. "Yes."

China Mary paused, the acid in her sudden smile cutting deep. "Then I will see, Mr. Dale."

"You'll see?"

Mary's face hardened. "I will see what I am able to discover. I will contact you if I am able to help you."

"But—"

"That is all, Mr. Dale. I believe our interview is ended."

Not able to accept the sharp reversal in their roles with grace, Harvey raised his chin in subdued anger. "I expect to hear from you soon."

Without response, China Mary walked toward the door in her characteristically short step. She opened it wide as she turned to him once more. "At *our* convenience, Mr. Dale."

Unable to resist a last glance toward Lily, Harvey saw her fine lips move in an emotionless echo of her mother's words: "At our convenience, Mr. Dale."

Shaken, totally subdued, Harvey Dale turned and walked out onto the street.

The door closed behind Harvey Dale, and China Mary walked to the window. Her gaze followed his halting, uneven step until he was out of sight. Turning, she studied her daughter's sober face. Without a word, she brought the palms of her hands together in a sharp summons that cracked in the silence of the room. In immediate response a slender, graying man appeared in the doorway. After a rapid exchange in their native tongue, the man disappeared back in the direction from which he had come.

Lily closed her hand around China Mary's arm. "The time has been long in coming, Mother, but it is almost here."

A flicker of a long suppressed fury moved across Mary's features. "The taste of victory is sweet, is it not, my daughter?"

Lily's smooth brow creased in a frown. "Is it wise to declare a victory that is not yet truly won?"

Mary turned toward the door, forestalling her reply, as a quiet Oriental entered the room. A mere shadow of a man, he moved without sound and paused in silence. His questioning gaze touched Mary's face.

"Yoong Tse," Mary said, "the time has come for your careful surveillance of Lai Hua and her lover to bear fruit. In a few days you will lead Mr. Harvey Dale to the cabin where his daughter is being held. You will cooperate with Mr. Dale and follow his orders. But until that time you will keep careful watch on the man who delivered the ransom note and still lingers in town. I would have nothing interfere with the progress of events toward which I have planned these many months. Toward this end, you will make yourself available to my immediate summons at all times. Is that understood?"

Yoong Tse nodded but maintained his silence. He turned
toward the doorway in a gliding, soundless step and within
moments disappeared through it as quietly as he had come.

China Mary turned to her daughter's concerned frown.

"A few days, Mother? Yoong Tse but awaits your command
to lead Mr. Dale to his daughter. My anticipation of the day we
are finally free of Mr. Dale is keen, and I chafe at such delay."

"I prolong our anticipation of triumph for good cause, daughter. I planned for this hour. It did not escape my knowledge that
Ross Morrison had obtained an early release from prison, and I
knew from the first who was stealing Till-Dale payrolls. When it
was reported to me that Lai Hua had taken Ross Morrison's close
friend as her lover, I could not believe my luck. I knew the
hatred that burned inside Ross Morrison would avail me of an
opportunity for revenge against Harvey Dale as well. I also knew
Lai Hua would not betray this man she loved, but I was certain
surveillance of her would eventually bring me the opportunity I
sought. As you know, daughter, my instincts proved true.

"But my desire to savor my triumph is not the only reason for
my delay. I have not forgotten that despite his present circumstances, Mr. Dale still has influence in high places. My true
concern is that we allow a plausible period of time to elapse so
Mr. Dale will believe we instituted a search for information
about his daughter at his request. He must be made to believe we
have triumphed over him not through an illegal act, but through
the unique position I hold within this community. Only then will
we truly be free of the risk of retribution."

Again Mary paused. A hard smile curved her lips. "But in
truth, daughter, I will savor this period of waiting for another
reason as well. I have nourished inside me a supreme hatred for
Mr. Harvey Dale that will not be easily satisfied. I wish him to
suffer a little longer, as I suffered when his hands touched your
chaste flesh, when he took your innocence, when he came to
know you intimately through no desire of your own. I would
savor the justice of Harvey Dale's unspoken fear in knowing his
bitter enemy holds his beautiful daughter as totally under his
control as he held you. It is true justice, indeed, that Harvey
Dale's misuse of his power over you will bring him to keener
appreciation of that which his daughter is undoubtedly being
made to bear. Ah, yes, daughter, sweet is victory over this man,
but sweeter still is the knowledge that he writhes in the same
pain he caused others. A few more days, Lily . . ."

Lily's dark eyes held her mother's gaze intently, fusing with its strength. A small smile flicked across her perfect lips. "A few more days."

The purple shadows of twilight were beginning to deepen across the endless expanse of rolling hills. Devina, almost fully recovered from her brush with death and again clad in the old shirt and trousers, was alone in the cabin. In the silence, Ross's image returned vividly to her mind, and she flushed at the spontaneous warmth of her own reaction. Her body, inexperienced and untutored in the ways of loving, reminded her in countless ways of Ross's unrelenting, loving attentions, but the tender aching of her soft flesh served only to return the recollection of passionate ministrations that had wrought it.

In an attempt to put aside the memories flooding her mind, Devina stood up and walked unsteadily toward the fire. She stirred the simmering stew and breathed deeply of its appetizing aroma. Uncertain of the exact moment he had entered the cabin, Devina was suddenly conscious of Ross's presence behind her just an instant before his strong arms closed around her from behind. His hands slipped up to cup her breasts through the coarse fabric of her shirt, and she leaned full back into his chest. His warm lips played against the side of her neck, sending small shivers down her spine, and she closed her eyes as a multitude of feelings assaulted her senses. The moist heat in the pit of her stomach expanded. It robbed her of her strength even as it moved to settle in the deep inner core of her being, the place no man had touched before Ross brought her to full, throbbing life. It was a part of her that was his and his alone, although she dared not openly declare it so.

Ross's lips moved to her ear. He whispered low, heated endearments, and she raised a hand to the hard planes of his cheek. She loved the feel of this man. She loved being in his arms. She loved having him inside her.

But who was this man she loved? That sobering thought made Devina stiffen, but Ross's knowing hands continued to caress her breasts, sending wave after wave of pulsing emotion along her spine. His gentle, loving lips cajoled her, tormented her into mindlessness once more. His strong arms turned her in their embrace, and his lips found hers.

Ross devoured her mouth with a passion that bespoke a hunger as deep and insatiable as her own, and Devina submitted to its driving assault. Her searching hands found his shoulders, her arms encircled his neck. She was merging, melting into the hard, firm body, which sought to consume hers with its loving strength.

But Ross separated himself from her, holding her at a distance even as he kissed her mouth, her cheeks, her eyes, the throbbing pulse in her temple. Seeking to feel him close to her again, Devina sought to be free of his restraint, only to realize that her rough shirt was being stripped away. It fell to the floor as Ross's mouth closed over the naked, engorged crests of her breasts.

Devina gasped, myriad searing emotions assailing her even as Ross's name rang over and over in her mind in an endless, loving litany: *Ross, yours is the mouth that has brought me love. Ross, yours are the hands that have brought me alive. Ross, you are the fulfillment for which I have longed. Ross, I know this now, I know this as surely as I know I will never be happy without you again.*

Ross's tender, burning touch moved to the soft flesh at her waist, and he unfastened the closure on her trousers. She felt the rough fabric slipping down over her hips and legs. Ross dropped to his knees, and she felt his lips following the path of his hands. She gasped again at the new emotions he raised within her. His mouth moved against the light curls between her thighs, and she gave an involuntary shudder.

Ross's passion-filled gaze rose to hers, even as he cupped her buttocks firmly, supporting her. His soft words rose to her ears as if in a dream filled with matchless beauty, "Devina, I want to love you completely. Give yourself to me, darling."

Unable to resist his impassioned plea, Devina relaxed in his arms, allowing his intimate kiss, his unexpected caresses. His mouth teased lips yet unawakened to his kiss, found the waiting bud of her passion, caressed it into full, flowering bloom. She was quaking under the magic of his touch, shuddering. Her knees buckled, and Ross lowered her slowly, cautiously to the floor before the fire. Smoothing her skin, fondling her, leaving not an inch of her warm flesh untouched, unloved, he returned to the warm, moist nest he had abandoned only minutes before.

With tender diligence Ross assailed her with his loving, raised her on great, billowing waves of passion until she floated high above them, drifting in the full, dazzling spectrum of colors racing across her mind's eye . . . pink, gold, red. Glorious, breathtaking. Then the colors burst, careening, streaking on a ragged, erratic course as she soared freely above the common plane, clutching Ross close. Her body pulsed with the magic he had wrought, and Ross devoured its homage to his lovemaking, drew that part of her inside him, his and his alone.

Devina was motionless as Ross moved to cover her with his length, his mouth touching hers. Her low gasp of acceptance resounded in her mind as Ross slid himself hard and deep inside, as he plunged again, again, as she met the violence of his loving measure for measure, in breathless wonder.

The pounding of Ross's heart reverberated in her mind, echoing her own, and she was raised higher into the ecstatic world Ross and she alone shared. The rhythm became more intense, and a racing anticipation stole Devina's breath. Abruptly the moment had come. She heard it in Ross's low groan of climax, she felt it resound within her as she was suddenly thrust from the pinnacle of sustained ecstasy, whirling, gasping, spiraling in a breathtaking plunge into the deep velvet abyss of total reward.

It was long moments before Devina was able to rouse herself from the lethargy of complete satiation. She was so very tired. Ross's dark eyes met hers as she raised her heavy eyelids, and a sudden anxiety touched her mind. What would happen when the world again touched them?

Ross caressed her cheek even as he lowered his mouth to hers for a deep, lingering kiss. Seeming to sense her unspoken fear, he whispered against her parted lips, "Don't worry, darling. Just a little while longer and everything will be settled. Everything will be all right."

Devina closed her eyes. Blocking out her anxieties, she allowed Ross's words to console her as she lay in the circle of his arms. She so desperately wanted to believe him.

CHAPTER XX

THE LAST GRAY wisps of dawn had surrendered to the brilliant gold of morning, but Charles was oblivious to the beauty of the new day. He reined his horse up in front of the office of the O.K. Corral and dismounted. He dropped his reins into Wilt Barrows's waiting hands with a tired nod, untied his medical bag from the saddle, and started walking home. It had been a long, hard night. Isabel Rigger's third child had reluctantly made his way into the world in the early hours of morning, and there had been moments when Charles had doubted the oversize infant would make it. But all his worries had been for naught. Both mother and child had been doing well when he left them, and if the enthusiasm of Harry Rigger and his two daughters for the first male child was an indication, they'd both be receiving more care than they could possibly need.

Charles abruptly changed directions. He needed a good meal under his belt, and the best place to get one was at the Can-Can. Then a few hours' sleep and perhaps the self-pitying, morose individual he had become in the past few days would be put to rest.

Refusing to allow his mind to venture further with that thought, Charles raised his eyes toward the small frame structure at the intersection of Sixth and Allen. The memory of brilliant red hair and dancing brown eyes returned, and a familiar anguish touched his heart.

Turning with great deliberation into the Can-Can, Charles sat down at the first available table. With a few unsociable words, he placed his order, and soon a cup of steaming coffee was delivered to the table. He lifted it to his lips, scalded his mouth, and muttered a low, appropriate curse.

His eyes wandered to the offices of Till-Dale Enterprises, visible through the window by which he sat, and Harvey Dale came to mind. Tension tightened Charles's stomach into knots. Harvey Dale was up to something. Too much time had elapsed since he had returned those files to Dale and given him the accounting Ross had demanded in the ransom note. The appropriate sum should already have been deposited in Ross's name in the bank, and the title to Brad Morrison's mine transferred and signed. Harvey Dale was stalling. Damn the man. Didn't he realize he was playing with his daughter's life?

Charles took a more cautious sip from his cup and swallowed carefully as he continued to stare at the steady flow of pedestrians moving along Allen. His heart suddenly leaping, he spotted a glimpse of flaming hair glinting in the morning sun. Cursing the tall cowboy who sauntered in his direction, efficiently blocking his view, Charles squirmed in his chair in an attempt to see past the fellow's oversize form. His breath escaped in a low gasp as Camille's lush form came into sight.

Hungry for the sight of her, Charles stared as she walked in his direction. His heart was pounding. She was alone.

On his feet before he truly realized his own intention, Charles took only a moment to signal the startled waiter of his return before walking out the door. He was crossing the street when Camille saw him. She frowned as he stepped up on the sidewalk beside her.

"*Bonjour*, Charles. I had not expected to see you on the street so early in the day."

Charles attempted a smile. "And I didn't expect to see you walking alone. Where's the Count? I don't often see you on the street without him these days."

"I suppose that is so. Pierre and I have been very busy shopping and making last-minute arrangements for our return to France."

Charles attempted to ignore the sinking sensation in his stomach that Camille's words evoked. Camille resumed her step, and he took up beside her.

"When are you intending to leave?"

"Pierre and I will leave Tombstone within the next several weeks. It is a long journey home, but I will be happy to see my family again."

Charles nodded. "Yes, I suppose your sisters and brothers will be just as pleased to see you."

"For the brief time that I will spend with them." Camille gave a small shrug. "I am no longer a country girl, Charles. I have accepted that. But Paris has much to offer, and I will make the most of it, as I always have."

They had reached the intersection of Fourth and Allen, and Camille paused. "I am on my way to the post office to send a letter to my family, so I must turn here."

Charles felt a moment's panic assail him. He was tired, depressed. He wanted to talk for a little while. Nobody made him feel as good as Camille did.

Charles took her arm.

"I was just having breakfast." Charles's voice faltered. His tone dropped a note lower as he continued, "Please join me. I've missed you, Camille. I'd like to talk to you, just for a little while."

Camille's face flushed. She averted her eyes, only to look back a moment later with a small, regretful smile. "No, Charles, I think not. There has never been anything but honesty between us, and for that reason I will speak to you without pretense. We have both made a pact with ourselves, have we not, Charles? You are tired. You are feeling very alone, and you want someone to talk to. So you seek someone who had always given you all of herself in everything you have asked of her. But it is not meant that a casual friendship should exist between us, Charles. If the contact between us is renewed, it would not long remain as you now wish. You would then hate yourself, and your agony would begin again."

Camille shook her head, her warm eyes holding his with a directness so typical of her character. "I do not wish to see you suffer self-recriminations, Charles. And neither do I wish a resumption of my own distress. The break between us has been made. We must both remember our original intentions, and we must both be strong enough to fortify them now. Anything else would be unfair to both of us."

Her unexpected refusal left Charles momentarily unable to speak. He raised his hand to her cheek to stroke back an errant curl as Camille raised herself on tiptoe and pressed her lips against his for a brief, lingering kiss.

"And so *c'est fini*, Charles."

With a tight lump in his throat, Charles nodded. "Yes, it's finished, Camille."

Her bright eyes lingering only a moment longer on his, Camille turned away. Her step was rapid as she continued up Fourth Street, and Charles watched her swaying form until she disappeared from sight. He turned away, his eyes touching on the entrance to the Can-Can. He remembered the breakfast waiting for him, but his appetite had left him.

Hatred laced with contempt reverberated through Harvey Dale as he saw Charles Carter disappear into the Can-Can Restaurant. He glanced up Fourth Street in the direction Camille DuPree had walked only minutes before, a vague satisfaction touching his mind. The petition he had initiated had been effective, and the red-haired French whore would soon be returning to France. If he was to judge from the look on the doctor's face, Carter was not taking the loss of the woman lightly.

Harvey resumed his rapid step. He could not afford to waste any more time thinking of Carter and his whore. He had received a summons from China Mary, instructing him to come to her quarters immediately. He cared little that the summons was more a command than a request. He had already surrendered his pride by appealing for help to that sly Chinese hag, and he knew he would do whatever else he had to do to get Devina back.

Harvey shuddered. A vision hovered in the back of his mind, driving him, giving him little peace. He had dismissed Morrison's hatred from his mind, the promise of revenge he had seen in Morrison's eyes when the sheriff had dragged him off to Yuma Prison three years before. But the memory had returned to torment him since Morrison had kidnapped Devina.

Harvey's heart jumped to a ragged beat. Even now Morrison could be taking that hatred out on Devina. Even now he could be hurting her, terrorizing her. Even now he could be touching her, forcing her to . . .

A sudden, uncontrollable spasm shook Harvey, and he missed his step. Managing to right himself before he stumbled, Harvey took a moment to regain his composure. The vision persisted, and Harvey started to shake. He had to find Devina.

Starting forward once more, Harvey increased his uneven step almost to a run.

As Harvey Dale crossed the intersection of Fourth and Allen, Jake cautiously stepped out of the entrance of the Occidental Hotel. He had had a close call a few minutes earlier. First he had almost come face to face with Charles Carter, and then he had almost run smack into Harvey Dale.

Jake pulled his hat lower on his brow and began to follow at a safe distance behind Dale, as he had for the better part of the week. Dale looked even worse than he had the day before. He looked seedy, exhausted, almost frantic.

Jake didn't like the way things were going. Dale was stalling, and Ross was probably madder than a hornet, waiting at the cabin with no news of how things were going. Jake would have to ride back to the cabin tomorrow to tell him something or there would be hell to pay.

Jake suddenly realized Harvey Dale was almost running down Third Street, and Jake rounded the corner just in time to see him step into China Mary's establishment. Jake slowed his step, abruptly filled with contempt for the hypocrisy of Dale's pretended concern for his daughter. Harvey Dale's Chinese mistress was a poorly kept secret, and it seemed the threat on his daughter's life had not lessened Dale's desire for her.

Disgusted, Jake turned back toward Allen Street. He'd give Dale one more day.

Ross lowered his head to trail his mouth over the graceful column of Devina's throat as she lay sleeping in his arms. He separated his lips against her delicate skin, tasting it, gently drawing it into his mouth. He had been aware that the emotions raging between Devina and him had altered drastically, but it was with particular difficulty that he had finally admitted to himself that he loved this beautiful woman as intensely as he had once thought he despised her.

Ross glanced at the morning sunlight slanting under the cabin door. A new day, and he knew he would not be able to avoid Devina's questions much longer. But they were questions for which he had no satisfactory answers. How could he tell the woman he held in his arms, the woman he had thoroughly loved, that his craving for vengeance against her father had not diminished? How could he tell her that when her father met the terms of ransom he had no intention of letting her go?

A flicker of movement crossed Devina's perfect features. Her delicate lids were fluttering, slowly rising, and Ross gave himself up to the tenderness that soared anew inside him. He had not thought himself capable of this depth of emotion. The strength of his love for Devina and the power it wielded intimidated him. In holding her in his arms, in loving her, he had discovered a new facet of passion, an incredible joy, a well of tenderness and caring within him of which he had been unaware. He realized for the first time that his bitterness and demanding need for revenge had made him less than the man he once was. He also knew that Devina could help make him whole once more. With these realizations came a driving certainty that without her he would never be whole again.

The glorious blue of Devina's eyes touched his face as she raised her hand to his cheek. He touched his lips to her fingertips, knowing that although the words had risen to his lips countless times in the past few days, he could not tell her he loved her. That would put her in a position of strength against him that he could not yet afford.

Devina's eyes drifted to the cabin door, and a pensive frown creased her brow. Ross felt the change her thoughts had wrought within her the moment before she turned back to him with a soft question.

"When are you going to take me back to Tombstone, Ross?"

The warmth within Ross turned cold. "Are you anxious to get away from me, Devina?"

"No . . . yes . . ." Devina shook her head and he could feel her heart begin to pound against his chest. Her confusion touched deeply protective instincts inside him, and he fought their debilitating effect.

Devina swallowed with difficulty, and Ross was aware of the effort she made at control. She gave a short shrug. "It's just that I don't know what to think. I can't believe my father is a villain."

"You mean you don't want to believe it."

"Ross, please." Devina took a deep breath. "I don't really understand any of this."

"How could you understand?" A familiar harshness touched Ross's heart. "You were brought up in luxury. You never had to work a day in your life . . . you and my brother, Charles."

The acknowledgment of Charles's and Devina's common bond stirred an aching jealousy in Ross, but he attempted to dismiss it with a short shrug.

"Your first memory isn't one of scratching in the desert sand at your father's side while he worked in the hot sun with a pick and shovel. You didn't grow up knowing your mother had left your father for another man without a backward look, a rich man who could give her more of the things she wanted in life. You weren't faced with the realization that she coldly left you behind as if you were so much excess baggage, but that she took her other son with her—the son the rich man wanted to raise. You didn't share your father's dream of finding the strike that would prove to her, the only woman your father ever loved, that he wasn't just a dreamer after all, that you and your father were both worth more than she had thought."

Ross paused, drawing his agitation under rein as he perused Devina's intense expression. "You didn't experience all of those things, Devina, so you couldn't appreciate what I felt when my father's letter reached me in San Francisco saying he had finally struck it rich. I had been on my own for a while; but it was as if I hadn't been gone a day. I took the first stage to Tombstone, and my father and I celebrated the strike."

Ross paused again. "Your father cheated that claim away from him, Devina." Devina's expression was suddenly stricken, and just as suddenly he realized that she believed him. Intensely grateful for that belief, he regretted the pain in her eyes, even as he recognized his need to continue.

"Pa and I tried every legal means we knew, but it was useless, Devina. I don't have to tell you what the realization that he had been cheated out of his life's work did to Pa. He hadn't told me how sick he had been, that he had been seeing that quack, Dr. Harlow, about his heart. The first I found out about it was when I came back to the shack Pa was living in and found him collapsed on the floor. There wasn't much anybody could do for him, considering his state of mind. I knew the only way to help him was to convince Harvey Dale, somehow, that he had to make things right."

Ross gave a short, bitter laugh. "I don't have to tell you how successful I was. Your father was very blunt about the whole thing. He said if my father was too much of a fool to protect his interests, then he deserved what he had gotten. I went kind of crazy when he said that. I warned him, made all kinds of threats. I told him he wouldn't get away with cheating my father, that I'd see he paid for what he had done, one way or another.'' Ross laughed again. ''As it turned out, I played into your father's hands by making those threats in front of witnesses. Your father capitalized on those threats when there was an accident in one of his mines in which six men were killed. He took the opportunity to get rid of me by laying the blame for that accident on me. By this time I had managed to establish a reputation for myself as a troublemaker and when Sam Sharpe, Wally Smith, and your father were done, the town was ready to lynch me.''

Devina's face was pale, and she attempted to speak, but Ross halted her words with a shake of his head.

''No, Devina, let me finish. I want you to know everything so you can understand.'' Ross stopped himself. It wasn't yet time for him to tell Devina he wanted her to understand so that she could trust him enough to love him as much as he loved her.

''That's when my brother, Charles Carter, first walked into the picture, after having ignored my father's letters and attempts to contact him for twenty-six years.'' The renewed interest in Devina's eyes caused jealousy to burn anew inside him. He could not restrain the acid tone of his remarks.

''No, Carter didn't come in and rescue my father and me from our stupidity, although I think he could have if he had wanted to. To tell you the truth, I don't really know how Carter happened to show up when he did. I can only think that word of Pa's strike got back to him and he wanted his share. If that's so, he must've had a big disappointment when he arrived in Tombstone. At that point, Pa was a poor, broken, sick old man, and I was hiding out, a fugitive with the whole town after my neck. Carter went to see Pa and then managed to contact and meet me. I found out later he went to see your father, too. And when all was said and done, he made his choice. He chose to believe your father. He asked me to meet him again, but the second time he brought the sheriff with him.''

''No! That can't be!'' Speaking for the first time, Devina shook her head in vehement denial. Her fair skin flushed as she continued emphatically, ''Charles couldn't do that! I know him. He couldn't do that even if he believed you were guilty.''

Jealousy flamed into pain at Devina's instinctive defense of Carter, and he refused to listen to the remainder of her protest.

"Don't tell me what my brother would or wouldn't do! You weren't there when the sheriff showed up at the door behind Carter, when the posse dragged me back to Tombstone and threw me in jail. You weren't there when my loving brother faced me through the bars and very calmly told me it was better that way."

When Devina made no further attempt to interrupt, Ross made an effort to draw his racing emotions under control. His smile was bitter.

Ross hesitated. "As for Carter, I still can't figure out why he decided to stay in Tombstone. I suppose the one thing I can thank him for was giving Pa a decent burial, or right now Pa'd be lying in a pauper's grave on Boot Hill."

Ross paused for a long moment. "But, as it turned out, Carter did me a real favor. If it wasn't for him, I never could have walked into your house the night of the party and taken you off to the garden. And you wouldn't be here with me right now."

Devina was momentarily silent while myriad thoughts moved across her pensive expression. Then she said softly, "I'm glad Charles didn't have any part in the plan to kidnap me. I knew he couldn't have from the first. Not Charles. He isn't that kind of man."

Devina's response pushed all thought from Ross's mind but the jealousy that consumed him. Gripping her chin roughly, he forced her to meet eyes hot with menace as he held her startled gaze with his own. "You believe everything I've told you about your own father, but you don't believe a word I've said about Carter. Why, dammit? Answer me!"

Devina shook her head, bewildered. "Ross, please, I—"

Trembling with rage, Ross gave her chin a hard shake. "Who do you really see when you look at me, Devina? Do you see me, or do you see Charles Carter?"

"Ross, you don't understand."

"Don't I?" He propped himself up on his elbow to glare threateningly down into her face. "I was just wasting my time, wasn't I, thinking I could explain, make you see? It's funny how a man sees only what he wants to see, until the truth is thrown in his face and he can't deny it any longer." Ross took a hard breath. "Charles is the man you want, the man you've always wanted, isn't he, Devina? He's the man you see when I hold you in my arms."

Not allowing her to respond, Ross continued in a low, threatening voice, "That's too bad, because you're never going to see Carter again. Your father will meet the terms of the ransom, no matter how difficult they are, but when he does, he's going to find himself cheated, just like he cheated my father and so many others like him. He isn't going to get you back at all, Devina."

Ignoring Devina's low gasp, he continued heatedly, "While he's waiting for me to bring you back, you, Jake, and I will be on our way to Mexico, where nobody will ever find us. We'll live well on the money Jake and I have accumulated from the robberies. In the meantime, all the money from Pa's mine will be in the bank in Tombstone, in my name, where your father can't touch it. Wouldn't you say that's a suitable revenge?"

Devina paled, but Ross refused to allow her lack of color to influence him. He prompted angrily, "You haven't answered me, Devina."

When Devina still did not respond, Ross pulled her closer. He was aware that she was shuddering, that fear had suddenly appeared in her eyes, and he regretted its presence. But his regret was only momentary. If he could not hold Devina with love, he would hold her any way he could.

Ross's voice was as cold as his gaze. "I'm not Charles, but I'm as close to Charles as you'll ever get. Keep that in mind, Devina, along with the promise that when you're in my arms I'll please you more than Charles could ever hope to please you. And I'll make you want me, the way you're wanting me even now. So close your eyes and pretend, if you have to." His eyes suddenly taking on a feral gleam, Ross rasped, "But I warn you. Don't ever mention Charles Carter's name to me again."

Devina's eyes were on his slowly descending lips, and Ross felt regret sweep his mind. He didn't want it to be like this between Devina and him, but he would have her this way if he could have her no other way at all. In the end, he'd make her forget Carter ever existed.

Ross adjusted Devina's small, trembling body against his as his mouth claimed hers. He allowed the warmth of that contact, the sweet taste of her to fill his mind. He allowed it to sweep away all other thought except the reality of the present, his love for the woman in his arms, and his unyielding determination to keep her there.

His face devoid of color, Harvey faced China Mary within the confines of her small office. He was fast losing control. Mary was smiling.

"You're certain you've located my daughter?"

"Yes, I am certain, Mr. Dale."

Harvey's patience expired with a snap. "Well, where is she, dammit! I want to go there now!"

"I will have one of my employees take you there soon, Mr. Dale."

"Soon isn't good enough! I want to go now!"

"I do not see any gratitude in your expression, Mr. Dale," Lily's clear, sweet voice interrupted. "Perhaps you do not fully appreciate that my mother has worked industriously in your behalf and has succeeded where all others have failed in finding your daughter."

Harvey's breathing grew labored, and he was visibly trembling. Lily's presence added more pressure to a situation that was already almost more than he was able to bear, and his humiliation was complete with the realization that Lily and her mother were enjoying his distress. Taking refuge in hauteur, he shot Lily a cold glance.

"Do you really expect me to express gratitude?" Harvey's laugh was scornful. "If you do, you are both fools!" He turned back to Mary. "I want to know where my daughter is now!"

Mary was still smiling. "In time, Mr. Dale. We have some business to transact first."

Barely restraining the desire to close his hands around China Mary's neck, Harvey nodded.

"The papers, is that it? I'll deliver them to Walter Sherkraut. He's a reputable businessman and can be trusted to turn them over to you if you can lead me to my daughter."

"No, Mr. Dale. Leave them with Roger Ball at the Safford Hudson Bank for safekeeping until you return with your daughter. Give Mr. Ball instructions to turn the papers over to me at that time. My patronage is valued highly in that banking establishment, and Mr. Ball will do nothing to endanger it."

"Crafty bitch!" Harvey stiffly nodded his head. "All right. I'll do it. Is there anything else you want from me?"

"Just confirmation, Mr. Dale. When Mr. Ball confirms that he is holding the papers, I will see that you are guided to the location where your daughter is being held."

"All right! I'll get the papers and take them there now. Is that enough for you?"

"It will suffice. You may have your men ready to travel tomorrow morning."

"Tomorrow! I'll get the papers now. You can tell your man to—"

"Tomorrow morning, Mr. Dale. And in the meantime, I would suggest you conduct your arrangements carefully, without drawing attention to your purpose if you choose to raise a group of men to rescue your daughter. We cannot be certain who is watching, can we?"

All but overwhelmed by the newest fear China Mary had planted in his mind, Harvey nodded. "All right, tomorrow." His eyes narrowing, Harvey impaled Mary with his gaze. "If you're bluffing, Mary . . ."

China Mary's smile broadened. "Like you, I am an honorable person, Mr. Dale. Like you, I can be trusted to keep my word."

Her subtle threat echoing in his ears, Harvey turned abruptly. Without another utterance he covered the few steps to the door and, within seconds, was striding toward his office. Mary's cautioning words returned to his mind, and he cast a suspicious glance over his shoulder before continuing forward with a lurching step. His humiliation, his defeat at the hands of the wily Oriental hag was but another price he had been forced to pay.

Harvey swallowed and breathed deeply against the heavy palpitation of his heart. His eye twitched uncontrollably, and he raised his chin in an attempt to regain control as he put his degradation behind him. It would all be worthwhile when Devina was safe once more.

Lai Hua walked swiftly, casting a glance towards the gradually darkening sky. She had made a difficult decision only a few minutes before and she hoped, very desperately, it was not too late.

Carefully avoiding the faster, more direct approach to her destination, in fear of being seen, she turned the corner of Third and Toughnut, and started toward Fourth. She was aware that her route did not stir the curiosity of passersby as she turned into an alley. Those of her race often used back alleys and back entrances in Tombstone when front doors were barred to them.

She had never been more grateful for that circumstance than she was at this particular moment.

Silently she scaled the rear staircase to the large frame building, opened the door at the top, and walked down a narrow hallway, following the room numbers intently. Her heart racing in her breast, she paused as the room she sought came into view. A momentary panic assailed her as she thought of the reception she would receive if the one she sought was indeed present.

The sound of her own heart racing in her ears, Lai Hua raised her small hand and rapped lightly. No response. She rapped again, disappointment and anxiety moving through her mind. A moment later a muffled voice sounded sleepily from inside the room. Before she could respond, the door flew open to reveal Jake Walsh's startled face.

Joy and relief coursed through Lai Hua, and she released a short, anxious breath. Her small face reflecting her uncertainty at the continued silence between them, she requested politely, "Mr. Jake, I may enter?"

Jake stepped back allowing her entrance, but Lai Hua was conscious of the restraint in his manner. She had expected as much. He closed the door and turned to face her, his expression sober. "You made yourself very clear the last time we met, Lai Hua. What are you doin' here?"

Lai Hua swallowed with visible difficulty, her eyes momentarily closing at the accusation in Jake's eyes. He was angry and hurt at what he considered her betrayal of the love she had professed for him. If only he knew how very deep that love was. She attempted a smile. "It has been many days since last we met and spoke."

"I didn't think there was much left for us to say to each other, Lai Hua. You made your feelin's very clear."

"I am glad that the intent of my actions was not misunderstood, Mr. Jake. I would not have you believe that my feelings for you are any less than they were before."

Jake's mouth twitched with discomfort, and Lai Hua shared his distress. If only there had been another way.

"Come to the point, Lai Hua. I have things to do tonight. I'm leavin' town tomorrow mornin' early."

Lai Hua felt his pale eyes, the color of the midmorning sky, touch the dark shine of her bound hair. She felt them move across her face, caress the skin of her cheek, her lips. Their warmth touched a familiar spot inside her, and her lips parted. The short, responsive intake of his breath echoed in the silence of the room, and her heart pounded anew. Jake's voice was hoarse when he continued. "Why did you nod, Lai Hua? Are you tellin' me you knew I was leavin' Tombstone?"

Lai Hua nodded again. "My heart told me it was so. I was uncertain if you would again return, and I wanted to say good-bye."

A short, bitter laugh escaped Jake's lips and Lai Hua felt his pain. He shrugged, but the emotion in his tense expression belied the casual gesture. "Good-bye, Lai Hua. Now, if that's all you came to say—"

. Lai Hua took a step forward, her courage almost failing. "I . . . I came to say good-bye in another way, Mr. Jake. A way more in keeping with that which we shared."

Jake's pale skin colored in a sudden flush. His expression was wary. His strong chest began a lightly agitated heaving.

"How many ways are there to say good-bye, Lai Hua? As far as I'm concerned, our good-byes are done."

A warm heat moved into Lai Hua's eyes. "If I might give you a parting gift, Mr. Jake, one from the heart."

Jake swallowed and paused before he attempted a reply. His youthful features were stiff, and his response was barely a whisper. "A gift?"

"A gift of myself, Mr. Jake."

Lai Hua took another step forward, the boldness of her actions reverberating within her as she stood a few feet from Jake's familiar strength. With slow deliberation, she released the first fastening on her jacket. Her trembling fingers moved to the second and then the third, her uncertain gaze never leaving his handsome, boyish face. Love shone from her eyes as she opened the garment, revealing her creamy skin, her small breasts. She slid the jacket from her shoulders and dropped it to the floor. The whisper of sound it created seemed unnaturally loud in the pervading silence. She moved her hands to the waistband of the cotton trousers that hugged her slender body. In a few moments they, too, were lying on the floor and Lai Hua stood naked in front of the man she loved. Still he did not move to close the distance between them.

Her voice tremulous, Lai Hua spoke into the void. "Do you refuse my gift, Mr. Jake? I give it to you with all my love."

Jake's low groan was simultaneous with his sudden movement as he closed the space between them. Joy coursing through her, Lai Hua was suddenly in his arms, scooped up high against his chest as he walked the few short steps to the bed. The mattress was soft beneath her back, still warm from his body. She lay, aching with anticipation as she watched Jake cast off his clothes until he stood as naked as she.

Within moments their flesh was pressed intimately close and a joy not without pain filled Lai Hua's mind. She felt his lips against her eyes, her cheeks, her mouth. She parted her lips to his kiss, welcoming its sweet intimacy. Jake tore his lips from hers to trail them down over her throat, her chest, her breasts. She clutched him close against her, giving him all she could offer. She encouraged his loving, allowing her own hands to travel over his strong hard body, to find the staff of his manhood, to stroke it warmly, lovingly. She heard his low groans, realized her mistake as Jake raised his eyes again to hers with a soft word of apology. Within moments he was pressing his throbbing tumescence against the moist, aching bud of her passion, then thrusting deep and hard inside her. She opened herself to him, reveling in the hunger that drove him, delighting in the wonder of his possession, realizing she had not felt truly alive since the last moment she had been so intimately joined to this beautiful man.

Then she was gasping, reaching the climax of the emotion he so faultlessly raised within her. She clutched him against her as his harsh rasps echoed in her ears, wishing never to separate from him as their bodies shuddered in mutual ecstasy, his filling hers, hers accepting and cherishing his.

Lai Hua heard the sweet words of love Jake whispered in her ears. She heard his apology for the swiftness of his culmination, his promise that he would surpass his poor effort and enjoy her gift many times before the night was past. He then set about to fulfill his promise, and she brimmed with love.

With great deliberation, Lai Hua turned her mind from the approaching dawn, and the awakening of another kind which would ensue. There was time now only for love . . . and how very much she loved this man.

• • •

The silver light of dawn was moving across the night sky outside his window when Harvey Dale's gray head snapped up at the sound of a sharp rap on his library door. The door opened to reveal a slight Oriental flanked by Sam Sharpe and Wally Smith.

His bearded face clearly reflecting his contempt, Sam motioned to the silent Asian in front of him. "This the fella you been waitin' for, Mr. Dale?"

Harvey met the man's gaze, then addressed him sharply.

"Are you the man China Mary told me to expect? Can you take me to my daughter?"

The Oriental bowed slightly in response. "Yes, Mr. Dale."

The chair on which he had been sitting lurched backward as Harvey Dale stood with a snap.

"How long will it take to get there?"

"A few hours, Mr. Dale."

"All right, then, let's get going."

Making certain to keep the Oriental in front of him, Harvey walked through the house and onto the porch to face the mounted men who waited outside. His eyes scanned the group, touching on Sheriff Bond and his four deputies, the two men of dubious reputation whom Sam Sharpe had hired at his request, and, at the rear, sitting on his horse silent and stone-faced, Charles Carter. Waiting until the Oriental had mounted his horse, Harvey addressed the men assembled.

"This Chinaman knows where my daughter is being held. He'll lead us there, and until we get there, he's the most important man in this group. I expect each and every one of you to protect him with your life. You'll be handsomely rewarded. You have my word on that."

Pausing to scan the group once more, Harvey walked toward the silent Charles Carter, aware that Sam Sharpe and Wally Smith were following at his heels. Halting to look up into Carter's sober face, Harvey fought to control the hatred shaking him. He addressed Carter in a low hiss.

"There is only one reason you're here with us this morning, Carter. That reason is my daughter, and my fear for her health. If Dr. Hastings had been available this morning, you wouldn't have gotten within fifty miles of this party. I won't risk my daughter's well-being because of my personal antipathy for you, but I warn you in front of these witnesses that if you try anything or attempt to help your brother in any way, I will have no more regard for your life than for that of a reptile crawling over the desert sand. Is that understood, Dr. Carter?''

Charles Carter gave a short nod. ''I only wish I had always understood you as clearly as I do now, Harvey.''

Turning to Sam Sharpe in a quick movement, Harvey instructed tightly, ''If he makes a wrong move, kill him.''

Sam Sharpe's thick lips curled into a smile. ''My pleasure, Mr. Dale.''

Turning on his heel, Harvey approached his horse and mounted. His heart pounding, his head strangely light, he raised his hand. An odd elation coursing through his mind, he ordered tightly, ''Let's go!''

Within moments the group was moving down Fremont Street toward the distant rolling hills. The thunder of hoofbeats faded into soundlessness as the dust raised by their rapid departure settled in the early morning mist.

Morning slitted through the shaded window, and Lai Hua stared toward the first brilliant rays of sunshine. She turned to the man who lay sleeping at her side, her eyes caressing his well-loved face. The night had been long, filled with tenderness, but she was aware that her ties to this man far exceeded the physical love they had shared. It was that love, and her fear for this man's life, which had brought her to him. It was that love which had caused her to compromise her honor, and it was that love which would force her again to leave him.

Slowly, with heartfelt reluctance, Lai Hua disengaged herself from Jake's arms. Her sorrow a deep ache within her, she slipped silently to the edge of the bed and started to rise, only to feel his hand slip around her wrist. His pale eyes rose to hers with loving warmth.

''Where are you goin', darlin'? I'm thinkin' there's no better way to begin the day than with a little lovin'.'' Jake's smile was almost apologetic. ''You're lookin' at a greedy man, Lai Hua. It's goin' to be a long time before I'm ready to let you go.''

Lai Hua's eyes remained intent on Jake's face. Her heart aching, she gently disengaged his hand. ''I must leave, Mr. Jake. I have accomplished the purpose of my visit.''

Jake's face went still. His pale eyes grew confused. He gave

his head a short, disbelieving shake. "Lai Hua, you didn't really
come here to say good-bye. Now that you realize what we mean
to each other, you can't leave again. You know I didn't betray
you, not intentionally."

Lai Hua stood beside the bed and reached for her clothes.
With quick movements she' stepped into her cotton pants and
pulled on her jacket. Securing the fastenings, she turned back to
Jake's astounded face. "I wish to speak these words fully clothed,
Mr. Jake, for I will leave immediately after they are spoken. I
know when I am done you will not resist my departure."

"Lai Hua, what are you talkin' about?"

"I am telling you that I spoke no deceit when I said my reason
for coming to you last night was to bid you good-bye. I did not,
however, speak my primary reason for the visit. You see, Mr.
Jake, I was aware of the time you had spent in Tombstone and of
the ransom note you delivered to Mr. Dale. I knew you would
soon return to Mr. Morrison and the place where he is holding
Miss Dale. I feared it would be this morning. True to my fear,
you spoke that intention when I arrived at your door last night. I
knew then the course I must take."

"Lai Hua, what are you talkin' about?" Jake made an attempt to take Lai Hua's arm, but she eluded his touch.

"Even as we now speak, Mr. Dale is taking his men to the
place where Mr. Morrison is holding Miss Dale."

Jake leaped from the bed to stand before her, his hands biting
into her arms, his voice harsh. "Explain yourself, dammit! And
do it now!"

Wincing at the pain of his grip, Lai Hua raised her eyes to
Jake's heated expression. "My position at the Dale household
has allowed me to learn that an informant of my people has
located Miss Dale. He is leading Mr. Dale, the sheriff, and a
group of his men to the hideout. They started out this morning at
dawn. I came here last night in fear for your life, should you
discover this intended foray against your friend. It was too late
for you to help your friend in any way, but I knew you would
attempt to save him, and I could not allow the wanton disregard
for your life that would ensue. I did not wish to see you die, Mr.
Jake."

Jake's mouth curled into a sneer. "So you came here, knowin'
I would forget everythin' when you offered yourself to me,

knowin' I wouldn't be able to resist lovin' you. Hell, you sure had me pegged. I played right into your hands, didn't I? Believin' everythin' you said, everythin' you did, thinkin' you had missed me as much as I'd missed you. Christ, and all the time you were laughin' at me.''

"I did not laugh, Mr. Jake. I but loved—''

"Love! That's a joke, isn't it, Lai Hua? You turn your love off and on to suit your purpose. That's a real useful love you got there. I wish I could manage the same thing.''

"Mr. Jake—''

"Tell me the truth, Lai Hua.''

Jake's hands were cutting into the soft flesh of her arms, but Lai Hua made no sound of distress.

"Tell me. Did your 'honor' make you choose Harvey Dale over me this time, too? Did you salve your conscience by makin' me betray my friend, just like you figure I made you betray yours? Is that what you did, Lai Hua?''

"No, Mr. Jake. I had no such intention! I—''

Jake thrust Lai Hua away in a quick movement that sent her stumbling toward the door, but there was no regret in his pale eyes. Instead, they burned as they stared into her face, and Lai Hua was stung by the fury in his whispered words.

"Get out of here, Lai Hua. I never want to see you again. You've had your revenge, and you've managed it very well. Congratulate yourself on your cunnin', because you are that, Lai Hua. Cunnin' and connivin' and everythin' I never thought you to be. And now that I know what you really are, I don't want any part of you. Hell, I never thought I'd see the day I'd say it and mean it, but get out, Lai Hua. Get out and don't ever come back.''

Jake's anger cut hotly into Lai Hua's heart. She paused, hoping to speak a few words to assuage his pain, but his rage was too complete.

"Dammit, get out!''

Turning swiftly, Lai Hua ran from the room and down the hallway. Tears clouding her vision, she made her way to the rear entrance, out through the heavy door, and onto the staircase leading to the alley. She was leaving the way she had come, never to again return.

Silence. Devina could not bear the silence.

She cast a furtive glance toward Ross, who stood near the doorway of the cabin. She did not know the man she saw there. The tenderness, the concern, the warmth she had experienced in his arms, the side of Ross she had begun to believe was the dominant part of his character, had disappeared as quickly as it had come. The old Ross Morrison had returned, the hard man filled with hatred and a need for revenge, the man whose cold black eyes menaced her every move. She missed the loving Ross. That man had worked his way into her heart and she loved him in a way she had not thought she dared to love. She wanted him back.

Devina approached him cautiously. She was within a few feet of him when he turned and saw her. The anger in his eyes caused a low regretful sound to escape her lips. "Ross, I don't want it to be this way."

Angry, his lips twisting into a bitter smile, Ross closed the distance between them.

"You don't want it to be what way, Devina? You don't want to spend the day avoiding my eyes. You don't want to feel this separation between us?" Ross pulled her close against him and cupped her chin roughly with his hand, forcing her face up to his. "Is that what you want? Well, now I'll show you what I want."

Ross's mouth closed over hers. His hand slipped around to the back of her head, his fingers tangling in her hair, twisting it with a sweet possession as he consumed her with his kiss.

Breathless under his assault, her mind reeling, Devina protested the mastery over her senses with which Ross attempted to subdue her, even as her lips separated under his. Tearing his lips from hers with a low, gasping breath, Ross trailed his mouth along her cheek, her throat. His hands caressed the womanly swells beneath her coarse shirt until she gasped at the conflicting feelings assailing her.

"No, Ross, please."

"Please what, Devina? Please make love to me? Please let me go? Tell me how I can please you!"

"Ross . . ."

His laugh was short, harsh. "You don't have to answer. It doesn't really make any difference, just as it doesn't make any difference whose face you see when you look at me. Soon you'll only see me, and when that time comes, you won't want to talk anymore. You'll only want to feel, just as I'm making you feel now, as only I can make you feel. You'll forget that there ever was another man with my face. You'll forget any other man ever existed, and you'll only want me. Then I'll—''

"Ross Morrison, this is Sheriff Bond. Your cabin is surrounded."

Ross's strong arms, holding her close, went suddenly stiff. Devina felt the shock of realization move through his body, even as it moved through her own, as her startled gasp echoed in the silence of the cabin.

"I know you're in there, Morrison," the voice shouted from outside the cabin. "And I know you have Devina Dale with you. I want you to send her out first, so we can see she's all right. Then I want you to come out behind her with your hands up."

Ross abruptly closed the door, plunging the cabin into semi-darkness. Devina felt a tremor of fear move down her spine as he reached for his gun, his eyes glowing with a heated fervor.

"It looks like I was wrong, Devina. You just might get to see your father again, and you may get the man you want, after all."

"Morrison," the sheriff shouted, "there's no way you're going to get away. I've got ten men with me. Do yourself a favor and send Miss Dale out. You don't want her to get hurt."

Ross moved to the window to peer out from between the boards. "Eleven horses. It looks like the sheriff isn't bluffing." He turned back toward Devina with a hard smile. "What do you think, Devina? Should I send you out to the sheriff?"

Fear coursed through Devina in sharp, quaking tremors. If her father was out there and if he had Sam Sharpe and Wally Smith with him, there would be no guarantee that they'd hold their fire if Ross chose to surrender. The memory of Sharpe's cold, lifeless eyes increased her shuddering. She sent Ross a pleading glance. "Let me talk to them, Ross. Let me tell them I'm all right."

As she watched Ross's face, she could see his resolution falter. Then his lips tightened into a firm line and he walked to the other side of the cabin. His deep, resonant voice filled the room as he shouted through the boarded window, "All right, Sheriff. I'll send Miss Dale out to you. Hold your fire."

"No!" Devina cried. "I'll talk to them through the window, but I won't go outside the cabin. If I leave you alone in here they'll—"

"Does it really make any difference to you what happens to me? Think a moment, Devina. You've been rescued. My great plans for revenge have fallen through. You won't have to go to Mexico, after all. You won't have to endure my loving. You won't have to pretend I'm Charles. All those plans I told you about were nothing but a dream, a lot of talk that never came out to reality, just like Pa striking it rich. You'll be able to go back to your father's beautiful house and the good life he has planned for you. You can go back to Charles. That's what you wanted, isn't it?"

Devina shrank from the anger in Ross's gaze. She had never seen such hatred and fury.

Ross gave his gun a quick last-minute check. Then, grabbing her arm in a painful grip, he dragged her to the door and attempted to open it, but Devina threw herself against it, forcing it closed.

"You're not going to surrender, are you?" Devina swallowed against the hard lump that had formed in her throat. "You're going to try to fight. You know you don't stand a chance. You know what'll happen."

Ross laughed, but the sound was devoid of mirth. "I made my choice a long time ago, Devina. I'm not going back to Yuma. I'll take my chances here and now."

Grasping her arm, Ross pulled her away from the door, but Devina fought his imprisoning grip. Kicking and punching with all her strength, she refused to allow him to open the door and force her outside.

"We're waiting, Morrison. Send her out."

Anger and frustration flashed across Ross's face, but Devina would not relent. Abruptly freeing himself from her with an angry thrust, Ross turned toward the doorway. "She'll be out in a minute, Sheriff. The lady doesn't want to be rushed."

Panic drove all thought from Devina's mind except the stark reality facing her. Ross was going to send her out, but he wouldn't surrender himself. He'd be killed.

His attention was still directed toward the armed men waiting beyond the shuttered windows. No! She wouldn't let him do it!

Turning, she scanned the room. The branding iron Ross had used for a poker lay beside the fireplace. Devina snatched it from the floor. Advancing silently toward Ross's back, she swung it with all her might.

Ross cried out sharply as the iron struck his arm, knocking his gun to the floor. He doubled over, clutching his arm in pain.

Quickly, Devina retrieved the gun and flung open the door before Ross could step forward. She was running toward the figures barely visible in the uneven terrain.

"It's all right," she shouted. "Don't shoot. He's unarmed. I have his gun."

Within moments, Devina was snatched up into familiar arms. She glanced up, a moment's shock shuddering through her as she glimpsed Charles's face.

Separating himself from her after a few moments, Charles drew back with concern. "Are you all right, Devina. Ross didn't hurt you?"

"No, but Ross is inside. I hit him. You have to help me get him out before they—"

"Take your hands off my daughter, Carter!"

Turning toward the sound of her father's peculiar rasping voice, Devina noted with alarm his livid color, the deep lines etched in his face. "Father!"

"I said get your hands off my daughter, Carter."

Her father took a step forward, but Devina turned away from his advancing step at the shout that echoed behind her.

"All right, Morrison, come out with your hands up or we'll come in after you."

Devina squirmed free of Charles's grip, her eyes darting toward the cabin. She turned back, panic in her gaze.

"Charles, he won't let them take him alive!"

With a low gasp, Devina halted her impassioned plea. Sam Sharpe was inching his way toward the cabin, a gun in his hand. She knew instinctively Sharpe wouldn't care if Ross was unarmed.

She started running back toward the cabin. The sound of heavy footsteps sounded behind her. One running step faltered and stopped, but the other continued on. She could not take time to turn. She had to reach the cabin before Sharpe.

She burst through the door of the cabin, knowing that Charles and Sam Sharpe were not far behind.

Ross's arm was hanging limply at his side, but he gave a low laugh, his eyes darting to the men behind her. "So you're back with your rescuers behind you. Don't worry, you did a good job. I couldn't pull the trigger of a gun right now even if somebody put one in my hand."

The posse filed past her through the doorway. Sharpe grasped Ross's arms, twisted them cruelly behind him, and bound his wrists.

She heard Charles's voice in sharp protest. "Watch what you're doing. He's been hurt."

Sam Sharpe's low sneer sounded in response as he pulled the rope tighter. "Not as much as he's goin' to be, Doc."

Devina felt Charles's supportive hand at her waist, and she realized she was shuddering. Her eyes trained on Ross, she was unable to move as he was pushed into motion and thrust roughly past her and through the cabin doorway.

Suddenly numb, Devina turned and followed him outside. She was standing in the late-morning sun when she saw her father walk unsteadily toward Ross. A jolt of fear penetrated her numb mind. Something was wrong with her father. His color was abnormally high. He was twitching, his handsome face distorted as he attempted to speak. She felt Charles's hand drop from her shoulder as a low sound of concern passed his lips. She walked faster, her eyes on her father's face as he stared into the venom of Ross's gaze.

"So you thought you'd win out over me, Morrison, and take my daughter." Devina was at her father's side, and she felt his arm slip around her shoulder in a weak, trembling grasp. "But I have her back, and you'll be sent back where you belong—to Yuma, Morrison, back to Yuma. You'll—"

A low gasp interrupted her father's tirade. A drop of spittle falling from the corner of his mouth, he strove to catch his breath, his handsome face distorting, twitching with more violent spasms. The arm on her shoulder went abruptly rigid as her father's body began to convulse uncontrollably. Devina attempted to support his crumbling frame, but it was no use. His eyes rolled up into his head, and he slipped from her clutching hands to the ground.

Unable to move, Devina watched as Charles kneeled at her father's side and began working vigorously over his prone figure. She raised her eyes as if drawn by a second sense to meet Ross's intense stare.

His low, bitter voice filled the void of silence. "So, there is some justice after all. Don't worry, Devina. You're your father's daughter, a true Dale. You'll—"

A quick, unexpected blow from Sam Sharpe's hand caught Ross across the face, knocking him backward. Blood spurted from his mouth, and Devina felt a drop hit her cheek. A peculiar light-headedness assailed her as her eyes touched on Ross's bleeding face. The sound of her father's rasping breaths grew louder. Unconsciously she touched the warm blood on her cheek and saw the stain on her fingers.

The world began whirling around her as fragmented pictures assailed her mind. Ross, her father, the sound of rasping breaths— each shardlike image stabbed her with excruciating torment until she sank slowly to the ground. The darkness accepted her, and her escape was complete.

CHAPTER XXI

CHARLES FROWNED AS the key grated in the metal lock and the steel bars of the door were drawn open to allow him entrance into Ross's cell. Sheriff Bond's low warning registered in the back of his mind as he met dark eyes so similar to his own.

"You only got five minutes, Doc, and don't try nothin' except for fixing his arm. Hear?"

Charles nodded as the bars slammed shut behind him and the key again grated in the lock. An uneasy silence followed the sound of the departing footsteps and the closing of the outer door.

"How are you, Ross?" Charles said finally.

The face looking back at him still amazed him with its resemblance to his own, but Charles was only too conscious of the marked differences now reflected there: a swollen lip and tight lines of anger and bitterness surrounding that bruised mouth. The realization that he was responsible for part of the bitterness reflected there was a burden he did not carry lightly.

The caustic tone of Ross's response was the only open indication of the anger he so carefully controlled. "Is that the doctor talking to me, Carter? I suppose it is, because I can't think of any other reason you'd be here right now."

Remorse stabbed at Charles's mind. Ross despised him. What else could he expect?

"Let me check your arm. You can believe what you want to believe, Ross."

385

"Since it's Dr. Charles Carter talking to me, I'll answer just as I'd answer any other doctor right now. There's nothing wrong with my arm that a few days' rest won't cure. I don't need anything from you."

Charles allowed a few seconds for that response to settle between them before he grasped the arm that hung lankly by Ross's side. His brother's gasp of pain brought a responsive frown to Charles's brow.

"Don't be stubborn, Ross. Even Sheriff Bond saw the need for you to see a doctor. If you don't want me to attend to you, I can call Dr. Hastings. But if your arm's broken, the sooner it's tended to the better."

"My arm's not broken."

"Devina will be glad to hear that."

Anger flared to open flame in Ross's eyes. His attempt to withdraw his arm from Charles's grasp caused another spasm of pain to cross his face. He uttered a low curse. "I'm not interested in what Devina will be glad to hear. Is that why you're really here, Carter? So you can report back to Devina how good a job she did?"

Charles held Ross's gaze for a few moments longer without reply. Realizing there was nothing he could say to alleviate the heat of his brother's anger, he carefully rolled up the sleeve of Ross's shirt and examined the muscular arm beneath.

"We may look alike, but I'll be damned if I ever had biceps like these," he said with a short laugh.

But Ross wasn't laughing. "Prison life builds a bigger, better man, Carter."

Charles met his brother's eyes again in silence. Returning to his examination, he finally pulled back with a satisfied expression. "Well, you're right. Your arm isn't broken. You'll probably be able to use it more easily in a day or so. It sure took a hell of a whack."

"I didn't need a doctor to tell me that."

Charles paused. "Devina regrets having had to do this to you."

Ross's expression turned suddenly vicious. "Spare me Devina Dale's secondhand regrets." He had pulled away and was fumbling in his attempt to roll down his sleeve.

Charles felt a familiar despair assail him. How could he tell his brother he'd been a damned fool? He took a deep breath. "Ross, I've been a damned fool."

Ross's head jerked up at Charles's unexpected statement. Suspicion moved across his face. "Have you, Carter? I'd say you were pretty smart. Here you are on top again, untouched by your criminal brother's actions and probably a hero in a lot of eyes. And you've even got Devina."

"Got Devina?" Charles was startled. "Devina and I are friends. She asked me to tell you—"

"I told you I didn't want—"

"She's coming later this morning to see you. Harvey Dale's had a stroke and she—"

"A stroke?" Ross gave a short laugh. "Hell, maybe there really is a God."

Charles frowned. "In any case, I didn't come here to discuss Devina. I came here to look at your arm and to tell you that I was a long time realizing the part I unwittingly played in this whole situation. Apologies don't mean much at this stage of the game but—"

"That's right, Carter. They don't mean much at all."

Charles took another deep breath, a deep sense of futility sinking into the pit of his stomach. "But I want to say it anyway. I'm sorry, Ross. I'm sorry I didn't believe you and our father."

"Like you said, Carter, your apology doesn't mean much. Pa's in the ground, and everybody believes he was nothing but an ignorant prospector who wasted his big strike. Harvey Dale got away with everything, and with his luck, he'll probably live to pull the same trick a half-dozen more times."

"I'm going to get you a good lawyer, Ross."

Ross laughed again. "Why? I'm guilty of everything they're going to charge me with, aren't I? Ask Devina, she'll tell you. I'm sure she'll be only too happy to repeat the whole sad story I told her." Ross laughed, his bitterness twisting the sound to hollow mockery. "But don't worry, Carter. They can try me and sentence me, but they'll never get me back to Yuma."

Charles shook his head. "What are you telling me, Ross?"

"I'm done talking, Carter, and you're done with my arm, so you can leave now."

"Ross . . ."

Turning, Ross called toward the outside office, "Five minutes are up, Sheriff! It's time for the good doctor to leave."

The outer door opened in almost immediate response, but Charles tried once more. "Ross . . ."

Ross stared directly into Charles's eyes, his expression resolute. "Don't come back, Carter."

"But—"

"I said don't come back."

Watching as Ross turned toward the window, Charles paused a moment longer. The hard voice coming from behind him was simultaneous with the sound of a key grating in the lock.

"Listen to what the fella says, Doc. He don't want you here no more, and that's that."

Charles slowly turned away.

Jake pulled his hat lower on his forehead and continued along Sixth Street in a casual step that belied his inner agitation. He swallowed against the knot of tension in his throat as he glanced toward the jail.

Christ, he couldn't rid his mind of the scene he had witnessed yesterday. It had been a real circus, Sheriff Bond's posse riding back into town carrying an unconscious Harvey Dale. Ross riding amid an army of guards, his face smeared with blood. And Charles Carter, a mirror image of Ross except for the cuts on Ross's face, riding close beside the beautiful, expressionless Devina Dale.

Jake remembered his panic when he first thought Harvey Dale was dead. He hadn't wanted that. The town would be all for hanging Ross. But now he realized the stupidity of that thought. Being sent back to Yuma would be worse for Ross than hanging.

Damn it all, the town was buzzing. The old story about Ross having caused the death of those miners had been stirred up all over again. Ross was being condemned a second time for a thing he had never done.

Jake's frown tightened. He had gone over everything again and again. There was no way out. He and Ross had the payroll money stashed away and were ready to make a fresh start, but now everything had gone wrong. Jake had more money than he'd ever know what to do with, but he didn't give a damn. Ross was the only family he had, especially now that he'd lost Lai Hua.

Jake's thoughts came to an abrupt halt as a tall, familiar figure emerged from the front door of the jailhouse. Jake gasped, only to realize his mistake a moment later. He stepped into the nearest doorway to avoid being seen as Charles Carter turned down

Toughnut and began walking in the opposite direction. Christ, he'd never get used to seeing Carter with Ross's face.

Waiting until Carter was out of sight, Jake lifted his hat, ran his hand through his perspiration-soaked hair, and replaced it firmly on his brow. He stepped down into the street and walked with slow deliberation toward the jail. Strolling slowly past, he cast an assessing eye toward the sturdy structure. His thoughts ran riot. He had to get Ross out of there. Ross wouldn't stand a chance in this town. It would be back to Yuma for him, as fast as Harvey Dale could manage it, sickbed or not. He knew the desperation Ross was feeling.

He and Ross could have used the help of Mack and Harry, both of whom were reliable and loyal, but those two had left town some time back and could be just about anywhere by now. Without them, Jake stood little chance of getting Ross out of that jail.

He knew, if the situation were reversed, Ross would never leave him to rot in Yuma. He had to do something.

Attempting to shrug off her exhaustion, Devina drew herself from the chair in the corner of her father's room and took a few steps closer to the bed. She watched Dr. Hastings as he finished his examination.

"Your father's condition is stable, Devina, but I can't give you a prognosis just yet. We'll know in a few days whether the paralysis is permanent."

Devina fought the sob she felt rising in her throat as she looked at her father's pale face. The high flush of color had faded, leaving him pale and gray, but the grim reminders of his condition were only too apparent. One side of his handsome face was cruelly twisted, his lips pulled into a grotesque angle, his eyelid similarly affected. His left arm lay useless at his side, and she knew his left leg suffered the same affliction. *Oh, Father, if Mama were here she'd love you no matter the extent of your disability. She'd care for you.*

"Devina. . ."

Her father was mumbling in his sleep, uttering a slurred pronunciation of her name. His eyes flickered open, finally focusing on her face, and his twisted lips parted as he struggled to speak again. Devina leaned toward him, attempting a smile.

"Yes, Father. You're all right and you're at home now. Dr. Hastings says—"

"Where is he?"

Devina shot a short glance toward Dr. Hastings. "He's right here, beside me, Father."

"Morrison . . ."

Devina swallowed tightly. "He's in jail."

"Did he hurt you?"

"No, he didn't hurt me."

"He'll pay."

"Father, please. It doesn't matter."

"He'll pay, I'll make him pay."

"Father, you mustn't excite yourself."

Glancing toward Dr. Hastings for support as her father's agitation increased, Devina felt her father's hand close over hers and tighten almost to the point of pain.

"Harvey, calm yourself," the doctor said. "You're not doing yourself any good. Devina's here, and she's going to stay here. Morrison's in jail, and that's where he's going to stay, too. All you have to do now is rest and allow your body to heal. You're a strong man, with excellent recuperative powers."

But Harvey continued rambling. "He took my daughter . . . all I have . . . He'll pay . . ."

Conflicting emotions assailing her, Devina searched her father's face. The threat he mumbled in his weak, slurred voice was not negated by his present physical state. A sharp stab of fear pierced her, even as she squeezed his hand in return, her voice a low whisper.

"Rest, Father. I'm here."

"So it's true." Devina gave a short, mirthless laugh and raised her shoulders in a gesture of helplessness. "I knew it. I just knew."

Covering the few steps between them, Charles curved his arm around Devina's shoulders and slowly drew her to the settee at the side of her father's study. He sat beside her and took her hand.

"Ross told me, but I didn't really want to believe him," Devina continued in a low, dead tone. "I didn't want to believe my father could have taken advantage of anyone in the way he took advantage of your father."

Charles hesitated. "It still feels strange when anyone refers to Brad Morrison as my father. I suppose a part of me still doesn't accept it. Wilson Carter was the only father I ever knew, and I loved him. I didn't find out the truth until just before Mother died. I never received any of Brad Morrison's letters. Mother confessed she destroyed them. She said she never got over her guilt for leaving Ross, and she was certain if she told me the truth, I'd hate her. She said that in the end she had only compounded her guilt by hiding the truth from me, and she wanted me to know the truth before she died. I suppose at first I was too shocked to react. I followed through with the burial, waited until the legal aspects of her death were cleared up. When I found myself clear of all those problems, I decided to look for Ross and Brad Morrison.''

Charles shrugged his broad shoulders. ''I put detectives on it. They finally located Ross and Brad Morrison for me, so I started out for Tombstone. I don't have to tell you, the timing of my arrival was damned poor. When I got here the town was up in arms against Ross and my father, and your father was regarded as the victim. I don't know why I reached the wrong conclusions and decided to take your father's word over Ross's. When I look back on it now, I can't imagine how I didn't see through your father.''

Charles shrugged again. ''I suppose I considered the files your father allowed me to read, the paperwork he had altered concerning his purchase of Brad Morrison's mine as conclusive evidence. And then there was Ross. He was so damned angry. He resented me for never having acknowledged my real father. He didn't want my interference and he offered no explanations. I suppose I reacted with similiar resentment. In any case, I didn't lead the sheriff to Ross, as he thought, not purposely. I was just too damned stupid to know I was being followed when I went to meet with Ross the second time. When the sheriff showed up, Ross was certain I had betrayed him. I don't suppose I can blame him for jumping to that conclusion. When I look back now, I can see that I was pretty damned pompous and insulted by his accusation. And I felt it was best that he was finally safe in jail, Devina. The town was out to get him. If the rabble in the town had gotten hold of him, he'd have been lynched.

''It all went from bad to worse after that. Ross was convicted and Brad Morrison died without Ross being able to see him to say his last good-byes. He said he'd never forgive me for that, and I don't expect I can blame him. But when it was all over and Ross was taken to Yuma, I couldn't make myself leave Tombstone. The whole thing nagged at the back of my mind. Somehow I felt I had to see it through. I deliberately cultivated your father's acquaintance, I suppose so I could prove to myself I had done the right thing. He didn't let me get too close, but he seemed to approve of me in a way he never approved of Ross. So I stayed on.''

Charles gave a short laugh. "It's amazing what a short memory a town has. Ross was written off within a year, and I was accepted into the community. Your father lent me his support while still keeping me at a distance. I suppose he figured he had an ally in me, or maybe he figured he had taken me in too completely for me ever to be a danger to him. As for Ross, I attempted to visit him a few times, but he wouldn't see me. I kept track of him, though. He had vowed to get revenge on Harvey Dale, and I think I always believed he would. When he was released after serving three years of his sentence, I figured he would return to Tombstone, and I would be able to talk him out of doing anything he'd be sorry for. I thought maybe we could be friends. But he never showed up. And then the robberies began.''

Charles took a deep breath. "I suspected from the beginning that Ross was behind the robberies. No one in Tombstone was aware that Ross had been released, so his name never came up. When you arrived in Tombstone after the stagecoach robbery and had that violent reaction the first time you saw me, you just about confirmed my suspicions.''

He paused and shot Devina a short smile. "I'm ashamed to say this, but I decided to use you, Devina, as an excuse to get closer to Harvey. I wanted to be in a position to help Ross. You know how things worked out. I inadvertently gave Ross just the opportunity he was looking for, and when you gave that party, he took my place. It was only afterward, when Harvey was forced to open his files to me, according to the demands of the ransom, that I found out how rich my father's claim really was and discovered how Harvey had duped Brad Morrison.

Devina rose to her feet. "I have to see him, Charles.''

Charles stood beside her, his expression concerned. "He doesn't want to see you, Devina. He said—''

"I don't care what he said, I'm going.''

"I'll go with you.''

Devina shook her head. "No, Charles, please. That would be a mistake. Ross thinks . . . Well, it doesn't matter what he thinks, I want to see him alone. Maybe I can convince him at least to accept your lawyer.''

"And if he won't talk to you?''

"He will, Charles. I'll make him talk to me.''

• • •

"I don't care what he says, I want to see him."

"I'm sorry, Miss Dale, Morrison don't want me to let you in. I'm thinkin' that's the way it should be. This ain't no place for a lady like you. And if you're wantin' to rail at him for doin' what he did to you and your father, then the place to do that is in court. He'll be comin' up on trial real soon. This town ain't goin' to stand for a fella like him stayin' in this jail for any more time than he has to. The place for him is Yuma Prison."

A knot tightened in Devina's throat. No, Ross couldn't go back there.

"I want to see Ross Morrison, Sheriff."

"I'm tellin' you, Miss Dale—"

"And I'm telling you, Sheriff . . ." Her voice regaining its old imperiousness, Devina raised her chin and stared directly into Chester Bond's eyes. "You are closely acquainted with my father, aren't you?"

"Closely acquainted, ma'am?"

"My father told me you were 'in his pocket.' "

Sheriff Bond flushed hotly. "Well, I don't know nothin' about that."

Devina gave a short laugh. "Perhaps I misunderstood him, but he seemed certain you would help me, that you'd go out of your way to do so, as a matter of fact."

"Just when did he say that, ma'am?"

"Just before I left the house. He's very much better, you know. As a matter of fact, Dr. Hastings thinks he'll be on his feet in a few days, and probably back to the office within a week or two."

Sheriff Bond frowned. "Is that so?"

"Yes, that's so. And he'll be very disappointed if I return to tell him that you've refused to allow me to see Mr. Morrison."

"I guess you're right, ma'am."

Devina saw victory in sight. "So, if you'll let me in . . . I'm in a bit of a hurry. Father is expecting me home in time for dinner."

Sheriff Bond hesitated a moment longer. "All right, ma'am."

Anxiety flickered through her as Devina stepped through the office door into the barred area behind. She approached the tall, dark-haired man in the last cell slowly. The coldness in his eyes chilled her.

"All right, Miss Dale. Five minutes, that's all."

Devina turned with an abrupt snap. "Let me into the cell, Sheriff."

Sheriff Bond's narrow, mustached face registered surprise. "Ma'am, that wouldn't be too smart. This here is a dangerous man."

"Not as dangerous as he was during the time I spent in the cabin as his prisoner, Sheriff. I wish to have Mr. Morrison see that I have no fear whatever of him."

"Just the same, ma'am, I'm thinkin'—"

"I'm not really interested in what you're thinking, Sheriff." Devina could feel the heat rising to her cheeks. She had no intention of talking to Ross with iron bars separating them. "Open the door, please. I have no objection to your locking me in for those five minutes you spoke of."

"Ma'am—"

"I'm in a hurry, Sheriff."

Stepping forward with an annoyed twist of his lips, Sheriff Bond directed a muttered statement to Ross as he inserted the key into the lock. "I'm beginnin' to wonder just who we rescued from who yesterday."

But Devina was not amused. She held Ross's intense gaze as she walked past the irritated sheriff and into the cell. The door closed behind her. She heard the key again grate in the lock. Sheriff Bond was making a fast retreat when Ross spoke for the first time.

"Well, I see the old Devina Dale has returned." Ross's voice was filled with contempt. "I would've recognized her anywhere."

His scorn cutting her deeply, Devina suddenly realized that the act she had just put on for Sheriff Bond's benefit was the sham she had lived most of her life. The realization was another rude awakening. "I suppose you would, Ross, although that person is a stranger to me now."

Ross's brows rose in mock surprise. "Really, Devina? Did our interlude affect you so deeply?"

Devina dropped her eyes momentarily, her gaze touching on the odd manner in which his arm hung at his side. Her eyes went back to his. "What's wrong with your arm?"

Ross gave a low snort. "You have a short memory."

Devina's face whitened. "I didn't realize . . . You were going to fight all those men. You would've been killed, and . . ."

"You were trying to save me, is that it? Or were you afraid that maybe Charles Carter or your father might be hurt if there was shooting?" When she shook her head in denial, Ross made a low sound of disgust. "What's the matter, Devina, isn't it enough satisfaction for you to see me here in jail, where I belong? Isn't it enough for you to know that a Dale came out on top again, that my threats and my plans amounted to nothing? What else do you want? Do you want me to tell you I meant all those things I said to you about making you forget Carter, about not giving you up? Well, I don't have much choice about it. You saw to that. That swipe with the poker came out of the blue, you know that? I wasn't expecting it or anything like it from you, not for a minute. I was so sure . . ." Ross paused, his eyes moving hotly over her face. A smile flicked across his lips. "But do you want to know something else? It wasn't as hard as I thought to face the fact that you took me in. But if you're wondering if you left your mark on me, Devina, I'll tell you, you sure enough did. It's right here on my arm, and it hurts like hell."

Devina was cut by Ross's devastating words, but she was determined not to allow him to know their full impact. "Is your arm broken?"

"You didn't do that good a job."

Devina was stunned to note that his eyes were filled with hate. Had she truly seen love reflected there? She supposed there was finally truth between them now, a truth unclouded by the heated emotions raised when they came together. But that truth wasn't complete. She hadn't told Ross that she still wanted him more than she had ever wanted any man.

She saw that Ross was waiting for her to make the next move, but she couldn't tell him any of those things. He didn't want to hear them, and she would not be able to stand it if he laughed.

"About Charles . . ."

Ross's eyes went cold. "I don't want to hear about Carter."

"He regrets everything that happened."

"I told you—"

"There's nothing between Charles and me, Ross."

Ross's chest was heaving with a new agitation. "You forget, I was there when you ran out of that shack and into his arms. I saw the relief on his face, the way he held you. Did you bother to tell Carter there's nothing between you? It might come as a shock to him." Ross laughed coldly. "Maybe when you marry Carter I'll be getting an even sweeter revenge than I ever expected."

"Ross, I—"

"Save it! I've heard enough."

Devina moved closer to him. Ross was hurting, aching in more ways than the physical, and she wanted desperately to soothe his pain. She wanted him to know that she knew everything he had told her about her father was true and that she was sorry.

Ross's breathing was ragged, his voice low and grating. "What else do you want, damn you? Haven't you had enough?

Why don't you leave?'' Grasping her arm, he rasped heatedly.
"Is this what you're waiting for?"

Unexpectedly, Ross pulled her tight against him, his mouth
crushing hers. He kissed her heatedly, viciously, his mouth
grinding into hers, his lips forcing hers apart. His tongue conquered her mouth, but there was no joy, no love in the familiar
intimacy. Tears were hot beneath her eyelids, but she forced them
back. She would not cry. She had revealed enough of herself.
She would not take that final step to humiliation.

Abruptly she was free, thrust back from Ross with contempt.

"Now you've had all you can get from me, Devina. Time to
go home. You said you were in a rush, didn't you?"

Ross raised his head, focusing his concentration on the outer
door. "Sheriff, the lady's five minutes are up!"

Booted feet were approaching the cell when Devina turned
away from Ross's unsmiling face. Her back to him, she waited
stiffly as the sheriff unlocked the cell door, then left without
speaking. She had walked through the office and outside before
the finality of Ross's words touched her. She had never thought
it would end this way.

Devina hurried toward Fourth Street, attempting to avoid the
gaze of a man approaching from the opposite direction. Her eyes
glanced off his face, returning a moment later with startled
recognition. The fair-skinned fellow stopped, his pale eyes holding hers, the freckles on his cheeks standing out darkly as his
face drained of color. She remembered those pale eyes moving
between Ross and herself in the prospector's shack, the discomfort they evidenced at Ross's harsh treatment of her. She remembered Ross's annoyance at the soft words this man had spoken in
her behalf. She remembered being startled by the concern and
affection Ross showed for him, an affection that was openly
returned.

Devina raised her chin. With slow deliberation she turned
away from the pale eyes and resumed her step. The breathless
silence over, she left the man standing, still unmoving, behind
her.

CHAPTER XXII

DEVINA RAISED HER hand to her hair in an effort to tuck a stubborn curl back into place, but her trembling fingers would not cooperate. Lord, how would she get through this morning? Her eyes touched on the small, concerned face peeking over her shoulder into the mirror. "Don't worry, Lai Hua. I'm all right. Please hand me my hat."

A month had passed since she had been rescued, and Devina was aware that Lai Hua considered the part she had unwittingly played in the abduction a blemish on her personal honor. Devina's reassurances had done little good. She supposed that scar would have to heal in its own way.

Devina accepted the hat from Lai Hua. It was a concoction of white lace, silk violets, and jeweled butterflies, a ridiculous confection she had purchased for an extravagant sum just before leaving New York. She remembered she had commented that it was the perfect accessory for the pale orchid gown she now wore, that the violets matched perfectly the embroidered flowers that adorned the bodice and short sleeves of the garment, that the lace was almost an exact duplicate of the trim that bordered the rather deep neckline and edged the neatly tucked waistline.

Devina placed the hat on her head. Hat. The former Devina Dale would not have deigned to refer to this extravagant headpiece as a hat. It would have been her *chapeau*. But it was just a hat to her now, and the stylish ensemble she wore was merely a way to disguise the anxiety that made her tremble.

A certain light-headedness and weakness assailed her. For a moment she doubted she would have the courage to walk to the courthouse and listen to the judge pronounce sentence on Ross.

Guilty. Ross had been found guilty of all charges against him, including armed robbery and kidnapping.

She supposed it made little difference that Ross had refused Charles's offers of help. The lawyer who had defended him had been adequate. Ross was, after all, guilty. He had not denied the charges.

Ross had appeared to be unaffected by the fact that she had been called to testify against him. She had not been able to ignore the summons. His expression had been hard, cold, when she had testified to the specifics of the kidnapping, and she thought she had read contempt in his eyes as she had carefully avoided any other comments as to the time they had spent together. She had held her head high, allowing the spectators to draw their own conclusions. She cared little what anyone said or thought.

She had leaned heavily on Charles for support for the duration of the trial, even knowing Ross read an entirely different meaning into the concern Charles showed for her. But she had had little choice, other than to stand alone in that courtroom, when she was uncertain that she could stand at all.

Her father had not been able to be there in body, but he had been in that courtroom in spirit. Devina took another deep breath, anger strengthening her. Harvey Dale was regaining his health steadily. His speech was improving, he was able to walk with support, and it appeared he would regain full use of his arm. Devina frowned. Dr. Hastings was uncertain if her father's face would ever completely return to normal. She hoped it would, for his sake. She knew how vain he was.

Devina did not wish her father ill, but her heart was frozen against him. Had it not been for his greed, Ross would not now be awaiting sentencing for crimes he was forced to commit for the sake of justice. It might have been so different between Ross and her.

Standing abruptly, she cast a last appraising glance in the mirror. She did not see the exquisite face framed with a wealth of shimmering silver-blond hair, the fragile features accented by the pale, perfect skin, the light shadows under her great silver-blue eyes, or the womanly proportions of her slender frame, fitted to perfection by the pale orchid gown. Instead, she saw the futility of wishing for something that was gone. She needed to go now, to face the reality of Ross's future.

With a determined step, Devina walked toward the door, smiling as Lai Hua opened it for her. She touched her maid's arm with affection, saw the tears in her eyes. She had not needed to explain her feelings for Ross to either Charles or Lai Hua. Close as they were to her, she had communicated the depth of those emotions without words, and she had seen acceptance there. They were friends. But friendship could not fill the void left by love unrequited.

Devina walked into the hall and started down the staircase, her eyes darting to the front door as Molly opened it in response to a summons. Charles's sober eyes moved immediately in her direction as he stepped over the threshold. He waited solemnly at the foot of the staircase, offering her his arm when she reached the last step. She saw him frown when he noted the trembling she could not seem to control.

She attempted a smile, only to feel it fade at the sound of her father's voice from his bedroom. He was calling her. Devina quietly asked Lai Hua to respond; she could not face her father this morning. Perhaps later.

Turning with an unsteady step, Devina walked toward the doorway. She was grateful for Charles's arm, for the strength of his presence.

Jake waited nervously in the brilliant morning sun, beads of perspiration forming on his fair brow. He stepped into a shadowed doorway and darted a quick glance up Third Street, noting that the curious were beginning to move in a steady stream toward the courthouse across the street. In a few minutes Devina Dale would walk down that street on the arm of Charles Carter, and Jake intended to avoid being seen by either one of them, as he had since the beginning of Ross's trial.

With a sense of incredulity which would not fade, Jake remembered the startling moment he had come face to face with Devina Dale outside the jailhouse. He remembered her shock at the moment of recognition, and he remembered his own when she turned with great deliberation and continued on her way. He had gone over that moment many times in his mind. The manner in which Devina Dale had withheld condemnation of Ross in her testimony, carefully stating only the facts of her kidnapping, had confirmed his suspicions. He had seen the emotion that moved between Ross and Devina Dale. It appeared that emotion had not been confined to anger.

From the back of the courtroom, Jake had glimpsed Ross's face the first day of his trial as his eyes had momentarily strayed toward Devina. Confirmation had been complete, and Jake had shared his friend's pain. He knew from personal experience that it was bad enough when the woman you loved was no longer available to you, but to see your own damned brother taking your place at her side . . .

Jake slipped farther back into the doorway. Devina Dale and Charles Carter were approaching. Recognition by Carter, or a sudden change of mind on the part of Devina Dale, would send the sheriff chasing after him, and Jake could not take that chance. He was Ross's last hope for freedom.

He pulled his hat down farther on his brow. The announcement made today would be crucial. After sentencing the judge would send Ross back to Yuma and provide the only opportunity Jake would ever have of breaking Ross free. They were sure to send a full contingent of guards to escort Ross to Yuma; Harvey Dale would provide the financing from his sickbed, just as he had managed to guide the direction of the trial. Jake wasn't a fool. He knew he didn't stand much chance of freeing Ross, but he also knew he had to take that opportunity or he would never be able to live with himself.

Jake watched Devina and Charles Carter disappear inside the courthouse. All was clear. He walked cautiously forward.

Ross rose to his feet with slow deliberation, aware of the breathless expectation of the spectators crowding the courtroom behind him. He flexed the muscles in his shoulders and gritted his teeth against the fury that burned through him as he awaited sentencing. His heated gaze was fixed on the overweight, perspiring judge who leafed through the papers in front of him.

Ross restrained the urge to glance behind him toward the handsome couple seated in the third row, the seats they had occupied since the beginning of the trial. One glimpse of Devina as she had entered the room had verified that she was still the most beautiful woman he had ever seen. An air of delicacy was now more a part of that beauty than he remembered, but the effect was an almost ethereal aura, a fragility that, despite his best efforts, stirred a familiar tenderness within him. His beautiful tarnished angel . . .

But in that one glimpse, he had also seen Carter's proprietary hand on her arm and the concerned gaze he turned in her direction at her whispered word.

Would the pain never stop? Ross wondered. Would he never stop wanting her?

"Ross Morrison . . ."

Ross's attention swung back to the sweating judge and the distaste obvious in the man's bloodshot eyes as he looked full into the defendant's face.

"You have been found guilty on all counts of the charges leveled against you. The sentence I am about to impose was not influenced by your previous record but by the severity of these crimes. It reflects my certainty that you were prevented from fulfilling the true, horrific potential of your crimes only by the diligence and unceasing efforts of Harvey Dale and Sheriff Chester Bond."

Devina's protest sounded behind Ross, but the perspiring judge ignored her as he adjusted his spectacles and continued with deepening severity.

"I think it is important for me to set a precedent at this time, to impress upon you and all criminals of your like, as well as on the spectators present, that the men of this territory value the welfare of their women and will not suffer their exploitation for criminal intent. And so it is with a true desire for justice that I sentence you, Ross Morrison, to serve twenty years in Yuma Prison, your sentence to commence not later than two weeks from this date."

Twenty years! The shock of the judge's pronouncement reverberated within Ross's mind, even as another low, shocked gasp echoed in the courtroom behind him. The judge pulled himself laboriously to his feet and, without another glance in his direction, turned away. A rough hand took Ross's arm in an effort to push him toward the side exit, but he shrugged it off with a brief warning sneer. At a flurry of movement behind him, Ross turned toward the distressed woman in the third row and to the image of himself who sat beside her, whispering to her as he stroked her hand.

The forceful grip clamped on his arm once more, pushing him

abruptly into motion, and Ross snapped his eyes forward. He continued toward the side exit. His mind was suddenly cold as ice, conviction firm within him. It made no difference the length of the sentence imposed. He would not serve it. He had decided long ago that he would never go back to Yuma. He was surer of that than he had ever been of anything.

"Tell him I can't come to him now. Tell him I don't want to see him."

Devina sank back against her pillow and pressed a hand to her forehead. She swallowed against the desolation that still assailed her, the raging despair that held her in its throes. She turned away from Lai Hua's concerned expression.

The last person in the world she wanted to see was her father. Right now even the threat of a relapse would not be sufficient to make her hold her tongue in his presence. She could not face him, knowing full well that he was the true criminal, knowing that because of him, Ross would spend twenty years in a place where each day was a lifetime.

The thought was more than she could bear, and Devina rolled to her side in an attempt to hide her tears. But her maid was soon beside her. Realizing the sincerity of Lai Hau's concern, Devina took her small hand.

"Go, please. Tell my father I can't come to him now. He knows about the sentence. Sheriff Bond reported to him while Charles was here. Tell him I'm not well, tell him anything you want. Damn him! I can't go in there and see the victory in his eyes."

Lai Hua left the room, and Devina closed her eyes in silent exhaustion and took a deep, steadying breath. The memory of the look in Ross's dark eyes as he had turned to her returned again, harsh, almost too painful to bear.

Ross . . . Ross . . . Why had she never told him she loved him? Why had she waited, hoping to hear those words from his lips? How very little it meant to her now, the uncertainty about his feelings for her. She would willingly endure it all again if she could only be in his arms once more.

Tears coursed down her cheeks in steady streams, which Devina brushed away with an impatient hand. This was all her father's fault . . .

"You're a Dale, Devina . . . a true Dale . . ."

Ross had meant those words as an accusation. She had seen that same accusation in his friend Jake's eyes when she glimpsed him outside the courthouse after Ross's sentencing.

Devina went suddenly still. Maybe Ross had been right. Maybe she *was* a true Dale. If so, why was she lying here lamenting Ross's fate? Perhaps only a Dale could fight a Dale . . .

Suddenly incensed by her own passive acceptance of the travesty of justice being practiced against Ross, Devina sat up straight as myriad thoughts assailed her mind. The sheriff would shortly be transporting Ross to Yuma. She could be no use to him then. If she was to do something it would have to be soon.

Devina's mind began working with a new clarity. She drew herself to her feet. Why had she not thought of this before? Why had she waited so long? If only it was not too late . . .

She turned as the door opened, and addressed her servant and friend with new determination, "Lai Hua, I need your help . . ."

The brilliant sun of midday shone on Lai Hua's uncovered head, as she slowed her step to cast a quick, furtive glance around her. Satisfied that her presence stimulated no curiosity on the well-traveled street, she turned down the familiar alleyway. Her rapid step took her to the foot of a staircase she had climbed once before, and she flung open the heavy door. Moving quickly down the dimly lit hallway, Lai Hua approached the numbered door and raised a trembling hand to knock on it softly.

The response was muffled, cautious. "Who is it?"

"It is I, Mr. Jake."

The door opened, and Lai Hua looked up into Jake's well-loved face. His voice was tense. "What are you doin' here?"

"I have come with a message."

"What message?"

Lai Hua bowed her head politely. "If I might enter . . ."

Jake backed up to allow her entrance, then closed the door behind her, his lips forming a tight line as he regarded her suspiciously, a brief flicker of emotion moving across his features.

"No more games, Lai Hua. I'm not up to them. You can consider that you've salved your honor. If I made you betray your friend, you've also seen to it that I've failed mine."

Unable to bear more, Lai Hua raised her guileless eyes to his. "I do not come here to cause you suffering, Mr. Jake. In truth, I share your torment, and would not cause you more of the same. But it is not only I who share your fear for your friend. Another, one who would help, suffers as well.''

"Another?" Jake shook his head. "What are you talkin' about?"

"I ask that you speak to this friend."

"Speak to him?" Jake gave a short laugh. "Who is this person? Why should I believe a word you say?"

Lai Hua lowered her eyes to shield her wretchedness. Her voice emerged in a low, shaken whisper. "I ask that you believe, Mr. Jake, because of all we have shared, for the many times you have loved my body and I have loved yours. I ask that you believe because my heart is filled with a love that will not fade despite all my attempts to shake it from my heart. I ask that you believe because I am a woman of honor, honor I have proved to you. I ask that you believe because I would alleviate your pain, and thus alleviate my own."

Lai Hua raised her eyes slowly to his. "I ask that you believe because my heart cries out to yours, Mr. Jake, to soothe the anguish I caused you when last I came here. I come to offer you a chance to help your friend, and thus relieve the burden of guilt you have assumed. I ask you to allow me to do this so we might both be free to remember, without grief, without regret, the times I came to you with love."

Jake's eyes grew moist and Lai Hua felt a similar moist heat gather beneath her own eyelids. She took a step toward him only to see his expression again harden with wariness.

"Who's this friend who wants to help Ross, Lai Hua?"

Lai Hua was suddenly still. "I would take you to this friend."

Suspicion again flickered across Jake's face. "His name?"

Lai Hua bowed her head without response.

A long silence prevailed before Jake's voice snapped Lai Hua's eyes to his once more. "All right."

Reaching out to grasp her shoulder, Jake held her still while his pale eyes assessed the joy that had sprung to life in hers at his assent, but his voice was low with warning. "Lai Hua, so help me, if this is a trick . . ."

"I would give my life before I would betray you, Mr. Jake."

Jake held her gaze for moments longer before his hand slipped from her shoulder. "Let's go."

Elation surging through her, Lai Hua turned without another

word. Leaving the room, she hurried down the hallway to the back entrance, Jake's footsteps sounding close behind her.

Charles turned from his desk at the sound of a knock at his office door. At his response, the door opened to reveal a familiar form hesitating on the threshold. Leaping to his feet, Charles strode forward and extended his hand. "Camille!"

Camille's warm, full lips moved into a smile. "Yes, it is I, Charles. I have come for a brief visit. I will not take much of your time."

Taking her hand, Charles drew her inside, swallowing against the formality of her greeting. This was the same Camille, beautiful, warm to the touch, but she was also a new Camille, reserved, subdued. He was well aware that during the past month, since her plans to return to France had been announced, her former duties at Blond Marie's had ceased. He was uncertain of the reason for the change, except that she had been seen constantly in the company of the Count. He had ceased his painful conjecture on the significance of that coincidence. All he knew was that he ached to hold her in his arms, to remember with fondness the old Camille, to experience the new.

When he tried to draw her closer, he suddenly felt the soft palm of her hand press against his chest.

Camille shook her head. "That would be lovely, Charles, but it would be unwise. Instead, I wish to express my unhappiness at the sentence pronounced upon Ross Morrison this morning. I could not allow this day to pass without speaking to you of my feelings, without letting you know that I remember well the grief you suffered at the estrangement between your brother and yourself. Circumstances have worsened, and I wish you to know that my heart is heavy with the unhappiness you have experienced this day. I also wish you to know that were it possible, I would change all this for you. I would have you realize the happiness of reconciliation with your brother, so that I might leave Tombstone knowing you are content."

Charles stiffened. "When are you leaving?"

"Pierre and I leave to return to France tomorrow morning."

"Tomorrow."

Camille's face was sober. "So, *mon cher*, I come to say a final good-bye. I could not leave without that small courtesy."

Charles felt the pain dig deeper into his heart.

"Let us make our good-bye short and sweet," Camille said, "a memory to cherish." Sliding her arms around his neck, Camille raised her mouth to his.

Charles savored the warmth in her glowing eyes, her breathlessness, drew from deep within him all the love and emotion stored in the long weeks of their separation. Closing his eyes as her lips touched his, he folded her lush warmth against him, losing himself in her beauty, in her glow, crushing her closer, closer still.

His mouth grew more possessive, responding to his need, but Camille withdrew from his embrace, separating herself from him. Her gaze was suspiciously bright as she gave a low, husky laugh. "It would be so easy, would it not, Charles? It is sad that it was not meant to be." Camille took a step backward. "But I would have you know before I go that my heart is with you, Charles. It will always be with you. *Au revoir, mon ami.*"

Unable to speak, Charles watched as Camille turned and slipped through the doorway, closing it behind her, as her bright head moved past the office windows. He released a low, shuddering breath as she disappeared from sight.

At the sound of a step behind him, Charles turned abruptly. "Devina, I'm sorry, I had forgotten you were in the other room."

"So it was true what Father said."

Charles paused. "If he said that I was seeing Camille, that it was more than a casual involvement for me, yes, it was true. But it didn't work out, Devina." He shrugged. "My loss, and a damned hard one."

"I'm sorry."

"No sorrier than I am."

At another rap at the door, Charles grew cautious. He waited until Devina had slipped back into the other room before responding. "Come in."

The door opened to reveal Lai Hua's diminutive form, and Charles released a short, tense breath as a familiar, youthful-looking fellow suddenly appeared behind her. "Come in, Jake. We've been waiting for you."

Advancing with caution, Jake closed the door behind him and scanned the room warily. He looked back at Charles. "We?"

"Yes, we," Devina answered from behind him.

At the soft, unexpected reply, Jake whirled around, then took an instinctive step backward. "I'm not so sure I like this."

Charles trained his gaze intently on Ross's friend. The man was little more than a stranger to him. How could he convince him that Devina and he wanted to help Ross? His gaze slipped to Lai Hua. He noted the manner in which her eyes assessed Jake's uneasiness. He saw her place her hand on his arm as she raised her soft voice into the unsettled silence.

"Miss Devina asked that I bring you here, Mr. Jake. She is the friend of whom I spoke. Dr. Carter also wishes to help."

Jake jerked his head in Charles's direction. "Ross doesn't want his help."

Charles stiffened at Jake's comment, but he restrained his instinctive anger, realizing his brother's friend had a perfect right to be suspicious. "I was a damned fool three years ago, and I haven't done a very good job of handling things intelligently with my brother since that time, either. I know I played a part in getting Ross into his present situation, but it's too late to lament my past mistakes. There's only one thing I can do to help Ross now, and I intend to do it with or without your help."

Jake turned toward Devina, his brow furrowing into a deep frown. He studied her expression openly as he spoke. "You're tryin' to tell me you're Ross's friend, is that right, Miss Dale? You didn't look much like his friend back there in the cabin, and you didn't much look like his friend when you stood up and testified against him in court."

"I didn't have any choice in court."

"And I'm thinkin' those weren't friendly glances Ross was sendin' you across that courtroom."

"I have no doubt Ross despises me. He believes he has good reason for his feelings. But those feelings are not returned in kind."

Jake studied Devina Dale's pale face. "You're tellin' me you want to help Ross—the man who kidnapped you and held you prisoner?" Jake shook his head. "What are you plannin', lady? I saw the way Ross treated you at that cabin, and I saw the hatred in your eyes."

"Do you see hatred in my eyes now?"

Jake paused, his eyes surveying her face once more. He gave a short laugh. "If you're anythin' like your pa, you're real good at actin'."

"Well, I'm not like my father . . . Not anymore, at any rate. And I know the truth now, Jake. I know my father cheated Brad

Morrison, and I know he was responsible for getting Ross convicted for the accident at the mine. Ross told me that, but I wasn't sure what to believe. Charles confirmed everything Ross said.''

Jake turned a short, knowing glance toward Charles. ''Yeah, Ross's honest, respectable brother.''

Devina, her anxiety obvious, reached out and gripped Jake's arm. ''We haven't much time. I can't spend any more of it convincing you that Charles and I want to help Ross. If you'll stop and think, you'll realize we have nothing to gain by bringing you here like this, except to help Ross. I'll ask you now, for the last time: Will you help us?''

Jake hesitated, and Charles felt the strength of his resistance. Damn, the fool was going to refuse. He would force them to go it alone and risk failure.

Lai Hua unexpectedly touched Jake's arm, and Jake turned toward her. She spoke softly into the tense silence of the room. ''Mr. Jake, we have been less than allies of Mr. Morrison in the past. Your suspicion is well founded. You are right to doubt and right to be cautious in protecting your friend's last chance for freedom. You also mistrust me, and the pain of that knowledge lies deep within my heart. But in the memory of all that has gone before between us, I ask that you trust those present now. I ask this of you with great humility and with the love I bear in my heart for you.''

Lai Hua's small face flushed with embarrassment at her outspoken words. She stepped back, allowing the silence to grow as Jake studied her bowed head.

Tension beginning to prickle along his spine, Charles restrained his anxiety. He glanced toward Devina's expectant face. She was pale and trembling. She could not take much more of this.

Jake's expression hardened, and he raised his chin, his decision obviously made. ''All right, tell me what you have in mind.''

Devina shot Charles a brief glance, the smile that lit her face leaving no doubt as to her reaction to Jake's response. Her first words were from the heart. ''Thank you for trusting us, Jake.'' She took another deep breath before continuing. ''Jake, I have a plan . . .''

                              *   *   *

Harvey Dale struggled to pull himself upright in the soft, overstuffed chair in his bedroom. A flash of pure fury suffused him as his stiff leg and dangling arm refused to aid his effort. He tried again, cursing his debility, cursing the man who had pushed him to this pitiful state, cursing the fates that had put Harvey Dale, always the master, in a position of dependence.

He gave a low snort. But if he suffered, he would see to it that he returned that suffering measure for measure. Today he had taken the first step in that retribution.

Harvey sought to control his elation. Ross Morrison—the low, thieving bastard, the totally worthless human being who had sought to avenge his fool of a father at his expense—would serve twenty years for the attempt. He would make certain that Morrison reached Yuma safely and on time. He had already arranged with Sheriff Bond to hire six guards. He cared little for the expense. Morrison would soon be firmly ensconced in his cell, and Harvey would make sure the bastard stayed there for the full term of his sentence, if he had to use every bit of political pressure he could exert.

He took a deep breath and attempted to rein in his rioting emotions. Devina was home with him, where she belonged, but he felt a measure of discomfort about her state of mind. She had not behaved normally toward him since her rescue. He had been startled by the condemnation he had read in her eyes, but he had not inquired as to its cause. He was not yet well enough to face her response. When he was, he would use his powers of persuasion, the charm that had never failed him, to subdue her unvoiced opposition.

And then, when he was on his feet, he would take Devina away from this damned savage frontier. He would take her to San Francisco, introduce her to society. He would see that she met and married a young man who was worthy of her, if indeed such a man could be found. She would have everything she wanted from life, everything he wanted for her. He would see to that, and he would see the warmth again enter her eyes when she looked at him.

Finding great satisfaction in his thoughts, Harvey smiled, but he knew that his once handsome smile was now distorted, grotesque. He raised his good hand to his cheek. The searching fingers found their way to the contorted flesh of his face, and he was repelled. No longer would his smile turn women's heads, except with disgust. Beautiful Lily . . . He had cherished a secret belief that he would be able to coax her back to his bed even though she was free of her obligation to him. But now she would view him with revulsion. Harvey's hatred soared. This, too, Ross Morrison had done to him.

Harvey took a deep breath and attempted to control his growing fury. He could not chance these thoughts. Dr. Hastings had said it would do him harm to upset himself. He must get well.

He struggled for a few moments longer with his helplessness in the overstuffed chair. Finally surrendering, repelled by the sound of his own slurred voice, he shouted, "Molly! Come up here and help me!"

Within a few minutes Molly's lumbering step could be heard on the staircase, and Harvey fought to control his impatience. He responded gruffly to the knock on the door, "Come in! I called you, didn't I?"

Pausing as Molly's oversize form moved through the doorway, he commanded, "Help me. I can't get up."

Responding to his command, Molly approached with a disapproving glance. "You shouldn't get yourself so upset, Mr. Dale. Dr. Hastings said—"

"I know what Dr. Hastings said!" Despising the quaking of his wasted frame as Molly helped him to his feet, Harvey questioned, "Where is Miss Devina? I haven't seen her all day. It's getting dark, and she isn't home yet."

Leading him across the room, Molly helped him to settle on the bed before responding. "She'll be home, Mr. Dale. She'll be home."

Harvey felt a flush of anger at Molly's patronizing tone. A telltale twitching began in his cheek. "All right, you've done what you've had to do, now get out!"

Ignoring Molly's tight glance, Harvey turned his eyes from the sight of her broad proportions as she ambled through the doorway. He heaved a deep sigh as she closed the door behind him. He was better off alone.

Damn, when was Devina going to get home?

Sheriff Bond looked at the covered tray delivered for his prisoner's supper. He inhaled the savory aroma and slanted a brief glance toward the tiny Oriental woman who turned to leave after depositing the tray on the desk. Frowning, he reached out and grasped her arm. His thick gray mustache twitched as she dropped her head in the traditional bow of subservience. Damn these Chinese! Didn't they ever look a man in the eye?

He addressed her with a narrowed gaze. "I ain't never seen you before. You new at Hagarty's Kitchen?"

The woman bobbed her head in response. "Yes, I am to take Lum Chow's place until he is again well enough to return to work."

"Yeah? I got kinda used to seein' him every day since I got this prisoner a month back. What's wrong with him?"

The woman bobbed her head again, and Sheriff Bond's lip twitched with annoyance. No wonder nobody trusted the whole lot of them. It was damned vexing talking to the top of their heads.

"It is an old malady," the woman said. "A stomach distress which prohibits him from working in the restaurant for fear of transmitting his illness."

Chester Bond took a step backward, immediately releasing the woman's thin arm. He cast a suspicious glance toward the tray. Hell, no telling what kind of sickness those foreigners had brought into the country. He'd make note not to eat in Hagarty's for a while. He wasn't anxious to get any of those foreign diseases.

"All right, you can go now. And you can remind Hagarty that I won't be needin' him to send any more meals after breakfast tomorrow. We're goin' to be transportin' the prisoner as soon as it's light enough to travel." Amusement touched the corner of Sheriff Bond's mouth and he gave a short shrug. "Hell, don't want no convicted criminals hangin' around this jail for too long a time. Liable to give this place a bad name!"

Thoroughly enjoying his own joke, Sheriff Bond waited for a reaction that did not come from the silent Oriental. His amusement slowly draining away as he stared at the top of the woman's bowed head, he scowled. Them Chinese didn't have no sense of humor, neither.

"All right, whatever your name is, I said you can go. Just remember to come back to pick up the tray. I don't like havin' dirty dishes hangin' around. Too many rats lookin' for an easy meal. I'm not about to go invitin' them in here."

"Yes, Sheriff Bond."

Watching as the girl turned obediently on her heel and disappeared through the doorway, Sheriff Bond again shook his head. He had wondered why the meal was so late tonight. Hell, it was almost dark. Not that his prisoner would complain. He didn't expect Morrison had much appetite anyway. He sure as hell wouldn't if he'd been sentenced to twenty years in Yuma.

Sheriff Bond took another look at the tray, a wary expression flicking across his face. He didn't expect a man could catch a disease just from touching the tray. He lifted the cloth with the tips of his fingers and peeked underneath in a ritual he had practiced three times a day for the past month. Nothing wrong there. As a matter of fact that stew looked damned good, and he always did like black bread. A cup of coffee, a spoon and fork neatly rolled in a napkin . . . Hagarty served a tempting meal. But sure as hell nothing would make him touch anything on that tray tonight.

Picking up the tray with considerable caution, Chester Bond held it a reasonably safe distance from his body as he kicked open the door to the inner room and walked in. His eyes touched on his tall, morose prisoner, and an unaccustomed sympathy flickered across his mind. It had to be hard being a young fellow and knowing you wouldn't be coming out of that hellhole of a prison until you were old and gray and your life was just about over. His sympathy softened his accustomed bluster as he snatched the keys from the peg near the door.

"All right, Morrison, step back if you want to eat. Yeah, all the way back to the corner, that's right."

Placing the tray carefully on the floor near the door, the sheriff drew his gun before putting the key in the lock. Holding it leveled at Morrison's stomach, he pulled open the door and slowly pushed the tray inside with his foot.

Turning with a small shrug, Bond walked the few steps to the door, hung up the keys, stepped outside, and closed the door behind him.

Looking up as the door opened and Deputy Larry Mills walked in, Bond raised his heavy gray brows. "About time you got here, Mills. I need a break." The thought of a cold beer was particularly appealing. He motioned toward the back room. "He's eatin' now. I'll be back in a half-hour. Think you can handle him while I'm gone?"

Mills's annoyed glance showed he didn't think much of the sheriff's little joke, and Bond's smile turned to a flicker of annoyance. He gave a low snort. It wasn't only the Chinese who didn't have a sense of humor. Bond shrugged again. "Like I said, I'll be back in a little while."

Not waiting for a response, Bond turned on his heel and walked toward the doorway. He was still annoyed as he closed the door behind him and started down the street.

Listening intently to the one-sided conversation that had progressed in the room beyond his cell, Ross heard the sheriff's departure and the squeak of the chair that indicated Mills was seated behind the desk. Satisfied he would have ample warning when Mills arose, Ross unrolled the napkin on his lap and stared at the small block printing that was Jake's distinctive hand.

He read the message for the third time and took a deep breath. The last sentence sounded over and again in his mind: "It's a slim chance, but it's now or never."

Sheriff Bond's step was leisurely as he approached the jailhouse he had left only a half-hour before. He looked up at the star-studded sky. Clear night, but not much moon. That was the main reason he'd walked back by way of Toughnut Street instead of cutting through the back alley as he usually did. He sure as hell didn't like tripping over the garbage that was always left all over the place, and he wasn't too fond of the scratching sounds he heard in the dark corners. Bond shook his head with distaste. Rats weren't his favorite animals. He could do without them.

One more night, and then that trip to Yuma. He was looking forward to it. He and the boys would push right through on the way there. He wasn't going to take any chances with his prisoner, but on the way back he planned to dally a bit. It was Dale's money. Mills would have to take care of things while he was gone. Bond grinned at the thought.

But what was that commotion near the jailhouse? Sheriff Bond strained his eyes in that direction just as two horses came tearing around from the rear of the building. One rider was fighting to bring his horse under control. The rider looked familiar . . . those broad shoulders, that black hair. Christ, it couldn't be!

Starting forward at a run, Bond drew his gun. He aimed it at the departing men just as the tall, dark fellow turned in his direction. Damn, there was no mistaking him! It was Morrison! He was getting away!

"Stop! Stop, Morrison, or I'll shoot!"

But Morrison wasn't listening to him! Bond leveled his gun even as he ran. He had as good a bead on him as he'd ever get. There was no way he could miss.

He fired once, twice. Morrison shook with the impact of the bullet that hit him, and Bond felt a thrill of elation. But, damn, he was righting himself, regaining control of the horse! Then he was bolting off, joining the other fellow, who was waiting for him at the end of the street. Damn, they were getting away!

Racing into the jail, Bond shouted at his deputy who stood looking into the rear room, a shocked expression on his pale face.

"What in hell are you doin' standin' there, you jackass? Get your horse! I'm goin' to get me a posse! We got some heavy work ahead of us tonight."

"Sheriff, I can't understand it! How'd he get out? I was here all the while. Nobody came past me and the cell's still locked!"

"Shut up, you damned fool! I don't care if he walked through them walls! Get to the corral and get them horses. And make it quick!"

Scrambling into motion, Mills headed out the door and Bond paused, his heart pumping.

Christ, there would be hell to pay over this!

Determined not to waste any more time, Bond followed his deputy out the door and headed toward Allen. He'd get him a posse and he'd get Morrison back in jail if it was the last thing he ever did!

From the darkness of the shadowed lot beside the jailhouse, two small figures stood watch as Deputy Mills came running out of the jailhouse, followed by Sheriff Bond. Waiting only until both men had disappeared from sight, the two figures moved closer to the street.

Holding tightly to a bundle she carried in one hand, Devina adjusted the traditional Chinese peasant jacket and trousers she wore and pulled her dark scarf down to cover her light hair. She glanced toward Lai Hua and nodded briefly. Together, Lai Hua and she stepped out into the light and entered the jailhouse.

Racing into the back room as Lai Hua watched the street, Devina snatched the keys from the peg inside the door and ran to Ross's empty cell. "Hurry! Get out of there!"

As she unlocked the door of the cell, Ross crawled out from beneath the low cot in the corner.

"Hurry!" she urged again, her voice husky and anxious. "They could come back any minute."

Ross drew himself to his feet, then froze as Devina's light eyes made contact with his. "What are *you* doing here?"

"We don't have time to discuss that now."

Handing him a baggy jacket and a tattered hat from her bundle, Devina instructed quickly, "Put these on and follow Lai Hua and me. Keep us in sight, but walk slowly. Slouch and weave as if you're drunk. But don't lose sight of us, Ross. Lai Hua's the only one who can get you out of Tombstone safely now."

Waiting only long enough for Ross to put on the jacket and hat, Devina turned toward the outside door. "Lai Hua?"

"All is safe, Miss Devina."

"Good. Let's go, Ross."

In a few quick steps they were out on the street, hurrying toward the shadows of the lot next door and then moving quickly toward the back alley. Grateful there was no time for thought, Devina followed as Lai Hua darted through the darkness. Hastening to keep up, she stumbled over an unseen obstacle. Immediately, strong arms closed around her from behind, steadying her. She felt their remembered warmth, and she swallowed deeply even as her heart raced with a new fervor.

"Are you all right?"

"Yes."

Quickly extracting herself from Ross's grasp, Devina continued on behind Lai Hua. Within moments they were standing at the entrance to the alley. Exchanging a short glance with Lai Hua, Devina turned briefly toward Ross. His dark eyes met hers from beneath the wide brim of his hat. "Remember, Ross, don't let us out of your sight."

Ross's response was immediate. "There's not much chance of that."

Ignoring her uncertainty at the odd tenor of his voice, Devina nodded to Lai Hua. "Let's go."

With short, quick steps, the two women stepped out of the alley and into the street.

Jake drew his horse up to a sliding halt in the darkness. The clatter of hoofbeats to his rear also drew to a halt. He dismounted quickly, darting a glance at the tall man who awkwardly followed suit, and then back toward the winding route they had taken around the town. He smiled, realizing they were still only a short distance from the bright lights of Allen Street.

The tall man swayed and Jake took a concerned step toward him. "You're hit!"

Charles Carter winced with pain. "A rotten piece of luck."

"How bad is it?"

"It's only a flesh wound." Taking his hand from his shoulder, Charles looked down at his blood-soaked shirt and gave a short laugh. "But I'm going to have a hell of a time dressing it."

Jake wasn't smiling. "Do you think you can make it?"

Charles's face hardened with purpose. "I'll be damned if I'll quit now."

Jake untied a jacket and Stetson from Charles's saddle. Watching as Charles struggled into the well-tailored coat, Jake carefully smoothed the shape of the hat, then placed it squarely on Charles's head. "Are you ready?"

"As ready as I'll ever be."

Jake slapped the rumps of their mounts with a low hoot that sent them cantering off into the darkness. He turned back toward Charles. "Let's go."

With a quick step, the two men turned back toward town.

Devina concentrated on keeping up with Lai Hua's rapid pace. She resisted the urge to check the progress of the unkempt drunk who was swaying along the street behind them. They had passed the intersection of Toughnut and Third and were walking through an unfamiliar section of Hop Town. The area deteriorated rapidly as they walked along the narrow winding streets, and Devina resisted the urge to turn her shocked gaze toward the rows of poor shacks they passed. She had not been aware of the deplorable conditions in which these hardworking people lived.

Lai Hua's step slowed, and without warning, she slipped into a dark alley, her small hand snaking out to draw Devina in behind her.

Breathless, silent, Devina waited in the shadows at Lai Hua's side until they heard a slow, uneven step approaching. Her heart pounding in her ears, Devina forced herself to remain still as the step drew nearer and, with a sudden turn, the tall, unkempt drunk slipped into the alley.

A low, relieved laugh, remarkably similar to a sob, escaped

Devina's lips as Ross's dark eyes met hers. She turned abruptly at Lai Hua's soft touch on her arm. Within moments they were moving again, along the narrow path between the two buildings, heading for a shaft of light at the end of the long corridor.

Lai Hua halted her as they approached an open doorway. The heat of Ross's body was warm against Devina's back as he stopped close behind her. She steeled herself against the appeal of his nearness, against her desire to turn, to lean full into his warmth, to feel his strong, familiar arms close around her. Those longings were remnants of another time, another situation. They had no place here in this dark alley where danger surrounded them.

She watched with heart-stopping fear as Lai Hua stepped into the brightly lit doorway and vanished inside the building for a few breathless seconds before appearing again to signal them to enter behind her. Devina took a tentative step forward, suddenly aware that Ross's arm had slipped around her, that he was sliding into a protective position beside her. As Devina stepped into the light, Ross poised in the doorway beside her, her gasp echoed in the small room.

"Come in, Miss Dale, and close the door."

A tall, exquisite Oriental woman whom Devina remembered well, stepped forward. In a gliding step, the woman covered the distance between them and with a gentle hand urged them into a room and closed the door behind them. She bowed politely, smiling as she looked from Ross to Devina.

"It is with utmost pleasure that I welcome you here this night, Miss Dale, Mr. Morrison. To both my mother and myself your presence is a personal satisfaction without compare."

Devina frowned, confused. She shot a brief glance toward Lai Hua, only to see that her attention was full on the beautiful woman's animated face. She glanced toward Ross, reading concern in his dark eyes. Devina's voice was halting: "I didn't know . . . Lai Hua didn't tell me . . ."

The beautiful woman looked pleased.

"So you remember me, Miss Dale?"

"Of course I remember you. I met you that day in the store during that embarrassing incident with my father." Devina flushed. "And you assisted in the preparations for my party. You arranged the flowers . . ."

"Yes."

Devina shook her head, her confusion growing. A small sound at the corner of the room drew her attention to a smaller, older woman. She remembered that broad smiling face, also.

"Welcome, Miss Dale, Mr. Morrison." Turning her attention toward Ross's silent presence, the woman spoke politely. "We have not met, Mr. Morrison. I am known as China Mary. This is my daughter, Lily." Ross nodded, and Mary continued in a soft voice. "You are tense. It is understandable. You are confused as to why Lai Hua has brought you to me. The answer is simple. It is because I instructed Lai Hua to do so, and because my protection, in this community where my influence is great, is essential to the success of your venture."

China Mary smiled more broadly, her round face creasing into myriad lines as she continued in a soft tone, "You now wonder at the reason for my daughter's and my concern for your safety, our satisfaction in your coming to this place, the obvious pleasure it gives us. The pleasure you see is twice as sweet for the dark feelings that preceded it."

China Mary turned toward Ross, her smile fading. "You are familiar with the desire for justice, are you not, Mr. Morrison? It has burned long and hard in your heart, has driven you to extremes of action you would not have contemplated for any other reason. A similar desire has driven both Lily and myself. I will explain."

Turning to Devina once more, Mary bowed her head. "Miss Dale, it is with difficulty that I cause you the pain of this disclosure, but it is essential to my explanation. You see, my beautiful Lily has long been the unwilling slave to your father's desires."

At Devina's startled gasp, Mary began her explanation.

"Mr. Dale desired my daughter, even though he considers us his inferiors. He used a very strong form of intimidation to force her to submit to his demands. I need not describe to you the depth of my daughter's humiliation."

Devina felt Ross's hand close around her arm in silent support as China Mary addressed him directly.

"The opportunity you provided brought my daughter freedom at last, Mr. Morrison. You see, it was I, through one of my employees, who located the cabin in which you held Miss Dale; and it was I who instructed my employee to lead Mr. Dale to you."

Devina felt the impact of Mary's words register on Ross's frame. "*You* were responsible for Ross's capture?" she cried.

Mary bowed her graying head. "Yes, it was I." She looked from Ross to Devina without shame. "Because, as I have said, Mr. Morrison unknowingly provided the means to free my daughter and myself from Mr. Dale's influence, we owe Mr. Morrison a debt of gratitude far greater than that which we can express." China Mary nodded again, her broad smile returning. "Which brings us to this night, this room, and the victory that Mr. Morrison has made available to us. For where is there a greater victory than to unwillingly provide satisfaction to one who is unworthy; and then, when he is about to savor it, to snatch it away? It is justice, Mr. Morrison, justice."

Devina was trembling. The picture of her father that China Mary had provided was very hard to face. "I am grateful for the aid you will furnish us, Mary. I have no words to express my feelings with regard to my father's actions."

"No words are necessary. Your heart speaks in your actions this night, and we are content to reverse the role we have been forced to play. We are content to win this victory over Mr. Harvey Dale."

Heavy, rapid steps sounded in the alley, and all eyes turned to the doorway. Instinctively, Ross stepped in front of Devina in a protective posture, his hard body tensed.

The door burst open, shattering the apprehensive silence, and Jake stepped into the room. A low gasp escaped Ross's lips as he saw Jake's white face, the blood on his hand and shirt. He was at his friend's side in a few quick steps, but Jake shook his head.

"I'm all right. This isn't my blood." Jake drew Charles Carter into the room. Carter's physical distress was immediately obvious. Ross's alarm was echoed by Devina's low gasp as she rushed to Carter's side, but Ross held himself back from a similar reaction as he assessed Carter's condition from afar.

Devina raised her hand to the dark red stain on the shoulder of Charles's jacket.

Charles made a strong effort to pull himself erect. He sent Devina a comforting glance before turning to Ross with a weak smile. "I guess you were right about me, Ross. Hell, I couldn't even do this right."

Abruptly moving to his brother's aid despite his conflicting emotions, Ross brushed off Devina's ineffective efforts in Charles's behalf. His voice was curt. "You're the doctor, Carter. How bad is your wound?"

"Probably not more than a messy crease. I think the bullet glanced off the bone, but I don't think anything's broken. It's a damned complication we hadn't anticipated, though."

"Charles, are you sure you're all right? What can I do?"

Ross felt a familiar tension tie his stomach into knots. Why did it still hurt to see how he dropped from Devina's thoughts the moment Charles appeared on the scene? Managing to quell the jealousy gnawing at him, Ross turned to China Mary. "We need some cloth, anything, so we can bind up his shoulder. Pressure ought to stop the bleeding."

Jake interrupted with an urgent warning. "There's no time for that now, Ross. Carter's a doctor! He can take care of himself. There're two horses waitin' in the alley, and if we don't get goin' now while that posse's still headin' in the other direction, we aren't goin' to make it."

Ross shot a short glance toward Carter, assessing his pallor. The realization that Carter had put his life in danger to rescue him, that the bullet his brother had taken had been intended for him, registered in his mind. He was reluctant to leave before he could be certain Carter was all right. He frowned as the face so similar to his creased in a wan smile.

"Jake's right. My shoulder has just about stopped bleeding. You don't have to worry about me. I can take care of myself. You'll have to get as far as you can by daylight. Sheriff Bond will soon get tired of riding in the dark. He doesn't have the reputation for being the hardest working lawman in these parts. He'll probably wait for daylight and then attempt to follow your trail. You've got a long night ahead of you, Ross, and you'd better get a head start."

Charles hesitated at Ross's silence. He gave a short shrug, wincing at the pain the effort caused. "Look, Ross, what's done is done. We can't change anything that's happened, or correct the mistakes we've both made. But just to set the record straight, I'm sorry I never got to know you or my father. I hope we can really get to know each other someday."

Ross nodded. Old resentments died hard, but there was no mistaking the effort Carter had made. Hesitating only a moment longer, he extended his hand. "Maybe that day will come."

Charles took his hand, and Ross felt the bond of peace finally seal between his brother and himself.

"Ross, we have to get goin'."

Ross cast another short glance toward Devina. He had the feeling she was deliberately avoiding his gaze. He wanted to see her eyes, to read her reaction to this whole thing. There were so many things he wanted to say to her.

"Dammit, Ross, are you comin' or not?"

Devina lifted her head at last. Her face was pale, but her gaze was direct. "It looks as if this is a time for apologies. I'm sorry, too, Ross. I'm sorry for everything my father did to you and your father, and I'm sorry for the unbreachable separation it's brought us." Walking to Ross's side, Devina raised herself on her toes and pressed her mouth firmly against his. Withdrawing quickly, her eyes suspiciously bright, she stepped back. "The horses are packed with supplies. You shouldn't have any problem getting out of the territory if you leave now."

Ross took a deep, shaken breath. He didn't want it to end this way.

Jake had walked to the door, was glancing out into the dark alley. Devina had returned to Carter's side and was clutching his good arm like a drowning woman, her knuckles white. Carter glanced down into Devina's face, and Ross could stand no more. He started for the door.

Within minutes he was following Jake down the alley toward the two nervous animals waiting at the end. He mounted up and turned, startled to see that Carter, Devina, and Lai Hua had followed them. He turned back in time to see Jake's expression as he stared at Lai Hua. He saw the flicker of hesitation in Jake's eyes, the sudden firming of his chin in the moment before Jake urged his horse forward and in a quick movement swept Lai Hua onto the saddle in front of him.

Jake's low, breathless voice carried easily to his ears. "We're leavin', and we won't be comin' back. I love you, Lai Hua. I want to take you with me. Do you want to come?"

A moment's silence and then the single word in response.

"Yes."

Turning his horse, Jake spurred him forward. Hesitating, his eyes moving to the spot where Devina stood, still clutching Carter's arm, Ross felt the desolation of loss overwhelm him. Gritting his teeth tightly shut, he turned and followed Jake's lead. He did not look back.

CHAPTER XXIII

CHANCING A SHORT glance, which she hoped did not betray her disguise, Devina frowned at the unsteady step of the tall man walking a short distance ahead of her. Her eyes again downcast, she followed his progress up Fourth Street with a worried frown. Still wearing the traditional cotton jacket and pants of the Oriental peasant, a scarf covering her fair hair, she had kept to the shadows and remained a respectable distance from Charles since they left Hop Town a few minutes earlier. Their progress had been difficult indeed as the signs of Charles's advancing weakness had grown clearer with each step. Would this night never. end?

Risking another brief glance, her gaze came upon the entrance to Charles's quarters a few doors ahead. It was almost over. She slowed her step as Charles turned toward the door. He was wavering weakly, and Devina felt her heart lurch into her throat. He could not collapse now.

Within a few moments Charles had entered his quarters and Devina walked past the door and turned the corner toward his office entrance. She waited in the shadows in breathless silence for the few long moments before she heard a step approaching from inside. The door opened and she stepped into the semidarkness of the room, her hands moving immediately to take Charles's arm, to usher him back into his quarters in the rear.

Releasing a short, shaky breath as Charles sank into a chair, Devina pulled off her scarf and lowered the shades to cover the windows. She lit a lamp and turned to face Charles, a low gasp escaping her lips as she saw the enlarged circle of blood staining his dark coat.

"Charles, the wound has started bleeding again."

He gave a low laugh. "It has, at that, hasn't it?"

"This is no time for levity! Tell me what to do."

"Are you sure you're up to it? The chore promises to be messy, and you won't do me any good if you pass out on me."

Devina did not bother to hide her annoyance. "If I haven't passed out so far, I won't now, Charles. Tell me what to do."

A few moments later Devina worked with steady hands to cleanse the wound.

"You're an excellent nurse, Devina. Now just pat it dry and apply the salve generously . . . That's right."

Biting her lip against the anxiety assailing her, Devina followed Charles's instructions. His next words, low with concern, had the effect of stilling her hands momentarily.

"You should have told him how you feel, Devina."

Devina's heart gave a small lurch. "I don't know what you mean, Charles."

"Devina, I'm not my brother. Maybe you can fool him about the way you feel, because he's so filled with anger and frustration, but I've been with you for the past month since your father brought you back. I saw the change in you. I know how you suffered knowing Ross was in jail, and I saw your face when sentence was pronounced this morning."

Devina gave a short laugh. "Was that only this morning, Charles?"

"Yes, only this morning. Does that give you any indication of how the days will drag now that Ross is finally gone and you have no hope of seeing him again? Devina, you should've told him how you feel."

"Why, Charles?"

"Why? Because you love him!"

Devina averted her gaze. She reached for the bandage and began dressing the wound with great concentration.

"Devina . . ."

"Yes, I love him, but it's hopeless, Charles. I don't mean to pretend Ross has no feelings for me in return. The problem is, how much of those feelings have to do with love, and how much with hate? Even when I was in his arms, I saw the shadows of hate in his eyes, Charles. I can't even be sure whether Ross made love to me because he wanted me or because he wanted to take revenge on my father in another, more personal way. Ross was so caught up in bitterness that I'm not certain he himself knows how he feels."

"Devina—"

"Charles, let me finish. I've gone over this in my mind countless times. I've asked myself how I can love a man who is filled with so much hate. There was no question of the feelings Ross stirred inside me when we were together, but the question was difficult to answer in the time since, when I lay in my room alone night after night, longing for him.

"It came to me then that from the first moment of our frightening, violent meeting, Ross was a part of me, impossible to forget. I don't know what kind of responsive chord he struck, how he managed to burn himself inside me, but he was there. Once that spot had been touched with life, it ached for Ross to assuage it. I suppose that's why I responded instantly to him the night of the party, in a way I never responded to you.

"After he kidnapped me, after the anger and accusations passed away, there was only love left inside me, Charles. Ross sealed that love with tenderness, with the revelation that he was capable of as much power in loving as in hating. My only mistake was in believing that those few days we had together had changed him, that love had replaced the hate inside him. I was wrong.

"Even now, Ross doesn't realize how very successful he was in his revenge. He doesn't realize that even though he's again a fugitive because of my father, he's won out over him. Father will never again know the confidence he had before. The pattern of his life, the quest for success and personal gratification at any cost, the single-mindedness with which he pursued that success, has been interrupted. I don't believe it will ever be fully restored. Father is a changed man, not only physically. He's come to realize he's not sufficient in himself, that he needs love. He's also come to realize that he's done very little to earn that love.

"Father's bitter. He never was before. His success, his supreme contentment with his life, had held him above such a common emotion. Father's bitterness also stems from another awakening Ross has forced upon him, the realization of the frailty of being human. It's a sobering realization indeed for a man who never even considered the thought.

"Ross succeeded in his revenge in another way, too, Charles. He doesn't realize how he's spoiled me for other men with that same supreme tenderness of which he's capable, how I suffer with the thought of the love that's going to waste inside him."

Devina's hands again stilled. Her voice was low, shaken. "Ross has so much love to give, Charles. I felt it rush through him, consume him, and it was beautiful. But it didn't last. It was eaten up by rancor, hate that flickered inside him every time he looked into my face and saw my father reflected there, every time he remembered my name. Ross needs someone who can make him forget revenge, put it aside forever, someone he can love without hating himself for loving her. That person can never be me, Charles."

Devina took a deep breath, determined not to discuss the matter any further. She knew she could not. She could not tell Charles how very intensely she wished she were riding with Ross right now, as Lai Hua was riding with Jake. She could not tell him that everything she had always considered important in her life fell flat and meaningless in the realization that Ross had ridden out of her life forever. She could not tell him that had Ross offered her the choice at that moment when he had mounted and prepared to ride off, she was uncertain what she would have done. But the emotion of that moment had passed, and reasoning was again strong in her mind. And with reasoning came the bitter truth that Ross had been beyond her reach even when she was in his arms.

"All right, it's done." Devina's smile was forced. "Only a little while longer and we'll be completely finished with all of this." Drawing back, Devina assessed Charles's pallor. "Do you think you can make it?"

Charles gave a short laugh. "Devina, if you think I'm going to let a little flesh wound get in the way of finishing this once and for all, you're not as smart as I think you are."

Pausing, Charles continued more softly, "Go in the other room and change. We're going to follow through with our plan. We're going to stroll back to your house after our 'pleasant dinner' and that 'lovely long walk' we took, and we're going to act utterly shocked when we hear that Ross has escaped. When tomorrow comes, everyone will be trying to figure out how Ross escaped and where he's headed. They'll soon find the two horses turned loose and grazing somewhere, but there'll be no sign of Ross, and they'll never find him."

Charles paused and tried another smile. "As I said, if you think I'm going to spoil everything now because of a little lost blood, you're vastly mistaken. Now go get dressed."

Devina smiled. "Charles, why could I never talk to Ross the way I can talk to you?"

"Because you love Ross, and love gets in the way."

The tears in Devina's eyes belied her annoyed response to his prompt reply. "Charles, you're too damned smart."

Turning she walked into the next room.

Charles watched as the front door of the Dale house closed behind Devina. Pausing only a moment longer, he descended the steps and headed home, his step lagging.

"Charles, you're too damned smart . . ."

Charles gave a short, self-deprecating laugh. Yes, so smart that he had outsmarted himself.

He looked up at the sky, realizing that it was not yet midnight. The realization startled him. The day had been so long, so crammed full of events of great magnitude that it seemed like an eternity since he had stood at Devina's side in the courtroom and heard sentence pronounced on Ross.

Light-headedness assailed Charles, and his step faltered. He raised a hand to his forehead and paused to take a deep breath. *Damn, hold on! You're all right. The wound is only a crease, and the blood loss was not significant.*

Charles felt the urge to laugh. Strange as it seemed, his debility seemed only to bring things into clearer perspective. His own stupidity, for instance.

He had seen the expression on Jake's face when he swept Lai Hua up onto his saddle, when he had declared his love for her. He supposed only a man similarly in love with a woman whom he had considered wrong for him could appreciate the full scope of Jake's declaration of love. And only a man similarly in love could appreciate what a damned fool Charles Carter had been.

Then there was the unhappiness that faced Ross and Devina, an unhappiness that could so easily be reversed if they could only manage to overcome the past. Wasn't there a lesson in that for him, also?

Charles winced at the pain that stabbed his shoulder. Firmly ignoring the new throbbing that ensued, he hurried forward.

He paused at the corner of Allen and Sixth and fixed his gaze on the small frame house ablaze with light. The escalated beating of his heart raised a film of perspiration on his brow. Damn, he was getting weaker, but this was no time to falter.

Stepping through the doorway of Blond Marie's well-attended establishment a moment later, Charles paused. His gaze swept the parlor and the two couples conversing there. Not seeing the face he sought, he raised his eyes to the staircase, toward the couple ascending, then toward the woman who stood at the railing above. He returned their greetings with an absentminded smile just as a step at his side caused him to turn to Blond Marie's startled expression.

"Dr. Carter, *bon soir*. We have not seen you here for a very long time. How may we help you?"

"I would like to see Camille."

Marie's expression stiffened into familiar lines. "I am sorry, Camille is no longer available. She leaves for France tomorrow, you see. The Count has decided it is time for her to go home. She has outlived her usefulness here."

Charles shot a brief glance toward the staircase, deciding suddenly on a different tack. "Then I would like to see the Count."

Marie stiffened further. "That is impossible. He is otherwise engaged. He is working."

A hot flush of jealousy coming to life inside him, Charles abruptly brushed past Marie's stiff figure and headed for the office beside the staircase. Marie followed protestingly behind, but he did not stop until he was rapping at the door with a heavy hand.

"Monsieur, I tell you Le Comte must not be—"

Marie's angry statement was interrupted by the abrupt opening of the door.

Pierre looked annoyed. "Marie, I told you I did not wish to be interrupted this evening."

"*J'en suis au regret*, monsieur. I could not stop him. He—"

"Marie's right, monsieur." Restraining his reaction to the smaller man's anger, Charles strengthened himself against the wave of weakness assailing him. "It's essential that I speak to you now."

Le Comte's eyes narrowed, sweeping his face, and Charles had the feeling the man was holding a deep animosity in check. Realizing his own animosity was just as deep in return, Charles flashed a short, tight smile. "Monsieur, I would prefer to speak to you before I speak to Camille."

"Camille is asleep. She must not be disturbed. We leave early tomorrow for France."

Charles was fast losing his patience. "Must we discuss this in the hallway, monsieur?"

Le Comte hesitated a moment more before stepping back with obvious reluctance as Charles walked past him into the room. "You are all right, Dr. Carter?"

Charles turned with a frown. "I'm all right, just tired. It's been a long day."

"And it is a strange time for such a call, is it not?"

"Maybe." Charles frowned more darkly. "But you won't be here tomorrow, will you?"

Le Comte's tight gaze intensified. "No, I will not. Come, monsieur, I have much to accomplish in the next hour. What is the reason for your visit?"

This time it was Charles's turn to assess the count. He remembered the way Camille had laughed up into this man's stern face, the way she had turned those hard eyes soft with her smile. He felt a new jealousy soar to life within him. "What are your plans for Camille?"

"Monsieur, Camille is my employee."

Charles made a low scoffing sound that grated harshly on the silence of the room. "You have many employees, monsieur, but only one Camille."

"You are correct in saying that. Camille is special; she always has been."

"So that's why you're allowing others to believe she's leaving for France because she has 'outlived her usefulness here'?"

"Who said that?"

"Marie said—"

"*Catin!*" Le Comte snarled the concise invective. "That woman and her jealousy."

"So it isn't true?"

"No, of course not! Camille is going to France with me because it is her wish to return. She has told you that herself, has she not, monsieur?"

Charles flushed. "You still haven't answered my question."

"What is the reason for your interest, Dr. Carter? Camille has not worked here for the past month, and she is not available to you tonight."

Charles tensed further. "Answer my question, damn you! What are your plans for Camille when you reach France? Do you intend to keep her for yourself or will you take her to one of your houses there? Tell me!" He took a threatening step forward, but the Count held his ground. He raised a gray eyebrow, a small smile curving his thin lips.

"Dr. Carter, I do not normally respond to such inquiries into my business affairs or into my private life, but since you are an old friend of Camille's and since you appear to be interested in her welfare, I will make an exception. I will tell you that I am a happily married man. I have not made it a practice during my marriage to maintain mistresses, nor do I consort with my employees."

Charles would not be silenced. "But for Camille you would make an exception to that policy . . ."

Le Comte paused. His eyes narrowed. "I might consider that possibility."

A flush of rage colored Charles's face. "So you still intend to use Camille . . ."

"Unlike yourself, Dr. Carter?"

"Bastard, you—" Charles was interrupted by a sharp knocking on the door and a frantic voice.

"Pierre! Charles!"

The door opened to reveal Camille's womanly figure. Blazing hair spilling over her shoulders, her lovely face concerned, she clutched a revealing lace robe over her sheer nightgown.

"Charles, Giselle told me you were here."

Le Comte reached out toward Camille, but Charles stepped in front of his outstretched hand. He saw Camille's startled expression, the glance she shot toward the Count and back to him. He laughed.

"No, I haven't lost my mind, Camille."

Taking her hand, he drew her closer, his eyes devouring her. How had he ever thought he could let her go? He attempted to inject a word of sanity into the rapidly deteriorating situation. "I came here tonight to talk to the Count. I wanted to know his plans for you. He's taking you back to France to work in one of his houses, Camille."

Camille raised a confused glance to Charles. "I know that, Charles. I have always known that. What have I said to mislead you into thinking otherwise?"

"It wasn't what you said. I saw the two of you together. I saw the way he looked at you, the way you looked at him."

"We are friends, Charles."

"He wants to be more than friends with you."

"Charles, my occupation suggests that kind of intimacy."

"Not anymore it doesn't."

"What are you saying?"

Neither of them noticed that Pierre had quietly walked out of the office and closed the door behind him.

Charles continued with a new heat. "Camille, I promised myself that if the Count wanted you to marry him, I would leave without seeing you."

"But Pierre has been married for many years, Charles."

"I know that now, and I also know I could never have left without seeing you. I must ask you to reconsider leaving Tombstone. I want you to stay here, with me."

"Charles . . ." Camille raised a trembling hand to her temple, pressed her fingertips against the light skin there where her pulse throbbed visibly. "Charles, we have said our good-byes. We have recognized that the feelings that flow between us—"

"No, Camille, we have recognized nothing of the sort. I have been fool enough to allow circumstances to color my feelings toward you, circumstances that came about long before I ever met you. I've had some time to think, and I realize that had it not been for those circumstances, you would not be here in Tombstone, I would not have met you and loved you. I would have spent the rest of my life searching for the woman who would bring my heart alive as you've brought it alive. I would have searched long and hard for the woman whose spirit would touch me, warm me, as much as the sweet consolation of her body. I would have been as empty as I have been this past month, thinking that another man was about to take the step I should have taken, that another man was bringing you from this house to his own house, where he could keep you as his own for the rest of his life."

"Charles . . ." Camille shook her head, her warm brown eyes searching his. "Charles, do you realize what you are saying, *mon cher?* You are asking me to leave this place and come with you. You are asking that the world see you, Charles Carter, the educated son of a wealthy man, a man with a bright future ahead of him, taking to live in his home a French courtesan, a common woman."

"No, you're wrong, Camille." Charles's broad hand stroked

back a few strands of fiery silk curling against Camille's smooth cheek. "I'm not asking that the world see me take you into my home. I'm asking that the world see me marry Camille, the woman I love."

"Charles, this is insane! I cannot!"

She thrust her palms against Charles's chest in an effort to break free of his tightening embrace. Her brows knit in a frown as a spasm of pain flicked across Charles's face and he expelled his breath in a short gasp, then staggered weakly against the desk. "Charles, what is wrong?"

Charles's hand moved to his shoulder. Her own hands followed suit, only to come in contact with wetness. She withdrew her hands, startled to find them stained with blood.

"Charles, you are wounded! What has happened?"

"Ross escaped from the jail a few hours ago. During the confusion a bullet creased my shoulder. Devina did her best to treat the wound."

Camille's heavily fringed eyelids dropped down to shield her reaction to the name. "Mademoiselle Dale was with you."

"Yes, she risked her life tonight for Ross. But, damned fool that Ross is, he didn't realize that she loves him."

Camille's gaze flew upward. Sparks of glittering gold came alive in the dark depths of her eyes. "Devina Dale loves your brother, Ross Morrison?"

"Yes, she does." Charles stared into Camille's eyes, fascinated by the dancing golden flecks as he continued softly, "And Ross Morrison's brother, Charles Carter, loves Camille DuPree."

The brilliant golden flecks were suddenly swimming in tears. "This Charles Carter, he is ill, feverish, suffering from loss of blood."

Charles drew her closer. "Will Camille DuPree take pity on him, come home with him, nurse him back to health, stay with him and care for him for the rest of his life?"

Camille focused her brimming eyes on Charles. Her voice was husky with emotion. "This Charles Carter, he has not asked if Camille DuPree loves him."

A tremor of anxiety moved down Charles's spine. He remembered the way Camille looked up into the Count's eyes, the warmth of the glances they exchanged. Suddenly serious, he shook his head. "It doesn't matter, Camille. I know you care for me, and that will be enough. Pierre can't offer you what I'm offering you. You said yourself he's been married for many years. He won't give up his wife for you. You'll forget him and come to love me, Camille.''

''No, you are wrong, Charles.''

A stab of pain pierced Charles's heart at Camille's words. The ache grew deeper as he held her sober gaze.

''I will not *grow* to love you, Charles, because I love you now. I have loved you from the first. I have never loved another man as I love you, Charles.''

A flush of joy moved through Charles. He held Camille close, but his attempt to cover her lips with his was interrupted by a wave of vertigo. He gave a short laugh, clinging to Camille's warm, womanly frame. ''I'm afraid this isn't the moment to show you how happy you've made me, Camille.''

Her expression concerned, Camille attempted to lead Charles to a chair. ''Come sit, *mon cher*. I will call—''

''No, call no one, Camille. I don't want anyone to know about the wound. There would be too many questions. I'm all right. I just need rest.'' Steady once more, Charles smiled. ''But I need you to come home with me tonight, now.''

''Charles, I must speak to Pierre.''

Charles felt a familiar jealousy twist in his stomach. He lowered his mouth to Camille's for a brief kiss. ''Tell him now.''

Camille turned and walked toward the door. She opened it and smiled at Pierre who appeared immediately.

''What is your wish, *ma petite?*''

Charles answered in her stead. ''Camille and I will be leaving now. She regrets that she won't be able to go back to France with you.''

Pierre glanced at Camille's face. ''Your bags are packed, Camille. Where would you have them sent?''

''To my quarters,'' Charles instructed.

Pierre ignored him. ''Camille? What is your response?''

Sliding her arms around Pierre's neck, Camille pressed her lips against his cheek. ''To Charles's quarters, Pierre. This foolish man wishes to marry me.''

The silence that followed was broken finally by the Count's low sigh. ''He would have been a far more foolish man if he had let you go.''

A quick turn of his head and a crisp order in his native tongue sent small feet scurrying, and within a moment Pierre was wrapping a great cloak around Camille's shoulders. Then, turning, he extended his hand to Charles. "*Félicitations*, Dr. Carter. You are a fortunate man, and I do not deny I envy you. But you must leave now, must you not? The wound in your shoulder . . . you would not wish to have it discovered by someone here so that all of Tombstone would hear of it by morning. Someone might then come to suspect there was some relationship between it and your brother's puzzling escape from jail this evening."

Startled, Charles relinquished Pierre's firm grip to curl his arm around Camille's shoulders. Surprise flickered momentarily across his face. "You are a very well-informed man, monsieur."

Pierre nodded. "*Oui*, but I will miss my dear Camille."

Charles's arm curled tighter as he urged Camille toward the door. "I'm sure Camille will write to you."

Le Comte's gray brow rose sardonically. "You are very generous, monsieur."

Charles gave a short laugh. "I'm in a magnanimous mood."

Within moments Camille was walking beside him along brightly lit Allen Street. Not speaking a word, he held her tight against his side until they reached his quarters. His expression sober, he looked into her face.

"Into my home and into my heart, Camille."

"Yes, Charles. That is all I ever wanted."

No other words needed to be spoken between them. Camille stepped into the room and into Charles's arms.

Devina tossed and turned restlessly. Exhaustion had forced her eyes closed, cutting off the thoughts whirling in her mind, but sleep had provided only a temporary escape. In her dreams, fragmented pictures of Ross continued to assail her: Ross angry, his expression cruel, unyielding; Ross concerned, bent over the wound on her ankle, drawing out the poison with his mouth; Ross hovering over her as she fought delirium, his low voice soothing; Ross loving, holding her, caressing her, taking her body with utmost tenderness; Ross startled, holding his arm in pain, staring at the iron in her hand; Ross hostile, his dark eyes anticipating a cruel twenty years stretching out before him; Ross determined, riding off into the darkness never to return. Each fragment was a sharp, piercing shard that tortured her as Devina continued to toss and turn.

But out of her desolation came a fragment of joy, a small circle of light, gradually growing to consume the pained reminiscences of her dreams. She smiled, experiencing it before it could be seen, hoping to catch it, to seal it within her sight, to watch it expand to envelop her completely. But it was glancing away, touching her lightly and fleetingly, feathering her forehead, her cheek, her fluttering eyelids. She felt its beauty on her ear, her throat. She felt it slide along her jaw, tease her mouth. She parted her lips with anticipation. The fragment of joy grew, becoming a living, breathing force. She wound her arms around it, held it close. She felt its breath against her cheek, heard its low whisper against her lips.

"Devina, darling . . ."

Abruptly, Devina was awake. Just as abruptly she realized the joy assailing her had taken human form. That human form was Ross. She gave a low, involuntary gasp, another part of her mind experiencing an emotion of another kind as the familiar warmth of Ross's body stretched out beside her.

"Ross, what are you doing here? You should be making your escape. If the posse trails you, finds you here . . ."

"Nobody will be expecting me to be back in town, much less in Harvey Dale's house. I'm safe, Devina, for a while. I'm not worried about the posse, not now."

Devina attempted to pull herself from the intimate posture Ross had assumed, his hard body flush against hers, his mouth brushing her lips as he spoke. She could not stand this torture.

"What do you want, Ross? Why are you here?"

"I asked myself the same question when I reined up my horse and turned back toward town, Devina. What do I want?" He gave a short laugh that reflected little mirth. "I suppose I was just as surprised as you are right now. After all, what more could I want than to be free of the threat of twenty years in prison? The answer to that isn't very simple. For more years than I choose to remember I was driven by only one desire, revenge. And only one emotion, hate, ruled my every waking thought and action. I don't have to tell you whom I hated. When I first saw you, you were only another object of that hatred . . . or so I told myself.

"But I could only fool myself so long. I was pretty good at convincing myself that I hated you—until you were bitten and I faced the threat of losing you. God, I was shaken. I was so panicked, so obsessed with your every waking thought and

breath after that that I almost tried to draw you inside me. I had
never felt the way you made me feel, Devina. I had never
despised a woman with as much fury as I despised you; I had
never lusted after a woman as I did for you; I had never raged at
a woman, fought so relentlessly with a woman, as I fought with
you; I had never tried to impose my will on a woman, to
dominate a woman the way I wanted to dominate you. I had
never been so confused by my feelings, so torn by the conflict of
a perverse desire to cause you the pain I had suffered while at the
same time I was overwhelmed by mind-shaking tenderness each
time you raised your eyes to mine."

Ross was trailing his lips over her chin, punctuating his words
with light kisses against her mouth, her nose, her fluttering
eyelids. Devina was becoming mesmerized by the loving words
with which he assailed her. She fought to overcome her growing
lethargy.

"Ross, you must go. You don't have time to—"

Ross swallowed her words with his kiss, devoured them with
his longing, erased them from her mind with his searching
tongue, his relentless caresses. Drawing away at last, he spoke
softly, caressingly. "A few hours ago, I thought I wanted nothing more than to be free of the prison sentence that hung over my
head. I blamed you for that, too. But I was wrong about that and
about a lot of other things. I didn't realize how wrong I'd been
until I was racing off into the darkness with fear at my heels and
an uncertain future before me. It was then that it occurred to me
how much you had risked to help me. It also occurred to me that
amid all the confusion, I hadn't even apologized to you."

Ross paused, drinking long and deep from her mouth, allowing his hands to move warmly over her, tracing the curves of the
warm flesh he knew so well. Devina felt the rise of his passion
against her, and she steeled herself against the response that rose
deep inside her. God, she must be mad . . . *He* must be mad to
be here now, touching her, loving her when his life hung in the
balance.

Tearing his mouth from hers, Ross rested his cheek against her
hair as he strove to rein in his riotous emotions. He closed his
eyes briefly, his voice low and intense. "So I came back to
apologize." His hand caressing her cheek, Ross raised Devina's
face to his. He consumed her perfect beauty with his eyes as she
searched his dark, pensive expression, seeing the uncertainty
there as he began speaking again.

"I'm sorry, Devina. I'm sorry for taking out my hatred and anger on you. I'm sorry I was too much of a fool to realize that it wasn't hate I felt for you, but love. I love you, Devina. I know that now. I also know I haven't done anything that would cause you to love me in return."

Ross swallowed deeply, his callused hand still stroking her cheek. "But I also know it's good for both of us when you're in my arms, when I'm loving you. Your body cries out to mine, darling, and that's something to build on. And now that I'm speaking honestly to you, I suppose it's time to tell you the real reason I came back was to take you with me."

Devina started at his words, and Ross felt her body's spontaneous reaction. He pressed with a fervent plea.

"I want to take you with me, Devina. I want it to be just the way I planned in the cabin. We'll go to Mexico, where no one will ever find us. I have enough money from your father's payrolls for Jake, Lai Hua, you, and me to live on comfortably for a long time." Ross paused, frowning. "I don't feel any guilt about living off that money until I can get a ranch going. I figure I have at least that much coming to me from Till-Dale Enterprises."

Ross hesitated, surveying Devina's solemn expression before continuing. "And I'll give you my solemn promise, darling. If you come with me, I'll love you, take care of you. You won't want for anything." Ross paused again, taking a deep breath. "And I'll make you forget Charles. He isn't right for you, Devina. He isn't really the man you see when you look into my eyes." Ross made a visible effort at control. "And even if you do see Charles at times, I can close my eyes to that, just as long as it's my arms that are holding you."

Ross kissed her again, long and lovingly. Drawing back at last, he looked down into her face. He saw the skepticism there, the doubt, and he gave a short laugh. "I want to hear your answer, Devina, and yet I'm shaking in my boots like a kid. I don't want it to be like the last time between us. I want you to come with me willingly. I want to know you want to be with me, even if you don't really love me yet."

Devina's frown halted Ross's words, allowing her the opportunity to speak. "Ross, love, or the lack of it, isn't the problem. It's hate that stands between us. You're not thinking clearly. You've forgotten the hate you feel for my father. You've forgotten the revenge you swore to get and haven't yet satisfied.

You've forgotten the last thing you said to me outside the cabin, before Sheriff Bond took you away. You said I was Dale . . . a true Dale. Can you ever forget that? Will you ever be able to forget that my father's blood flows in my veins, that no matter how far I run, he'll always be a part of me?'' Tears springing to her eyes, Devina continued hoarsely, ''Will I wake up one morning, Ross, and find that you hate me because, looking into my face, you're unable to forget my father?''

Ross's arms were suddenly hard and tight around her, and Devina yielded to their strength, her arms moving around his neck to hold him close against her. ''I do love you, Ross. I've known that for a long time. Charles is only a friend to me, a good friend. I knew that the first minute the 'Charles' at my party took me into his arms.''

Ross was drawing back, the tense planes of his face softening, but Devina shook her head. ''No, Ross, our problems can't be solved so easily. I won't go with you unless you can tell me that the battle is over between you and my father. I don't ever want to see hate in your eyes for me. Not again. I couldn't take it, Ross.''

Ross's dark eyes looked directly into hers, and Devina felt the full impact of their intensity. His low whisper was filled with the heat of his emotions. ''Devina, it came to me when I was riding off into the darkness tonight that freedom was suddenly flat and meaningless to me. All it meant was a succession of long, empty days when I'd still be a prisoner of my own hate, of my own thoughts. It also came to me that if that was so, I'd be granting Harvey Dale a greater victory than he had ever hoped to win. I'm not about to do that, Devina, and I'm not about to give up the only woman I've ever loved. He's not worth it, and he's not going to win.''

''I'd say that statement is a bit premature, Morrison.''

A low, slurred voice sounded at the entrance to the room as the door swung back on its hinges, slamming against the wall with a resounding clap. Light from the hallway streamed into the room, and Devina stared with disbelief at her father's bent frame outlined in the opening, at the gun held securely in his hand. She felt Ross's body stiffen, saw his face harden into that of the Ross of old. No, it couldn't end this way.

''Get out of my daughter's bed, Morrison, and make it quick! Stand on your own two feet instead of hiding behind her. That is, if you're man enough to do it!''

Ross slowly rose to his feet, and Devina stood up beside him, her eyes on her father's twisted, hate-filled face.

"Father, please, put the gun down. Ross isn't—"

"You're right, Devina, Ross isn't going to take you away with him." Harvey darted his daughter an angry glance touched with incredulity. "I never thought I'd see the day I'd say my daughter is a fool, but you are a fool, Devina! Don't you see what he's trying to do? He's getting back at me through you! He doesn't love you! He hates you, just as he hates me! If you went with him now, he'd make your life a living hell, and my life would be hell, too, just knowing that you were suffering with him. That's his aim . . . that's what he wants! He doesn't want you!"

"You're wrong, Dale. I don't want Devina because she's a Dale. I want her in spite of it."

Harvey gave a short laugh. "Really? Well, you aren't going to get her at all. All you're going to get is—"

"No, Father!" Devina's eyes went to her father's hand, to the finger tightening on the trigger of the gun, and she jumped in front of Ross. "It's not going to be this way. You're not going to make me responsible for Ross's death!"

Fury moved across the twisted lines of Harvey Dale's face. "Get away from him, Devina! Get away! You won't be responsible for Morrison's death. He's a convicted felon! He deserves to die. I'll only be helping the law, saving the territory the cost of confining him for the next twenty years."

Devina shook her head. "No, Father, I will not."

But Ross's hands circled her waist. Devina felt his fingers tighten a split second before he pushed her out of the way and lunged at her father.

The two male bodies met with a sudden impact. A gunshot exploded in the veil of semidarkness!

Frozen with fear, Devina remained motionless as her eyes slowly distinguished a sign of movement on the shadowed floor. A low gasp escaped her throat as a tall, erect figure drew itself to its feet, gun in hand.

"Ross!"

Darting a glance toward the shadowed floor, Devina heard her father's voice, low and venomous.

"Go ahead, Morrison. Shoot! Show my daughter the kind of man you really are. Show her how sincere you were about forgetting your vow of revenge."

Ross remained unmoving, the gun still in his hand, and Harvey went on in a lower tone, "Remember how I cheated your father, Morrison. Remember how he died all alone while you begged to be released from jail. Remember those three long years you spent in Yuma, dreaming of the day you'd hold a gun in your hand as you are now, pointing it at my head. Remember, Morrison, and pull that trigger. Pull it, damn you!"

A tense, breathless silence followed Harvey's venomous tirade. Extending his hand toward Devina, Ross clasped her tight against him when she ran to his side. His low voice penetrated a stillness that, until now, had been broken only by the sound of Harvey's labored breathing.

"No, Dale, you caused the death of one Morrison. I'm not going to let you cause the death of another. The war's over for me. I have the feeling it'll never be over for you, and I suppose I couldn't ask for a sweeter revenge."

Turning, Ross looked down at Devina. "Are you coming with me?"

Not bothering to respond, Devina snatched up her robe from the foot of her bed, then turned toward the broken, rasping shadow on the bedroom floor. "Good-bye, Father. Molly will take good care of you, if you let her."

"I don't want Molly; I want you, Devina . . ."

But Devina was no longer listening. Leaning full into Ross's guiding embrace, she ran down the staircase and out of the house at his side, then let him lift her astride his horse.

Seated in front of Ross as he spurred his horse into the darkness, Devina felt a rush of night air against her face, felt Ross's strength at her back, and she knew that, whatever the future held, she was home at last in the arms of the man she loved.

EPILOGUE

"ROSS, NO, DON'T!"

But it was too late. Ross had already pinned her against the wall with the weight of his body and was running his mouth over the white column of her throat, brushing her lips with his, pulling her arms up around his neck, urging her cooperation as his kiss grew more intense. With a soft groan, he parted the barrier of her teeth, urged her closer still, curling one hand around the curve of her buttocks, fitting her tight against the rise of his passion.

Losing herself in the heat of Ross's embrace, Devina felt his kiss deepen, searing her until it was she who clung, she who protested his sudden withdrawal from her.

A low laugh sounded in Ross's throat as he lowered his head for another kiss, but this one was brief, glancing her lips.

"That's all you get for now, Mrs. Morrison. I just want you to know what's waiting for you tonight after you send our guests home."

Devina gave a low gasp. Lord, for a moment she had actually forgotten she had guests in the next room!

Ross laughed again, tightening his embrace once more as he drew her to him, fitting her close against the hard length of his body to bury his face in her silky curls. His voice was suddenly intensely serious. "I love you, Devina. I don't know what I ever did to deserve you, but there's one thing I do know: I'm never going to let you go." Ross drew back unexpectedly, his dark

440

eyes touching her face. How she loved it when he looked at her that way, as if he never wanted to stop.

Devina flushed, remembering that he had looked at her the same way last night as she lay naked in his arms. The heat of his gaze had touched her skin with the power of a physical caress. They had just made love, but he not been sated. Somehow the fire inside him had burned hotter than before. She did not fully understand his raging, insatiable desire for her. He had told her many times in the year of their marriage that she was all he ever wanted, all he ever needed, that she had given a true purpose to his life. He told her she was the most beautiful woman he had ever seen, the only woman he would ever love. But she didn't really believe that, not now.

A small smile touched her lips. She had a competitor for Ross's love. Another woman . . . well, one day she'd be a woman, anyway. And that very vocal competitor was now sounding a lusty cry from her cradle in the next room. Devina turned toward the sound, only to have Ross stay her attempted flight.

"Just a few minutes more, Devina. It's been a long evening. I just wish you weren't so addicted to parties."

"Ross, I'm not!" Indignant, Devina shook her head. "This is our first party, and you can't really call it a party with the few people you agreed to invite. But Melinda Lee does deserve some sort of a celebration for her christening, doesn't she?"

"Just as long as this party doesn't end up with a lusting cowboy carrying you off to his isolated cabin where he'll keep you prisoner and make love to you until he can no longer stand."

"Ross!"

He lowered his head to whisper in her ear. "You do know that's the way I intend to spend our first anniversary in a few weeks."

"That's impossible. The baby . . ."

"Lai Hua will take care of her."

"Jake will have your head. Lai Hau will deliver her own baby in a few months. She needs her rest."

"Then Camille—"

"If you can talk Charles into letting her out of his sight." Devina shook her head. "I've never seen a man so obsessed with a woman."

"You haven't?"

Devina gave a short laugh. "Well, maybe it runs in the family."

Carefully, Devina extricated herself from Ross's embrace, although she was as reluctant to leave those strong arms as those strong arms were to relinquish her. Damn, whose idea was this party anyway?

Devina turned to lift the coffeepot from the stove, aware that her husband's dark eyes were following her every move. How had she ever felt fear at the touch of that gaze? Why had she not immediately recognized the love welling there, waiting to be coaxed to life?

All that was in the past now. She only knew that she loved Ross Morrison, former convict, former wanted man, former escaped felon. And she was proud of Ross Morrison, officially pardoned for past crimes because of extenuating circumstances; Arizona rancher, father, responsible member of society, husband— loving husband.

Devina lifted the coffee tray carefully. Taking his opportunity, Ross slid his arms around her narrow waist and tucked his head into the curve of her neck. Devina uttered a soft protest as he nibbled at the soft flesh there, unable to resist a smile as he finally released her, then followed her into the next room.

"Well, at last . . ."

"I was beginnin' to think you two had taken off."

Devina flushed. "Ross, uh . . . Ross wanted to make certain the coffee was strong enough."

"Yeah, sure. I can understand that." Jake turned to Lai Hua, who now held the cooing, fair-haired Melinda Lee in her arms. His expression was suspiciously sober. "Can't you understand that, darlin'?"

A small smile turned up Lai Hua's lips. "Yes, I can, my husband."

"Well, I was getting damned tired of waiting."

At Charles's comment, all heads turned in his direction. He laughed suddenly, reaching out for Camille's hand. "After all, when a man has an important announcement of his own to make . . ." He turned to look at his brother's expectant expression. "Ross, you're going to be an uncle. Camille and I—"

Not waiting for his brother to finish his announcement, Ross took two long steps forward and reached down to draw Camille to her feet for a short, hard hug. "Camille, you've made a human being out of this man. Now you're putting the finishing touches on the product.''

"Just as Devina did for you, *vraiment?*''

Ross's low laugh was echoed by the entire group. "True, Camille.''

At the sound of a carriage drawing up outside, Devina felt a tremor of apprehension move down her spine. Her smile vanished as she hurried to the window. Sensing rather than hearing Ross's step behind her, she paused, biting her lips as a stiff gray-haired figure stepped to the ground with obvious difficulty. She swallowed tightly as Harvey Dale turned to lift a gaily wrapped parcel off the seat of the carriage before walking laboriously toward the house.

The room, formerly filled with laughter, was suddenly silent as Devina looked up into the dark eyes of her husband, seeing there the shadows of old hatreds, old wounds again stirred to pain. She paused, glancing toward the child Lai Hua was placing in her arms. She saw Ross's gaze follow hers. She felt hope rise within her as Ross slipped his arm around her waist, as her baby nuzzled seekingly at her breast.

She whispered softly, "Ross, we have so much love, more than enough to share.''

The tight line of Ross's lips softened. He glanced up at the knock on the door. He walked with her as she started forward in response. Devina felt her heart swell with love as he attempted a smile.

Dear Reader,

I hope you enjoyed *Tarnished Angel*. Devina and Ross's story
was a joy to tell, and the colorful events of the Tombstone
frontier were an exciting experience for me as a writer. The
diverse characters in this book, both real and fictional, became
friends to me. I hope you feel the same.

Those of you who are familiar with my books and have
written to me in the past, know I take great joy in pleasing my
readers. I have so much more planned for your reading pleasure
in the future. I am excited at the prospect of introducing you all
to the characters I have waiting in the corners of my mind, and
transporting you to all the periods where their thrilling, tender,
and sometimes very poignant, stories unfold. I hope your
anticipation is as keen as mine.

I'd love to hear from you, both old friends and new. It will be
my pleasure to get to know you better.

Best regards,

Elaine Barbieri

Elaine Barbieri
P.O. Box 536
West Milford, NJ 07480